LALDASA: BELOVED SLAVE

ALSO BY
MAYA KAATHRYN BOHNHOFF

THE ANTIQUITIES HUNTER

STAR WARS: THE LAST JEDI
with Michael Reaves

STAR WARS: SHADOW GAMES
with Michael Reaves

MR. TWILIGHT

The Mer Cycle
THE MERI
TAMINY
THE CRYSTAL ROSE

THE SPIRIT GATE

SHAMAN
(A Collection of Short Science Fiction)

ALL THE COLORS OF TIME
(A Collection of Short Science Fiction)

LALDASA: BELOVED SLAVE

A TALE FROM THE ASOK TREE

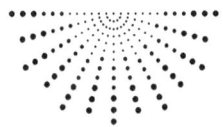

MAYA KAATHRYN BOHNHOFF

BOOK VIEW CAFE

A Book View Café Original
Ebook edition 2009
Audiobook edition 2013
Paperback edition 2022

Cover design by Maya Kaathryn Bohnhoff

Ebook ISBN: 978-0-9828440-8-3
Paperback ISBN: 978-1-63632-031-1
Audible audiobook ASIN: B00FR151MO

for Cynthia McQuillin

CHAPTER ONE

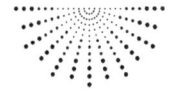

SHE EXPERIENCED her emergence through the layers of darkness and pain as an uphill struggle through an oppressive storm. Every breath came at a price; every movement was agony.

Had she lost her breather? She didn't remember. She gasped for air, expecting the sting of wind-driven sand on her skin, the taste of it in her mouth. But the air was too thick, too warm, too humid.

How could that be? It was autumn. Snow and ice were the only forms of moisture natives of the Kedar knew at this time of year.

Up through the muddle of sensations she climbed, groping toward light. She smelled vegetation, lush and sweet, heard the soft trill of water over rocks.

Wrong—that was wrong. Surely she was hallucinating.

Adrenaline seeped into her veins. She knew, too well, one familiar scenario that would account for hallucinations—that she had fallen through an old sink shaft into a pocket of manda gas. She willed the adrenaline to rouse her; manda fumes were slow poison. They fogged the mind, befuddled the senses, and eventually destroyed both.

She saw light and leapt after it. Made out indistinct shapes—a play of sunlight and shadow. But the sunlight was too bright, the shadows too dark.

She came to on a surge of near panic, disoriented by surroundings that made no sense. She was lying on a bed of grassy turf, overshadowed by softly waving greenery. Ferns—alien, and dripping with dew.

Wrong. Oh, wrong. There were no plants like these ...

She tried to lift her head and all but swooned again at the pain. Memory rode the storm of agony. Fragmentary, but complete enough that she knew she was not on a mountain slope in the Kedar. She was not even on Avasa. She had come to the inner planet of Mehtar to ...

There the memory failed. She rolled onto her back, slowly, carefully. Her right hand and forearm plunged into cold water.

Gasping in surprise, she rolled again onto her right side, bringing all her senses to bear on the stream. It was no more than a rill, wending its way through the foliage, sparkling where the sun kissed it. But it was clear, cold, and liquid.

She brought her face close to the surface of the water, used a cupped hand to fling it into her face, carry it to her mouth. Her senses steadied and cleared. The pain in her head steadied too, seeming to subside with every breath she took of the warm, moisture-laden air.

The nape of her heck stung when she trickled water over it. She touched it gently with trembling fingertips. They came back spotted with blood. How had that happened?

She breathed, drank water, bathed her face, and waited for the answer to come. It did not. Finally, she dared to sit up. She was at the bottom of a little slope in a tree-shaded glen choked with ferns. The air was heavy with the sweet perfume of alien flowers. Sitting, she was challenged to see over the nodding fronds.

Above her, clouds roved the sky, fat with the threat of rain, now masking the sun, now revealing it. Below her a jumble of colorful carts, tents, and stalls were scattered across an open meadow. People scurried around and between the little nomadic shops, rolling out awnings, setting out wares. On any world that was recognizable as a bazaar.

Memory fluttered. She had come to Mehtar, to the capitol city of Kasi, to buy mining supplies.

The flutter became a flood. She had had money, but no more. It was gone along with her pack, her cloak and—she put a hand to her throat—the necklace that had held her leaf, her personal identification.

Despite the warm air, a hard chill settled in the pit of her stomach. She knew who she was—she was Anala Nadim of Onan, Kedar province, but on this alien world she was no one. She had no identity, no money, no family, no friends. And she had no idea what to do or where to go.

But go, she must.

Shakily, Anala got to her feet and stumbled down slope toward the bazaar. Before she had taken two uncertain steps, it began to rain.

∿

Aridas, in the midst of clearing the breakfast dishes, was still rattling on when Jaya Sarojin left the morning room. The door slid shut behind him, cutting off the flood of words in mid-sentence. Aridas was a man of a strong and numerous opinions. Jaya was certain he must have heard every one of them.

This morning the subject had been the growing friction between the Kasi-Nawahr Consortium and Avasa's Guild of Independent Miners. Aridas had been following the story closely in the heralds and had developed copious opinions about it, as with all things.

Jaya Sarojin grimaced, pulling a thick cloak around his shoulders and checking the pale grey sky through the skylights overhead. He'd taken more than one critical sermon on the social evils of allowing das to have opinions about anything. Society seemed compelled to keep things as they were. It was rita, said the pundits, the natural order of things. Stagnation, he called it.

He reached the end of the broad, light-washed hallway and left the house. A damp wind hit his face, making him catch his breath. He waved away his Horseman, who had appeared to hover at his side.

"I'll walk, Kenadas. Thank you."

He took deep sips of the wet breeze, savoring its crispness. Even a residence the size of the House Sarojin could become stifling. No, size was irrelevant; it was the Sarojin name that made it oppressive —the centuries of tradition that laced its atmosphere, the political responsibility that encrusted every molding, the social grandeur that gleamed from every inch of polished floor and column. He had grown up with it. For his own survival, he had various escape routes. He was taking one now.

Tomorrow morning he would be in the Council chamber poring over petitions from the Avasan Guild and the Consortium, and would probably be there every morning after that, indefinitely. So today, he escaped, wishing he could relinquish his seat on the Vrinda Varma to Aridas the Opinionated. Ari obviously had more interest in the subtleties of government than his master.

He walked. Paths of pink-veined kumuda gave way to coarser stone, then to sun-baked brick, then to dirt and grass. He stopped at the top of a gentle rise and gazed down the lea and smiled at last. Here was life at its most chaotic. Colorful flags and rags fluttered damply over the ridgepoles of a thousand billowing tents and garish stalls.

Here, there was only foot traffic. No aircars scorched the grass with their dragon's-breath or flattened it with their air cushions. No cycles rutted the fresh earth. Only the merchant's wagons came here. The Bazaar was technologically sacrosanct—one of the few traditions of Kasi society Jaya Sarojin applauded.

Each breath sucked in a thousand-thousand teasing, tempting smells. His steps were quick now, and brought him to a well-known stall of pungent and pleasant fragrance.

A round, shiny face peered out at him from under the striped awning. "Nathu Rai! Lord!" The face lit up like a hundred candles. "It's been a week! Have you been ill?"

Jaya laughed. "I'm healthy enough. Only my humor is ill."

"Well, then let me cheer you." The woman waved a chubby hand at her baked goods. "What'll it be this morning? Choose quickly, before it rains."

Jaya threw a glance at the silvery sky, but his eyes were drawn quickly back to the table full of temptation. He chose two pastries and bought a cup of hot channa. Then he wandered.

People who recognized him, or at least recognized the signature of rank on the breast of his cloak, greeted him amiably or respectfully, depending on their own station. He bought gifts for the family das and for his grandmother, the Jivinta Mina, who loved such things as the hand blown glass falcon he found.

It was too early for the tent shows and he was contemplating a second mug of channa when the clouds broke.

The rain was relentless. When it became apparent it would continue, Bazaar dismantled itself tent by tent and disappeared into the colorful wagons that had brought it here. The stalls pulled in their wares and closed their awnings.

Jaya Sarojin watched it all with lazy fascination and a little disappointment, standing under the broad leaves of an ancient tree—watched the merchants and hucksters scurrying to fold and pin and lock down tight.

Something caught his eye—something that seemed out of rhythm with the orderly chaos of the disintegrating Bazaar. Just below where he stood at the edge of the wood, a tall, slender figure in mud-stained blue staggered, fell and rose to stagger forward again. It was a woman, he realized. She was clutching her head and obviously injured.

Jaya left the protection of the trees. Drawing nearer, he saw, out of the corner of his eye, that the woman was under surveillance by two Sarngin—guardians of law and order—who were even now moving toward her. Curious. He wondered what she might have done to merit their interest.

Jaya stepped into her path as she stumbled on a tuft of grass. Grasping her shoulders, he steadied her when she would have fallen. She stared at him, mutely, through eyes the color of the clouds where Mitras burned. A wave of hot static swept down through his body, granting him a moment of intense, if pleasant, surprise.

She was truly exotic—skin the pale gold of a freshminted coin, hair the hue of black cherries, eyes in which one could imagine he saw a winter storm. He took her to be somewhere in her twenties. Her clothing—a blue, one-piece coverall made of rugged material—suggested she came from a rural region, or even from Mehtar's sister-planet, Avasa. She wore no id at either her neck or wrists. That she had once possessed it, Jaya surmised by the thin, red line of welts on her neck. He took her left hand and turned it palm up. It was innocent of markings.

The Sarngin were hurrying toward them now. Impulsively, Jaya pulled off his cloak and threw it around the woman's shoulders. The Sarojin crest gleamed even under the clouds. Grimacing, he hugged her to his side as the Sarngin drew level with them.

Their eyes had not missed his scanning of her palm, and would understand the gesture of the cloak in that context. They knew what he knew—the woman was yevetha—unmarked, unregistered. Their eyes told him that as they each gave a crisp rendition of the respectful greeting.

"Good day, mahesa," said one of them, a sergeant in rank.

"Our blessings, Nathu Rai," murmured the other.

Jaya smiled and nodded. "A good day to you, friends," was all he said and mentally urged them to simply move on.

"The day is rather cool and wet for Chaitra," returned the first officer, "but you don't mind the rain, I see."

Jaya let his gaze flick to the woman's stricken features. "No, Sarngin. Rain brings blessings."

The sergeant nodded and bowed, a slight gleam of irritation entering his eyes before he averted them. "Then enjoy your blessings, Nathu Rai Sarojin. Peace."

Jaya inclined his head. With the Sarngin gone, he released the woman, turning her so he could see her face. The static curled below his stomach as he checked her eyes for dilation.

"Are you all right?" he asked and got no answer but a blank stare. It was followed momentarily by a slight nod. When he continued to search her face, she nodded again, more emphatically, and managed something that might have been intended for a smile.

The Sarngin still watched, and Jaya suspected they would follow him for no other reason than to see the law was obeyed by the Taj caste as well as shaped by it. He considered his options for a moment. He could attempt to elude the Sarngin and get the woman to the House Sarojin. He might then be able to help her recover her id or have some fabricated. Or he could obey the law and take her to a dalali for processing.

That felt wrong. Legal, proper, but wrong.

Jaya began to walk, holding the young woman at his side, half-supporting her tenuous steps. The Sarngin moved at a distance, shadowing. Well, he would at least go through the motions of taking her to a dalali. Once inside, he could wait the length of a processing and exit again. The thought of circumventing caste law was a perversely pleasing one, and Jaya Sarojin savored it.

Meeting the road to the spaceport, he hailed a public aircar, which carried him and his dazed companion back into Kasi. Here, her eyes scanning the buildings beyond the vehicle's windows, the woman finally spoke.

"Where am I?"

Jaya smiled, hoping to put her at ease. "At last! Words! I was afraid you'd been knocked dumb. You're in Kasi. Did you mean to be in Kasi?"

"Yes ... but not like this."

"What happened?"

"Thieves," she said.

He nodded as the car slowed to a halt before the dalali of Ashur Badan and Kareen Devaki. "They took your id," he said, and felt her stiffen.

Her face went white as she raised a hand to her neck. "I know. I go to prison?"

He paid the driver and helped her out onto the gleaming walk. "No. You go here." He turned her to face the dalali's glistening facade with its intricate pattern of inlaid tiles. As he did, he saw the Sarngin again, getting out of their blue aircar up the street. His reputation must have preceded him: Nathu Rai Sarojin, disrespecter of order, who treated das as if they were free men.

"What is this place?"

"A ... brokerage. Come."

He led her gently, still thinking, still watching the Sarngin, into the sumptuous foyer. From behind the long gleaming service counter across from the doors, a clerk saw the Nathu Rai Sarojin and rang upstairs for the proprietors. The whisper of his name brought them both down to the foyer.

Jaya saw them at the top of the green-carpeted stair—Ashur, short and fat; and the svelte, handsome lady Kareen Devaki, still beautiful though graying. He smiled, then saw that the Sarngin had come into the foyer behind him. He nearly swore aloud. No faking then, unless he dared use his status to induce the brokers to run a bogus processing.

He gritted his teeth. No. He would not ask a law abiding business to break the very law he was honor-bound to uphold, even if that law itself soured his stomach.

Next to him the woman, her eyes on the couple descending toward them, murmured, "Who are they?"

Jaya's hand tightened on her arm, trying to soothe the fear he could hear in her voice. "Trust me," he said. "Do as you're told and you'll be all right. What's your name?"

"Anala. I'm not going to prison?" she asked again.

"No prison, Anala. Just follow instructions. Good day, friends." He spoke loudly for the benefit of the Sarngin and held his hand out to be taken by the two dalal, each in turn.

"This is a rare privilege, Nathu Rai. How may we serve you?" asked Kareen, appraising first him, then his companion. Her eyes, as always, told him he attracted her, and sent an invitation he always refused, though graciously. It was almost a ritual by now, having taken place at every meeting since he'd reached fourteen years.

Ashur Badan was more interested in the woman. "Yours?" he asked with characteristic bluntness.

"It would seem. I found her wandering without id. She'll need processing."

Ashur took Anala's hands and turned them palms up. He grunted delicately. "Unmarked."

Jaya feigned affront. "You think me a thief?"

"You think me a fool? But you do have a reputation, Nathu Rai."

"Not for pirating dasa. I would have purchased her."

"You, mahesa, have never purchased a dasa in your life," said Ashur, with the familiarity of one presuming on an old family acquaintance. "This we know. You merely surprise me." He turned his gaze back to the woman, assessing her with an expert eye. Breath hissed between his parted lips. "Exotic! Her coloring, her eyes. She would bring a rare price at auction, Nathu Rai. Would you—?"

"No." Jaya cut him off, disgust leaving a sour taste in his mouth. "I need to have her processed." Jaya sent the two watchful Sarngin a meaningful glance.

Following it, Kareen raised her artistically shaped brows. "Can it be that rita has finally caught up with our rebellious Sarojin?"

"Well, convention has, at any rate," admitted Jaya wryly. He lifted off his personal id leaf and draped it around the woman's neck. "How long?"

"How much do you want done?" asked Ashur. "She has a natural beauty—won't need much painting. So pale. Is she Avasan?"

"I don't know." Jaya surveyed the silent woman. "She needs bathing—clothing."

"Consider it done." The dalal fingered the medallion at Anala's throat. "Your personal seal?"

"Yes."

"As you wish." He signaled a clinician to his side and sent the woman away with her. "Will you wait here? We have refreshment..."

"No, I have some business to do next door. I'll come back for her."

Jaya replied to Anala's last, pleading glance with one he hoped was reassuring.

Anala's present circumstance terrified her in a way the dangers she had faced almost daily on Avasa had never done. She had been in a mine when a pocket of manda gas was loosed; she had piloted a sandcat through a red blow. This was nothing like that. This was worse. Her mind felt muddy, her thoughts tangled, her body weak. There must have been at least one chance for escape—a chance she could have taken.

All she had to hang onto at the moment were the assurances of a total stranger that she was not destined for a Mehtaran prison. Now she was being led away from even that contact—denied the only hint of safety she'd known since the thieves had attacked her.

She fought her fear under control and clutched the cloak closed over the medallion. Those had to mean she'd be returned to him. He seemed kind. At least, she hoped it was kindness she saw in his face. He was obviously someone whose words were more than casually heard.

The clinician guided her through an archway into a nearly sterile corridor of white tile that opened into an equally immaculate warren of dazzling white and chrome. Steam rose from a myriad shower nozzles along the walls where clinicians bathed their female charges or watched them bathe themselves.

"Please disrobe."

Anala turned her head too quickly and staggered against her attendant.

"You're injured. Here, let me see."

She was seated on a tile bench while gentle but businesslike fingers made an inspection of her forehead.

"Quite a lump. Fortunately, the cut is not deep and it's above the hairline. It won't be seen. We can dress this with ointment. Now, your clothes."

Those were summarily peeled off and her personal garments tossed into a bag. Her protector's cloak and necklace, however, were carefully handled by a young white-robed attendant whose sole task seemed to be their safekeeping.

Two women guided her now, taking her to a shower and washing her with embarrassing thoroughness. Her hair was cleansed, her wound cared for, and her body and hair both dried by a device that spewed warm air. Then she was perfumed from head to foot. It was all dizzying—all relaxing. She wanted to sleep, but her tenders kept her on her feet.

The bathing over, she was drawn into yet another tile chamber. Her eyes rebelled at the glare of white unveiled by steam. They closed against it.

"No inspection for this one," said a half-familiar voice. "Nathu Rai Sarojin will be back shortly. Process her and dress her..." A hand captured her chin, then brushed her cheek. "And put some blush on those cheeks. She's deathly pale."

"Yes, Devaki-sa."

It was the woman from the foyer.

"And those cuts," the woman went on, briefly touching her neck, lacerated where the chain of her id had cut. "They'll need to be covered. She's to have the mahesa's personal seal."

"Yes, Devaki-sa."

A swirl of skirts and the fading of her pungent scent signaled the proprietress's departure, and Anala was guided forward again. She was stopped before a vicom terminal with a luminous dome cabled to it. One clinician took her left hand and placed it atop the small dome, holding it there. The other woman touched the terminal's keys, calling an image to the screen before her. Nodding in approval, she tapped a final keystroke.

Anala jumped as the dome blazed with light, sending a burning tingle through her palm and up her arm. The hand was then turned palm up and a rod of purple light passed over it. To her surprise, her palm glowed with an intricate golden pattern.

Still tingling from the light globe, Anala was taken to a carpeted room with walls the color of an ice lake. Her eyes opened wide to take in the racks of bright clothing. Nearby, clinicians tried shimmering prints on a dark-skinned girl with a cap of curly black hair and a sullen expression. Around the room others were being fitted before large mirrors.

Anala was led to her own mirror to have a variety of materials tried against her complexion while her attendants debated which colors suited her best. They decided on a deep saffron dress, fitted her with undergarments and shoes, touched up the scars with flesh paint and her cheeks with tawny color. Minutes later, she stood dressed, curried and perfumed in a staging area near the dressing room.

"Good," Kareen Devaki approved her. "The mahesa will be pleased. Hold her here until he returns."

∾

Carrying a new cloak and a package of roasted nuts, Jaya Sarojin entered the dalali through the long foyer to have a grinning Ashur Badan appear to escort him.

"Your timing is perfect," enthused the dalal. "She's ready and waiting. If you will follow me, please?" He led the way to a small, but sumptuous gallery with a stage and walkway.

"Very grand," commented Jaya wryly.

The dalal was obviously pleased by the compliment. "We're justifiably proud of it. We just bought out Asta Kagum, next-door. That makes Bedan-Devaki the largest dalali in Kasi—and the most prosperous. We now have eight showrooms. Three on the ground floor and five upstairs—plus private facilities. We guarantee every purchase ... if it passes our inspectors, of course," he added, "in the case of this girl..."

"I understand. This is one of your showrooms, then?" Jaya glanced around the small gallery and up the carpeted walkway.

"One of our private showrooms," explained Ashur. "We have a larger gallery which we use for our regular auctions. This room, you understand, is only for clients of the Taj. Now, please sit, and we'll bring your dasa to you."

At a signal from the dalal, the curtains parted and a black-robed attendant led the dazed Anala down the walkway to the circular pedestal at its end. There, she was turned about so Jaya could see the transformation.

He caught his breath on a wave of pure sexual attraction. He'd thought her exotic before, now she was stunning—a jewel of garnet and topaz. But the jewel was flawed; the silver eyes screamed terror.

He stood and moved forward, gesturing at the attendant to bring her down the carpeted steps to floor level. The new cloak went around her shoulders immediately.

"How much do I owe you?" he asked the dalal.

"One hundred dagam for partial service, mahesa."

He paid in cash, retrieved his own cloak and medallion, and the bag containing Anala's effects and took her to a waiting car. She was silent. Thinking she must be starving, he offered her the roasted nuts. Her hands shook as she put the nuts into her mouth. Three handfuls was all she took before she was sucked into a seemingly bottomless sleep.

He carried her into the House, directing Aridas to have a meal ready for her waking, and assigning Ari's wife, Helidasa, to be her attendant. Then he retired to his personal quarters, feeling irritable and morose. When he caught Aridas glancing at him warily, he laughed.

"Sorry, Ari. I'm finding new rooms in life, is all. And I'm not sure I like them very much."

He got out the presents he'd bought then, still safely stored in his belt cache, and gave them to Aridas to present to his family, all indentured servants of the House Sarojin. The little glass bird he took himself, carrying it reverently to the wing of the House occupied by Jivinta Mina.

He found her in her dayroom, enjoying a break in the clouds. She sat in pillows beneath a skylight, holding her sharp featured face to Mitras's brief smile.

"Jivinta," he said softly.

Her bright eyes opened and snapped to his face. She was bird-like in her movements—sprightly despite her advanced age.

"Gauri!" She smiled and a thousand tiny wrinkles transformed her face into a thing of art.

He didn't mind the childish pet name from her—or from Aridas, who also used it in private moments. He would always be their Golden One; it would be useless to protest.

"A present, Jivinta." He held the glass bird in a shaft of watery sunlight and watched her eyes sparkle at it.

"A bird!" She took it from him. "Ah, a falcon! How like you it is—the sharp eyes, the proud head."

Jaya laughed. "And I thought how like you it was."

Mina Sarojin was pleased. "Well, we are of a kind, you and I ... You got this at Bazaar?" At his nod, she leaned forward as if conspiring. "Take me with you next time you go."

"Jivinta, your leg won't carry you over that rough ground," he protested.

"Then we'll take a palanquin. Promise you'll take me."

Jaya smiled. "All right, yes, I promise..." His smile knotted itself into a grimace.

"What is it, boy? Tell your Jivinta."

Boy. He sat at the edge of her hassock, scratched at his close-trimmed beard, and mused that every hair in it would be white before Jivinta Mina would stop calling him 'boy' and expect him to share all his secrets with her. And he would share them—every last one. There were no secrets between him and Jivinta Mina.

"I found a woman at Bazaar today and brought her home."

"A woman? What kind of woman? Why am I not meeting her?"

"She's sleeping."

"You wore her out already?"

He ignored that. "I found her wandering—hurt, confused, without id. That was stolen. I think she may be from Avasa, by her coloring."

"Is she pretty?"

"She is..." He tilted his head from side to side. " ... stunning would be the right word, I think."

The old woman's eyes sparkled. "Ah, and you rescued her!"

He shook his head. "Unfortunately, the Sarngin saw her. I had to take her to the Bedan-Devaki."

Mina laid a wrinkled hand firmly over his. "Poor Gauri. And you vowed not to take any dasa to yourself. Well, you can always return her to the brokerage."

Disgust was quick to engulf him. "What, and have her sold into some ... business?"

"A kaladan," said Mina bluntly. "You can say the word—I've heard it before."

"To a kaladan. Or as cunnidasa to a private owner."

"And what will you do with her? Your mother has wanted you to take a cunnidasa for some time. Perhaps this is an opportunity to appease her." She tilted her head to study his averted face. "Does she attract you, this woman?"

He nodded. "When I look at her, Jivinta, it's like..." He chuckled, making a gesture of dismissal. "I can't describe it."

"What? My grandson has never felt lust before? Liar."

"Not lust ... sakti ... the force of life." He grimaced. "Maybe it's past time for a cunnidasa."

"Cunnidasa are for the management of lust—for exorcising such demons as cloud perception. Lust clouds, sakti illuminates. Know what you feel before you act on it."

He smiled at her and she smiled back, adoring him with her eyes. "I've heard father and Uncle Namun both say that."

"Ah. And where do you suppose they got it?"

"Are you always right, grandmother?" he asked her.

"I try to be," she said.

CHAPTER TWO

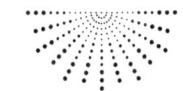

Jaya was on the shaded patio overlooking Aridas's artfully curried garden when Helidasa appeared in the doorway behind him.

"She's wakeful, Nathu Rai."

He glanced at her, only half seeing her at first, then focused on her face. It was set in almost prim lines.

"Have I earned your disapproval, Heli?" he asked.

"I'd have no business disapproving a Lord, Nathu Rai." Only the words were meek.

Jaya sighed. "Yes, Heli, I have taken a dasa. And yes, I do remember that I swore not to. But it was against my will."

Helidasa's eyebrows rose questioningly. "How does one enslave another against their will?"

"One finds a stranger wandering, injured and without id, through the Bazaar, and one gets to her just before the Sarngin do. Your next question would be, 'Why does one take the stranger to a dalali?'"

"That dascree in her palm be hard to remove," Heli replied, admitting that her curiosity had led her to a close inspection.

"I know. I'm sorry about that. But the Sarngin were watching our every move. They followed us all the way into the dalali."

She nodded, unbending a little. "She's very beautiful. What will you do with her?"

"First, I'll find out what she was doing in Kasi—if she has any family that can produce more id leaf for her. Then-" He shrugged.

Helidasa glanced back over her shoulder. "Well, you'll be hearing about that soon, then. Shall I bring her meal out here?"

His gaze going past Heli into the interior of the solarium, Jaya realized his foundling had come downstairs. She was standing near the door to the entry hall, looking out at them.

"Yes," he said, "bring it out here." He nodded toward the stone table set like a jewel in the center of a pastel mosaic saroj, a scene from the creation of the universe worked into each of its pale blue petals.

"And you? You are hungry also, Jaya Rai."

Jaya smiled. It was more command than question. "A little. Thank you, Heli."

The dasa grunted, satisfied, and went into the morning room. Jaya watched as she directed the other woman toward the mellowly lit patio. Anala emerged into the late afternoon sunshine, her gaze taking in the gardens in a wide-eyed sweep. The setting sun caught the deep copper hair and saffron gown and turned her to a pillar of flame.

Lust clouds, he reminded himself. Sakti illuminates.

"You have a beautiful palace, Lord," she told him. Her eyes met his and retreated behind a wary screen. "Sarojin ... That's the Taj House of Kasi. Your father holds a seat on the Vrinda Varma?"

"I hold a seat on the Vrinda Varma. My father is in the arms of Tara-rama."

"He is blessed," Anala responded automatically, pressing her palms together over her heart. "Why am I here?"

Jaya smiled wryly—blunt. "It was your best option."

"The others being?"

"The others being sale to the highest bidder or to a kaladan."

"A what?" She stopped by the stone table, her attention shifting from the bird-filled trees to his face.

He averted his eyes and gestured for her to be seated, then moved to sit across from her. "A kaladan."

She shook her head. "Is that some sort of prison?"

"Some sort of prison, yes ... You seem to have a fixation with prisons."

The woman shrugged, causing the soft sunlight to dance in the folds of her gown. "It's what my brothers told me could happen if I was stupid enough to lose my leaf."

"Where did they hear this?"

"On Mehtar, I imagine. They've both been here several times."

"Well, they were misinformed. We don't imprison idless people on Mehtar. We have work-farms and kaladans and large houses like this one that need das to run them as their masters require." His sarcasm was not lost on his guest.

"You mean domestics?" She jerked her head toward the house. "You have them. How can you sound so disapproving?"

"Ari and Heli are family das. I..." He hesitated. He'd been going to say, 'I don't have any,' but that was no longer true. He wondered if Anala understood her position. "Do you have das on Avasa?" he asked.

"We don't call them that, or consider them that. My family has a large compound, so we've had to hire domestics and hands. They do become like family after a while ... How do you know I'm from Avasa?" She shifted in her seat to watch Helidasa emerge from the house with a food-laden tray.

"Where else? Thank you, Heli." He accepted a bowl of sliced fruit with a nectar sauce glistening atop it. "You know very little about Kasi, you had no cree in your palm—you'd have to be from an extremely rural area at the very least. But then you refer to Mehtar as if you've never been here, so the only logical answer is Avasa. Besides, your ... coloring is ... unusual, as is your accent. Anything I missed?"

"I have an accent?" Anala paused in the act of biting into a fat, red berry. "You have an accent." She bit into the berry and chewed it thoughtfully. "Is it unpleasant?" she asked after a moment.

"What?"

"This accent you say I have."

He chuckled. "No, it's very pleasant."

She nodded. "Yours doesn't grate the ears either."

"Thank you." He studied her, considering what tack to take. "Do you understand what happened today?"

She snorted. "I was robbed. I understand that perfectly well."

"At the Bazaar?"

"No. Close, though. On the avenue that comes in from the spaceport." She shook her head in disgust. "Stupid. I was so freighted down in that winter cloak—I was trying to juggle my pack and take the cloak off at the same time. I didn't expect it to be so warm here."

"It's actually cool for Chaitra."

"Cool is fine—our summers are cool—but I was wearing an insulsuit under that cloak. My brother said it was winter in Kasi this time of year. It's more like late summer."

"Well, that entirely depends on your point-of-view. I suppose compared to what you're used to, Kasi winters might seem rather mild."

"I should have expected that, of course, but I'd thought with the elliptical orbit..." She shrugged.

He was surprised she understood that sort of thing and let it show in his expression.

"We're not savages on Avasa, despite what the Consortium wants everyone here to think." She hesitated, giving him a measuring look. "You'd be surprised, Lord, at how civilized Avasa is. We are an honorable people-"

"And a rebellious people," Jaya inserted for the sake of argument.

Anala flushed, ignoring the remark. "We have much to offer as an independent-"

"Mostly a lot of trouble to the Consortium, it appears."

"Are we not justified?" She slammed her fist down on the table top, nearly upsetting a bowl of stewed nuts.

Jaya grabbed the bowl. "Eat the kuri, don't bludgeon it."

Surprisingly, she laughed, then returned to her story. "So, there I was, struggling to get out of this fleece cloak, when four men pounced on me and knocked me senseless. All I remember after that is trying to follow them. Falling down a hill. Everything is a blur. Even meeting you, the dalali..." She shook her head. "I'm not sure what I dreamed and what really happened. All I know is, my id is gone—which I suppose means I'll have to leave Mehtar—and my money with it—which means I'll leave empty-handed." She was suddenly grim. "I'm ashamed to have to go back to father like this. After all his talk about how competent I am."

"Competence or lack of it has nothing to do with what happened to you, Anala." He avoided the issue of her return to Avasa for the moment and asked, "What were you to have brought home with you?"

"Mining equipment. Nandin drill bits. That new chemical spray that's supposed to neutralize manda fumes. Protective gear."

Jaya nodded. "How much money did you lose?"

"Twenty thousand dagam. Damn!" she added, feelingly.

"Why come all the way to Mehtar for mining equipment? Why not buy it on Avasa? Surely they sell it there after nearly two hundred years of mining."

She gave him an odd look. "It was sold on Avasa, up until about six months ago. Then the Consortium stopped its import."

"Just like that?" he asked. "They stopped it?"

"Yes."

She was telling him the truth, he was convinced of it—or at least she believed it was the truth. It was an accusation that the Consortium was putting economic pressure on the Avasan colonies even as it worked to stall their independence through legal means. If that was true, it could mean an indictment for arbitration violation.

He suspected guiltily that if he'd half kept up with the briefs for the upcoming Council sessions, he'd have already known about the import situation.

He shrugged the niggle of concern away and realized he was staring at Anala's hands. They were strong hands with short, neatly filed nails. Workers' hands. Her arms were bare (surely proving that even hot and cold were relative concepts) and unusually muscular. He recalled that her legs were, as well.

"So," she said, "when do I go back to Avasa?"

Jaya found meeting her eyes very difficult, but managed it. He ignored the tightening sensation under his breast bone and said the words bluntly: "You don't."

She was so still, she might have been part of the stone bench she sat on. "I don't," she repeated finally. "Can you explain that?"

"That's difficult. The fact is, Anala, you're now ... part of my household."

Her eyes dropped to her hands. Mouth grim, she turned the left one palm up and flexed the fingers back, exposing a faint golden design the shape of the Mehtaran river lotus—the saroj.

"I see. What you mean to say is—or perhaps what you've been trying not to say is—you own me."

"Yes."

"I see."

"Do you? Do you see that it's not something I wanted? Do you understand that I didn't have a choice? I made a decision when I was of The Age not to own das-"

"What are they, then—peris?" she asked, jerking her head toward the house.

"They're family das. Their family has served mine for centuries. To me, they ... they are family."

"If that's true—that you want no slaves—then let me go."

"I can't, Anala." He willed her to look at him, so she'd know the depth of truth in him. "With that mark in your hand, you can't leave this planet unless you leave it at my side."

The pale eyes lanced through him, almost making him catch his breath. "You could take me to Avasa, then."

He shook his head. "Not now, I can't. The Vrinda Varma is just beginning to hear petitions in the case between the Consortium and the Avasan Guild. You're from a mining family, you know how important that consultation is. At this time of year the turnaround to Avasa takes the better part of a week. I can't vacate my seat for a trip of that length."

She snorted. "Least of all with the daughter of Rokh Nadim."

He was stunned. He tried to hide it and failed.

"I see Father is a celebrity even on Mehtar."

"You could say that."

"So." Anala folded her hands in front of her on the table.

There was an entire discourse on resignation in that one word—in that simple gesture. Jaya was almost awed by it. No tears, no histrionics, no anger. Just "so."

She met his gaze again. "I am part of the household of Nathu Rai Jaya Sarojin. I thank you for helping me escape another fate. What now, mahesa? What will my duties be?"

She was steeling herself. He could see it in the slow straightening of her spine.

"Your first duty," he said, "will be to take twenty thousand dagam into Kasi, buy the mining equipment you were sent to get, and ship it to Avasa on the next freight shuttle."

Clearly it was not what she'd expected to hear. "What? Why?"

"Because ... because your family needs it."

"Nathu Rai-"

"Kasi stole your money—and more. You didn't gamble it away or lose it carelessly. Kasi is my city. I am only returning a small part of what it took. I can't return the greater part. It's not in my power. I can only apologize ... for everything."

"I'm ... more than grateful, mahesa. You seem to have saved me twice today."

Jaya grimaced. "Hardly. All I've done is contrived to make the disastrous merely intolerable ... Anala, would your family be able to produce duplicate leaf for you?"

"I should think so."

"Then, we can send a message over with the equipment asking your mother and father to appear with it. The Inner Circle should be able to declare your freedom on the strength of that. And your father will very likely be appearing before the Vrinda Varma to argue AGIM's case-"

Anala was shaking her head. "Father's position is very much like yours, mahesa. He can't leave Avasa right now. He won't leave unless he's ordered to testify before the Vrinda Varma. The Guild needs him at home now, and there's every chance, if he did come, that his life would be endangered. The same is true for my brothers. They're too well known. Why do you think they sent me for equipment? No one knows me in Kasi and father said Mehtarans underestimate women. I'd be just another young dustbrain coming to Kasi for fun and pretty clothes."

Jaya had missed half of what she'd said. "What do you mean, your father's life would be endangered?"

She lowered her eyes to her lap. "He's received threats."

"From whom?"

She glanced up. "The Consortium, of course. Who else?"

"Anala, you know I sit on the Vrinda Varma. Are you sure you're not-"

Her eyebrows rose. "Exaggerating? No, mahesa, I'm not. My father and the other Guild officers have all received threats. They're also under surveillance. As I said, I was able to come only because I'm female. My father will send one of his officers to speak for him."

"How do you know the threats are from the Consortium?"

"Who else would they be from? Who else would want to keep us in thrall to Kasi-Nawahr?"

"I don't know and I'm not going to conjecture. Now about your leaf-"

"Could they send it by packet?"

He shook his head. "Bad idea," he said. "Any mail coming from an Avasan Independent to me or any other Varmana would be intercepted and checked."

"If the Consortium learns of the position I'm in on Mehtar, they'll jump to use it to their advantage."

"Then they'd best not learn. We'll make sure your message to your father is well hidden among your drill bits."

"And what will my message say?"

Jaya stood as the house lamps came on in the purple twilight. "That you're safe, but unable to return because you lack id. That you're under the protection of a Lord who will return you when he can. Shall we go in? I'd like you to meet my Jivinta, Mina Sarojin. I think you'll find her a friend."

"Two new friends in one day. I am blessed, mahesa." She rose, pressed her palms together again, bowed and smiled.

He grimaced. "I'd rather you not call me that."

She looked at him quizzically. "What should I call you then, Nathu Rai Sarojin, that won't scandalize your family?"

"Jaya?" he suggested.

She looked at him doubtfully.

"Jaya," he repeated.

"It seems disrespectful for a slave to address her lord-"

"Let's not dwell on that shall we?" He moved toward the house, pausing when she didn't move with him. Annoyance pricked him. "You don't have to walk three paces behind me," he said, without looking at her, and continued toward the house.

She was beside him when they reached the sliding glass panels that opened into the solarium, and gave him an odd look when he held them open for her. He led her through the core of the palace toward the wing occupied by Jivinta Mina. On the second floor she nodded at one of the uniquely decorated doorways.

"That's the room I woke up in." She hesitated a moment, then asked, "Is yours in this part of the house?"

"Yes," he said, and gestured at the one next to it. "That one."

A look at her very expressive face told him she hadn't asked the question with the intent of offering to share her bed; a disappointment. Now she appeared to be rummaging through an obviously troubled mind for something to say.

"What, Anala?" he asked. "Speak plainly."

"Nathu Rai," she said, "I realize that as my ... lord you can command me as you wish. But, I would beg you-"

"You don't need to beg, Anala. Your honor is as sacred to me as it is to you." It was an ambiguous statement, but it seemed to satisfy her. He'd be a liar to deny the kinetic attraction he felt to her, a hypocrite to protest that he would not act on it if the opportunity presented itself. That oath left the sacredness of her honor entirely up to her.

~

Mina Sarojin was enjoying a light supper when Jaya brought Anala into her suite. He hadn't gotten a word out before her bright, raptor eyes found and fixed on the Avasan.

"Ah! You are right, Gauri, she is stunning. Such coloring!" She swung aside the carved wooden tray that held the remains of her meal and sat eagerly forward in her cup chair. "What's your name, child?"

Anala, immediately impressed with the Jivinta, presented her with the respectful greeting—palms out, palms together, a slight bowing of the forehead to her fingertips. "It's Anala, Rani."

"Anala." The old woman nodded as if she liked the feel of the name on her tongue.

Anala had the sudden impression that if her name had not met with the Jivinta's approval she would have simply changed it on the spot. Everything about her spoke of royalty, from the erect posture to the long hair she wore like a silver diadem.

"And you will call me Jivinta Mina," the old woman decided. "The distinction of Rani in this household goes to my bonddaughter. Unlike her, I prefer names to titles. So, what is the story of Anala? Are you to be a guest of the House Sarojin?"

Anala shot Jaya a fleeting glance. "A while, I think," she said. "It much depends on the Nathu Rai's kindness."

"Well, he's long on that quality. Your while here should be pleasant if it's his kindness you depend on."

Jaya smiled at his Jivinta. "Ah, and this is where I jump in with a proof of my kindness. Jivinta, could I impose on you to take Anala into Kasi tomorrow for some shopping? She needs to purchase some mining equipment and some new clothes. That dress and a torn insulsuit is all she's got at the moment."

Mina's sculptured silver brows ascended delicately. "Mining equipment and new clothes? An interesting combination. Well, I'd be very happy to take our new friend shopping."

Anala stirred uneasily. "Nathu Rai, please don't trouble your Jivinta to buy me a new wardrobe. If I could have my insulsuit mended I'd be more than grateful. And I'm sure I can find the equipment broker on my own."

Jaya's reply was blunt. "Anala, I'm going to be honest with you. I know your desire to get home is fierce. I don't want you to be tempted to try to return on your own. You simply wouldn't make it. Not with that dascree in your palm."

Ana felt her face suffuse with heat. "You don't know me, so I won't take that as an insult. I couldn't possibly leave Mehtar with your money in hand. Besides which, I'm honor bound to repay your kindness to me. If I left without doing that, I couldn't face myself, let alone my family."

The Nathu Rai flushed and opened his mouth. Whether he meant to equivocate or apologize, Ana was not to know; chimes sounded from the com-unit at Jivinta Mina's elbow.

The old woman glanced at it only briefly before returning her eyes to Jaya's flushed face. "Yes, Ari. What is it?"

"Some visitors for the Saroj, Jivinta. The Vadin Bel Adivaram and the Lord Kreti Twapar. They say it is urgent."

"I'll be right down," Jaya said and threw Anala a rueful grimace. "While I'm closeted with my guests, try to think of something I can do to merit forgiveness for that ignorant remark."

"So, Anala," said Mina Sarojin when her grandson had left her rooms, "Come, sit. Tell me about Avasa. Is the air as dry and sweet as I've heard?"

Jaya wasn't particularly pleased to have government business brought into his private quarters, but turning away Adivaram and Twapar would be considered an extreme rudeness. To them the governing of the Mehtaran Commonwealth and the concomitant political existence was the center of their universe. To one who didn't even want a political existence it was at best a duty, and at worst an imposition.

By the time Jaya reached the Court Salon reserved for the reception of Mehtar's elite, Aridas had already provided his guests with refreshment and was standing by to hear his Nathu Rai's pleasure.

"Channa please, Ari," Jaya told him, and did not miss the oblique glances of his fellow Varmana. Their raised brows marked his indiscretion silently. He ignored them and followed a perverse urge to compound the social gaffe. "Oh, and Ari, you can just leave the carafes. I'll serve."

Aridas bowed slightly, a smile playing at the corners of his mouth, then went to the kitchen to fetch his master's channa.

"I wish, Nathu Rai, you would not amuse yourself at our expense." Vadin Bel Adivaram studied the fluted stem of his wine goblet distractedly.

"At your expense?" Jaya asked, seating himself beside the opulent hearth. He chose a low, comfortable chair and chuckled inwardly when his guests both glanced toward the ornate and infinitely less comfortable throne he was expected to use on such occasions. "I fail to understand how Ari's humor cost you anything."

"Then you fail to understand much," mumbled Kreti Twapar. "Every time you elevate a das, by neglecting to use his varnal name, for example, you demean yourself in his estimation. When you make it a joke between you, you demean yourself even more—impair your dignity, impair the dignity of your station. In this instance, you have included us in the joke."

"I've impaired your dignity?" Jaya asked. His answer came in the form of two eloquent glances. "Well then, aren't I demeaning myself even more by allowing you two to lecture me—a Sarojin?"

Vadin Adivaram set down his goblet with a distinct click. "Nathu Rai, demeaning you was not our intention. Think of us merely as a couple of fond old uncles bent on imparting their wisdom to a favorite nephew."

"I'll do that," Jaya promised. "Now what brings my two fond old uncles out this evening?"

"You've read the petitions?" Bel Adivaram came right to the point.

"Yes." That wasn't quite true, and Jaya felt just a little guilty in professing that it was. He had read the Focus Document and scanned the individual petitions tendered by the several chapters of the Avasan Guild. Of the Consortium's counter-petition he'd read only the synopsis.

"And have you formed an opinion?"

"Not one I should discuss."

"I'm not asking you to discuss your opinion," returned Adivaram mildly, "just to comment on whether you've formed one."

Aridas' return with his channa gave Jaya a moment to ponder his reply. Opinions, he didn't have. He hadn't read the petitions well enough for that, nor had he paid strict attention to their presentation in Assembly. He had leanings—an instinctual belief that if the Avasan miners thought they'd be better off without the over-lordship of a Mehtaran corporation, they were probably right—but nothing more solid than that. However, if the Consortium's methods of dissuasion were what Anala claimed ...

"Thank you, Ari. This is excellent, as always. No, I don't have any opinions. I haven't heard both sides in Session yet."

"Well," drawled Lord Twapar, "I'd say we've all heard the Consortium side often enough. It's rather hard to avoid it when every social event seems to center around bringing Kasi-Nawahr officers and stockholders together with Varmana. The Consortium, understandably, does not want the competition. Independents are one thing, united Independents are quite another."

"What do you think Kasi-Nawahr would do if the Vrinda Varma grants AGIM some form of legal status?" asked Jaya.

"Obviously, they're hoping it won't," returned the Vadin.

Jaya glanced at him. "Obviously, but would they do more than hope, do you think?"

Kreti Twapar sat forward in his chair, clasping veined hands before him. "What do you mean by that?"

Jaya shrugged. "They have a lot to lose. I wonder what they might do to protect their interests on Avasa."

"Are you suggesting something less subtle than lobbying?" queried Bel Adivaram.

"Subtle? I've had to avoid too many growling, whining Kasi-Nawahr associates at social gatherings to call it subtle. Although, very few of them go far enough to warrant a sanction being placed on them. I was thinking of something more secretive ... and more serious."

The two guests shared a significant sidelong glance before putting down their glasses in near unison.

"I think it's time to come to the point," said Adivaram. "The Consortium, as you suggest, is more than eager to maintain its hold on Avasa. But it is not the Consortium we come to speak of. We come with a warning, Nathu Rai. You may well be approached by ... a group of people who are willing to do a bit more than whine."

After a moment of silence, Jaya prompted him. "Approached?"

The two older men continued to gaze at him without replying.

"Am I to construe from that an unlawful query as to my opinions, or something else?"

He glanced from one closed, watchful face to the other, hearing only Kreti Twapar's raspy breathing, the snap of flame from the hearth and the tell-tale click, click, click of Bel Adivaram's fingernails against the arm of his chair.

What in the name of Sanat-Ram were they trying to do, frighten him?

"What is it we're not discussing, uncles?" he asked. "Bribery? Threats?" He gestured around the room. "Bribery hardly seems likely, considering my circumstances. Promises of political promotion are equally ludicrous. Threats, then? Is that this evening's purport of the word 'approached?'"

Bel Adivaram cleared his throat. "I'm not sure how much we dare say."

"Were you approached?"

"Possibly." Adivaram glanced sideways at Twapar.

"You couldn't tell?"

"We're not certain what to do. It was so vague, so nebulous." Twapar made a fluttering gesture of helplessness and trained sorrowful eyes on his Nathu Rai. "Nothing, you understand, that could be pinned down ... quite. We wondered, Nathu Rai, what you would do in such circumstances."

"I can't tell you. I don't know what the circumstances were. Were you threatened or not?" Jaya felt a tickle of irritation. What did these two think—that he had the Jadu and could read minds?

"Not threatened, precisely," said Adivaram. "It was suggested that there are advantages to deeming the Avasan position unlawful."

"Unlawful?" Jaya got up and moved away from the hearth,

putting his back to them. "That suggests that the Vrinda Varma should declare the Avasan Guild asat."

"That was what I inferred also," admitted the Vadin. "Apparently, the Consortium is preparing an addendum to their counter petition that demands AGIM be declared a subversive organization and officially disbanded. And, of course, if AGIM is asat, it would keep the issue of their independence from ever being raised again."

"Leaving all AGIM mining interests open for KNC appropriation," murmured Jaya. How amazing are the workings of the political mind, he thought, and was grateful he didn't have one.

"Excuse me, Nathu Rai?"

"Never mind." He turned back to face them. "Who approached you?"

"They called themselves WoCoa—the Workers' Coalition," said Twapar. "They indicated they felt that any decision favoring AGIM threatened their jobs and incomes. They suggested that supporting the Consortium's counter petition is the best thing for all concerned. They were quite vehement."

"Vehement, but nebulous, eh?"

Adivaram scowled. "As I said, we were unsure of how much we should say."

"Well, what did you say to these suggestions?"

"We didn't know what to say to them," protested Adivaram. "What would you have said?"

Jaya shrugged. "I'm not sure. Maybe I would have thrown the suggestion-makers out of my house. Then again, maybe I would've asked to hear more."

They stared at him and he chuckled. "Did I shock you? Sorry. Just consider it a function of my infamous eccentricity."

Kreti Twapar's stare twisted into a grimace. "Your eccentricity, Lord Prince Sarojin, is sometimes inappropriate."

Jaya raised his eyebrows in amusement, but the Vadin Adivaram misread him. "Forgive our irascible old Lord, mahesa. He's becoming cranky with his years." He shot his confederate a withering glance.

"Yes, Nathu Rai," mumbled Twapar, with about as much contrition as Jaya felt for being eccentric. "Please, don't take offense. I forgot myself."

"No offense taken," said Jaya blandly. "You see? My eccentricity can also be a blessing. I've forgotten you, too."

For a moment Kreti Twapar's face drained of all color—lacking even its natural yellowish tinge. Jaya's pleasant laughter seemed to restore it somewhat, and he laughed, as well.

"Why haven't you reported this to the Inner Circle? You are members, after all."

"We ... didn't want to muddy the waters with mention of this WoCoa matter. If you've read the petitions, you've no doubt realized how complex this situation has already become."

"Very complex." *You have no idea.*

"So," said Bel Adivaram finally, "you would advise us to say nothing of this before the Vrinda Varma? Or should we register a complaint?"

"I wouldn't presume to advise you," returned Jaya. "But I do see the point of not lodging a formal report. If I were 'approached' by anyone, I probably wouldn't be inclined to complain to the Vrinda Varma right away. Silence can give instruction even to the wise." He'd heard his father say that often enough. He could only assume he'd gotten it from Jivinta Mina.

The two old ones nodded and hummed and then excused themselves, leaving Jaya alone in the Court Salon. He wasn't alone long— a grinning Aridas joined him, chuckling as he collected the glasses and cups from the room.

"Ari, you'll burst if you don't share that grin with me. What did my two 'old uncles' do to amuse you?"

"'Ay! Silence can give instruction even to the wise, he says!'" The imitation of Kreti Twapar's gritty, wheezy voice was eerily accurate. "'How dare that insolent young whelp sound so damn sage? Nathu Rai he may be, Sarojin he may be, but he's got a head full of air and ego!'"

Jaya laughed. "Air? Something as benign as that? I'm amazed. I would've expected they thought it was full of something else."

Ari shook his head. "Someday, Jaya Rai, you should land upon those two old scoffers with talons. You tolerate them so well, they're getting bold and toothy."

"Why should I do that? I don't care how toothy they get."

"But I do," chided Ari. "Their das know what disrespect they feel for you, mahesa. Heli and I have to put up with their foolish mockery, you know. It's not easy."

"Ah, and of course you defend me loyally."

"Of course," Ari assured him. "It's our duty and privilege. But you could help by quashing them occasionally." His reproachful expression twisted into a leer. "It'd scare them to eternity, mahesa."

"And you'd like to be there to see it, of course."

The leer was still hanging in the air when Aridas was halfway back to the kitchen with his tray.

The Rani Melantha Sarojin was curious about her son's visitors. She made an abortive attempt to pump Helidasa for information, but got absolutely nowhere with the woman. She should have known better than to waste her time trying, she realized, pulling off her gloves in the front hall. Her late husband's das were fiercely loyal to his son and imagined that loyalty extended to keeping all his affairs secret from even his own mother.

She paused to study the closed doors of the Court Salon, considered stepping closer to listen to the conversation she could just barely make out, then saw Aridas coming down the corridor with a carafe-laden tray.

She collected herself and headed for the grand staircase, hoping the das hadn't seen her lingering there like a common snoop. It occurred to her, as she mounted the stairs, that her bond-mother might know why there were Varmana sitting in their Court Salon— Varmana who were also of the Inner Nine. She hoped Mina Sarojin would be in one of her chatty moods. With that in mind, she turned right at the top of the stairs and passed down the central corridor to the dowager Sarojin's quarters.

The Rani was surprised to find that the old woman also had a visitor. The young woman was quite beautiful in a wild, vivid and somewhat alien way. Her dress was exotic but tasteful and made the most of her rather pale skin. She remembered Bel Adivaram's seemingly endless supply of young female "relations" and wondered if this was one of them.

She was faintly amused by the two pairs of eyes that stared at her as she stood in the doorway of her bond-mother's suite. They could have belonged to children caught whispering in the Asra during prayers.

"Pardon my intrusion, Mata," she said. "I didn't mean to interrupt your visit. May I be introduced?"

Mina Sarojin collected herself and fixed the Rani with a brittle smile. Her veined hands, still strong and supple, caught the young woman's possessively between their palms. "Of course. Melantha, this..." Her smile swung to her young companion, warming. "This is Ana Sadira, a new, but already dear friend of mine. Ana, I present the Rani Melantha Sarojin."

The younger woman made a visible attempt to free her hands from Mina's to offer the respectful greeting, but Mina held them immobile, a frozen smile aimed at the Rani.

Ana Sadira nodded, embarrassed, and said, "I am honored, Rani Sarojin. The hospitality of your House is as the kindness of Tara-Rama."

Melantha accepted the greeting and compliment with a slight raising of artfully painted brows and an even slighter nod. "You are related to one of my son's guests?"

"No, Rani, I am not."

"She's a friend of Jaya's," said Mina. "That should please you."

"Yes, it should."

The Rani studied her bond-mother's guest a moment more, then smiled briefly and left them. On the opposite side of the translucent curtains that separated her bond-mother's sitting room from the anteroom, Melantha turned for a last look at the pair. The vivid young woman was staring into her palm, while Mina Sarojin remonstrated with her.

Odd. The Rani wondered if it had anything to do with Mina's refusal to allow her guest to offer the respectful greeting. Bemused, she turned away and left the suite.

"Jivinta, may I speak with you for a moment?" Jaya stood just inside the curtained door of her bedroom, his eyes on the pool of light that washed the shallow bowl of velvet padding she slept in.

She laid aside her book and shifted to face him more directly. "Of course, Gauri. Come." She patted the lip of the bed.

As if I were still a small boy with bad dreams, thought Jaya, and moved to her side.

"I like her very much," answered Mina, before he could phrase the question. "She is not prim about spiritual things. You know how I loathe religious primness. And I think she is to be trusted. I should mention that your mother has met her."

A terrifying thought. "How?"

"She paid me a visit this evening—I can't imagine why, unless it was to see if I knew anything about the business downstairs. Naturally, she was fascinated by Anala."

Jaya shifted uneasily. "What did you tell her?"

Mina chuckled. "The Rani is under the impression that our young friend is also a Rani—of the family Sadira."

Jaya was not certain whether to be relieved or worried. "Not my cunnidasa?"

"I refused to let Anala offer her the respectful greeting."

"That was wise."

"I thought so."

"So, she's Anala Sadira, now."

Mina's smile deepened. "Ana Sadira. Ana of the Lotus Tree. I thought it was appropriate. I hope your mother doesn't take it into her head to check up on her."

"Why should she?"

"Maybe she suspects a wedding is being plotted behind her back." The look she gave him was coy.

"I'm ignoring you, Grandmother."

"Mmmm. But can you ignore Ana?"

"Grandmother, you are an incorrigible match-maker! The woman is Avasan—the daughter of a miner."

"So?"

"So where's your Mehtaran pride? Aren't you supposed to be bringing me quality Taj-daughters of Mehtar? Dark-skinned Ranis, Devas-"

Mina made a rude noise. "That's your mother's job. Quality doesn't come with breeding, titles, citizenship ... or racial heritage. It comes with character. The daughter of an Avasan miner is just as likely to have that as any woman on Mehtar, regardless of her rank."

"Her father is Rokh Nadim." Jaya watched his Jivinta's expression. It didn't change.

"Yes, I know."

"She told you?"

"She told me many things." She paused, assessing him. "Did you know she was Rohin—a bhakta?"

Jaya was surprised. That explained why, despite her apparent acceptance of her situation, she'd dared to let him know his sexual advances would not be welcomed. He was relieved that he hadn't pressed the issue. Even a member of a Taj House generally watched his manners with a devotee of the Upward Path.

Mina was watching his face with raptor gaze. "I hope you didn't embarrass yourself, Grandson."

He smiled. "Only slightly."

"What do you think the Rani would make of all this ... if she knew?"

Jaya could just imagine. The knowledge that the daughter of Rokh Nadim had come into the possession of the youngest member of the Vrinda Varma would probably be the most important piece of gossip Melantha Sarojin could ever hope to pass along. Since her current male companion was Kasi-Nawahr's Legal Representative, and since that particular gossip would have the greatest impact in his quarter, she would pass it along to him.

"You were wise to give her a new name."

"I try to make a habit of wisdom," said Jivinta Mina. "What will you do if the Rani presses the issue? Who is Ana Sadira that she should suddenly be living under your roof?"

"Why should I have to comment? If it pleases me to suddenly invite a beautiful woman into my house-" He shrugged.

"But not into your bed? Highly suspicious."

"She's in the adjoining suite. I can make sure the door is unlocked in case the Rani or one of her das should wander into my quarters."

Mina nodded. "And if the Rani sees the palm of her hand?"

"That's more difficult. I can't, in good conscience, pass her off as a cunnidasa, knowing she's Rohin ... We could fake an injury to her hand."

"And when that wears thin?"

Jaya opened his left hand and studied the palm thoughtfully. "With a little alteration, the dascree could be made to look like a raicree. Change the color, a line here and there ... ." He illustrated, tracing the faint scarlet imprint in his own palm.

"An unknown branch of the House Sarojin? From where?"

Jaya shrugged. "Darupur?" He named a city halfway across the continent. "The Saroj is a far-flung clan."

Mina was skeptical. "Darupur? With her coloring?"

"Ah ... one of our distant relations moved his family to Avasa."

"I will relish watching you come up with a credible reason as to why any sane man would do such a thing. Just how do you propose to get this cree 'fixed?' Who do you know that owns the proper machinery ... that you can trust?"

"Badan-Devaki?"

Mina snorted. "Those maggots! I said, 'that you can trust.'"

Jaya feigned shock. "Jivinta! Such language!"

"Such people! Do you think either of them would keep that damaging knowledge to themselves? They'd sell it, just as they sell the poor creatures who have the misfortune of coming into their possession."

"There's a cree imprinter at the Asra."

Jivinta Mina was amused. "Do you think the Deva will be persuaded to let you use it? What will you do, pose as God?"

Jaya was cornered and knew it. "The Deva Radha is not as legalistic as some of the Rohin."

Mina didn't say anything, but merely quirked an eyebrow at him. He knew the look well after over two decades of these sparring matches. She was giving him a second chance to make a better parry.

"If the situation gets desperate," he said, "I can always take her to the Inner Circle for sanctuary. They could make her their ward. No one would dare touch her then."

"True. They would likely give her sanctuary. They know the sanctity of a covenant."

"So, who is Ana Sadira?" asked Jaya, wondering how many points he'd made.

Mina shrugged. "She's a Sarojin cousin whose grandmother, a native of Avasa, moved to Mehtar for reasons of health and married a member of the Saroj from Darupur. He returned the family to Avasa when ... his bond-father died, leaving an estate to his only daughter. Ana is in Kasi for a holiday."

"And her hand?"

"Ah, leave that to me. Helidasa can do wonderful things with her herbs and dyes."

Jaya kissed his Jivinta lightly on the cheek, then rose to leave. "Well, this story at least saves the Rani Sadira having to leave her bedroom door open at night. She wouldn't like that."

"No, she wouldn't."

She said it with such vehemence that he had to laugh. "Am I that repulsive?"

"Repulsive? You?" She scanned his face, her eyes mocking him. "Your father was called 'the Golden Lotus,' and you are your father's son. You know this—you've heard it often enough. But Anala is Rohin. That is something you may not be able to understand, even if you try."

Jaya smiled wryly. "You're being mystical and sage, Jivinta. I hate it when you're mystical and sage."

"Phht! You love it, and have since you were a boy. When you're my age, you'll be mystical and sage too. Then you'll see the other side of things."

"I hope I enjoy it as much as you do."

"You will," she assured him. "Especially if your audience stands raptly in wide-eyed wonder, never doubting a word you say."

"I doubt," said Jaya. "I am simply too polite to say so."

That was a lie, he thought, as the door of her suite closed behind him. He'd never doubted Mina Sarojin for a moment.

The room was dark, lit only by a fire in the hearth and the light that breached the vast expanse of windows and squeezed through the brocaded drapes from outside.

Anala parted them and caught her breath. From the second floor she overlooked the walls at the front of the palace—now a line of indistinct black—and saw the broad avenue beyond sweep away downhill, ablaze with street lamps. At its end, Kasi spread before the House Sarojin like a litter of vari-colored gems on black velvet— a tribute. Or like a jewel-bedecked pet tethered to its master by a chain of light.

Tethered, as she was tethered.

A smoky curl of anger roiled for a moment in her heart. She took a deep breath and blew the fire out, unclenching her fists in a deliberate stretching of muscle and bone. She pulled the drapes fully open and knelt on the window seat.

She focused on the litter of light and kept her eyes there until they blurred. Then she closed them and began to pray.

"Sanat-ji, Tara-ji. Please visit this, Your daughter. You know, O my Lord, what has befallen me. I have been lost, but found; enslaved, yet freed; mistreated, but kindly. I am frightened, yet comforted; alone, yet among friends. I do not yet see Your purpose in these things, O Lord, so I await Your guidance. Do with me as befits Your grace, O Most Gracious One, and is worthy of Your glory, O Most Glorious One."

She was silent for a moment, listening; and still, waiting. Waiting for the Sign that her prayer had been heard. There ... within three heartbeats, the warmth of certainty blushed outward from heart to hands and up into the very roots of her hair. She couldn't recall a time the Sign, when asked, had not been given.

She lay down, then, to watch the lights of Kasi until sleep came.

CHAPTER THREE

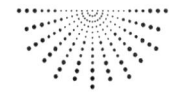

MORNING BROUGHT SUNLIGHT AND WARMTH. But the winds were capricious, gentle one moment, unkind the next. Sitting at the head of the breakfast table in the Morning Room, Jaya watched the tall evergreens in the garden shrug off the rough teasing, their topmost branches shying first one way, then the other.

He was alone, and Helidasa moved almost silently in and out of the room, laying out the meal. He smiled at the sheer amount of food she was assembling on the sideboard.

"Heli," he said, when she appeared with a huge bowl of fruit, "are you planning to feed a team of rattle-ball players?"

"I am feeding three people," she said, setting the bowl of fruit in the center of the arrangement. "Maybe four." Catching his questioning glance, she continued, "The young lady will be down. Which means your mother will most certainly be at table. Jivinta Mina tells me she will be down as well."

The soles of her soft shoes padded lightly across the tile floor of the solarium as she returned to the kitchen, disappearing through the broad, corner-cut doorway.

Jivinta at breakfast—now that was an event. She'd stopped coming down to breakfast months ago, claiming her leg was paining her. Jaya suspected that in reality, it was the Rani Melantha that was paining her. Conversations at breakfast didn't always go pleasantly with Mother there—especially since she'd taken up with her newest beau. She tended to echo his philosophies and viewpoints, which was usually enough to send Jivinta into a temper and Jaya out of the room.

A soft cadence of footfalls told him Helidasa was returning. Something in the whisper of sound made every hair on his body rise up. He chuckled and turned to tell her she'd have to walk less like a cat, then froze in the torrent of electricity that poured through him.

Anala stared at him from the doorway, her cloud of blackcherry hair ablaze in the bold wash of sunlight from the tall solarium windows.

Were he a religious man, he might have claimed her as a vision of the Mother God. He wasn't, but the name dropped from his lips before he realized it had slipped out. "Tara-ji."

Anala shifted uneasily. "Mahesa?"

He felt immediately foolish. "Sorry, Anala, I wasn't taking one of your God's names in vain. There's a painting of Her Holiness Tara-Rama in our family shrine—for a moment, you reminded me ... with the light..." He gestured past her.

She turned her head, glancing at the sun-washed tiles. "Ah. I'm flattered, Nathu Rai. Thank you, but you do no honor to Tara-ji with the comparison."

"That's debatable."

She blushed, averted her eyes and moved to take the seat he indicated. "Please, Nathu Rai. You're making me uncomfortable. I'm unused to flattery."

"I find that hard to believe."

Anala's eyebrows winged upward. "Nathu Rai, I don't know what you imagine life in an Avasan mining community is like, but it doesn't give one many opportunities to wear the sort of clothing that draws compliments."

"I wasn't complimenting the clothing, Ana."

Anala stared at her empty plate. "Nathu Rai..."

"Jaya."

She shrugged. "My life on Avasa hasn't prepared me for any of this." Her gesture took in both her surroundings and circumstances.

"You must tell us about your life on Avasa, my dear."

Jaya's eyes flew from Anala's face to his mother's and back again. He was torn between mirth and chagrin—compromised with a choking cough.

The Rani Melantha crossed from the doorway behind Ana's chair and rounded the table to take a seat to her son's right, her expression quizzical.

"I'm sorry, Mother," he said, recovering himself. "You startled us."

"Indeed," said the Rani pleasantly, her eyes on Ana's face. "I had not imagined anyone's eyes could get that large. Yours are most unusually pale, as well. Almost ... colorless, in fact. Have you ever considered ... cosmetic coloration? I hear it is quite safe."

"Oh, no, Rani. This eye color has been passed down through generations of the family Sadira," returned Anala, glibly. "It allows more light to enter the eye, thus enhancing the sight. My father's eyes are white as snow. They call him 'the Bat.' He can see well enough in the dark to shoot the petals off the black jambu on a moonless night."

Jaya only just managed not to laugh. Quick. He wondered at how easily the story had fallen from her lips.

"That ought to answer your arrogance," observed Jivinta Mina dryly. She entered the room on Helidasa's arm, her ornately carved cane tapping firmly on the tiles of the floor. Taking her seat at the head of the table, she signaled Helidasa to serve.

"A moonless night?" murmured the Rani, her tawny skin flushing with rose. "Unimaginable. I'd heard Avasa was a dim world. But no moon?"

"On moonless nights, we have the Upala Ratri—the Night Jewel —to light the sky."

"The Upala Ratri?" repeated Jaya.

"A colorful aurora caused by suspended ice crystals in the atmosphere. It's quite beautiful. When I was a child I would pretend they were angels dancing for Tara-ji."

That was truth, Jaya thought, but could not explain why he thought so.

The Rani cast her son a bemused glance. "Your coloring," she commented after a moment, "is quite ... striking. Is this to be blamed on the Avasan environment?"

Again, Anala failed to rise to the obvious insult. "It's due mostly to the climate in the Kedar. It's a mountainous place—thickly forested, most often snow-covered. There is little sun."

"You were born on Avasa?"

"Yes, Rani."

"But, Sadira..." She looked to Jaya. "I am not mistaken, Jaya. Isn't that a distant branch of the Saroj clan?"

"It is, Mother. It seems Ana is a remote relation."

The Rani's lips curved in a bemused smile. "From Avasa?"

"Ana's grandmother was from Avasa. She relocated here—to Darupur—for reasons of health, and there met the man she would marry. The family returned to Avasa when Ana's great-grandfather died." Jivinta Mina put another stitch into their fabrication.

Ana neatly tied it off. "My great-grandfather owned a number of prosperous businesses—lumber yards and paper factories. When he died, he bequeathed them to my grandmother. My grandparents refused to be absentee landlords, so they made their home in the Kedar."

"I have considered a trip to Avasa myself, recently," said Jivinta. "Ana says the air in the plains is quite dry and sweet. The air here is getting worse every day." She gazed pointedly at her daughter-in-law.

The Rani wrinkled her perfect nose and glanced apologetically at Anala. "I hear it's dry and sweet only when it's not dry and dusty —and unbearably cold. You may have Avasa, my dear. I would be terrified of waking up one morning to find myself the color of cow's milk." She touched one flawless, tawny cheek.

"I think a little less sun would do you good, daughter," said Mina, sugaring her tea. Her eyes lifted to the Rani's face. "And I can't believe all your dyes and tints are good for your skin."

Melantha Sarojin did not offer a retort. "How do you come to be with us, Ana? I may call you 'Ana?'"

"Of course, Rani Sarojin. I have just finished my schooling, so Mother and Father thought a holiday would be in order."

"Your schooling?" repeated the Rani, glancing obliquely at her son. "What sort of schooling does a young woman obtain on Avasa that would extend beyond her fourteenth year?"

"I studied forestry, land management, and environmental law."

It came off her tongue so readily, Jaya wondered if it was true.

The Rani's expression said that she considered the idea preposterous. She did not, however, offer her opinions on the woman's place in society. "So, was your visit to the Saroj unexpected, or did my son merely neglect to tell me you were coming?"

"A whim on God's part, Rani. Nathu Rai Sarojin and I met quite by chance near the spaceport."

The Rani's neat brows ascended with bird-like grace. "Quite a chance, I must agree, that two so distant cousins should meet accidentally in such a large city as Kasi."

Jaya studied his plate, teasing an innocent and unresisting melon with the tip of his knife. "One might almost think Ji had arranged it," he said wryly.

"One might almost," agreed the Rani, studying Anala again. "But to what purpose?" The question hung, full of innuendo, until the Rani asked: "So, your family has prospered on Avasa, then?"

Jaya could well imagine her thought process: Down and out tendril of the Saroj vine arranges chance meeting between lovely leaf and the Heart of the Lotus. A move calculated, of course, to infuse new life into the poor distant tendril.

"Father tells me he is the richest man on Avasa."

"Really?"

Jaya put his cup down with a thud and coughed, trying to get Anala's attention. What was she doing? Claiming not to be down and out was one thing, but this-

She was smiling. "You would have to understand my father, Rani. He has always said a man's wealth is in his family."

"Not in his forests?" The Rani shook her head and emitted a musical, shallow trill of laughter. "Pardon me, Ana, but I find the idea of a Sarojin in a lumber yard ludicrous."

"He had an opportunity to go into government ... or was it politics? I always get the two confused. I note that both are lucrative in the extreme. But my father is an honorable man and therefore felt it necessary to earn his bread in an honorable way."

"How ... noble of him," said the Rani and withdrew into her bowl of fruit.

"Do you really think governance is a dishonorable means of earning one's keep?" Jaya asked Anala later. They waited in the great Entrance Hall for Jivinta Mina to join Ana for their outing.

"Did I say that, mahesa?"

"Not directly, but you implied it. Also that the Vrinda Varma confuses politics and government. I assure you, it does not."

"Forgive me then, mahesa."

"Jaya. My name is Jaya. Not Mahesa or Nathu Rai or Master."

"I would never call you 'Master,'" said Anala. "Sanat-ji is my Master. My only Master ... mahesa."

She was being deliberately antagonistic and it annoyed him. "Please, call me by my name instead of a meaningless title."

Anala's vivid brows tilted slightly. "Your titles aren't meaningless, you know. Being a Varmana is a sacred privilege ... and a responsibility—one which has nothing to do with politics."

"You are the second person to remind me of that in as many days." Jaya was annoyed with the direction the conversation was taking. "I am not a political, Anala. I inherited my wealth and title in the same way I inherited my seat on the Vrinda Varma. I didn't ask for either. But since I have them, I do try to give them the serious consideration they deserve." That was so close to a lie, he was surprised he didn't choke on it.

"You sound as if you would just as soon be an indolent beggar as the Lord Prince of Kasi."

"No, but the responsibility of my position does sometimes..." He raised his eyes to the Sarojin crest, mounted in gleaming splendor at the head of the hall. " ... weigh a lot."

"I don't see you trying to crawl out from under the weight."

"Actually, that's what I was doing when I met you—crawling away, escaping. For a while."

"But not permanently?"

"If I escape this,"—he gestured at the grandeur of the sunstrewn hall—"I also escape my dignity, my family honor, my responsibility to my father's household ... my Jivinta. Can you honestly see me abandoning her? Or depriving myself of her?"

Anala sobered, lowering her eyes. "No, I can't. Forgive me for making light of your honor. I misjudged you, Jaya Rai."

Jaya Rai. He awarded himself an imaginary point.

She caught the expression on his face and said, "Well, your das call you that—your other das."

"You aren't-" But she was. He started again. "You are the Rani Sadira, a distant cousin to the Saroj. Do you mind me calling you 'Ana?'"

"My family calls me 'Ana,'" she said.

"That's nice, but that wasn't the question. Do you mind me calling you that?"

"It seems that you are family now, too."

Exasperation tickled his temper. "Is it a function of being Rohin that you answer every question indirectly?"

She seemed to consider the question seriously. "No. I think it is a function of being uncertain."

He felt swift guilt, then brushed it aside with the reasonable argument that there was nothing else he could have done. Had the Sarngin reached her first, she would still be in that dalali, or worse.

Jivinta Mina chose that moment to appear at the head of the hall. She moved briskly, despite her cane, and swiftly herded Ana into her coach.

The shopping expedition dispatched, Jaya found Heli and Ari's eldest son, Ravi, waiting for him in his study, his lord's chamber robes—in the blaze and blood of the Sarojin colors—draped over one arm.

Jaya grimaced. "Am I going to be late again?"

Ravi smiled. "No, Jaya Rai. But I wanted to be sure you were not. The senior Varmana were a bit disgruntled the last time you took your seat in the middle of the invocation."

"Took my seat? Fell into it, you mean."

Ravi laughed. "Just as the Dandin said, 'May the blessings of Sanat-ji descend upon you."

"Damn robes will be the death of me, Ravi." Jaya flicked a golden sleeve with one finger.

Ravi was immediately sober. "I suspect the robes had less to do with it than the wine, Jaya Rai."

"I was feeling father's passing rather acutely that day."

"Understood, but it seemed to those who watched that you made light of the responsibilities that go with inheriting your father's station." He held the robes out for his lord to put on.

Jaya discovered, again, that there was an element of pain involved in allowing friendship to supplant ownership. "Ravi, you're beginning to sound like your father."

"If my father has told you that, then I'm happy to repeat him. He's right ... on occasion." He fastened the closes on one crimson shoulder drape, then arranged his own matching cloak and waited.

Jaya looked at him a moment, his mind framing a sarcastic suggestion that they trade robes and position. The remark died before it reached his lips. This morning, he didn't really mean it. This morning, he was anticipating the session. Between Anala's accusation of Consortium foul play and Adivaram's veiled suggestion of coercion by some mysterious coalition, Jaya Sarojin's curiosity was kindling rapidly.

"You won't believe me, but I'm actually looking forward to the assembly today."

Ravi blinked. Of all the things his master might have said to him, that was possibly the least expected. Jaya scored for himself another imaginary point.

"Of course I believe you, Nathu Rai," Ravi said finally. "You wouldn't lie to me." It was almost a question—suspecting, if not a lie, at least a jest.

Jaya chuckled, clapped a hand on Ravi's shoulder and steered him out to the waiting coach.

～

The Sarojin box at the Kiritan was a second floor gallery, small enough to provide intimacy and warmth, and large enough to hold a good-sized party of guests. Anala and the Jivinta Mina entered it from a beautifully carved door of the same general proportions characteristic of those in the House Sarojin.

Anala smiled wryly. In her experience, one stooped to get through most doors. The small apertures, with their curved cowling and inner membranes and baffles shunted the stinging assault of the chill vayu winds. Only in the mild equatorial climes of the Sagara or the old-growth thickets of the Kedar did unprotected doorways exist. Her own home was in the rocky passes at the tree-line and just below the high Sita Plateau, so called because its barren earth was so bleached, it always seemed to be covered with snow.

She directed a smile at the servant who seated her at the large, graceful table, then almost gasped aloud when he drew the curtains that covered one wall, opening the box to the room below.

"Half-open please, Naru," Mina told him. "We will have iced nectar to refresh ourselves before the meal."

The man bowed and smiled, not insincerely, Anala decided.

There was legitimate pleasure in his handsome face. Mina Sarojin was evidently a favorite patron.

"What do you think, Ana?" she asked when the server had disappeared to bring their drinks.

Anala's eyes made a thorough assessment—the splendid box, the view of the beautifully laid-out restaurant with its fountains and greenery and statuary. What she had once taken as luxurious surroundings—the channara of the Hotel Gaesa in Raratok—seemed colorless in comparison. "It's beautiful," she said.

Mina quirked a silvery brow at her. "And extravagant?"

"The soul has as much need for beauty as the body does for food. What could be better than to feed both at the same time?"

"Well put. And,"—Mina glanced over the carved balustrade—"one can also feed one's curiosity. Most of the crowns of Kasi society have boxes or booths or standing reservations at the Kiritan. Not to mention some from Nawahr and even Vatapur. From here, I can see much. Ah ... Namun!"

Ana followed Mina Sarojin's eyes as she sent a cheerful wave to someone below. A tall, slender gentleman with finely cut features and streaks of silver in his dark hair had just entered the main dining area from a side room and glanced up, smiling broadly in return. His somewhat mismatched clothing looked as if it had been an after-thought—careless enough that he looked as out-of-place as Ana felt. Mina beckoned to him and he began to move toward their balcony.

"Namun Vedda," Jivinta Mina explained. The twinkle of her eyes told Anala that here was another of her favorites. "Jaya's godfather. A delightful man. Very erudite. He once taught at the college here in Kasi, but he has left academic life to devote himself to research."

"Research?" repeated Anala. "He's a scientist?"

"Yes. He owns his own company, too. A company my son helped him start. They were like brothers. When Bhaktasu was killed, I think Namun nearly died with him. He's unmarried." She gave Ana a sly glance out of the tail of her eye. "Quite a catch for some intelligent and engaging woman. Oh-!"

The disappointment in Jivinta Mina's face caused Anala to drop her gaze back to the floor below. Vedda-sama had been waylaid by another man—a handsome, impeccably dressed fellow with quick mannerisms and an air of great intensity. They were a study in contrasts; this newcomer was gesturing emphatically with his hands —Veddasama had stuffed his into the large pockets of his tunic. It was clear that this other demanded his attention and just as clear that he was much annoyed at the demand.

In the end, he waved his regrets to the Rani Mina and returned with his companion to the room he'd only just left.

Mina's expression was one of barely veiled disdain. She made a clucking noise and shook her head.

"You don't care much for Vedda-sama's friend," Anala guessed.

"An understatement. I despise him. He is my bond-daughter's current ... companion. I had thought better of her than that. I had, in fact, hoped she and Namun..." She shrugged eloquently and let the subject drop.

"I see our drinks hurrying this way," observed Anala. "Should we order?"

In the end, the alieness of the dishes convinced Anala to have Mina order for her. It sounded like more than she could possibly eat, but Mina assured her that between the cook and the server, they would receive amounts proportioned to their respective appetites.

"A good server," said Mina, "is a master at knowing his patrons' preferences and appetites. This first time he serves you he has only your size, age and gender to go on, but as you return, he will note which are your favorite dishes and in what proportion."

"Is he das?" asked Ana.

"Naru? Oh, no." Jivinta Mina seemed almost scandalized at the thought. "The service people at the Kiritan are free—every one. Highly educated in the culinary arts as well as the spiritual disciplines. Giving pleasure is an art, Ana. But of course, your discipline as Rohin has taught you that."

Anala discovered that one could, indeed, blush to the roots of one's hair. "My bhakti is of the simplest kind, Jivinta," she said. "I observe devotion to Sanatji, the pursuance of the Intellectual Arts. My knowledge of the Pleasure Arts is-"

"Ana," interrupted the old woman, almost reproachfully, "I was not implying something about you I know is not true. I am aware that there are those who call themselves Rohin and are little more than glorified cunnidasa. I am also aware that you are not one of them. There is much of that on Mehtar," she said thoughtfully, "but perhaps the Path is clearer on Avasa."

"The Path is becoming unclear there, too. In the cities—even in a place as small and out-of-the-way as Onan—I've met bhakta who make a devotion of giving pleasure to male pilgrims in the Asra. The men joke and call it Josha—the Path of Satisfaction." She looked away from Mina's sharp gaze to the arcade below. Delicate sounds mingled with delicate perfumes rose upward to their aerie.

"Don't concern yourself with them. Only your bhakti, Ana, concerns you. Not theirs ... What's wrong, child?"

Anala barely heard the question. Her entire attention was on a familiar face in the room below. Where had she seen that face, and why did it matter? His clothes didn't seem right ...

She nearly jumped out of her chair. "That man, Jivinta!" She pointed. "The one just crossing the room—no, he's stopped again, near that small fountain."

"I've never seen him before. What about him bothers you?"

"That's one of the thieves who stole my father's money."

Mina didn't ask if she was certain. Instead, she turned raptor eyes on the man as if to memorize him. "Shall we pursue him?" she asked. "Have him stopped?"

"On what charge, Jivinta? How can I stop him without revealing myself? Besides, who would believe that a man of such obvious means would steal money from someone like me?"

"What is he doing here, I wonder?"

"Could we find out?"

Mina smiled and rang the service bell.

Naru appeared almost immediately with a platter of breads, a slight frown in his eyes. "There is something wrong, Rani?"

"Not a thing, Naru," Mina told him. "Your service is exemplary, as always. But I've seen someone I know I should recognize, but cannot match with a name. One of my grandson's many friends. Is he still there, Ana, dear?"

"Just leaving, Jivinta." Ana's voice betrayed none of her desperation.

Naru took the cue and moved to stand behind Mina's chair, his eyes on the premiere floor.

"There," said Mina, "just passing the first table."

Naru squinted, frowned and shook his head. "I've seen him before, but I know nothing about him."

"He came out of that doorway over there." Ana pointed to an elegantly decorated portal of only slightly less grandeur than the one they'd entered to reach the Sarojin box.

"He might be acquainted with someone who has a box in that section. Then again, he might just be a general patron."

Anala sighed in frustration. Fate had granted her a gift and she had failed to accept it.

Naru's face brightened. "I could give him a message, if I should see him again."

"Oh, no," said Mina, "that would never do. Then I should have to make the embarrassing admission that I've forgotten his name."

"Well then, I shall ask the other servers if they know him."

"If you would be so kind. If I'm going to put the man on my invitation list, I must have his name." Mina smiled engagingly and Naru bowed his way back to the serving cart, clearly pleased to assist her.

The meal was wonderful and Anala managed to lose herself in enjoyment of it, though Naru didn't discover anything about the Nathu Rai Sarojin's mysterious "friend." He promised continued attention to the matter as he escorted them to the Sarojin carriage.

"I will find out this man, Rani Sarojin," he vowed. "You shall have him at your next dinner, I promise you."

"Yes, as the main course," murmured Mina.

Naru laughed and bowed as the carriage pulled away from the Kiritan's front curbing.

CHAPTER FOUR

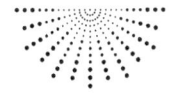

Jaya Sarojin shifted uncomfortably in his seat and tried to concentrate on the petition being read by the Kasi-Nawahr legal representative. Legalese always numbed him; he made an effort to focus on its intent. The KNC document was purposefully obscure, but he caught the intent easily. If it was accepted, the Avasan Guild would be obliterated and its miners reduced to virtual slavery.

In obscure manner, it set strict percentages on the amount of ore Avasan mines must sell to the Consortium and gave the Consortium first refusal on all output. In convoluted language, it barred Avasans from selling their ores directly to KNC customers, from setting up their own refineries and even from shipping their freight on any but Kasi-Nawahr vessels. There was, of course, a perfectly good rationale for each provision. The KNC was merely protecting the interests of its customers and the economy of Mehtar.

Jaya scanned the faces of his fellow Varmana and wondered how many of them understood what was couched so carefully among the twisted clauses. It was clear the Deva Radha did. The pensive disapproval on her dark face as she accepted a copy of the document from KNC Speaker Duran Prakash was eloquent; her fingers seemed to disdain the touch of the light-tablet as he placed it in her hand.

"We will, of course, thoroughly review this document at length before coming to any decision regarding its merit." She handed the tablet to one of the Vrinda Varma's couriers to have it downloaded to the Council data system, then faced Prakash. "Have you anything further to add to this reading?"

The man smiled, teeth glistening as if oiled, and Jaya tried not to imagine his mother kissing him.

"Only to comment, Deva, that the Consortium is confident your decision will not allow the forces of anarchy to rob Mehtar of its greatest resource."

"Whether this petition is granted or not," said the Deva, "we will certainly not allow the forces of anarchy to rob Mehtar of anything."

Jaya's mouth twitched. Deva Radha had a delightful way with words ... and eyes. Just now she had locked hers with Prakash's and held him standing before her dais like a stick doll on a string.

Finally, she released him to glance at her notes. "You may return to your quarter." She looked to the AGIM box on the left end of the semi-circular room. "We will now hear the presentation of the Avasan Guild of Independent Miners."

The AGIM representative rose and strode to the central witness box.

"Pritam-sama." The Deva acknowledged him. "We expected Rokh Nadim to speak on behalf of the Guild. Where is he?"

The room was silent but for the shuffling of feet and paper, and Taffik Pritam used that silence to dramatic advantage. Mounting the docket, he scanned the curving chamber, his eyes striking the faces of the Varmana like a pale blast of winter wind. He made a full circle with those freezing eyes, the bells at the hem of his prayer sash singing in a soft, holy whisper.

The windroughened face turned at last to the KNC quarter. His arm rose with the sudden thrust of an accusing finger directly at Duran Prakash and the Vice-director of the Kasi-Nawhar board, Ranjan Vrksa. The tiny bells let out a burst of song. "They know why Rokh Nadim is not here, Deva. He's not here because he's not safe on Mehtar. His life has been threatened, not once, but several times; it has been made clear to him that if he were to come to Mehtar, misfortune would befall him."

At a look from Vrksa's frigid eyes, the KNC Speaker came

languidly to his feet. "And do you suggest, sama, that we are responsible for these alleged threats?"

"I do not suggest such a thing, sama, I accuse."

Jaya sat forward in his seat, along with nearly every other Varmana.

"This is a serious charge, Taffik Pritam," said the Deva Radha.

"I have others to go with it," he returned. "First, they cut off our supplies, forcing us to the expense of sending to Mehtar for the most basic equipment. Then they refused to let our vessels transport that equipment to Avasa. Then they prohibited their freighters from carrying it unless a member of the Guild accompanied the shipment—as a paying passenger. Our earnings do not run to frequent space passage, Deva. When we pooled our resources, sending one Guilder to stand for collective orders, we were told that every Guilder who places an order must sign for it, in person, at the freight dock on Mehtar before the resources can be released."

"We are only trying to protect our associates, Deva," interrupted Speaker Prakash. "The Avasan ships are ancient and unreliable-"

"They are entirely reliable!"

"-and sending expensive equipment to Avasan retailers in the hope that it will be sold is not profitable. What are we supposed to do if someone orders a drill rig, then never shows up to pay for the shipping?"

"That has never happened!" objected Pritam.

"We propose that it never will."

Taffik Pritam smiled acidly. "How very prudent of you."

"It would also be very prudent, Prakash-sama," interjected the Deva, "if you would take your seat and allow Taffik Pritam to continue with his presentation uninterrupted."

Prakash bowed his head deferentially and sat. Ranjan Vrksa immediately began to whisper in his ear.

"Do continue, Pritam-sama." The Deva favored the Avasan with a nod.

"Thank you, Deva. I also lodge official complaint against the Kasi-Nawahr Consortium for deliberately standing in the way of our legal free enterprise. They have blocked shipment of our independently contracted ores, which has caused us to default on at least two hard-won contracts. We are trapped, Deva. Even when we can contrive to get the equipment to Avasa to get the ore out of the ground, we cannot ship to more lucrative markets because Consortium associates own the ships on which it must be freighted. Since their Quality Control discounts at least forty percent of our yield as inferior or impure grade, we are left with no choice but to sell to the Consortium at a substantially lower price."

"Naturally, we pay inferior prices for inferior ores," muttered Prakash, just loudly enough to be heard.

Before the Deva could utter censure, Pritam rounded on him. "There is nothing inferior about our ores! We have independent analysts who will testify-"

"Then sell your ores to them. The choice is yours."

"If we are to feed our families, we have no choice!" His face flushed with emotion, Pritam turned an impassioned gaze on the Council. "Noble Varmana, members of the Inner Circle, all we ask of you is the protection of our right as citizens of this Commonwealth to pursue our livelihood unfettered by Consortium interference. Our ancestors migrated to Avasa as adita—free as the world they found. The Consortium would now enslave us. We ask only that you allow us our freedom under Mehtaran law."

The comment light on the front of the KNC box lit up momentarily.

Deva Radha acknowledged it. "The Consortium Speaker requests leave to comment. Do you object, Pritam-sama?"

"No, Deva. Let him speak."

Prakash saluted his opponent with a mocking bow. "How kind of you. Let me start by reminding Pritam-sama that Avasa's status, under the law, is far from certain."

"If you are going to speak to Pritam-sama," interrupted the Deva Radha, "speak to him, not around him. However, I'd rather you address your remarks to the Vrinda Varma itself ... if you don't mind."

Prakash colored slightly.

Was it possible the man was embarrassed? Or did he merely possess the good sense to fear incurring the displeasure of the Inner Circle? The former wasn't likely, so Jaya decided the good Prakash had finally realized that Deva Radha was not just a "frigid harpy with a sharp tongue," or whatever he'd had the poor judgement to call her at dinner three nights ago. Jaya had long ago decided that the man was a pompous idiot, but realized a number of people, Duran Prakash among them, thought of Jaya Sarojin in the same terms.

Just now, the pompous idiot was favoring the Assembly with a deep, courtly bow. "My humble apologies, Deva, Noble members of the Inner Circle, respected Varmana. I meant no disrespect. The issue here is a critical one. An emotional one. I lost my temper at these insulting charges. I meant only to say that the legal status of Avasa is in question. Our petition speaks directly to that uncertainty. Surely it is apparent, Noble One, that the citizens of Avasa no longer consider themselves Mehtaran. They are Avasan. Over time, they have become increasingly independent."

"May I remind you, Prakash-sama," said Deva Radha, "that they yet hold Mehtaran citizenship."

"Yes, but they handle many of their own judicial and legislative matters. They have selectively altered timehonored and established systems and customs. They have even elected their own Colonial Council."

Jaya gathered from Prakash's dramatic delivery that this last bit of news was supposed to be earth-shaking. It was not.

"As they were instructed to do upon petitioning the Inner Circle for the privilege," the Deva informed him.

Consternation rippled across the representative's brow. He glanced aside and met Vrksa-sama's dark blue and glittering gaze. It was the KNC Vice-director who spoke.

"The Consortium was not aware that the permission of the Inner Circle had been given."

"The Inner Circle was not aware that it was required to inform the Consortium of administrative decisions that do not effect them."

"Surely, Noble Deva, it does affect us. It renders our position as a corporate entity rather ambiguous when we don't know whether we're dealing with subject colonies of Mehtar or a sovereign power. However, that's less important than the fact that the Avasans have obviously taken the bestowal of such a privilege as a signal to challenge the authority of the Circle."

"As your associate pointed out," said Deva Radha, "the political status of Avasa is ... in flux. But there is no challenge to our authority in that—overt or otherwise. What is obvious is that Avasa is challenging the authority of the Consortium. If you are honest, Vrksa-sama, you will admit that to be your prime concern. Don't try to cloud the issues here by identifying yourselves and your concerns with the Vrinda Varma. There is a difference between government and business, sama. A difference that shall be preserved."

"Deva, I did not-"

"It is rita," continued the Deva inexorably. "It is the order of things. Government may often direct business, set its priorities and define its limits. Business should never attempt to reverse the role."

There was silence from the KNC box.

The Deva removed her light pen from its holder. "Now, if one of you gentlemen would kindly speak to the Consortium's concerns, so that we may consider what are ours."

"Yes, Deva." Prakash bowed deferentially, while Ranjan Vrksa reseated himself, his broad face an unbecoming shade of purple. "Our concerns should be obvious. If the Guild of Independent Miners is sanctioned, and if that Guild is allowed to become truly independent, it could result in the Consortium's ruin. Clearly, the first thing they will do is attempt to obtain higher prices for their ores. Prices we will be forced to pay regardless of quality. If they are allowed to sell any amount of ore to any bidder, there is no guarantee that KNC Associates will get the ore they need to do business.

"If they are allowed to ship their products on any vessels at their disposal, then that is just one more revenue the Consortium will be deprived of. Besides which, their ships are not safe. They're old and decrepit. The loss of one vessel would severely cripple monthly ore quotas."

"Pardon, Deva," Taffik Pritam interjected. "May I speak to the issue of safety?"

At a grudging nod from Prakash, the Deva signaled the Avasan to speak.

"Our ships are old because that is what we can afford—with few exceptions. But we keep them in the very best condition."

Prakash objected. "They do not meet with our safety standards."

"Your safety standards are unduly strict," countered Pritam. "You will note the Guild proposes that the Vrinda Varma appoint a

Safety Council made up of reputable and expert members of the Engineering Guilds who will inspect and pass all ships that carry ore consignments. We propose that the standards"—he glanced at Prakash—"be set jointly by the Consortium, the Guilds and the Vrinda Varma. We then propose that the Miners' Guild be allowed to ship ore on any vessel passed by the Safety Council."

"Why should the Vrinda Varma go to that sort of expense when the safety inspectors we provide are already doing the job adequately?" Prakash asked.

"They are doing it prejudicially. They are rejecting our vessels on the basis that they lack a new technology we cannot afford."

"They are rejecting your ships, sama, because they lack a reliable magnetic stabilizer system. The keels of your vessels generate unstable and even volatile fields."

"Your inspectors specify the VT-255 trim system, which is prohibitively expensive. The old technology is neither obsolete nor unstable. It is merely not the newest system available, which the Consortium has arbitrarily decided to be the only system allowable."

"There was nothing arbitrary about the decision. The VT255 is the best stabilizer available. We simply cannot allow such precious cargo to be shipped in vessels equipped with anything less trustworthy. The Guild ships must meet our equipage standards ... and they don't."

The Deva interrupted. "Are the specifications for the VT-255 system available to us as part of your counter-petition, Prakash-sama?"

The KNC Speaker seemed taken aback. "They are ... not with the package we presented, Deva."

"If you would be so kind as to make them available? Pritam-sama, if you would do the same for the trim system or systems currently in use on Guild vessels?"

Pritam bowed. "I would be pleased to do so, Deva."

"Very well, now, Prakash-sama, have you any further remarks to address to your original subject?"

"Indeed I have. My original subject, which you may have forgotten during Pritam-sama's rambles, was the financial damage that granting the AGIM petition would cause the Consortium and, in turn, the Mehtaran market and economy. Some consequences are easy to predict, others are more subtle. AGIM is attracting more and more of our independent suppliers. We have even..." He paused, seemingly reluctant to continue, and glanced back at the KNC box as if seeking a signal. He got one in the form of a curt nod from Vrksa-sama.

"We have even," he repeated, "lost some of our employees to Guild mines and foundries. Last month, three of our best pit-lords, two factory administrators and a key marketing manager jumped to Guild establishments. We stand to lose more key personnel and more money if this continues. This issue affects not only every business involved in the Consortium, but it will also be extremely hurtful to Mehtaran consumers, who will be forced to pay much more for the products they need to survive. We foresee that the situation AGIM would thrust upon us will cause a drastic increase in the price of KNC goods and services. I cannot emphasize this enough. The total independence of Avasa could mean the devastation of the Mehtaran economy."

The Deva nodded, her light pen moving delicately across her monitor. When Prakash fell silent, she looked up. "You have concluded your comments, Duran Prakash?"

"Yes, Deva."

"Very well. Taffik Pritam, the docket is still yours. I am interested in hearing more of these threats you mentioned."

The KNC comment light flashed angrily. Before Deva Radha had done more than glance at him, Duran Prakash was on his feet with his mouth open.

"This is a travesty! Don't listen to the ravings of these anarchists!"

"The only ravings I hear presently are yours, Prakashsama." Deva Radha's voice was like a cool, wet, and heavy stone. "Please seat yourself."

Prakash sat reluctantly.

As Taffik Pritam spoke, Jaya studied Prakash's face, trying to pry from it some indication of how true the Guild's accusations might be.

"Rokh Nadim has received no less than five threats to his life," the Avasan claimed. "I, and the other members of the Guild's steering Committee, have also received threats. These threats have been communicated by post, by vicom and via notes tucked into the orders of equipment and provisions we receive from Mehtar."

A query light flashed on a console three seats to Jaya's right. Behind the console, Kreti Twapar perched like a fat, aging bird on the lip of his seat. "Have any of these threats been delivered in person by people claiming association with the Kasi-Nawhar Consortium?"

"We have been visited by KNC 'ambassadors,'" replied Pritam. "They substitute words like 'repercussions' and 'consequences' for the more straight-forward terms of the covert messages."

Jaya pressed his own query button and got an immediate electronic nod that displayed as a blinking green icon on his monitor. "What terms did the covert messages use?" he asked.

"A week ago, Rokh Nadim's daughter went to check incoming messages on the family vicom and found this..." Pritam consulted his own light-pad. "'If you visit Mehtar, Rokh Nadim, Yama-Death will visit your household. A death for a day. At the end of two days, you will have no sons. At the end of three days, Yama will enjoy your daughter. At the end of four, you will be a widower. When you return to Avasa you will find your family in Yama's Black Palace, underground. The mines you live for will be their death.'"

Nadim's daughter ... Ana had intercepted that message. Jaya shook his head, clearing the image. "So Rokh Nadim stays at home to guard his family?"

"Yes, Lord. He has put his family above all, and the Guilders respect his decision. His children and wife go about armed and with friends and servants watching their every move. No one leaves the compound without protection."

No one but Anala, thought Jaya wryly. He half-wondered if Rokh Nadim knew that his daughter had come alone to Mehtar for his damn drill bits ... or if he thought the KNC had gotten her. Sending a clandestine message seemed more imperative than ever. He eyed the Guild spokesman speculatively.

"I am in complete sympathy with Nadim-sama's concern for his family," said the Deva, "but this turn of events makes it even more imperative that we meet with him. How may we accomplish this?"

"Come to Avasa. Or put his family under your protection ... day and night."

She nodded. "We shall consider those options, sama. Tell me, have any of the threats against you been carried out?"

"There has been vandalism at several of the mines. The stream that feeds one of our largest reservoirs was poisoned—a heinous crime on any world. Water is more precious to us than even the ores we mine. To poison that resource is to toy with our lives." The remark was accompanied by an eloquent glance at the KNC delegation.

Prakash half-stood. "Deva, this vandalism is entirely too convenient."

"Is this documented, Pritam-sama?" the Deva asked, raising her hand to silence Prakash.

He nodded. "In an attachment to the document I delivered to you today, Deva. We have included signed affidavits from the owners and pit-lords of the vandalized mines and the local Sarngin commander, as well as vipics of the damage."

"Vipics?" The Deva looked up from the notes on her screen. "May we view these vipics now?"

"If it be your wish, Deva."

"How votes the Council?" she asked the membership. "Do we wish to view this evidence now?" She glanced down and counted the flashes of gold and red on her console. Looking up again, she said, "Do the nay-sayers wish to comment?"

Bel Adivaram flashed his courtesy light and was recognized. "It only seems to me, Deva, that these alleged threats against the Guild are an entirely separate matter from the petitions before us."

"Not," countered the senior Dandin, Sri Elui, "if they are the result of the petitions."

"Does anyone else wish to speak to this point?" There was no response, and the Deva went on. "There were five dissenters. We will view the evidence now, Pritam-sama."

She nodded to the Council courier who stood silently by, and the young man swiftly produced the Guild's petition package. Radha withdrew a data wafer and slipped it into her console. The lights dimmed.

The Council Chamber was suddenly silent, but for the minute riffle of fabric. The two dimensional image of three wrecked sand-cats dominated the view screen at the open end of the curving room. The machines had obviously been ripped by a violent explosion and huge pieces of metal lay strewn over the amber Kedar sands.

"As you can see by the chemical analysis on your displays," said Pritam after allowing the sheer devastation to sink in, "the explosive used is a relatively new compound known as Niraybar 4. NB4 is not used in any of our mines, nor will you see it on any AGIM associate's shipping manifest or inventory. This is because it is not yet on the market."

"May I ask if you had this analysis done on Mehtar?" asked Bel Adivaram.

Pritam ignored the implication behind the question. "It was done at the Asra of Sciences in Onan. The Head of the Order, himself, oversaw the work. You will note that his seal accompanies the data."

"Still," persisted the Vadin, "a Mehtaran lab would certainly be more-"

"We expected that objection, so we took the additional precaution of having a second analysis done by Vedda Technologies. They confirmed that NB4 was developed in their own laboratories and is currently licensed for use solely by Ahurajas Incorporated, an associate business of the KasiNawahr Consortium."

"But it could, of course, have been used without a license," observed the Vadin Narudin, his tone neutral.

Pritam nodded. "I grant you that, Noble One. But the implied accusation by Prakash-sama is that we did this damage to our own equipment. We would hardly sacrifice expensive, vital resources to cause the KNC discomfort. Nor would we poison our own water. Deva, if we may view the next pic."

Radha keyed her console and the image on the screen changed to show the further results of sabotage. Along a sparkling, clear stream lay the decomposing bodies of what had been a herd of goats. Between and around the dead goats were the carcasses of other animals that had drunk the poisoned water.

"That stream feeds into a reservoir that provides water for three settlements and a number of mining compounds. So far, there have been eight deaths. Were it not for these unfortunate animals, there would have been more." Pritam swept a cold gaze about the chamber. "Does anyone honestly think we would kill our own people to discredit the Consortium? I tell you, Holy Ones, we would rather spend eternity imprisoned by the KNC than cause the death of one innocent person. We are not capable of this."

The KNC comment light flashed and Prakash was on his feet. "This is an outrage!" he croaked. "You accuse the Consortium of this-this hideous vandalism? I've no doubt it was perpetrated by your own juvenile delinquents!"

"There are no juvenile delinquents in a mining community," retorted Pritam. "Mischief is the province of the idle. Our youth work from the Age of Reason—boys and girls alike. They don't know what idleness is."

"Are they saints, then?"

"They are not vandals! If they were, they'd hardly be capable of the level of damage our mines have sustained. Whoever did this had machinery capable of breaking solid hacovite beams and crushing wall bracing to dust. And they had a sandcat to haul that machinery to the mines they vandalized."

"Sandcats can be stolen," said Prakash.

Pritam uttered a sound like the breaking of a dry branch. "Let us suppose for one moment that a youth gang could break into one of our yards without tripping the alarms. I won't ask you to explain why they'd want to do such a thing. Let us also suppose they had the time to either find a sandcat rigged with the equipment they needed or load one themselves. Let us suppose further that they could get the sandcat out of the yard without being seen or heard. Now, tell me how they could arrange for it to be in two places at once. None of our machinery has gone missing, Prakash-sama."

"Such certainty!" Prakash's voice was scathing.

"We are not the unsophisticated savages you would like people to believe we are. Our yards are well-manned—all day and all night —by trained Sarngin."

Duran Prakash's expression changed with the fluidity of oozing oil. "We have not doubted your sophistication or your shrewdness," he said. "We suspect you are shrewd enough to destroy your own property to incriminate the KNC and win your war for autonomy."

"Our war? OUR war?" Taffik Pritam was livid. "No, Prakash-sama, not our war. We want peaceful coexistence. We want the authority to control what we produce. We don't want a fight. Not with the Consortium, not with anyone. We did not start this battle, but we will finish it!" He turned back to face Radha. "We don't need

to incriminate the KNC. This"—his hand swept toward the screen
—"is enough to incriminate them. Deva, if you would cue the next
image."

The next image was a close-up of the rear of a sandcat that had
been driven straight into a mine entrance and was all but buried in
debris. There was a word scrawled across the green haunch in thick,
uneven letters: WOCOA, it said.

Jaya glanced at Bel Adivaram, but it was too dark to read his
expression. He said nothing and Jaya said nothing.

"WoCoa?" said the Deva. "What is that?"

"We don't know, Deva," admitted Pritam. "This is the latest bit
of sabotage and it is the first time a signature has been applied.
Since the only pressure we have felt so far has been from the
Consortium, we must assume that this is their work."

"Heinous lies!" exclaimed Prakash emphatically. "Our ambassadors to you have done nothing but attempt to negotiate. How
dare you characterize it as-as threat?"

"How dare you characterize your threats as negotiation?"

The Deva waved them down. "Enough, both of you. You have
stated your wishes, made your accusations, and laid before us your
petitions and counter-petitions. I would like, at this time, to
adjourn this session so that the detailed documents can be analyzed.
That is, unless any member of this Council has questions they
would like answered." The query lights were dark. "In that case, the
delegates may leave us to our study."

Three hours later, Jaya left the Assembly hall with copies of all
petitions, charges and evidence, a growing dislike for the Consortium, and a growing lack of respect for Bel Adivaram and Kreti
Twapar. They could have said something about WoCoa. It had been
the perfect opportunity to speak of it.

Jaya's conscience pricked him. You could have said something,
too, it said. Except of course, that it was their experience with the
Worker's Coalition that would have been at issue; if he'd lit up and
divulged what little he knew, it would have embarrassed them.
Wondering if he had committed a sin of omission, Jaya stepped out
of chambers and into the Hall of Ancestors.

As fate would have it—or more likely design, Duran Prakash was
waiting in the Hall with Ravi when he emerged from the inner
chambers. He put himself firmly in Jaya's path.

"Nathu Rai! Jaya!" Prakash settled comfortably on the intimate address. "I hope you aren't finding this whole business too tedious."

"Not at all." Jaya eyed the older man speculatively. "I find it most interesting."

"Really? I wouldn't think this sort of dry legality would have much allure for a young talon like yourself."

Jaya declined to take offense at the veiled insult, reflecting meditatively that this was the second time in two days someone had compared him to a bird of prey. He said as much.

"I'm not surprised," Duran Prakash informed him. "You have about you the look of a predator. The air of a man who is the guardian of his own best interests. Bad business this," Prakash informed him, seeming to change the subject. "Kasi-Nawahr Associates stand to lose a great deal if AGIM can make a case for itself. You wouldn't have any KasiNawahr holdings?"

Ravi growled.

"No," Jaya said mildly, "that would be a conflict of interest. My family held part of a passenger service associated with the KNC. I put the holding in suspension and sold it to my Uncle Namun."

"Ah, of course." Prakash nodded. "Well, I am not so fortunate. As Consortium fortunes go, so go mine. I only hope they go well. For your mother's sake, especially."

"My mother?"

"I mean that were she to marry me and were the Consortium to ... fail drastically..." He shrugged.

Jaya made a barely successful effort not to react to the casual mention of marriage to his mother. "I'm sure the Rani's fortune would support you both well enough."

"The Rani's fortune is tied up quite extensively in KNC holdings and sub-holdings. I wonder if I should encourage her to sell." His eyes flicked briefly to Jaya's face.

"And how has my mother's fortune become so entangled? I would have advised her against any investment that was in conflict with our House's position of neutrality."

"Well, naturally, these investments were made long before this case was ever brought to Council. The Rani Melantha had no way of knowing that her son would be adjudicating a case involving the KNC."

Jaya unclenched his jaw with some difficulty. "Of course not," he said. "Nor would she have any way of knowing that the person who encouraged her to purchase these holdings had something other than her personal profit in mind."

Prakash looked scandalized. "Oh, I'm sure-"

"How much of her fortune is invested, may I ask?"

"Oh, I'm sure I couldn't say, Nathu Rai. I'm not privy to that information. You'd have to ask the Rani, herself."

"I will," Jaya promised, and left Duran Prakash standing in the middle of the Hall without farewell.

"I swear, Jaya Rai," hissed Ravi, hurrying after him, "if he calls you a talon one more time, I will personally gut him."

Jaya stopped in the sunlight that poured into the huge courtyard of the Asra Complex and considered Mitras's position in the sky— the way its glow was reflected in the golden dome of the Asra.

"Well, maybe he sees something in me I don't. Maybe I have talons and only hide them from myself."

"He sees nothing in you, Jaya Rai, except a means to an end. The man is a vulture."

"If he is a vulture," said Jaya, "what does that make my mother?"

"Jaya!" The Rani Melantha jumped and spun away from her mirror. "You scared me to death! What is the matter?"

Jaya Sarojin stopped about two feet from his mother's glass-topped vanity and caught sight of himself in the tall mirror. Eyes dark and hard, he was as terrifying as her expression suggested. He hardly cared.

"I just had a very interesting conversation with Duran Prakash."

The Rani's expression shifted to a point between wariness and amusement. "I didn't think that was possible."

"Neither did I, but he had some information he suggested I corroborate with you."

Now the expression was completely wary. "Oh?"

"First, he intimated that you might marry him."

Rani Melantha stared, then she laughed. "That idiot! Of course I'll not marry him. Great Mother, he's a-a corporate toady! He's not even a Vadin, and stands very little chance of becoming one. What would possess the man to think I'd marry him?"

Jaya folded his arms across his chest and took a deep, calming breath. "Perhaps the increasingly intimate relationship you share. He's been with you day and night for the last eight months."

The Rani glanced aside, running a gold-tipped nail over the shining glass of the vanity. "An exaggeration. But he pleases me in some ways." She shrugged and watched the nail etch a pattern in the reflective surface.

"I hope that Prakash-sama is a better cunnidas than he is a diplomat." He ignored his mother's angry exclamation and went on. "He implied that in marrying him you would effectively be marrying the Consortium. And, of course, as their fortune is his fortune, it would be yours, as well."

"I'm not marrying him," said the Rani flatly.

"I'm relieved. Being married to the Consortium could damage your health. I doubt even your sexual forces are up to that much of a workout."

The Rani came to her feet, dark eyes blazing. "How dare you speak to me that way? If your father were alive-"

"If my father were alive, you wouldn't be bedding KNC lawyers with political aspirations."

"That is all I'm going to take from you, Jaya Sarojin. You may leave."

There was fire in Jaya's head; he fought it, imagining a reflecting pool with not a wind-ripple to mar it. "Not yet. Another bit of information the good Prakash-sama gave me was that you've invested heavily in KNC holdings."

The look of a cornered animal swept across Melantha Sarojin's beautiful face, making her son feel he was once more playing the raptor, staring his victim down over a set of blood-stained talons. He didn't care. He could insult and offend and terrify every atom of her being and not care.

"Suppose that to be true," she said finally. "What of it?"

"What of it? Your son is a member of the body adjudicating a situation that could adversely affect Consortium holdings."

"They're not your holdings—why should you care?"

"They are holdings purchased with my mother's private funds. Isn't it conceivable I'd be partial to the KNC keeping its assets intact under those circumstances?"

The Rani's eyes evaded him. "Our lives are separate. I can't imagine the Inner Circle would see a conflict."

"Uncle Namun should have seen a conflict. Didn't you ask his advice before you did this?"

She shook her head. "Namun doesn't know. He takes this whole conflict of interest thing as seriously as you do. He told me he's not even certain he should see us socially until this is all over. He's even spoken of missing the Mesha Festival for the first time ever. Oh, honestly, Jaya I really don't see a conflict. We're two adults-"

"You're my mother, and even if the money you used wasn't part of father's estate, it's still Sarojin money."

Her eyes skittered aside again. The gold nails pecked at the sleeve of her gown.

Jaya felt a cold tickle of suspicion under his breastbone. "You used family money."

She did not deny it and, thereby, confirmed it.

"Mother, how could you? For that matter, how did you, without me knowing it?"

She had the good grace to look guilty. "You extended me some funds for that winter cottage in Dagpur. I didn't buy it. Jaya, I was fully extended and there was this one holding I desperately wanted to own. A couture—one of the finest—with outlets in the best stores."

"How much, mother? How much did you invest in your couture?"

She shrugged. "About five million."

Jaya wanted very much to sit down. "Five million dagam," he repeated.

The Rani nodded. "Which I fully expect to see doubled."

"Sell it."

"Jaya!"

"Sell all of it! Now! Every last thread of it!"

"I can't! I won't see any of my investment until summer when the new line of clothing is out."

"And why, in the name of Rama, not?"

"That's the way the contract is structured. Duran said I would see the greatest profit if I opted for delayed returns. It gives the couture working capital he can count on through the big trade shows."

"Duran! Of course."

The Rani paused in mid-excuse and gave her son her full attention. "What are you implying?"

"Isn't it obvious? Your lover has steered you into investments that will only thrive if the Consortium thrives. I'm one of the people in a position to decide whether it does that or not. Long ago, when only the KNC knew the situation on Avasa was escalating, when only they knew about this damned petition to shut down AGIM, Prakash bought you into a KNC investment that you either had to hold onto for some time or sell at a huge loss. And he did it knowing that I'd be caught in this position. The only way to save your investment, Mother, is for the KNC to maintain its current control over Avasan resources. Without that monopoly, there's no way the Consortium can avoid some loss."

"So, what's wrong with them keeping their monopoly?"

Any blood remaining in Jaya's face drained away. "I can't discuss that with you, but I am not about to vote in favor of the KNC just to save your assets. Which is what Duran Prakash was hoping I'd do."

"How can you be so sure?"

"He made a point of bringing all this up today. Hints about conflict of interest. Hints about how much money you had sunk in Consortium business. He's pressuring me, Mother. Trying to wield influence over me through your illtimed spending spree."

The Rani sat down slowly. "He's been using me. That's what you're saying isn't it? Using me to get to you."

Her bemusement and deflation were so ingenuous, it was almost funny. "Oh, admirable, Mother. What wonderful insight."

"Don't abuse me, Jaya."

"I don't need to. You do a fine job of abusing yourself."

She held up both hands in a gesture of defeat, but the look in her eye belied it. She shook her head, raising her eyes to his face. "I can't—by Tara—I don't believe you. Oh, he may be trying to manipulate you; I don't deny it. But I will not believe that is the only reason he's interested in me. He desires me, Jaya. You can't make me believe he doesn't."

Jaya stared at the beautiful, perfect oval face and felt a surge of boiling anger rush to his head. "You are the most shallow, vain, pretentious woman I have ever known. No—" He took a step toward her, forcing her back into her chair. "You've become that. I used to love you. I used to have reason to love you."

He turned his back on her, left her cowering before her mirror.

She made a sound that was halfway between a cough and cry. "You arrogant bastard! How dare you speak to me like this?"

He stopped at the door, swinging back to face her. "You should know," he said tartly. "You're not faithful to Father's memory. Why should I believe you were faithful to him while he lived?"

The Rani was on her feet again. "Because I tell you I was! Your Father was the center of my life. But he's dead, Jaya. Dead! And I'm still alive. I will not be married to a ghost!"

"I don't expect you to be. I wouldn't mind if you married again—even some cork-brained schemer like Duran Prakash, if you really loved him. But ever since Father died, I've watched this endless string of 'companions' parade in and out of your rooms."

"It has not been a parade, damn you, Jaya!" the Rani contested. "There have been a few men-"

Jaya slammed his fist against the door post. "This is my Father's house and you have the-the effrontery to bring your damned cunnidas into it."

"Stop calling them that!"

"It would be bad enough," Jaya continued, his voice rising to a shout, "if you entertained them in their homes. But no, you have to bring them into my father's bed!"

The Rani shrank from his fury, cowering against her vanity. It pleased him to see her cower.

When she broke the strained silence, her voice was barely audible. "You've never spoken to me like this, Jaya. He's been dead nearly five years and you've never even hinted at how you felt."

"Oh, I've hinted, Mother, you just never noticed. And I ... I wasn't sure I had any right to tell you how I felt."

Her eyes kindled again, the hauteur creeping back into them. "Well, you were right, my dear son. You don't have a right to lecture me about my behavior—to come into my quarters and vilify me." She began to tremble with suppressed rage. "I will consider what you've said about my investments. I'll see if I can disencumber some of your precious family money. That's all I plan to disencumber. Duran Prakash, for all his idiocy, has consummate skill in the Plea-sure Arts. I find that skill a source of great satisfaction. I'm not done with him yet." Her eyes met his unwaveringly. "But I am done with you. Please leave me."

Jaya gritted his teeth against a strong desire to scream childish insults at her. Tears, hot with equally childish disappointment, pressed for release.

"With pleasure," he said and left, slamming the outer door hard enough to flutter the curtains around the bed.

He did not see the Rani tremble in that frail breeze, nor did he hear the sound of her weeping.

CHAPTER FIVE

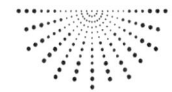

Ana reflected that the coach in which she sat and rocked was the perfect metaphor for her current state. She moved, but not of her own will, the reins were in someone else's hands and she could only fold her own in her lap, sit impotently and watch the world go by outside. Jivinta Sarojin might think the mountain of parcels in the carryall represented a sort of progress, but to Anala it represented only distraction from purpose.

"I'm sorry about the drill bits, Ana," said Mina softly.

She pulled herself from her study of the blur beyond the window. "I'm being discourteous," she said. "Forgive me."

"Nonsense. You aren't being discourteous, you are being absorbed. I know the look. I've seen it on my grandson's face often enough."

Ana smiled. "You're very kind, Jivinta. It's just so frustrating. To have to wait two days for those bits!" To have to sit here, like a lump while the situation on Avasa deteriorated, she didn't say. To be separated from my family, from news of my family.

"Perhaps Jaya could check into the delay."

Anala uttered a crack of laughter. "Wouldn't it seem very odd for the Taj Prince of Kasi to take a sudden interest in drill bits?"

Jivinta chuckled. "A good observation. Well!" She sat back. "I'll tell you what. To take your mind off your father's machinery, we'll get Helidasa working on that dascree when we get home."

Ana grimaced and glanced at her palm. "That would be nice. I can't wear gloves everywhere I go. Of course, I could just stay in the house."

Mina's eyebrows arched in amusement. "My dear, it isn't even safe for you to be without gloves in the Saroj. Even a Rani is expected to give the courteous greeting to a Deva or a Dandin, and you may meet either in our halls. In fact," she added, "there will be a reception at the Saroj on Bhaktar-eve for the Mesha Festival."

A cold tickle of fear fluttered beneath Anala's breast bone. "But surely I won't attend."

"Ana, you are a member of our household. The Rani assumes you to be of the Sarojin Clan. Your presence will be expected."

"What shall I do? About my hand, I mean."

"Don't worry," Jivinta Mina reassured her. "Helidasa has magic you cannot imagine."

Half an hour later, with her new wardrobe being put away by Helidasa's capable daughters, Ana came downstairs in a soft body-suit, beyond relief to be rid of that alien bit of amber fluff she'd been wearing. It felt good to have her arms and legs covered.

Mina met her in the solarium, eyeing her with approval. "Green is a good color for you. Are you more comfortable now?"

"Yes, Jivinta. Thank you."

"Good. Now, come along to the kitchen. Heli has a concoction she's sure will help."

She led the way down a short corridor and through a wide, swinging door. The room was huge, spotlessly clean, and flooded with sunlight. At its center, at a tile-topped table, Helidasa stood with a variety of items spread out before her. Grinding away at something in a small mortar, she looked like one of the witches of Ana's childhood fantasy, surrounded by the odd tools of her mystic trade.

She smiled when she saw Anala and Mina, and beckoned them to join her at the table.

Anala peeked into the mortar. "What is it?"

Helidasa dumped the yellow powder into a bowl and added an amber liquid that looked like tea. "A powder made of saffron," she said.

"A table spice?"

"Which also makes a fine yellow dye. And this" —she held up a bottle of tan powder—"is another herb that makes a pale stain. Put them together and one would have to have a creescan to tell whether one wore a dascree or raicree or no mark at all."

"If it's that easy to disguise them, then why haven't you changed your own and escaped?"

"Escape?" repeated Heli blankly. "Escape what, Rani? What is there I should escape?"

Ana remembered Mina Sarojin's presence; her face tingled with embarrassment.

"This is my home," continued Heli. There was no offense in her voice or expression, only motherly patience; as if she was forced to explain a bemusing concept to a small child. "It was my mother and father's home and the home of their parents before them. And of the Mata Jivinta before them. I am dasa, Rani Anala. It is rita. But you are not dasa—you are free, no matter what the mark in your palm says. For me it's a truth. For you, it's a lie."

Ana nodded, pretending to understand what she did not. Had this woman become content with slavery, she wondered, or had slavery, in her case, transmuted itself into something she did not recognize as such? From her studies as a bhakta, Anala well understood the spiritual concept of servitude. Was this what Helidasa believed her existence to be, or had she, with the words, 'it is rita,' simply relinquished all thought of freedom? Instinct told Ana that slavery was slavery, no matter how pleasant, and freedom was worth any sacrifice or hardship.

Yet, something in her empathized with the dasa. She found that disturbing.

Jivinta Mina, watching Ana's face with opaque eyes, brought them back to the matter at hand. "So, Heli, how is the lie to be removed?"

"First, the yellow dye." Heli began the process of carefully mixing ingredients. "We fill in the areas inside the pattern of the dascree so the skin has an even, yellow tint, then we dye the other palm as well, so they match. And then, the pale stain covers all. It should darken the skin very little. When that has been done, a very fine red dye will do to retrace the pattern and add the taj, making you a Rani of the Saroj."

"Since few people would have the audacity to aim a creescan at the palm of a Sarojin," Mina added, "the chances of you being found out are thin."

An hour and twenty minutes later, Anala surveyed Heli's work with amazement. "It looks so natural."

Heli nodded, satisfied. "And only you know how much lighter your palms were before. To anyone else..." She shrugged.

"Still..." said Mina, turning Ana's left palm into the bright light from the overhead lamp, "Still, perhaps a little more camouflage for the party. A hand-dazzle, I think. We purchased several today. And we must fabricate an id wristlet or necklace for you—a leaf with the Sadira legend on it. Until then, I have a brow stamp that should suffice to announce you to the casual observer." She patted Ana's hand. "Jaya should be home. See what he thinks of Heli's little miracle."

With much to tell him, Ana tracked Jaya to the garden where he stood, flinging stones into a deep, clear pool separated from the patio by a band of low trees and shrubs. She observed him silently for a moment, noticing the tiny tongues of silver, flame and crimson that darted beneath the surface of the pond at the fall of each stone.

Ana chuckled inwardly. Even the Sarojin fish flew the Clan colors. "Meditation might more profitable, Nathu Rai."

He turned, eyes sharp, almost angry. They met Ana's and the anger twisted awry. "But not nearly so satisfying," he said.

"Are you sure? When was the last time you meditated?"

"A long time ago," he admitted. "I'm sure you'll tell me I should try it again."

"I would suggest it, yes."

The almost-anger flickered again briefly in his eyes. "I'd be happier if I meditated, I suppose?"

Ana cocked her head slightly and eyed the now serene pond. She did not think the anger was directed at her, but it was hard to tell. "I don't know. But the fish certainly would be."

Caught unawares, Jaya laughed.

Anala watched him silently, her hands clasped behind her back, until the laughter spent itself. Better.

"Damn, that was a relief!" he said, wiping tears from his eyes. "I was all set to be furious with you."

"Forgive me," said Anala, "for whatever I did that angered you."

She solemnly gave the respectful greeting, drawing it out like the sinuous moves of a Kunda dance.

Jaya stared. "Your hand!" She held it open in the afternoon sun so he could inspect it. "That's amazing! Heli did this?"

Ana nodded. "With herbs and oils. She says it should last three or four days before needing to be restained. Do you think I'll pass inspection?"

"The most discriminating eyes will pass you as the Rani Ana Sadira, on holiday from Avasa. A cousin of mine—blossom of the Saroj." He glanced again at Heli's masterpiece and shook his head.

"Good. But, now hear what I have to tell you. At lunch today, I saw one of the thieves who attacked me!"

"What? Where?"

"At the Kiritan. I saw him walking below us in the main dining room. Jivinta Mina asked our server if he knew the man, but he didn't. Only that he'd seen him before."

"How in creation did he get into the Kiritan?"

Ana pulled her hand away and moved back a step. "Through the front door, I imagine. That's the way he left."

"Ana, will you be serious? The Kiritan doesn't usually admit thieves."

"He didn't look like a thief. He looked like a respectable sama. A Lord, even."

"A successful thief, apparently," commented Jaya wryly.

"If my 20,000 dagam was an average day's taking, he must be."

"There must be some way of finding out who he is."

Ana shrugged as they turned in unison and started back to the house. "Naru is keeping watch for him. Jivinta Mina told him the fellow is an old friend of yours and that she needs his name so she can send him a dinner invitation."

"Even if he did get a name, Ana, there's no guarantee it would be a real one."

Idiot. "I hadn't thought of that," she admitted.

Jaya laid a hand on her shoulder. "I'll see what I can do."

≈

What Jaya did was coax Anala into yet another outing at the Kiritan. She resisted at first, giving in only when he pressed the idea that she might see the thief again.

She didn't. She saw only a restaurant full of strangers, all of whom seemed to be staring at them. She quickly wished she hadn't come. She had felt casual curiosity from the room when she had been here with Jivinta Mina, but this was different. There was an undercurrent to the interest their appearance together evoked that she did not like.

There were, inevitably, those who had to breach the privacy of the Sarojin box to discover who Nathu Rai Sarojin's dinner companion was. Notably, the portly, over-dressed Vadin of the Port Zone, Bel Adivaram. He was polite, flattering and very interested in the Sarojin "cousin." He seemed to take their fabricated relationship at face value, amused at Jaya's description of how a piece of baggage bearing the Sadira-Saroj leaf and colors had brought them together at a hotel near the spaceport.

"I knew I didn't own a piece of luggage like that," Jaya lied (something he seemed to do easily). "Yet, there it was, wearing my clan leaf. While I was standing there, staring at it like an idiot, this beautiful young woman arrived to claim it."

"Ah!" purred Adivaram, beaming. "And you then discovered you could claim her!" He tilted an eyebrow at Anala. "Congratulations, Rani, on finding your way into the warm embrace of your Mehtaran family."

Ana said "Thank you" in a voice that was not at all thankful. The Vadin did not seem to notice.

When he finally excused himself, Jaya sagged exaggeratedly into his chair. "That man is one of the most efficient gossips in the Seven Provinces. I guarantee you that by Bhaktar-eve, the entire Port Zone and adjacent districts will know that I have a young, beautiful, unmarried, female cousin under my roof. So, at our Coming of Spring reception there will be a plethora of scheming parents and hopeful daughters ... and now hopeful sons, as well."

"A display of ego, Nathu Rai?"

"Hardly. I have no illusions that either scheming parents or hopeful daughters are the least seduced by my charm and great beauty. I am, however, a Sarojin and a Varmana and, therefore, considered a good match."

Ana's lip curled against her will. "Should I be impressed, mahesa?"

"I'd be disappointed if you were."

She studied him and decided that he was serious. She was also compelled to acknowledge that he would be perfectly justified in a display of ego. He was a Sarojin, after all, and a Varmana. And he was, despite his self-deprecatory remarks, a strikingly beautiful man. His hair tumbled to his shoulders in waves of gleaming black; his eyes were a dark, liquid brown. If she had met him in a channara in Onan or Raratok, she would have admired his looks. In fact, he would have probably taken her breath away at first glance. She would have been warmed the first time she surprised the child hidden in the man's eyes. But here, in this place, everything was different. She felt ... unnatural, alien.

"You surprise me," she told him. "Most powerful men are at least a little impressed with themselves. Your Vadin was impressed with himself. You seem ... dissatisfied." It was a rude, even unkind thing to say and she felt immediate contrition. "No, forget I said that."

"But you're right ... in part. All that I have was given to me. I did nothing to achieve it. I have yet to accomplish anything of my own." He shot her a wry smile. "Maybe that's why I want to buy your drill bits and catch your thieves. I want to accomplish something."

"Being a Varmana isn't accomplishing something?"

Jaya gazed at his rice bowl as if he expected it to do something fascinating. "Being a Varmana is something I inherited from my Father. It was his achievement, not mine."

"What you're saying, then, is you don't want to accomplish anything."

His eyes met hers sharply. "Of course that's not what I'm saying."

"No? Then, I don't understand. Surely, accomplishing something on the Vrinda Varma is your decision. You're certainly in a position to accomplish a great deal."

His eyes were instantly wary. "Such as grant the Guild independence from the Consortium?"

The silence sat between them like a wall of thick glass while Ana struggled with her temper. "If you feel the Guild deserves independence—if it is right for all concerned—yes."

"You can't possibly be that objective."

"I can try."

"Without wanting to beg me for help? Without wanting me to plead your case?"

"I must try to be objective."

"Because you're Rohin."

He was half-trying to incite her temper, she thought. He would fail. She refused to rise to the bait, merely inclining her head.

Jaya's eyes dropped to his food again. "You take that very seriously."

"That surprises you?"

He nodded, smiling. "It's hard to imagine a woman of your age—and beauty—choosing a life of asceticism."

Caught off guard, Ana let out a peal of surprised laughter. "Asceticism? Who said anything about asceticism? A Rohin is not an ascetic."

"No?"

"No. The Upper Path is not about deprivation, it's about ... detachment, and devotion. Detachment isn't 'not having.' It's a lack of attachment to 'having' or 'not having.' In a word, balance." She was suddenly amused. How like someone with much material wealth to equate spirituality with poverty. "So, you thought I lived alone high on some barren mountain, wearing sail cloth and eating the bread crumbs dropped by passing birds."

"Something like that."

She had embarrassed him and felt a perverse gratification in it. She did not yet wish to temper that gratification with contrition. "Well, you were wrong. Mice."

"I beg your pardon?"

"My bread crumbs are brought by mice." She shook her head, pulling a concerned frown across her face like a party veil. "Jaya Rai, someone has been telling you stories!"

"Yes," he said, and the corners of his very serious mouth twitched. "Indeed they have."

There! There was the child again. She'd surprised him out of hiding. She laughed, warmed, and wishing that she had, after all, met him in a channara in Raratok.

CHAPTER SIX

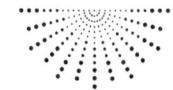

EARLY, Anala was up and fed and begging a drowsy Kenadas to allow her to take a horse from his stable. He declined and drove her himself in the two-coach, knowing if he didn't, there would be demons to pay when the mahesa found out.

The Nahar Zone was a place of disagreeable smells and fog and chill. It was named for the canal that cut across its drab flank, giving the air a heavy, sodden quality. Rheumy mists drifted up from its glistening, grimy streets, making Ana gaze wistfully at the cloud-draped southern mountains of the Lake District just visible here and there through the gaps between indistinguishable buildings.

The streets were already filling with the sorts of people who frequented the Nahar. Miners, dock workers, and bargemen—even darumen, down from their wooded slopes. They, too, outfitted themselves in Kasi, buying whatever it was darumen bought to fell their trees. Ana decided she'd have to do some research in that area if she was going to make her cover story work.

She knew a little of the commercially used trees on Avasa—a bit about the use of their wood. Manzan trees were the most populous varieties in the temperate zones. Technically they were tall enough for board lumber, but their spindle trunks were dense and knotted and hard enough to dull a Nandin saw. Hakwood were short, thick, gnarled things unsuitable for the lumber trade, but used much for craft work and sculpture. Only the rangy varieties of conifers that gave the Kedar region its name were harvested in any amount. The Environmental Covenants assured that hey were used carefully and just as carefully replanted.

Ana stared at the darumen as they wended their way through the miners and beggars and waremongers. They were different— from their rugged clothing to the way they carried themselves. There was an arrogant tilt to the head, a length of stride that demanded more ground than the poor Nahar streets had to give, a sensual quality that was comfortingly earthy, as if they had grown up out of the roots of their trees. They didn't fit in here any more than she did. Oddly, they reminded her of Jaya Sarojin—or rather, she corrected herself, the Jaya Sarojin of her Raratok channara.

She stopped watching the darumen, realizing suddenly that they were staring back at the cherry-haired girl in the out-of-place coach. Her fingers drummed on the padded arm of her seat. Kenadas drove slowly through the jostle and the coach seemed to creep.

Ana caught her fingers in mid-beat with a stifled sigh of frustration. She closed her eyes and concentrated her senses outside the coach, listening to the rhythm of foreign words falling from a score of foreign tongues, the distant clip-clip of the horse's hooves, and an occasional bell clap from the airtruck behind them, which could only proceed as fast as her coach would allow.

By the time they reached the Korba Industries warehouse, Ana was apparently calm, serene, and quiet of heart. Only she could tell how much nervous energy vibrated in her breast.

Kena drew the coach up in a sandy lot and held her door while she alighted.

"Rani Sadira," he said most respectfully, "are you certain you must come here?"

"Yes, Kena, I'm certain." Her eyes scanned the park with unintentional wariness. There were people who would call the Kedar wild or hostile, but the wildest reaches of the Highlands had nothing on this place—hemmed in with walls, teeming with people who looked at each other as if they were cataloguing the contents of purses and pockets.

She caught Kenadas following her gaze with worried eyes and grinned at him, clapping a hand on his shoulder. "Remind me to tell you about the time I fought a red chandi cat singlehandedly."

After a moment of uncertainty, Kenadas grinned in return. "He must have made a fine coat, Rani."

"'Ana,'" she said, and crossed the park toward the blocky gray building with a consciously breezy stride.

The small sales room of the Korba warehouse was nearly empty, but Ana's presence caused a stir among the few customers. The young man behind the gray plastic counter looked her over in a way that was at once flattery and insult, and eagerly offered his service. Unfortunately, he knew nothing about her order and had to call the floor manager.

"I was here yesterday," Ana told him. "I'm sure you remember me."

The man nodded, eyeing the silver and flame saroj imprinted between her brows. "Ay, we don' get much like you down in Na'arzun, Rani. Never done business with a 'ooman, m'self."

Ana ignored the remark. "Are the bits in?"

"Wayl, some is an' some i'nt. See, it's those big 'uns—the Number Twenties. Had a run on 'em about two week ago. Fact'ry han't sent me more'n enough to fix my reg'lars. An' you i'nt a reg'lar." His eyes strayed back to the saroj, then slid down to assess what he could see of her over the counter.

She met his gaze, pulling his eyes back up to her face. "I realize that, but you said they'd be in today."

"Maybe they will. Check back."

The younger clerk had been trying to get his boss's attention. "Dabu-sama, we have some Number Twenties ... on the dock."

"Ay, them's for the Mitra-Karka Combine. Ordered last week. They're reg'lars."

"I could go somewhere else, I suppose," Ana said.

"Could."

No, she couldn't. Korba was one of the few independent warehouses in Kasi that didn't fly the KNC banner from its rusty ridgepole. More to the point, it was the only one her father had deemed safe. If she went to one of the myriad well-stocked Kasi-Nawahr houses, they'd be bound to ask for id and she had none. The chain around her neck held only charms. There was no where else to go, and she suspected Dabu-sama knew it.

"I'll check back later," she said.

Out on the sidewalk, she stood for a moment, trying to keep her temper from boiling over.

"Rani?"

Ana glanced up to find the two-coach right in front of her, a concerned Kenadas frowning down at her from the box. She grinned ruefully. "No luck. I've got to come back later. He says they don't have the whole order."

"Home then?" Kena asked hopefully.

She nodded.

Kena was off his box in a second, relief all over his craggy face. He helped her into the coach and hopped back up, clucking the team into a fast walk. It was stop and go again, even though Kenadas took a route he thought would be less populated with pedestrians. Ana gazed moodily out the window, watching the traffic on the walkways.

As they neared Kasi Spaceport, she began to see people who reminded her of herself two days ago—carrying sofpaks and walking with their feet not quite touching the ground. Their heads swiveled every which way as they tried to take in their new surroundings. Their clothes also marked them as being from out of town or outprovince or off-continent or off-world.

Ana smiled, wondering if she'd really looked that awestruck at the sight of the lush greenery and pale, glistening, buildings soaring like giant hand-carved ornaments from ground to cloud.

The smile froze on her face at the sight of a lone, stationary figure scanning the passersby with seeming disinterest. This time, there was no mistaking him. This time, he looked like a thief. He turned and began to move down the street.

Frantically, she threw open her window and yelled for Kenadas to stop. She didn't wait for him to comply, but leapt from the moving coach. Glancing up into Kena's startled face, she gestured at the curb. "Pull over and wait for me!"

Her eyes caught the street banners as she sailed past them in pursuit of the thief—Kaveri Cross at Dockrow.

He was moving at a leisurely pace and she drew up to keep him just ahead of her. He seemed to be wandering aimlessly, giving shop windows along the warrow the most casual of glances.

Damn! she thought. He's probably looking for a place to spend my money!

He paused on a street corner at a news stand, crossed his arms over his chest and appeared absorbed in the events on one of the kiosk's several viewscreens. Ana meanwhile, pretended interest in the contents of a leather shop, keeping one eye on the thief.

She was close to screaming in frustration when the viewscreen suddenly lost the man's attention. His head swiveled to follow something out of Ana's line of sight. After a moment of intense study, he glanced back over his shoulder and made a subtle gesture to someone. Then he moved off down the side street. Ana glanced at the street banner and followed.

Now the pace became more purposeful. Anala tried to look ahead to see who the thief was tailing, but without success. There were too many people on the walks. What she did see—or thought she saw—was a second man across the street echoing both the thief's pace and the direction of his gaze. When he turned right, down a narrow side street, his shadow crossed the street and followed.

Trying to look purposeless, Ana padded after, her eyes shifting from the thief to the walk ahead of him. She saw him then—the target of all this skulk and scurry. The young man carried a sofpak and wore clothing that, while obviously of fine quality, set him apart merely by its simplicity. He had skin of deep gold and hair that was nearly the same color—exotic by Mehtaran standards. He appeared to be in his early twenties and was extremely attractive.

The thieves shadowed his every move, matching his pace, turning away when he scanned the street. When he stopped to buy a bag of roasted nuts and a tea ice, they did the same at a booth across the street.

Before he left the booth, the young man engaged the monger in conversation. From the gestures involved, Anala guessed he was asking directions. When the monger shook his head, another man, who had been standing at one corner of the kiosk reading a herald, became involved, adding his own series of gestures to the conversation. Finally, the young man drew a card from his pack and showed it to the others. The monger shook his head again, but the second man nodded, obviously recognizing where the young man wanted to go. He gestured broadly one way, then another. The youth smiled briefly and nodded, then set off, munching his snack.

Ana glanced about, looking for the thieves. They had vanished. Shrugging away unease, she shadowed the young Avasan.

On a brick and tile back street with pleasant but poor white-washed rows of tall houses, he slowed his pace and began glancing at the card he carried. He seemed confused. He stopped before an ancient rowhouse whose unkempt front garden was separated from the street by an ornate, vinestrangled pike fence. He glanced around uncertainly, as if in search of someone to consult, but the street was empty.

Ana felt the hair rise up on the back of her neck as the young man laid his hand on the gate latch. It lifted with a metallic shriek and he pushed the gate open on rollers that complained loudly of the abuse. Frowning, he entered the garden and mounted the steps to the front door. After a moment more of hesitation and a backward glance, he entered.

Ana knew a moment of dire indecision, an emotion that brought swift annoyance in its wake. She took a deep breath and started into the street, but the sound of running feet made her reverse course.

Two men dressed in dunnish clothing appeared from the mouth of a narrow alley on the opposite side of the way. They loped down the walk and through the gate of the old rowhouse, padding swiftly up the front steps and pausing only to open the door with great care. They slipped into the house, closing the door behind them.

Ana's thoughts tilted grimly; one of the two was the fellow who had given the young man directions in the warrow. This was obviously no spur-of-the-moment robbery they were contemplating. Clearly, it had been well-planned.

Ana saw only three paths before her: she could break in behind the thieves, risking her own life to the bargain; she could go to the Sarngin—also a risk; or she could wait until the thieves left and take their victim to the Saroj. She quickly ruled out the first two paths as untenable, and waited, tightly reining in her desire to act.

She had spent thirty or forty seconds in enforced meditation when the thieves reappeared—four of them, now—and scampered, laughing, down the front steps of the house. Her own attacker was among them, which meant that he had known exactly where his target would end up and had preceded him there.

Ana felt her arm gripped suddenly and tightly.

"Rani!" Kenadas was at her side, his face wearing the map of his recent and anxious journey. "Rani, what are you about? We must leave this place. Now," he added for emphasis.

But Anala was distracted anew and signaled him just as emphatically to silence. A pair of Sarngin had come around the corner at the top of the street and would pass right by the thieves.

She growled in frustration, unconsciously scraping her marked palm with her fingernails. "I can't even tell them!"

"Tell them what, Rani?"

Ana watched as the Sarngin passed the thieves with a nod and continued down the street. At the open front gate of the rowhouse, the pair turned and entered without so much as pausing to discuss the move.

Ana gaped and Kena, eyes going from the Sarngin to the house to her face, murmured, "Rani Ana, whatever is wrong?"

Adrenaline racing, Ana came to a quick decision. "Stay here," she told the coachman, and slipped out of the access and across the street. He obeyed for perhaps a second, then matched her stride, putting himself at her shoulder. She could not help but wonder if he was this disobedient to his mahesa.

There were still few people about—some children had come out to play further down the block and a couple strolled hand in hand across the intersection where the thieves had disappeared. Ana adopted a lazy gait and meandered idly up toward the rowhouse. She tried not to react when the Sarngin led their prize from the premises, his hands bound at the wrists with securweb. She feigned curiosity as they drew abreast of her.

"Excuse me," she said, turning a puzzled gaze on the group.

The senior officer gave the respectful greeting, his eyes lighting as they swept up Ana's body to her face. "Rani," he said, smiling. He glanced over her shoulder at Kenadas, who had drawn up about a foot behind her, and his smile evaporated.

"I have never seen an arrest being made before," Ana said, affecting sultry curiosity. "Is this young man a real criminal? What has he done?" She fixed the Avasan with an interested gaze. "Is he very dangerous?"

"Well, he's not precisely a criminal, Rani," the officer explained patiently. "He's yevetha. No leaf. No cree. Not a mark on him. Now, as to how dangerous he is..." He shrugged. " ... there is no way of knowing. I suspect he's from Avasa, in which case he is likely wilder and rougher than he looks."

"Ah, I see." Anala nodded, hiding her insistent anger behind affectation. She tossed back her hair and shifted her weight from one foot to the other, drawing the Sarngin's eyes to the subtle movement of her hips. "What will happen to him?"

The Sarngin read her interest and grinned. "It's to a dalali with him, Rani. Badan-Devaki, to be exact. You can visit him there, if you've the urge."

Repulsed by her own behavior and the assumption she could readily see in the Sarngin's eyes, Ana looked the Avasan man over from head to toe, speculatively. He sent back a gaze that was at once defiant and frightened. A muscle in his jaw clenched and unclenched.

"I don't suppose," she said, "that you could just let me have him." She made her voice like nectar and made the most of her pale eyes, hoping her growing rage was tucked safely out of sight.

The officer lingered in her eyes for a moment, but ultimately glanced at his partner and shook his head. "Sorry, Rani. I would delight in your pleasure, but the law says I must take him to a dalali."

"Oh. Too bad." Ana pouted prettily, then shrugged. "Well, at least, as you say, I can find him there. Badan-Devaki, you said?"

The officer nodded.

Ana gave the prisoner a hard glance. "What is your name, pretty man?"

"Hadas," he said, his voice a low growl. "Hadas Gupta."

The junior Sarngin chuckled. "That'll be 'Hadasdas' before too long."

Ana ignored him. "You're Avasan by birth, are you?"

"Yes ... Rani." He bowed his head and stared at the ground. There was nothing subservient in the gesture; he, too, was hiding rage.

"You are very pretty, Hadas," she said. "I will see you again." To the Sarngin she said "Good day to you. May your careers be interesting."

And short, she added mentally as she left them and continued on to the top of the hill, Kenadas striding in her wake. Once there, she glanced back. The Sarngin and their hapless charge were just turning the corner below.

She felt Kena's eyes on her face. "He was lured to that house, Kena. Lured there, robbed of his identity and sent into slavery."

"This is what happened to you, isn't it, Rani?"

She nodded. "Very nearly. And now I wonder, to how many others has it happened?"

"We will not concern Jaya with this just yet."

Jivinta Mina paced her grandson's study without the aid of her cane, which sat propped against a couch near the hearth. She was impressive and Ana was willing to be impressed by such a woman.

"You and I will look after it, Anala. After all, what would Jaya do? Buy the young man back! I can do that ... as a gift for my darling grandniece." She smiled conspiratorially at her 'grandniece.'

Ana was stunned by the suggestion and not a little queasy at the thought of returning to the dalali. She had imagined that she would tell Jaya of this latest development and he would simply take care of it. She saw the irony in that, but it failed to spur her conscience.

"I can't go into Badan-Devaki, Jivinta. Someone might recognize me."

"No one will recognize you, Ana. Trust me."

Two hours later, standing in the Badan-Devaki foyer with her hair bound in a red turban, her hands covered with matching gloves and her skin dusted to a deep, creamy gold, Ana thought her own family wouldn't have known her.

The Sarojin Matriarch took it upon herself to do all the talking, while Ana, fake tendrils of straight, black hair peeking from beneath her turban, glanced archly about like the Rani she was reputed to be. "As you can see," said the Sarojin matriarch archly, "my grand-niece has the famous Sarojin coloring. I want for her a young man that will complement her beauty. Someone exotic. Someone close to her in age. Someone fresh and possessing a certain innocence. Do you have anyone like that?"

They did, in fact. They had several such young men. Ashur Badan showed them vipics. Several of the youths might have been

Avasan. One of them was golden of face, hair and eye. Young, handsome and exotically fair.

Mina and Ana both expressed interest, prompting Ashur Badan to lead them to a tiny gallery that reminded Ana of nothing so much as the inside of the jewel box that sat upon her dressing table at the Saroj. She shivered reflexively and concentrated on the cluster of auction items.

Badan singled out Hadas and removed him from the group. He moved with the lethargy of the drugged, his amber eyes showing not even a spark of the defiance Ana had seen in them just hours before.

She forced to her lips a plastic smile of admiration. "He's lovely," she said. "Let's get him."

In the end, Mina Sarojin paid a steep 8,000 dagam for Hadas ... and another 1500d for Item ***25—a young girl who had caught her eye. She loudly proclaimed the girl would be a godsend to her poor overburdened house-das.

"Damn broker," Jivinta grumbled to Ana as she paid for her purchases. "They push the legal age of das down every year. That little girl couldn't be more than twelve."

Ashur Badan's all-hearing ears caught the comment. He padded solicitously to her service. "Is there a problem with your purchases, Rani Mina?"

"This girl." Mina pointed to the blank-faced child she had just collected. "Are you sure she's above the minimum age for permanent service?"

"I assure you," said Badan, "that all is quite legal. The Non-Separation Code does not extend to orphans. This girl had no family to separate her from."

Something that flickered momentarily in the child's dark eyes made a lie of that statement; Mina snorted and turned toward the foyer.

"Excuse me," said Ashur Badan, halting her. "But since meeting your lovely grandniece, I am haunted by the feeling that we are already acquainted. What was your family name, again?"

Ana shot Mina a flickering glance, using all her resources to remain calm.

"Sadira," she said, tilting her head up so she might look down at the dalal. "From Darupur, originally. I'm certain we've never met. I could not forget such a man as yourself, Badan-sama."

He preened, flattered where no flattery had been given. "Ah, well. Then, we have met only in my dreams. Every man has a vision that haunts his sleep."

"Never forget such a man as that, eh?" muttered Mina Sarojin as they climbed into her coach. "You're sly, Ana. That man is as slimy as the underside of a moss snake."

"Which, of course," said Ana, "was what I meant."

Chuckling, Mina seated herself on the padded bench with a regal flourish and eyed her two acquisitions as they slid in across from her.

"Go ahead and laugh, child. It's permitted," she told the girl, then asked, "What's your name? I can't keep calling you 'girl' and 'child.'"

"My name is whatever pleases the Rani."

"Completely proper. And completely idiotic. What is your given name?"

"Dana, if it please the Rani."

"'Dana' pleases 'the Rani' very well, thank you. Now tell me, Dana, are you an orphan?"

The girl's eyes displayed anger, unease, and resignation in swift succession. "I'd make Badan-sama a liar."

"Badan-sama is a liar already. You can't make him one. I want the truth, Dana. Do you have a family?"

Dana lowered her eyes, blinking rapidly. "Yes, Rani."

"Where is your family, then? Kasi?"

"Kalpali," she said. "My mother and two little brothers."

"How did you come to be in the Badan-Devaki?"

"My father was killed two year past in a logging accident. Mata tried t'work, but it's hard with the baby so young. I thought I'd do some, but there isn't much doing for a girl my age ... not that's blessed by Tara-ji. One day this woman shows at our place and says she can find work for me in a Big House in Kasi. Take one load off Mata's hands, I figured. Ma didn't want t'do it," she added defensively, "but they had to eat. So I say, 'yes.' Wasn't til we were on our way here in the skycoach I find out where I'm going. I tell them I'll go to the Sarngin, but they say I'm legal to them 'cause I'm an orphan by law."

"What?" Ana exclaimed. "But you have a mother—"

"A new interpretation of the law," commented Jivinta Mina wryly. "And a new interpretation of 'family.' A family without a father is no longer a family. It's a body without a head—it ceases to be." She looked, again, at Dana. "Tell me, child, what skills has your mother?"

The girl's eyes lit up and she nearly smiled. "She paints things, Rani. Tiny, tiny things. Whole villages in porcelain spice cups and palaces in the bowls of spoons. She paints me a cup once that's a flower inside and out with a green stem for a handle and a little, tiny wood-deva in the center..." Her eyes swung away suddenly. "They took it. Said it wasn't allowed, to have things from before."

Ana gritted her teeth. Violent, black rage boiled in her heart, and for a brief moment she imagined Ashur Badan and Devaki-sa sold, homeless and friendless, into ignominious slavery. Contrition followed, swiftly.

Mina said, "You must tell me how I may contact this talented mother of yours, Dana. Perhaps she could paint some things for me." Then she poked Hadas's knee with her jambu-wood cane. "What about you, young man? Where are your people?"

Hadas jerked his eyes back from their glazed stare out the coach window and brought them to Mina's face. He seemed to have difficulty focusing.

"What?"

Ana grimaced, doubting Hadas Gupta had been the most quiescent of acquisitions. "You're from Avasa, aren't you?"

He nodded, visibly pulling himself together. "Yes. Peradnatok. In the Sagara. My parents ... run an inn ... the Blue Pearl."

"I've heard of it," said Jivinta Mina. "A very fine, very beautiful inn, if the brochures are to be trusted."

Hadas fixed her with a knife-sharp gaze. "What will happen to us?"

"You must understand that you will not be treated as das in my House and the House of my grandson, the Nathu Rai Sarojin. We have not purchased you for that purpose—either of you. We have purchased your freedom that we may return it to you. You will be reunited with your families in due course. That's easy for Dana, but not so easy for you, I fear, Hadas."

"Why?" asked Hadas, voice and jaw tightening. "Why not so easy for me?"

"Because you're Avasan, " Ana answered. She pulled the turban and wig from her head, allowing her fat, cherry braid to fall to one shoulder.

Hadas reddened. "You!"

Ana grinned at his expression. "I told you I would see you again."

They spent the afternoon outfitting their guests with new clothing and disguising Hadas's palm. Jivinta Mina sent Kenadas back to the dalali to collect Dana's belongings. Her clothing and other personal effects had been destroyed, but one of the attendants had kept the flower tea cup. Kena returned with it in hand, presenting it almost reverently to his mistress. It was exquisite and displayed considerable talent. Mina admired and praised it highly before returning it to its rightful owner. Then she set about assigning aliases to her new charges.

Dana, whose age, accent and lack of education precluded her passing as anything but a rural child, was placed in Heli's able hands to help about the household. Hadas became another member of the Sadira clan, newly arrived from Avasa on holiday. He and his "cousin" Ana spent some time getting their stories straight, then went to their rooms to dress for dinner.

When she told him what they had done—that yet another Sadira 'cousin' had joined the household—Jaya was stunned to silence. It was a condition Anala took advantage of by steering him into his study. He slid into one of the chairs flanking the massive black fireplace, watching her warily while she danced a dance of sheer excitement.

"Jaya Rai, it was him. It was them! The same men!"

"Who did what, Ana?"

She paced the rug in front of the hearth, making emphatic gestures with her hands. "Who lured Hadas into a house near the warrows, took his id and left him for the Sarngin. Sound familiar?"

Jaya sat forward in his chair. "You're implying what happened to you—what?—wasn't a simple robbery?"

"Not at all simple, Jaya Rai. I had assumed it was my money they were after, that somehow I had tipped them to the fact that I was carrying it. But today, I watched them tail Hadas, offer him directions, even, all to lure him to a particular place so they could attack him. He wasn't carrying a large amount of money-"

"So they misjudged the situation. In your case-"

"In my case, they got lucky. I was wearing a money bag around my neck, when they grabbed my leaf, they got that as well. Jaya, they took Hadas's id. He said they didn't even search him for anything else. The id is what they were after all along."

She was losing him. "Why?"

She stopped pacing and came to crouch, cat-like on the carpet before him, her pale eyes imprisoning his, "To make yevetha, Jaya Rai. To create exotic fodder for the dalalis. What could be more perfect? Avasans wear no cree. On Avasa, this isn't a problem, we lose our leaf, we get new. But here..." She shrugged. "We are dispossessed."

"How-?" he began, and she told him how. Described seeing her own robber again, following him, stalking him as he stalked his own prey. And while she told him these things, Jaya felt as if a chill wind swept direct from some blasted Avasan plain through this, his inner sanctum.

"And if you catch them, what? If you make a complaint to the Sarngin, you'll have to have your palm read as well as submit leaf you don't have. You can't be the one to report this, Ana."

"I'm not sure, Nathu Rai, that it would do either of us any good to report this." She proceeded to tell him, then, about the pair of Sarngin who arrived on cue to take Hadas Gupta away to the dalali. "There was no discussion. No hesitation. No searching. They passed the thieves in the street, went in, secured him, and came out again."

The wind grew ever more chill. "You think the Sarngin were in league with the thieves?"

"So it would seem. They take Avasans off the street and put them into dalalis."

"So then, who's making it worthwhile for the thieves and the Sarngin? The dalalis?"

"One dalali is, anyway. Badan-Devaki."

"How did you happen to trace him there?"

"I didn't have to trace him. They said they would take him to Badan-Devaki and so they did."

She had his complete attention. "They said to whom? You spoke to them?"

She rose and turned away, made an odd wagging gesture with her head. "I wandered by and asked what dangerous thing such a nice-looking young man had done. They explained and I expressed a certain interest in Hadas." She moved to gaze from the atrium doors overlooking the gardens.

He couldn't see her face; she was taking special care with the arrangement of her tunic's thigh-length skirts.

"I understand," he said, counseling his rising temper to patience. ""They told you you could obtain the object of your desire at Badan-Devaki. So you simply went there."

"I wanted to contact you, but your grandmother decided to take things into her own hands. You know how she is."

"Only too well. But you went along–"

"I didn't want to, at first, but I had to identify Hadas."

"Who saw you—Kareen Devaki?"

"No. Ashur Badan was on the floor today. I was very well disguised."

"Were you wearing a veil?"

"No. But I was made up quite heavily."

"You weren't disguised, Ana. A man doesn't forget a face like yours—it haunts."

She shivered at how close those were to the words of Ashur Badan. "You shouldn't say such things to me."

"Why, because you're Rohin?"

"Because of our circumstances, Nathu Rai. Our worlds were not meant to collide."

"No? Then why did they? You're Rohin. You're supposed to believe that some all-knowing, all-seeing deity is in control of our destinies."

"I do believe that."

"Then we must have been intended to meet for some reason."

"Yes. Before we met, you didn't really care about what happened on Avasa or to Avasans. Now you do."

Jaya considered that. "I wouldn't say I didn't care," he said finally. "I would say I didn't want to care. I didn't want to get involved."

"And now you do."

"And now I do." Though not, perhaps, with what Anala Nadim would consider pure motives.

"Our meeting has served a purpose, then. An important purpose."

"That's too pat an answer, Ana." He turned to watch her face in profile, feeling her pull, tide-like, at him.

"It's the only one I have."

He was drowning, he thought. Drowning in metaphysical nuance and religiosity ... and desire. "Look, let's confine this conversation to practical issues for the moment. I need to extract a promise from you."

She was at once wary. "A promise? What sort of promise?"

"That you won't pursue this matter any further on your own."

"I wasn't on my own," she prevaricated. "I had Kenadas at my side this morning and was in the capable hands of your Jivinta this afternoon."

He came to his feet on a wave of impatience. "You're sidestepping the issue, which is one of character. You are very likely to take it upon yourself to pursue this. I ask you not to."

"You ask?" She was regarding him slyly out of the corner of her eye.

"I ask."

"When you could command?"

"As I said, it's an issue of character—yours. I appeal to your Rohin sense of responsibility." He at once regretted how very sarcastic that sounded.

Her eyes, mirroring his impatience, picked at his thoughts. "Responsibility, Nathu Rai? To what? To whom? I am responsible, by my own choice, for finding out who is assaulting Avasan travelers and selling them. Other than that, I am responsible for my own actions to God and to no one else."

"My grandmother has grown very fond of you, Ana. I won't let you be reckless with her affection."

She seemed scandalized. "I would never willfully hurt Jivinta Mina. If you don't know that about me, your own lack of insight is at fault. Jivinta is part of my responsibility to Sanat-ji. The two are not separable. Besides, Jivinta is behind what I'm doing. She supports me in it."

"Implying that I don't?"

Ana made a futile gesture. "You're always angry. I begin to believe it's your natural state."

He had to ponder that for a moment—to check the set of his face, wonder what she read in his eyes. Anxiety was there, he was certain. Impatience also. Did those things appear to the outside world as anger?

"Odd," he said. "I've always stood accused of being good-natured to the point of frivolity—of taking too little seriously. Until now," he added wryly, "my life has been relatively free of irritants. I haven't found it necessary to be angry. I'm not very good at it."

"Why is it necessary now? Why not stop being angry before you do get good at it?"

What did he say? What could he say? That he was jealous of her adventurous nature? Or worse, that he had the sudden, insane conviction that in threatening her own life, she threatened his as well?

"What's the matter?" she asked, and sounded more concerned than sarcastic.

He shook his head, his anger oozing away like water from a cracked bowl. "You are the matter," he said, half to himself.

"Do you to intend to begin fasting, or shall I have Heli serve your meal?" Jivinta Mina stood in the doorway, her eyes daring Jaya to challenge her for her day's work.

He didn't. All he said was, "And what are we doing to do with our new foundling, Jivinta? I must assume you don't mean to keep him as das."

"I intend to get his leaf replaced."

"Falsified leaf?"

Mina's brows formed a snowy exclamation. "Of course. We could hardly get the real article on demand."

Was this woman speaking so calmly of circumventing the law really his grandmother?

"What kind of leaf was he wearing? It would be next to impossible to fake one of these." He pulled his own id out of the neck of his tunic. The delicately faceted oval crystal spat varicolored fire into the room.

"He had metal leaf," said Ana. "Most of the colonies are still using the old id system."

Jaya was unconvinced. "Even so, he couldn't get off-world. He couldn't pass the id-scan."

"But he can go freely about Kasi," said Mina. "As long as he doesn't try to use his community credit, no one would have any reason to subject his leaf to a scan."

"Then what?"

"We'll have to get word to his family somehow. Try to get someone to bring the id to Mehtar. The Gupta family isn't involved in this thing with the Consortium—at least not directly. His family owns an inn."

"Rani Sarojin," said Ana quietly, "every family in the mining provinces are involved in this thing with the Consortium. Whether they are miners, darumen, or merchants. Nor, I think, do these thieves ask whether we are in the Guild before they steal our lives from us. There is no guarantee the leaf would reach Hadas safely and having it ferried here could put yet another life in danger."

"But, if we can't bring duplicate id from Avasa-"

"Then," said Ana, "we must catch the thieves and get our id back."

Jaya laughed. "Just like that?"

"Why not? Now I know approximately where they strike—between the spaceport and the Nahar. And I know who they strike. And why."

"It's unlikely they'd keep the id, Ana. Chances are they destroy it. Or perhaps they've found a way to make more money from it. They could sell it to people who need to assume a false identity for some reason ... fugitives perhaps. Or they could ransom it to your families, who would then have to buy your freedom. Remember, these are people who will squeeze what benefit they can from any situation."

"I paid 8,000d for Hadas," said Jivinta Mina dryly, "but only 1500d for a healthy young Mehtaran serving girl. I think that clearly illustrates the economics of the situation. An exotic item brings more profit. I can only imagine how much Ana would have brought at auction."

Jaya suppressed the urge to glance at Ana's face. He kept his eyes on his grandmother, recalling how keen Ashur Badan had been to impress him with the dalali's success. Had Badan-sama and Devaki-sa worked out a unique way to gain a competitive edge? Nausea circled the pit of his stomach, restless, looking for a place to lodge. In spite of this, he asked Jivinta Mina to have Heli serve, promising he and Ana would be in shortly.

"Your promise?" he asked when his grandmother had gone.

"I have made no promises," she returned quietly.

"Ana, please. I am trying to be respectful of you. I am trying not to make demands."

"I am trying not to make promises I can't keep."

You're trying my patience, he thought wryly. "And I am attempting not to make threats I don't want to keep. Ana, make me this promise—don't make me force the issue."

"It is said that force is the refuge of the desperate."

His patience evaporated. "Damn your Rohin platitudes! Stop throwing them in my face."

She rounded on him, pale eyes frigid. "You are willing to throw my 'Rohin platitudes' in my face when it suits you, mahesa. You call so eloquently on my honor, my virtue, my honesty—when you have need of them."

"I don't consider your honor a platitude. Do you?"

"Excuse me, Nathu Rai. I believe my dinner is getting cold."

He stopped her when she would have gone—blocking her path to the door. She turned away, fluttering between him and the windows like a trapped bird. He watched her for a moment, pondering his next move, his next words. Whatever they were, most likely they would drive her further into her pious fury. He chose to be conciliatory.

"I'm sorry, Ana. I don't mean to lose patience with..." That didn't sound conciliatory. "May we start again? I believe that if you give me your word you'll keep it. I trust you to be both honest and honorable with me."

He cringed, realizing he was doing exactly what she had just accused him of. That this had not escaped her registered clearly on her very expressive face.

"Will you at least promise me this: that you will not leave this house without letting someone know where you are going?"

She turned slightly toward him, her eyes assessing, her expression not quite contrite. "If I make you this promise, will you be less angry?"

He was surprised into laughter. "Would you have me make a promise I can't keep?"

"I suppose that wouldn't be fair, would it?" She took a deep breath. "Yes, I promise I will not leave this house without letting someone know where I am going. And now, Nathu Rai, if you are ready for dinner, I would like to introduce you to my 'cousin,' Hadas."

～

The next morning, when Ana would have gone to the Nahar Zone for her drill bits, Jaya sent Ravi instead, armed with enough money to offer the bribe he was certain the equipment broker had been holding out for.

Ana was disgusted. "I am beginning to think this entire society runs on bribes and threats," she told him. "Are you often forced to conduct business this way?"

Jaya raised his brows in mock surprise. "You don't do business like this on Avasa? Tsk. How uncivilized."

"Oh, we're horrible savages on Avasa. We sell mining equipment to women all the time, without extorting any extra gain from them."

"Now, according to the travel services, you Avasans live a pretty mean existence. What was it I read? 'An existence pried out of the miserly earth by brute force.' Something about a 'desperate struggle for survival,' 'frontier lawlessness,' 'pagan life styles.' Very exciting."

Ana laughed. "Have you ever been to Avasa?"

"Once, to a private resort in the Sagara."

"Ah, the Garden Spot." Ana nodded. "I was there once, myself. I stared at the ocean for hours. I couldn't believe how big it was."

Jaya smiled wryly. "By Mehtaran standards it's a large lake."

"We are impressed with it, and so I guess are many wealthy Mehtarans, or they wouldn't be buying up the sea shore for their private resorts."

Jaya felt a surge of guilt lock in combat with a warring sting of annoyance. It was a brief scuffle won by neither. "Yes, I do feel shame when I compare my life with what some other people have to endure," he said baldly, answering her veiled accusation. "I also feel a slight twinge of resentment that you insist on reminding me of the disparity."

"I'm sorry, mahesa." She changed the subject. "Can we tour the Port Zone?"

Jaya shook his head. "I have a Varmana assembly later. But we could breakfast at the Kiritan."

Breakfast was not all they got. Naru had some information about the thief. His name was Parva Rishi, or at least that was the name he used when he dined at the Kiritan. He didn't seem to have any particular friends among the regular patrons, but he was on nodding terms with several of them. Not, Naru added, that those people seemed overly pleased to see Rishi-sama. When asked for his impression of the man, Naru disclosed that he ate too much and had questionable table manners. And he only left gratuities for the more well-endowed female servers.

It wasn't much. In fact, it wasn't anything at all, to Ana, but Jaya had a resource very few of his class would appreciate. He knew a madman named Govinda.

CHAPTER SEVEN

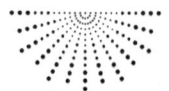

THE ROOM WAS dark and close, full of the sweet, warring perfumes of a variety of tobaccos. Candles flickered in the darkness, their inconstant light picking out bits of faces—the curve of a cheek here, the gleam of an eye there. Jaya came down the short flight of steps into the dingy grotto and headed for a stall in a far corner.

He was not himself tonight. No one would recognize the dark, rough-looking young man in the scuffed leather coat as the lord of anything. A woman smelling of a thousand night flowers brushed by him and tried to draw his eyes to her. He offered only a sly glance—the merest hint of a smile—then continued on this way.

"I'm glad you're a man of habit." He slid into a badly padded seat and grinned across the table.

The answering grin revealed a set of impossibly white teeth, slightly uneven due to a chip on one incisor.

Jaya noticed it. "That's new. Been fighting, Govi?"

"Not me. Got nothing to fight over. Someone thought I needed to relocate my cozy, is all."

"You disagreed?"

"Not a bit. I saw their superior reasoning immediately. I was just a grain too slow in moving, is all."

"So you're not in the alley behind Badan-Devaki anymore."

"Nah. Someone else is at home there now."

"I'm sorry to hear that."

Govi shrugged. "T'was getting a bit busy back there anyway. What brings you into Marketzone?"

"Parva Rishi. Heard the name?"

Govi was nodding. "Smalltime thief, bigtime schemer. That's not his real name."

"I didn't suppose it was. What others does he use?"

"Pel Ruche, Pidar Rel ... a few others. Got idea none which is the real thing."

"All with the initials P.R.."

Govi shrugged again. "He's consistent. Or maybe just superstitious. He's also the one who rushed me out of my cozy behind B'n'D. Him and his three thugs."

"Why? Surely he didn't need a place to live."

Govi laughed outright. "That's God's promise! That boy's got funds!" He rubbed his palm illustratively.

"Where does a 'smalltime thief' get funds?"

"This escapes me," Govi admitted. "Guess he's made some schemes pay. Why d'you ask?"

Jaya hesitated, considering how much he wanted to confide. "I know someone who had an experience with Rishi-sama that was a lot like yours."

"Rushed out of their cozy?"

"Rushed out of their id and 25,000 dagam."

Govi whistled. "Sarngin get 'em?"

"Very nearly."

"What's the plan?"

Jaya shook his head ruefully. "No plan. I was just trying to figure out what Rishi's up to."

He paused long enough to order drinks from the girl who loomed suddenly out of the darkness beyond the lamplit table. She took their order, then stayed overlong to play the coquette. Jaya flirted in return, and hinted that he might be around after her shift.

"He's up to his ears in money, from what I've seen," commented Govi when the girl was gone. "You really gonna wait that out?" he asked, jerking his head at the server's swaying hips.

Jaya shook his head. "Just being polite. How does Rishi come to be up to his ears in money? He doesn't seem to be stealing that much of it." Jaya leaned across the table and lowered his voice. "My friend saw Rishi strike twice. Both times he was after his victim's leaf. The first time the money just happened to get discovered. It was on a thong around her neck—so was her leaf. They lifted both. The second time they didn't even look for money. They went straight for the id. The Sarngin arrived to take the victim into custody—obviously by pre-arrangement—and brought him to the Badan-Devaki. My friend thinks the two things are connected."

Govi's face had puckered into a comic frown. "That's an odd one. Why would Parva Rishi be stealing id?"

"Possibly to help one of the dalalis make das that are cheap to obtain and sell for a high price."

"I don't track."

"They target people who don't have cree and whose legal rights on Mehtar are, shall we say, not that well-protected. With the leaf gone-"

Govi whistled. "Instant yevetha."

Jaya nodded. "I take it you don't know anything about this."

"No, would you like me to?"

"It would be very helpful to my friend."

"If I find out something, how should I get to you?"

"You know where I live."

Govi looked skeptical. "They call me the 'Crazy Beggar,' but I'm not so crazy I'd walk right up to the Sarojin Palace and ring."

"Why not?" asked Jaya. "I just invited you to."

"Jaya Rai, the existence of our friendship proves you an eccentric man. An invitation into your home proves you a demented one. Are you sure you want the whole city of Kasi privy to this?"

"I don't really care," Jaya admitted.

"Stone bet your mata do."

"The Rani may care all she wants, that doesn't mean I have to."

Govi's shiny, black eyes took on a particularly knowing gleam.

Jaya saw it and shook his head, grinning wryly. "No, I am not embarking on a token rebellion against Melantha Sarojin's shallow values. You're a friend, Govi, not a challenge to the Rani."

"Ah, this is true. I am your friend. But have you not, like your father before you, embarked on a crusade against rita?"

Jaya's face flamed with sudden embarrassment. He hoped Govi couldn't see the blush by candlelight. "I'm not a crusader, Govi. I would never presume to follow my father in that."

"Ah, well, it is a token rebellion, then."

"I pray it's not a token anything. I'm simply weary of hearing rita used as an excuse for injustice."

Govi laughed. "So you pray, do you? To what god does an atheist pray?"

"I was speaking figuratively."

"Ah! Then what figurative injustice do you speak of?"

Jaya's patience was beginning to stagger with exhaustion. "The injustice is completely real, Govi. Someone I know was free three days ago. She set foot on Mehtaran soil and was robbed of a stupid piece of metal. According to rita, the thief who stole it also stole her identity and her freedom. The loss of that worthless trinket makes her suddenly and mysteriously less than human—a commodity. Subject to the whims of someone like me."

Govi's face was finally completely sober. He was, himself, yevetha, an idless non-entity—but he was that by choice.

"And she's now a dasa in your house, this someone?"

Jaya glanced warily over his shoulder before answering. "She's in my household, but not as a dasa."

Govi nodded slowly, knowingly. "The young princess you were about with this morning. The Rani Sadira. Rumor makes her your cousin."

"Rumor is supposed to make her my cousin."

"A milk-skinned beauty ... from Avasa?"

Jaya nodded, watching the server make her way toward them with their order. Both men were silent until she had done flirting and was out of earshot.

"Then she has no cree," guessed Govi.

"She does now," said Jaya grimly.

"Dascree?"

Jaya nodded.

"What leaf?"

"Saroj."

Govi's brows fluttered to a perch beneath his scraggy fringe of graying hair. "You marked her?"

"It was that or turn her over to the Sarngin."

"Ah, a dilemma. So, now you try to retrieve her stolen identity. A worthy cause. Consider my assistance your right."

To someone else the assistance of a half-mad indigent might be beneath contempt. To Jaya it was invaluable.

In the misty quiet of the late night streets, he wound his thoughts through Anala's predicament, trying to separate it from the KNC and AGIM. It would be dishonest to deny that he had already lost the neutrality that was the ideal for a member of the Vrinda Varma. How could anyone remain neutral around Ana?

He amended the question: How could any man remain neutral around Ana?

He returned his horse to the stable and meandered into the House. Eyes on his thoughts rather than on his path, he nearly collided with Helidasa and a tray of channa and cakes. He apologized, she scolded him respectfully, he apologized again and asked if Anala was still awake.

Heli lifted the tray slightly. "This is for her."

"I'll take it," he said, and did, not quite oblivious to the sudden change of Heli's expression.

He went to his own suite first, divested himself of his cloak and the ragged coat beneath it, and knocked on the connecting door to Ana's rooms. That, he figured, would at least give her some warning in case she was in a state of undress. He side-stepped the thought, listening for the click of the door latch. He didn't hear it and the door came open silently, making him jump.

She stood a little inside her room, fully dressed in a long robe of Saroj crimson, only the tips of her toes showing beneath the hem. He couldn't see her hands.

"Nathu Rai?" she said and waited for him to speak.

"I-I didn't hear the latch," he said irrelevantly.

"It wasn't locked."

"Oh." He raised the tray and bowed slightly. "Tea, Rani?"

"Are you practicing to be das?" Her eyes mocked him and her hands appeared, reaching for the tray.

He pulled the tray away. "Sit down. I'll pour."

The hands retreated beneath the sleeves of the robe. "That wouldn't be appropriate, Nathu Rai."

He brushed past her into the room, moving to deposit the tray on a table before her hearth. "I was 'Jaya Rai' yesterday and 'Jaya' earlier today. What happened?"

She followed him, cautiously, watched as he poured the tea and took the cover off the cakes. "I'm sorry. I forgot myself this morning."

"I encourage you to forget yourself more often," he said and handed her the cup. "Ravi got your drill bits, by the way."

"Thank him for me ... and thank you."

She sat in one of the chairs that flanked the hearth, watching him, seeming to mark his less than lordly appearance. If she thought it odd that his hair was lying unbound on his shoulders and his clothing was common and plain, she didn't remark on it.

"How do we get them to Avasa?"

Jaya sat down opposite her, ignoring the question. "Ana, do you trust Taffik Pritam?"

Her eyes pinned him to the back of his chair. "With my life. He's family. Married to my cousin, Rafeen. They live in our compound."

"Then he'd be a good person to deliver a message to your father?"

"Yes! He's here, then? Taffik is here on Mehtar?"

Jaya nodded. "He's acting as chief negotiator for AGIM."

"Father ... ?"

"Your father is fine. Apparently he's in hiding."

Ana was on her feet, heading for the writing table under its now darkened skylight. "I'll write a note." She stopped at the table and turned, frowning. "What do I tell him?"

"Tell him anything you want, but start with the fact that you're safe. After the threats on your family he's bound to be worried about you."

Her gaze became more intent. "So you believe there were threats."

"Yes. And I believe there was sabotage. I'm just not sure the Consortium is guilty of it."

"Who else could it be?"

Jaya changed the subject. "How were you supposed to have contacted your family when you got here?"

Ana let the subject of the Consortium's culpability go. "I was to check into the Voyager hospice as Agni Kedara as soon as I got into Kasi. That's where I was headed when the thieves attacked. Father planned to trans-chat the Hospice and ask if Agni Kedara had checked in."

"Why didn't you say something, Ana? If I'd known, I could have checked somebody into the Voyager under that name."

She shook her head. "By the time you found me, it was already too late. There was a prearranged time window for the transchat. I wasn't there. Now, with no id, chatting back is out of the question."

"Not for me."

Ana tilted her head and gave him a look that questioned his sanity. "Lord Sarojin of the Vrinda Varma is going to trans-chat Rokh Nadim's compound? The Inner Circle will be interested to know why. So will the Consortium. No, mahesa, you were right the first time. A note to Taffik is the best channel. He's expected to contact my father."

"I'll get this done tomorrow. Your father is probably frantic by now."

"He won't be the only one. Hadas's visit here was not taken for pleasure. It seems his elder sister, Belia, has gone missing. She came to Mehtar almost three weeks ago to purchase some furnishings for their family inn, and disappeared. I think we may have a good idea of what happened to her."

The universe inside Jaya's head became suddenly still and hushed, and it occurred to him to wonder why he had never before considered—really considered—the minute and individual implications of the caste system that had having been dismantled in ages past on the mother world, had re-emerged, on Mehtar. Somewhere, long ago in the dimly recalled past of that other world this had been the way of things—but this way had perished as the words of newer Avatars prevailed and cultural values and views changed.

The first people to come to Mehtar had not been a race of masters and slaves, and Jaya realized with dim shame that, though his father had spoken to him of how caste had crept back into the culture, he could not recall it. He had not been inclined to listen. A boy has other things to fill his head than history, and a man can tell himself with comfort that to simply eschew owning another human being is a righteous enough protest.

Now Jaya struggled to remember his father's words. Mehtar, Bhaktasu Sarojin had said, was a world in need of an Avatar. Jaya could not help but agree, if only metaphorically. Perhaps Ram-ji had lost track of his people in their travels. If no Avatar arose, was that excuse for inaction?

Eons ago, on another world, the Avatar Krishna had stood above a battlefield and told His Lord Prince Arjuna that one could not merely let oneself out of the battle. Inaction and wrong action were the same; in deciding not to choose, one yet made a choice.

Jaya raised his head above the flood of epiphany and looked at Ana, forcing himself to imagine what her fate might have been had he not gotten to her before the Sarngin. Here, she was desired by one man who could, legally, force himself upon her, but would not. Elsewhere, any number of men would have already bedded her. That, he supposed, had been the fate of Belia Gupta, and would have been her brother's fate as well, were it not for Ana's impulsiveness.

How many Belias were there in Kasi at this moment, or scattered among dalalis and kaladans and private houses throughout the Seven Provinces? Jaya's desire quailed before his awakened conscience.

Ana had picked up a stylus and was rummaging about the desktop for a vellum. "You know, Taffik-sama could get the drill bits sent back, too. That way no one from this House has to have their seal on any transport paperwork."

Jaya nodded and rose to go. "That's a relief. My brain has gone lame trying to figure out how I was going to get that stuff off-world without someone tracing it back to me ... and to you."

"You won't be doing anything unethical, will you? By passing the note to Taffik, I mean."

"Unethical? What could be unethical about letting your family know you're not lying in a charnel house?"

She paled at the reference. "If anyone saw you pass the message, they might think it had something to do with the AGIM petition. You're neutrality could be questioned ... your honor."

Honor again. "I am capable of being discreet—even sly."

Ana's face suffused with sudden color. "I'm certain," she murmured, staring at the intricate pattern in the carpet beneath her bare feet.

Jaya moved automatically toward the door.

"Thank you, Nathu Rai."

He stopped and turned to look at her. She was still studying the carpet, curling her toes in its plush weave.

"Are we back to that nonsense, Nadim-sa?"

Her eyes met his, sending a wave of static down his spine. It lodged in his groin.

"Jaya," she said and the static sparked a fire.

He felt part of himself being sucked toward her like a leaf caught, unresisting, in a whirlpool. His body stayed rooted to the polished wooden floor—giving the appearance of solidity. Inside him, there was nothing at all solid. Rita had dispossessed his segment of the cosmos and left it in chaos.

He watched her stare at him and wondered what she felt. Did she feel this current arcing back and forth between them like a static tide? Or was it only arcing forth?

He opened his mouth (he thought), and said (he heard himself say it), "Ana, there's something ... I feel..." He extended a hand toward her, groping in the current for words. "Sakti. Something. Here. Around us, between us, in us." He'd never sounded so incoherent in his entire life.

She lowered her eyes and murmured, "Something cold and hot and moving and still. Something creeping and soaring and whispering and raging."

"You feel it, too. Tell me you feel it."

Her eyes rose again. "Yes," she said.

Witch, he thought. Deva. "I want you," he said.

"Yes." She lowered her eyes and waited.

He stared at her for a moment, feeling every inch of himself— cold/hot, moving/still, creeping/soaring, whispering/ raging—mostly raging. He could taste her, feel her, almost divine her thoughts.

"If I asked you to come to my bed..."

"I would refuse, Jaya Rai."

"If I commanded you—"

"I would come, Nathu Rai." Her head dipped in a gesture of submission.

Anger swept upward from his groin and burned itself suddenly out, leaving ashy defeat. He nodded. "Because of a legality."

"Yes."

"If you were free?"

She raised her head. "No doubt I would find the most valuable object in this room and hurl it at you. Breaking it, if possible."

He chuckled, relaxing slightly. "No doubt you would," he said, and turned to leave. At the door, he stopped. "Remind me, in the morning, to tell you about Pidar Rel."

"Who?"

"Your thief. That's another of his aliases."

Ana nearly leapt at him. "How do you know that? What have you found out?"

"In the morning," he said, and closed the door between them.

He did not sleep right away. Instead, he went down to the study, loaded the AGIM and KNC petitions onto a reading tablet and carried it upstairs to his bed. After a moment of thought, he added a volume of history.

Hours later, when he'd read through both court documents—some parts twice—he set the reader aside. He closed his eyes, but his mind refused to rest. How, he wondered, had the Avasan mining community become so completely indentured to the KasiNawahr Consortium? Was it some cosmic echo of the caste system? He realized his knowledge of the history of Avasan settlement was as sketchy as his knowledge of history in general. He resolved to educate himself.

He slept, finally, only to dream of frozen deserts and mine cave-ins and blasted sandcats. It was a sleep that did anything but refresh.

CHAPTER EIGHT

THE MESSAGE SAT HEAVILY in the inner pocket of his coat. He felt it there all during the invocation, barely remembering to murmur "Ya, Ramji" at the appropriate times. He listened drowsily to the opening comments of the Dandin, Sri Elui, rousing himself only when the Deva Radha raised the Branch of Oration.

She lifted the Branch from her console and turned it absently between her fingers as she spoke. "We have had several days to look over the petitions brought before us by the Kasi-Nawahr Consortium and the Avasan Guild of Independent Miners. You have no doubt begun to form opinions about the ethics of this situation and the spiritual and moral issues involved. Now is the time to voice those opinions."

She glanced around the chamber, finally singling out Jaya. She held out the Branch. "Nathu Rai Sarojin, what principles do you see involved?"

Jaya was struck by swift dread. Why had she come to him first? Did she intuit something about his manner; had she heard something of Ana? He shook himself free of the paranoia. That line of thought was pointless. He had, in any event, done much thinking in anticipation of that question. It was necessary to answer honestly, but without bias. Necessary and difficult.

He took the Branch from the courier who brought it to him and folded his hands around the stem, ordering his thoughts. Two seats to his right, Bel Adivaram snickered, and Jaya could only assume it was because this new sober mien did not at all suit him in the Vadin's eyes. It was also difficult, the Lord Prince of Kasi found, to feel truly and fully mature in the presence of peers who had the advantage of age and experience. He was nearly thirty years of age and they still looked at him and saw a frivolous youth.

Jaya marshaled his thoughts. "Dignity," he said. "Freedom, independence of thought, the right to pursue a livelihood. The right to ... an identity. These are the principles I see that must inform this discussion. Honesty is at issue here, as well. Trust and trustworthiness, generosity, simple courtesy. Balance and moderation."

At the Deva's nod, Jaya passed the Branch of Oration to his right. The Dandin beside him spoke of justice and equity and greed before passing it on to Bel Adivaram.

"Greed is certainly a factor," Adivaram said. "And ingratitude. Equity and justice must be the guiding factors in our adjudication."

So it went—each of the twenty-seven members of the Vrinda Varma speaking in turn. Once the Principles of Justice had been compiled, consultation began, the order of oration now being reversed. The eldest Dandin, Sri Elui, began by expressing his disappointment that the Consortium thought so little of human rights that they would try to bind their fellow men and women to economic stagnation.

A senior Lord, Vivekand, expressed similar sentiments, adding that the situation transcended politics or economics.

"I feel it is critical that we bear the human values at stake here constantly in mind," he concluded.

The first of the Vadin to orate was old Narudin, who spoke, as was worthy of a Vadin, of due process and protocols and legal precedent. He suggested the KNC's current policies for dealing with AGIM be reviewed.

The sentiments expressed by the next Dandin speaker, a young Deva, though framed in more metaphysical terms, were the same, as were those of the next series of Varmana—Lord, Vadin and Holy Ones alike. Many only nodded or murmured "I concur" when the Branch passed into their hands. Two young Vadin abstained from comment.

So it was that Kreti Twapar's oration came as a complete surprise to the entire assemblage. He took up the Branch and held it for a moment, watching it tremble in his hands. He cleared his throat no less than four times and finally managed to raise his eyes to the assembled Varmana. Clearing his throat a fifth time, he said, "I agree with this Council about the principles here involved, but I don't—I mean, that is, I have to ... I'm forced to disagree with their application. I do not see the Consortium's demands—that is, their requests—as excessive. No, I quite agree with their attempts to protect the Mehtaran economy. I empathize with-with their concern for their own resources. I don't feel it unreasonable for the KNC to wish to control the flow of goods to and from the Avasan mines. Nor do I feel it is unreasonable to expect that the Guild should ... should show special consideration to the Consortium. It is by the largesse of the Consortium that they have flourished on Avasa in the first place."

The Lord Twapar warmed to his subject, developing a sense of drama. "Surely," he said with doleful passion, "they cannot have forgotten that their forebears traveled to Avasa on KNC vessels or that it was the KNC that supplied them grain to plant and food to eat until their crops were selfsupporting. Or that every last peg and pot of mining equipment was imported under the auspices of that same organization. The Guildsmen owe the Kasi-Nawahr Consortium much. Indeed, I am saddened that they choose such a treacherous way of repaying the kindness and generosity of a benefactor."

He closed his mouth suddenly, oration apparently at an end, and sweated.

In the silence that followed the monologue, Jaya stared at Kreti Twapar. So did nearly every other Varmana present, except the nine Holy Ones, who never stared. All, Jaya wagered, were wondering what strong emotions had driven the timid but opinionated old Lord to such outspokenness.

Twapar, evidently unnerved at being the object of intense scrutiny, quailed and silently passed Oration to Bel Adivaram.

The Vadin scowled. "I find myself, for once, in agreement with Lord Twapar. We must not let our emotions run away with us. Freedom and justice and humanity are all mighty principles, but we must not be misled into seeing oppression where there is none, or label as oppressed a group of people who wield perhaps more power than we suppose. I urge this Council to caution. It is clear to me that the Avasan Guild could exert a strangle-hold on the Kasi-

Nawahr Consortium that would ruin its fortunes. Their conception of free enterprise could easily become blackmail."

Jaya exhaled, wondering what he was missing. Were there elements here he was failing to comprehend? Was he letting his emotions run away with him? Was he biased against the Consortium because he had come to think of the Guild in terms of Anala Nadim and the Consortium in terms of Duran Prakash? Was he incapable of objectivity?

He listened very hard to the consultation after that, not offering much comment and taking copious notes.

It was a long session. Consensus evaded them. Kreti Twapar doggedly insisted on interpreting the Consortium's position as self-defense and AGIM's as treachery, and Bel Adivaram stolidly insisted he could be right. The two abstaining Vadin joined them, and a small but vociferous core of concord formed.

It was generally agreed that the Safety Council proposed by AGIM was a good idea, but it was not agreed that the Vrinda Varma should oversee it. It was generally agreed that an independent Quality Control would be ideal, but it was advanced, on the other hand, that it was prejudicial to imply that the quality control measures of the Consortium were insufficient or biased.

Late in the session, Duran Prakash and Taffik Pritam were called in to clarify a few points. There were words exchanged between the two, at which point the Deva intervened and sent Pritam-sama from the chamber until the Varmana should be done with the KNC Speaker. Both men received stern warnings about their behavior.

Prakash was the soul of rationality and discretion after that. He even sympathized with the Guilders. Of course they wanted their freedom. Of course they wanted their own mines, their own lands. That was why the Consortium document included a provision for the Independents to be able to purchase the properties they were currently mining, farming, and living on. Naturally, the KNC couldn't be expected to sell the properties to its avowed enemies, so only those miners and settlers who were not affiliated with AGIM would be considered for ownership.

The Deva reminded Prakash-sama that KNC ownership of Avasan mining concerns had not been determined, and Prakash-sama reminded the Deva that the KNC had, after all, bank-rolled the initial exploration of the planet, paving the way for settlement.

Later, given a summation of Prakash's commentary, Taffik Pritam was outraged. "We reject the idea that we must buy our properties from the KNC!" he exploded. "We have already paid for our holdings on Avasa in blood. Our families homesteaded that land. We have sweated and starved and died for it—carved our graves out of its rock. And now they would have us pay a second time? It is too much, Noble Ones. It is too much."

The Deva excused Pritam-sama at the conclusion of his remarks, then asked for further consultation. There was little of that. The Vrinda Varma seemed to be at an impasse. There was no way to even attempt to negotiate compromises—Taffik Pritam was not authorized to make command decisions for AGIM. Only one man had been granted that right and he was in hiding on Avasa.

"I don't see how we are to resolve this issue," said Bel Adivaram at the end of a fruitless round of commentary, "without speaking face to face with Rokh Nadim. I feel we must request— no demand —his presence here. I myself will offer a team of Sarngin from my Zone to protect him. There are no better forces anywhere."

"Oh, but there are," said the Lord Mandal. "There are much better forces at our disposal." His eyes quickly picked out the other members of the Inner Circle, then returned to rest on the Deva, who was its Head.

She nodded. "What say the members of the Inner Circle?" she asked. "Shall we assign the Balin?"

"Surely that's not necessary," objected Vadin Adivaram mildly, amid the rustle of commentary that question evoked. "The forces under my command—under the command of any Vadin—should be sufficient. Under the circumstances-"

"I believe the circumstances may warrant the special disciplines of the Balin."

"The Sarngin are well-trained," offered one of the younger Vadin, defensively.

"Vadin Pangum, it is not a matter of training. It is a matter of doctrine. The Balin have the discipline of Orders. Do you suggest mere military training is superior or equal to that?"

The Vadin reddened. "No, Holy One. I would never suggest that. By all means, if the Circle feels this Rokh Nadim's safety warrants the use of the Balin-"

Sri Radha turned back to the Circle. "I put it to the vote. Shall we assign a team of Balin to Nadim-sama's escort?"

They nodded, each in turn—the two remaining Dandin, the three Vadin, the three Vasin. The last of these, Kreti Twapar, hesitated momentarily and seemed to consider declining, but in the end he, too, nodded his assent. It was unanimous: Rokh Nadim would be escorted to Mehtar by a contingent of Balin—the select Guard of the Inner Circle.

When the session closed, Jaya went quickly to where his coach waited in the circular court central to the Asra Complex. Ravi was already waiting for him there.

"Pritam is registered at the Inn of the Golden Lota," Ravi reported as he helped his Nathu Rai out of his chamber robes. "Room 4-75."

Jaya glanced down the broad, flowered avenue that led from the Complex. He could see the artistically lit facade of the Lota from here. This was luck. The Inn had one of the finest restaurants in all Kasi and he dined there often enough after Varma sessions to be considered a regular; his appearance tonight would cause no speculation.

"We'll walk," he said and glanced up at the driver's box. "Join us, Kena?"

"No, sir!" said Kenadas in his usual tone of scandalized reproach. "I'll go to the Coach House, Nathu Rai, as is my habit."

Jaya chuckled. Someday Kenadas would break down and dare to cross the bounds of caste, if for no other reason than that his curiosity would get the better of him.

Their robes stowed in the coach, Jaya and Ravi strolled to the Inn of the Golden Lota where they were seated in the opulent dining room with great ceremony and where the patrons whispered to each other about how scandalous it was for the young Nathu Rai to bring his das to table with him. They ordered their meal, then Jaya excused himself to go to the men's grooming salon, leaving his companion to peruse the dessert menu.

The salon was accessed by a broad, subtly lit hall that gave onto the lift-well at its nether end. A cross-corridor there led right, to the lobby, and left, to the back firestair. This was a fortunate arrangement. What was not so fortunate was that when Jaya reached the hall, a group of gentlemen of his acquaintance was clustered about the salon entrance chatting. He could not get to the lift-well without drawing their notice.

In fact, he realized, they'd noticed him the moment he set foot in the hall. Cursing silently, he drifted up to them, said "good-evening," exchanged a few pleasantries, and confirmed that he would look forward to seeing them Bhaktar-eve at the Mesha banquet. Then he excused his way into the salon.

The outer room was not empty. A man stood before the wall-length mirror, grooming his substantial beard.

Jaya fumed, took out his hairbrush, loosed his hair and began a careful currying. He glanced sideways. Damn all vanity! The fellow had begun to braid a lock of silver that stood out of the contrasting black. Jaya gritted his teeth.

"Excuse me," said the beard-braider, "but is that natural?"

Jaya looked at him blankly. "Pardon?"

"Your hair, mahesa. Is that the natural color?"

"Yes, it is."

"Ah. Very unusual. Very striking. Almost ... blue black, isn't it? I had to have this done." He indicated the black curtain that framed the lone silvery lock, then went immediately back to braiding it.

Jaya glanced up into the mirror—his eyes on the door behind him. Maybe ... A roar of laughter told him the corridor was still well-guarded. He resigned himself to patience, carefully rebound his hair, then got out his kohl kit and seated himself at the vanity bar. He then embarked on a painstaking refreshment of the Sarojin tiliq between his brows.

He was running out of things to touch up when at last the Bearded One finished his task and left the room. Jaya felt a wave of relief wash through him. It was rudely strangled by the muttered "excuse me's" that greeted the Beard's passage into the hall outside.

He sat, silent, listening, as the voices seemed to fade. In a moment there was silence.

Jaya quickly reassembled his grooming kit and tucked it away inside his day-coat. He was halfway across the salon when the door swung open and a young Vadin came in. Jaya froze and pretended to search for something in his pockets, his eyes on the swinging door. Through it he could see that the outer hallway was empty. He all but bolted for the corridor.

In the hallway, he strode swiftly to the lift-well and took the empty basket to the fourth level where it stopped with a swish of air brakes. The fourth floor corridor was empty. Jaya stepped out onto the plush turquoise carpet, then froze as a couple strolled arm in arm through the cross corridor. Intent on each other, they didn't even mark his presence. He moved quickly to room 4-75 and pressed the chime.

It took only seconds for Pritam-sama to arrive at the door—to Jaya it seemed like minutes. He saw the surveillance light go on above the chime button and felt a stab of nerves, knowing he was being watched.

The light went out and the door slid open, revealing Taffik Pritam. Jaya slipped into the room before he was invited.

The Avasan regarded him warily, ice-pale eyes narrowed. "Mahesa. To what do I owe this honor?"

Jaya pulled Ana's note from his wallet and offered it to him. "A message for Rohk Nadim ... from his daughter."

Pritam's hand froze halfway to the note. His eyes penetrated Jaya's like a deep blue frost. The hand hovered, snatched. He opened the note and read it, then read it again.

"This is her handwriting," he said finally. "Where did you get this? How?"

"Ana is safe. In my home. She's ... posing as my cousin Ana Sadira from Avasa."

Pritam-sama frowned. "How did she come to you?"

"That's a story I don't have time to tell. I'm dining downstairs and need to get back. I'm supposed to be in the men's salon."

"Why does she need duplicate leaf? Can you tell me that?"

"Hers was stolen."

Taffik Pritam's face went pink. "She's yevetha?"

Jaya shifted uncomfortably. "Worse, I'm afraid. She's carrying a dascree."

"What?"

"We've managed to doctor it so it looks like a raicree, but she needs her leaf if she's ever going to get home."

"Get home? With a dascree in her palm?"

"No one expects an Avasan to have any cree at all, Pritamsama. With the proper leaf, no one would have any reason to check her palm. The problem is getting the leaf to Mehtar."

Pritam nodded. "Not something that can come by packet. It

would have to be carried over on someone's person. And that—the expense of passage-"

"Is not a problem. I'll pay it. Can you get the message to Rokh Nadim that his daughter needs duplicate leaf?"

"Of course."

"Then that's all that needs to be done. He can bring it with him when he comes over."

"Comes over?" The Avasan was immediately suspicious. "How is that? He would make himself an instant target if he were to leave Avasa."

Jaya colored in embarrassment. "I'm sorry. I shouldn't have said that. I'm not at liberty to discuss it."

Taffik Pritam studied his face. "They want to kill him, mahesa," he said at last. "They want to smoke him out and kill him."

"That won't happen," said Jaya, side-stepping the issue. "Trust me. The arrangements for his well-being will be to your satisfaction. Can he be told that Ana needs the leaf without arousing suspicion?"

Pritam nodded. "There are ways. No one outside the family knows Anala is on Mehtar. Messages about her will not be expected to come from me."

"Where is she, supposedly?"

"She went up to the camp at Tibi and took ill. As far as the KNC is concerned she is still there, fighting a case of vapor chill. She smuggled herself out of camp in a shipment of ore." Pritam-sama's eyes glinted speculatively. "Perhaps we should not be so hasty to get Ana home."

"Why not? Surely, Nadim-sama is worried."

"Oh, yes. He is that. The whole family is frantic, but I can put their hearts at rest with my next trans-chat. Think, mahesa. On Avasa Ana is in danger. Here ... ?" He shrugged.

Jaya nodded. "She's anonymous and probably a good deal safer. Yes, I see your point."

"But you, Nathu Rai. If you are afraid of being found out-"

"I'm afraid only of what might happen to Ana. If she's safer in the Sarojin Palace, then that's where she'll stay. Now, I'd better go." He turned, then paused. "Be careful what you say over the trans-chat, Pritam-sama. Someone may be listening."

The Avasan grinned mirthlessly. "Have no fear, mahesa. We

Guilders have our own peculiar language. Peace to you. And may Tara-ji smile on all your undertakings."

A most composed-looking Ravidas was enjoying his food when Jaya returned to the table. A quirked eyebrow formed a question mark.

Jaya smiled and tackled his own meal. "I feel much better, having satisfied my vanity," he said. "You will note my Saroj is now delivered of that purple smudge."

"Ah, yes," replied Ravi, squinting at his Nathu Rai's forehead. "I am relieved."

So was Jaya, and he settled back to enjoy his meal.

Ana's day had gone much less smoothly than Jaya's. Despite his concern about her being out on her own, she spent most of it wandering the Port Zone, following this new arrival or that. Jivinta knew what she was about, and had been surprisingly discouraging, but she had not tried to stop Ana from leaving the Saroj.

Ana saw a number of people from home, but the thieves never appeared to dog their tracks. She thought of approaching the Avasans herself, passing them notes asking them to contact her at the Sarojin Palace, but caution and courtesy got the better of her. The thieves might be watching. It would do her no good at all to be seen, perhaps even recognized by them. Besides, she thought, watching Mitras's orb slide, crimson, toward the skyline, she could hardly give away the Nathu Rai's address as if it were her own. The last thing he needed in his present circumstances was to have the Sarojin Palace turned into a camp for Avasan refugees.

In the sunset of a fruitless day, Ana mounted the horse she'd slipped from Kenadas's stable and rode slowly toward the Sun Crescent. She despised her black mood. Gloom did not come naturally to her.

Passing the Asra Complex, she felt a swift need for intimate conversation with Something beyond herself. She stopped the horse and studied the magnificent dome of the Asra where it sat jewel-like amid its ancillary buildings—the Council Hall, the Hall of Knowledge, the Hall of Records. Surely, she could manage to enter unseen. Her clothing was inconspicuous and dark. But what if she was noticed? The Sun Crescent was Sarojin home turf. The Dandin of the Sanctuary would certainly know every soul in their community. A stranger would stand out like ... like an Avasan on Mehtar.

In the end, she gave in to her inner need. It was dark when she entered beneath the lamplit archways and she tried to keep to the pools of shadow that eddied along the curving back wall of the Most Holy. There were few worshippers here at this time of day and most of those wore the silken robes of Orders. There were several older women in street clothes offering veneration at the feet of the Flower Altar, and a Dandin, still in the heavy chamber robes of the Vrinda Varma, knelt in a wall niche.

She surveyed the heart of the Asra. The circle of cushions around the Rama Fire was empty but for one very young bhakta whose half-shaved head and black robes marked him as one of the ascetic Asen.

Taking a deep breath, she moved silently to sit as nearly opposite the youth as she could, figuring that the Rama Flame itself would seclude her from him. Once cross-legged on her cushion, she pulled her prayer beads from around her neck and draped them over her head, pressing the large, faceted central crystal between her brows before allowing it to dangle there.

The firelight pierced the facets in a dizzying spray of hues. She followed them for a moment, allowing her eyes to play, unfocused, in the swirl and dance of colored lights. Her mind began to calm. She gazed past the crystal to the Flame that danced in its silver bowl. Light and heat ... life of souls and planets.

She began a soft chant, her body rocking to an internal rhythm. The tension and frustration flowed out, light and heat flowed in. Time was meaningless here. It melted upward with the tongues of flame, curled toward the vaulted ceiling, and dissolved in tiny wisps of scented smoke. Deep in the spiral weave of meditation, Ana confronted the shame of being yevetha and was solaced: There is no shame save in breaking faith.

She had begun to swim toward outer consciousness, clutching that thought as if it was a Sagaran pearl, when she knew she was being watched. She opened her eyes and removed the beads from her head. Across from her—or nearly so, for he had moved—the young bhakta stared at her gravely. Seated on the cushion next to her, sat a Deva of the Cloud Order, arrayed in silver and white. Her waist-length hair was so close in color and sheen to her robes, it seemed to melt into them.

Ana bowed her head and quickly gave the respectful greeting. "Deva," she said.

The other woman nodded in return, her dark, colorless eyes searching. "You have agitated my young associate," she said. "He is not used to having young women appear suddenly at the Rama Fire and perform devotions ... least of all if they are not in Orders."

Ana couldn't help throwing the bhakta a slightly pointed glance. "I am Rohin, Deva," she said respectfully. "I wasn't aware that this Asra was reserved for the Orders."

"It isn't, but..." The Deva's mouth twisted wryly. "Mehtaran custom does not make your actions ... common."

"Is my devotion not acceptable to Tara-ji?"

"I am sure it is more than acceptable to Her."

"Then, may I not offer it here?"

"You may offer it wherever you are called to offer it. I speak only of custom, not of Law." The Deva's eyes glided to the young ascetic's face, then back to Ana's. "You're Avasan, are you not?"

"Yes, Deva."

"Yet, you wear the Saroj on your brow. I know the Sarojin clan very well. I was not aware of an Avasan branch."

"A remote branch, Deva. We are called Sadira. We have been two generations on Avasa, now."

The Deva nodded, making an "ah!" with her mouth. "Am I correct in assuming that on Avasa no one would blink at a young female Rohin offering bhakti at the shrines?"

"You are correct, Deva." Ana's eyes found the bhakta's face again.

Again, the Deva nodded. This time, she also smiled. The bottomless, black eyes came to life. "I shall inform Brother Dru of this fact."

Ana dared an answering smile. "I am sorry to have disturbed his devotions."

"Dru-sama disturbed his own devotions, Rohina. I will suggest to him that a slight difference in custom should not be allowed to spook the steed of contemplation and unseat the Rider."

"If I might be so bold, Deva—I have found recitation and

contemplation of the Seven Vales to be most helpful in learning to keep one's seat."

The Seven Vales was a highly mystical allegory of the soul's quest for meaning revealed by the Kalki Avatar. It gave novice bhakta fits until they found the comprehension that came only through experience. Ana somehow doubted the unfriendly bhakta's life in a Mehtaran Order had run to that experience ... yet.

She knew there was a red gleam in her eyes. Her mother had always called it her demon. Oh, but it couldn't be a demon, because there it was, echoed, in the Deva's eyes and then, in her smoky, incense-scented laughter.

"That is an excellent suggestion, Rohina Sadira. May I assume you are able to perform such a recitation, yourself?"

"I am able, Deva. And to provide commentary."

"I would like to hear that commentary someday," said the Deva, "but now I feel the need to be expedient in giving my young associate his lessons."

She rose with fluid grace, the yards of silver-silk hair billowing with the movement.

Ana looked up and smiled beatifically. "I'm sure he'll feel well-rewarded by such great bounty."

The Deva nearly grinned. "Oh, most certainly." She moved a few steps away, then turned. "You will visit us again, Rohina?"

Ana bowed her head deeply. When she raised it, the Deva was already taking the bhakta aside, her face as unreadable as a festival mask.

Ana chuckled inwardly, feeling much better about everything ... except ... She glanced up into the capacious rotunda above the Asra's Heart of Flame. "Forgive me, Sanat-ji, for judging the bhakta, Dru. And for crediting him with so little inner sight. I pray he is at least as enriched by the Journey through the Vales as I was."

Her conscience somewhat appeased, she left the Asra and returned to the Sarojin Palace.

When she entered the Evening Room, some twenty minutes later, Kenadas was receiving a heated lecture on responsibility. It took her a moment to realize that she was the cause of the lecture, only a second more to feel profoundly guilty.

"Nathu Rai," she said.

His head whipped about so briskly, she imagined she heard his neck snap.

"Please, Nathu Rai. Don't take Kena to task on my account."

Jaya obliged. He dismissed Kenadas, then turned to toss his ire in her direction. "Where were you?"

"I borrowed a horse and went for a ride," she returned demurely. "I ... needed to clear my head. Sort things through. I told Hadas and Jivinta Mina where I had gone." It was not quite a lie; she merely omitted where she had ridden. "Ram-ji has always seen to my safety quite well," she added.

"Ram-ji is, in all likelihood, a mass illusion incapable of protecting a dust mote. You need to look after yourself."

Her cheeks felt scorched, but she chose not to answer his disbelief.

He changed the subject abruptly. "I saw Taffik Pritam this evening."

Ana's stomach did a somersault. "You gave him the message?"

Jaya nodded. "He promised to pass it on to your family at the earliest opportunity."

"Then I will soon be leaving Mehtar."

Jaya hesitated just enough to make Ana squirm, then he said: "Pritam-sama and I discussed that. We agreed you would be safer here."

Anala's ire kindled. "You agreed?"

"He brought to my attention that as long as your father's enemies suppose you're on Avasa, they won't be looking for you here."

"Then you needn't be so concerned about my comings and goings."

"Don't be smug, Nadim-sa. I'm not worried about the KNC recognizing you and you know it. They're not interested in what happens in the streets of Kasi, but Parva Rishi is. Neither of us knows to what lengths he would go to protect those interests."

Anala blushed. "I didn't mean to be smug, Jaya Rai. Forgive me."

Jaya motioned at the chairs by the nearest hearth. "Will you sit down and have some tea with me?"

"Thank you, I could use some."

Ana made herself comfortable in one curving cup, then watched the leap of flame as Jaya seat himself and used the chair-side com unit to ring Heli for tea.

"Did you inform Cousin Taffik of my status in your household?" She felt his gaze on her and decided she would never get used to that sensation.

"I told your cousin your id was stolen. I told him you were masquerading as the Rani Ana Sadira—my cousin."

Ana picked at a stray thread on her seat cushion. "Then you didn't tell him I was your dasa?"

"I value my life, Anala. I don't think Pritam-sama would have reacted well to such news. And you are not my dasa. You were fortunate to have been stumbled upon by someone who doesn't believe in slavery. Why do you persist in provoking him?"

Well, that was an honest enough question. "I don't know. I suppose it's my nature. I am trying to overcome it," she added.

"Are you, indeed?"

"I went to Asra tonight."

Jaya laughed at her. "To pray for forgiveness?"

"I always pray for forgiveness," she told him. "I went ... to sort things out. To get a different perspective."

"And did you?"

She nodded. "My difficulties are insignificant. I see that. But the same difficulties are being inflicted on others—only God knows how many others. As you pointed out, I was fortunate. I was found by you and not by the Sarngin ... or worse. Hadas was lucky, too. But his sister was not. What happens to her? To the others like her?"

Jaya shifted in his chair, his eyes following hers to the fire. "Why ask me?"

"Because you know. You know something about kaladans and slavery."

He was not a man without conscience; she knew that. Last night she had sensed in him the opening of a new level of comprehension. They spoke of people, of lives—not of commodities, nor ciphers on an inventory sheet, nor even the strictly faceless "other." These commodities had names—Ana, Hadas, Belia. She pressed him purposefully, now, wanting him to see this reality as she saw it, feel it as she felt it. She wanted him to walk, if only for a moment, in the way of the casteless—to imagine being free one moment and enslaved the next. She watched his face, wanting it to reveal his comprehension. It revealed nothing.

"I think you understand very well what might have happened to you, Ana. You were in that dalali long enough."

"I was there long enough," she said, "to know I'd like to see such places closed down."

His mouth twitched. "That will never happen. The dalali is an institution in every major city on Mehtar. It's how we handle people who ... who fall from the structure of society."

"Fall?" repeated Ana. "I didn't fall, Nathu Rai, I was pushed. As other of my people are being pushed. I am not part of the structure of your society. It should have no claim on me."

Jaya drew his eyes from the flames to give her his full attention. "It thinks it does, Ana. Generations ago, it seemed necessary to mark and track every man, woman and child in the world due to the diseases they might carry or the politics they might breed. Some believe it is necessary still. Some believe it necessary that every man be able to look at every other man and immediately know his relative place and relationship. It is a ... a convenience, a shortcut. If I know you are of a lower caste, I don't have to bother myself with establishing a relationship with you—that relationship is already established and defined. If I know you are higher, likewise, I need not worry myself with relationship, but only bow and offer the customary rituals of respect."

He stopped speaking, but continued to look at her as if trying to work something out.

"But how can this happen?" she asked, and thrust her hand at him, palm up. She bored into his eyes, demanding him to give her an answer that made sense to her. "You were born to station; you are part of this world. I'm not. I'm Avasan. How can this happen to me?"

He looked away. "The laws of Mehtar don't acknowledge true castelessness. You fell through the cracks, Ana. You all fell through the cracks."

"You are a mahesa, a Lord, a member of the Vrinda Varma. Will you tell me that nothing can be done about this injustice?"

When he looked at her again, she saw her anger reflected in his eyes. "A week ago I might have told you that," he said. "I might have half meant it. I can't tell you that now, because I think something must be done."

Ana nodded. At last, she thought. At last I have reached him.

"Thank you, Jaya Rai."

"But," he added, "it will not be done in the back ways of Kasi by a lone woman. Promise me you won't go out again, alone. Promise me you will take someone with you. Promise as a Rohina."

This time, Ana accepted both the logic and the urgency of the request. "I promise."

He was surprised at her easy capitulation. "No argument?"

"I try not to argue with common sense. It's foolish. I dislike looking foolish."

Helidasa entered just then with their tea. They spoke of the Mesha party after that and said no more of conspiracies or slavery or of men who could steal lives without taking them.

CHAPTER NINE

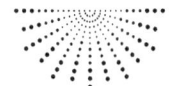

Hᴀᴅᴀs ᴡᴀs ᴀʟʀᴇᴀᴅʏ at the breakfast table, disassembling and eating clusters of grapes, when Jaya entered and took his seat. After a moment of obvious indecision, the Avasan gave a sketchy rendition of the respectful greeting, showing Jaya the carefully tinted Sarojin raicree on his palm.

"It seems Heli has been at work again," Jaya commented dryly.

"Did I do well?" Heli the Ever-Present carried a carafe of jambu to the table and poured the amber liquid into his glass.

"Thank you. Frighteningly well. You might consider going into business, Heli. I'm sure there would be no end to the parade of people who'd line up to have their cree altered."

Heli's expression carried censure. "That would be illegal, Jaya Rai."

"And this isn't?"

Her head wagged this way, then that. "This is different. This is to fix an injustice. Since our laws provide no justice, legality is irrelevant." The dasa turned on her heel and returned to her kitchen.

Jaya pondered that momentarily but, feeling Hadas's eyes on him, he glanced up to meet the other man's gaze.

"You will not punish her?" Hadas asked.

"For what?"

"For doctoring this cree?" He held up his hand. "For speaking to you with such disrespect?"

"There was no disrespect. Heli is a firm believer in rita. Rita dictates that you should be free. Therefore, Heli considers it inappropriate for you to carry a dascree and takes it as her duty to adjust reality to suit rita. I am not a believer in rita. Therefore, I consider it inappropriate for anyone to carry dascree. And, since I have no imperatives strong enough for me to argue with Heli's impeccable sense of duty, I find myself in complete agreement with her solution."

"Very well-put, politically speaking," commented Hadas. "You commit to a view without committing to anything."

Jaya did not answer that no doubt intentional jibe, but instead asked, "Has my grandmother arranged for you to contact your family?"

Hadas merely blinked at the change of subject. "Yes, thank you. They were much grateful for your assistance. They are also distressed by the disappearance of my sister. Like me, they are certain that what happened to me must have also happened to her."

There was something sharp and watchful about the younger man's eyes and Jaya wondered (as he had often wondered recently) what was expected of him. "I will make every effort to find your sister, Hadas. Although I'm not sure what or how much I can do."

Hadas reddened. "You are a mahesa—more than that, you are the Lord Prince of Kasi. What is there that you cannot do?"

"He cannot pry into the workings of a private business without a legitimate reason. If he did, it would almost surely draw unwanted attention and possibly censure." Ana stood in the doorway of the morning room, half shadowed by a cascade of artful foliage.

"What are either of those things beside slavery?" Hadas asked as she moved to take her seat.

Jaya answered him. "If I am exposed as someone who subverts the law by passing das off as members of a royal family, I will be little good to your sister or any other person who was seized illegally."

"Then, if you cannot help us, who can?" Hadas asked, temper flashing in his eyes.

The question hung awkwardly in the air as Heli re-entered the room with a large platter of tiny cakes, which she set carefully at the center of the group at the table. Her new assistant was right behind her with a tureen of fruit sauce.

Jaya realized with a start that he didn't know the girl. He gave her his most disarming smile, asking, "And who is this?"

"This is Dana Kapivastu," said Ana, watching the child react warily to Jaya's obviously unexpected warmth. "She's helping Heli in the kitchen. Dana, this is-"

"Jaya," he finished for her. "Where did you come from, Dana?"

"The Badan-Devaki dalali, Jaya. Your Jivinta, the Rani Sarojin, purchased me this afternoon."

"My ... Jivinta purchased you?"

"And why not?" asked the voice of that Venerable One from the doorway. "Did you expect me to allow a child her age to be sold into the ranks of some kaladan? Not likely!" She rapped her walking stick sharply on the tiles of the entry. "Now, will someone help me to my chair, please? This old body has not yet awakened fully."

Hadas jumped to her assistance with nimble ease, settling her reverently into a chair beside his own. She patted his hand fondly, then turned her sharp gaze to Heli. "It looks like a lovely repast you've prepared, Heli. May we see the rest of it?"

Heli colored slightly and gave a quick bow of the head before shepherding Dana back to the kitchen.

"Hadas has asked a most important question, Gauri," Mina Sarojin said, and Jaya knew she did not use the pet name without intent. "Who is able to help him extract his sister from Niraya Hell?"

"Jivinta, I can't-" Jaya began.

"I can," Mina said. "If, as Ana suspects, this traffic in Avasan yevetha is according to some plan, then it is most likely that Belia Gupta was processed at Badan-Devaki just as her brother was. And if that is the case, then she will be easy to trace."

"And your reason for doing this?" asked Jaya.

"I'm the eccentric old matriarch of a Taj House. I don't need a reason. I need only that I like Hadas's looks and wish to have his sister in my household as well. A matched set, if you will. Or perhaps my grandniece's new das is pining away for his lost kin and I cannot abide his misery or the thought of their separation. It matters very little what reason I give the dalal. He will look up Belia Gupta in his well-kept records and he will direct me to her owner, who will not refuse to cater to the whims of the old Sarojin mata ... for a sum of money."

Hadas looked upon his benefactress with obvious admiration and gratitude. "Rani, I don't know what to say."

"Save what you will say for your sister. She will need your words much more than I do." The old woman looked at him with sharp, searching eye. "She will not be the girl you knew, Hadas. You must understand this and prepare yourself for it."

Hadas lowered his eyes and colored. "It will not matter."

"It will matter to her," Mina told him.

"My, what a serious group," exclaimed a new voice. "Ah! And who might this be?"

Conversation was swallowed in a silence as profound as the hush before sunrise. All eyes turned to the entry. The Rani Melantha laughed charmingly and floated into the room in a cloud of silk and scent.

"Well, don't all talk at once. Who is this lovely young man and how does he come to be among us?"

"This is Ana's cousin, Hadas," Jaya supplied smoothly and wondered how much the Rani had overheard.

Introductions were made and stories recited. At the end of it all, the Rani shook her head and sighed. "I suppose I really should pay more attention to what goes on in my son's life. I'm so out-of-touch I don't even know who he's invited to live under our roof. Well, since the company is so charming and lively—" Her bright eyes came to rest on Hadas. "I believe I'll change my plans and stay in for breakfast. Helidasa!"

Heli, hovering in the kitchen doorway with a bowl of rice, jumped guiltily. "Yes, Rani."

"Do get on the vicom and send my regrets to Prakash-sama's residence. Tell him I'll see him later today." Her glance flicked to Jaya and she smiled. "Now, I must hear more about our newfound cousin, Hadas."

Breakfast was an ordeal. If Ana was unlettered in subterfuge, she made up for it in inventiveness. Ignoring Jaya's tightlipped watchfulness, she regaled the table with tales of snows and storms and deadly flora and fauna in the forests of the Kedar.

When Hadas observed that he was glad such things didn't figure in the relatively quiet life of a hotelier's son, he had the Rani's complete attention. "Your father owns hotels, does he?" she asked sweetly. "In the Sagara?"

"Well, actually he–"

"Uncle owns hotels and inns all over the Territories," interjected Ana. "He winters in the Sagara and summers in the foothills of the northwestern spur of the Kedar, near our family estates."

"Really? I don't suppose family members receive any sort of special consideration..."

Hadas smiled. "Family members stay free of charge at our inns."

He learns quickly, thought Jaya, and tried not to notice how the Rani stroked the back of his hand. He caught Jivinta's grimace. She did not seem to be enjoying her breakfast any more than he was.

Jaya's comfort level took a steep downward turn when Hadas turned to Ana and said, "I had been meaning to ask, cousin, if your trip into Kasi yesterday yielded much fruit?"

Ana colored and glanced obliquely at Jaya. "None, I'm afraid."

"Did you see our friends?" Hadas persisted.

"No, I didn't." The words were accompanied by a look that could have frozen water.

"Did you try the spaceport as I suggested?"

"Yes, Hadas. I saw no one."

Hadas subsided, but Jaya was already thoroughly alarmed and annoyed. He could see that his mother found the tension between their Avasan "cousins" amusing. He got to his feet so quickly, Ana jumped.

"A word with you, Ana," he said and headed for the gardens.

He heard a chair being pushed from the table, a murmured apology from Hadas and his mother saying, "My, what could possibly have triggered that? Jealousy, perhaps?"

His grandmother said something in reply, but the closing of the door cut it off.

"You lied to me," he said.

She spoke from behind him. "I did not lie. I borrowed a horse and went for a ride. I simply–"

He swung around to face her. "You simply lied! You weren't out clearing your head, you were looking for Parva Rishi."

"I went into Kasi merely to look, to watch. I saw nothing—no one. I spoke to no one."

The anger he had promised himself he would try to expunge blossomed in his breast. "You rode through the streets of Kasi alone. After dark."

"I was only out after dark because I stopped at the Asra to pray. Surely, there is no safer place."

"It is not the Asra that is the problem; it is the journey. If you decide to take another ride, Kena goes with you."

"Kena treats me as if I were his virgin daughter. He will not leave my side."

"Good."

"Not good. There are those who might talk to a lone Avasan woman who will not talk to a Rani with an attached bodyguard."

"Hadas then."

Ana moved to stand at the balustrade beside him, her hands flying in a dismissive gesture. "Hadas is a hot-head."

Jaya laughed. "And you're such a fountain of calm wisdom." The mirth was not strong enough to overcome his anger; the words came out twisted with sarcasm.

She turned to face him, leaning against the balustrade. "I don't understand you," she told him. "I have become a thorn in your side. My presence here threatens your political life, disturbs your household, necessitates lies that I know you find distasteful. If I were to go into Kasi and to disappear there, surely your life would be much more serene."

His juggernaut anger stopped in its tracks. He searched her eyes, looking for some indication that she was trolling for compliments or for a declaration of love. He saw none. Her gaze, as always, was direct, if bemused, and searching.

"Serene, yes," he acknowledged. "But perhaps not as full. Nor as ... challenging. Nor as interesting. You say you don't understand me —well, the feeling is mutual. Neither do I understand you, but I must admit I'd like to. More than that, I'd like to understand..." He paused and searched, momentarily, for some appropriate words. He could not, and ended up by making a vague back and forth gesture between them. "This," he said. "I would like to understand this—whatever it is—that exists between us."

"Attraction?"

"A weak word."

Ana lowered her head. "Then, you have me at a disadvantage, Nathu Rai. I have never felt 'this' before."

"Ah. I suppose you think I have?"

"You are a man."

Now she was toying with him, surely. Jaya's anger circled, looking for an opening, he elbowed it aside. "Jivinta said something to me the day I brought you here. She said, 'Don't confuse sakti with lust. Lust clouds, sakti illuminates.'"

Ana turned her extraordinary pale eyes on him. It was like looking into the sun.

"Are you illuminated, Nathu Rai?" she asked, scorching him.

He held her gaze. "My name is Jaya," he said, "and I think I've just recently begun to know who that is."

"He knows God who knows his own Self," she said softly.

He recognized the words as scripture. "Don't."

"Don't what?"

"Don't hide behind your Rohin wisdom."

There was a flash of angry fire in the pale eyes. "Hide?"

"Hide."

The fire flickered and went out. "Yes," she admitted and looked away from him. "Yes, I'm hiding."

"Why?"

"You terrify me."

He hadn't expected that. It first shocked, then disappointed, then angered him.

"I will not rape you."

"You can't rape me," she said and turned her left hand palm up and held it out to him. "Not as long as this is in my palm."

"Stop it. Please." He closed his eyes, giving his temper another shove. "I'm tired of being angry, and tired of getting slapped across the face with that"—he grasped her wrist and shook it—"every time I talk to you."

"I'm sorry."

"So am I. I'm sorry you feel compelled to run from hiding place to hiding place when we're together—your proper Rohin wisdom, my anger, that dascree."

"I've done that, haven't I—made you angry so I could hide more easily ... Camouflage."

"It won't work. I'm beginning to be able to see through you."

She smiled wryly. "I'll have to find a new place to hide."

"You could learn to trust me."

"I do trust you. You're a man of honor and candor. I trust that."

She lapsed into silence, turning her head to watch the tall evergreens dance in the rising breeze.

He was also silent, wondering what would happen to her trust if she knew how often in the last couple of nights he had stood at the door connecting their rooms, his hand on the latch, listening to his body's loud demands that he exercise the rights rita accorded him. He fought her in those moments; he fought himself and he fought the current that washed between them. Then, he wondered why he bothered to fight it at all—why he didn't just surrender to it as he knew she would surrender to a direct command.

He wondered ... and saw the answer in terms of a chain of Karma, a sequence of repercussions, a path littered with distrust and recriminations and bitterness.

The first time he'd stood against that door, he'd remembered a bit of advice from his father. Bhaktasu Sarojin had given it to him in the form of a parable about the Asok tree—the mythic fruit of non-sorrow.

The fruit of the Asok is luscious beyond compare. Its juices give birth to bliss. In the spring, its blossoms are beautiful and fragrant with promise ... but a man cannot eat blossoms. Eagerly, he watches the tree—the blossoms fall, the fruit appears, and he waits for its ripening. If he is patient, if he waits until the Asok's time is complete, his first taste of its fruit will yield the sweetness of bliss. But, if he is impatient, willing the seasons to hurry, and picking the fruit before its time is complete, his first taste will yield nothing but bitterness.

It was good advice—as good as Jivinta's. He had little doubt where his father had gotten it.

Ana sighed and stirred then, and Jaya realized he was still holding her wrist. She didn't pull away when he moved his hand to hers and squeezed it, but simply returned the gentle pressure. He left her watching the trees perform their dance.

Patience, he thought.

~

The assembly lasted only a half-day and consisted of the presentation of ancillary evidence by the concerned parties. It ranged from the highly technical to the financial to the legal.

Jaya was no engineer. Fortunately, he was not alone in that; the specifications for magnetic stabilizers would go to the appropriate experts, as would the financial and market projections which, while not technical, were shrouded in legalese.

Jaya downloaded copies of the documents nonetheless, then, at loose ends, took Ravi to the Kiritan for the mid-day meal. He was impatient, wishing the experts could be prevailed upon to hurry. His impatience made him a poor companion, and Ravi, to his credit, waited for several minutes before saying anything about his mahesa's mood.

When he did speak, he said simply, "If it would help to talk, Jaya Rai, I would be pleased to listen."

Jaya said, "I want to do what is right and just, but I wonder if what is right and just for Ana and her people is what is right and just for Mehtar."

"The Avatars—may my life be a sacrifice to Their glory—have said that truth is but one point, which we have multiplied. Surely, this may be applied equally to justice, for justice hinges upon the truth."

Jaya shook his head. "That sounds like something Ana the Rohina would say."

"No doubt."

"You think it's really that simple?" Jaya glanced idly over the room below the Sarojin box; faces turned away from him and eyes dropped before his gaze.

They were no longer surprised at the appearance of Ravidas at his lord's table, perhaps, but they still allowed themselves to be scandalized by it. The silent censure bred a peculiar satisfaction in Jaya's heart and this worried him. Did he subject Ravi to this public display as a token form of rebellion? Did Ravi suppose that he did?

"Ravi, are you uncomfortable here?" he asked abruptly.

The dark eyebrows winged upward. "No, Jaya Rai. I am quite comfortable. You have made it so."

"Your father would say I dishonored myself by taking a position that others of my caste would ridicule or despise."

The other man grinned waggishly. "My father would change his tune if he were to ever dine here."

"Ravi, you're my friend. Almost my brother. We grew up together. We were raised in the same house."

"But not in the same caste."

"I have never understood that boundary. I think that's why I've chosen to deny its existence."

Ravi nodded. "And that is why I am comfortable here. In your company, that boundary does not exist, truly. You fear I think you insincere. I do not. We have known each other too long for that, haven't we?"

"I've often thought ... I could give you your freedom ... "

"To what point, Jaya Rai? If I were free, I would still work for you and would mostly likely draw similar wages. No doubt you would have me continue to live in your house, and eat the food prepared by my mother. What could I do as a free man that I cannot do as I am?"

"Marry a free woman?"

A flash of something like surprise crossed Ravi's face, but was quickly gone. "I am not likely, mahesa, to meet a free woman that I would care to marry."

"Unless you were a free man."

Naru arrived to serve them then and, while he did not dare show overt disapproval, he was less than cordial with Ravi. Jaya was, for the first time, embarrassed by something he normally met with wry humor.

The impatience bubbling in his soul expanded and took on nuance. He wanted the AGIM/KNC dispute to be over; he wanted his mother's relationship with Prakash to end; he wanted the caste structure to crumble.

He wanted. He wanted. Truth. Wisdom. Patience. Enough power to change the world in the blink of an eye.

When he saw a familiar face in the room below, he thought of one way in which his impatience might be assuaged and asked Naru to invite Namun Vedda to the Sarojin box. The older man hesitated only briefly before joining his godson. His smile was genuine and slightly conspiratorial when he saw Ravi there, as well. Namun Vedda, himself a freeman of the merchant caste, had echoed Bhaktasu Sarojin's views on Mehtar's convoluted social system since Jaya could recall; it was one among a myriad points of agreement the two men had shared.

It occasionally occurred to Jaya to wonder if Uncle Namun were disappointed in his godson for not being his old friend in any but the most insignificant ways. He looked like his father, had his father's voice and mannerisms. But in other, more important, intangible ways, he was a watery image of the man—Bhaktasu Sarojin reflected in a troubled pool. He supposed he could claim to hold the same values the older Sarojin had espoused, but he held them more loosely. What had been passions in Bhaktasu Sarojin were, in his son, merely convictions. Jaya wondered if he might raise them to the level of passions sometime before he died. He had loved his father; he loved his father's memory, but it was difficult to exist as a rippling reflection of another man's vivid greatness.

Jaya did not speak of either convictions or memories, however. After the obligatory exchange of pleasantries, he turned his mind to demystification. "Uncle, might I assume you understand something of magnetic trim systems?"

Namun seemed amused by the question. "Considering the fact that I help design them, I should hope I know something."

"Ah. I take it that means you helped design Star Trim?"

Namun nodded. "Why the interest in mag-stabilizers, Jaya? I hadn't thought that one of your particular avocations."

"It's not. But it is one of the points of contention between AGIM and the KNC. The KNC claims the trim systems on the Guild vessels are antiquated and sub-standard—the standard being the Star Trim system. This makes them dangerous, which makes them a poor risk for shipping materiel important to the Consortium associates. That, at any rate, is the claim."

"I see. Is your next question whether I consider that claim to be justified?"

"Is it?"

Namun leaned back in his chair and studied the fruit arrayed on his plate. "We developed the Star Trim stabilization system because of inherent inefficiencies in the older designs. The AGIM ships are less fuel-efficient than ships with Star Trim—much less—but that doesn't mean they're necessarily less stable."

"Then the KNC claims are false?"

"Let us say, they are highly exaggerated. Yes, a less efficient keel is potentially more prone to magnetic fluctuation, which can be a problem during rotation. But I think the accident records should speak to that; surprisingly few ships experience major problems during lift-off."

Jaya nodded. "Thank you. The Council is having experts look over the presentations, but I..." He shrugged. "I seem to be impatient."

"You weren't afraid I'd be partial to the KNC? After all, they are easily Vedda Technologies' best customer."

"You're a scientist and a visionary, Namun, not a businessman. If I asked you how much money the Consortium spent at V-Tech last year, I'd be willing to wager you couldn't tell me."

Namun laughed. "You have me there. No, I couldn't tell you. But I could tell you the exact thickness of the magnetic plating necessary to generate a smooth mag-field for a 100,000 ton freighter."

Jaya raised his hands. "Don't, please. I have all the information I need about mag-keels. I would like to ask your opinion on another aspect of this, if I might."

Namun shrugged. "Of course. If you think my opinion is worth anything."

"What's your sense of the Consortium claim that a free-market Avasa and a truly independent Miner's Guild would be disastrous to the KNC and our economy?"

"I honestly don't know. I have a suspicion they might be right about their own fortunes, if only for the reason that, given the choice, many of those who have been forced to deal with the Consortium in the past will no longer do so. And that, Jaya, speaks less of market imperatives than it does of Karma." He patted a napkin to his lips, his eyes unfocused.

The look was familiar to Jaya; he had seen it on his father's face often enough.

After a moment of thought, Namun continued. "There are very few people and organizations outside its immediate family of companies that Kasi-Nawhar has not stepped on or aggrieved in some way. I believe there are those who would sooner pay more for needful services than do business with the KNC. I can't say I blame them."

"You do business with the KNC," Jaya observed.

"They need me—or at least, they need V-Tech. Because they need V-Tech, they have always been generous and above board with me. Better, they leave me alone and do not meddle in or steer my research. Which is not to say they don't try to take the tiller now and again. But then, I simply remind them of their need. Take the

Star Trim system, for example. With a fleet as large as theirs the efficiencies it buys them result in significant savings."

"Can AGIM hurt them?"

"As I said, they've hurt themselves. If they were bigger men, more honest men, in a word—more spiritual men—they would be afraid of neither AGIM's defection nor it's power."

"Afraid?" The words seemed absurd applied to Ranjan Vrksa or Nigudha Bhrasta.

Namun smiled, perhaps a bit wickedly, and said, "Yes, even men in that position of power count fear among their possessions. It is not quite like being a mahesa of the House Sarojin."

Jaya considered that. "I believe my father proved that even a mahesa of the House Sarojin has reason to own fear. No one can live without fear, excepting perhaps a saint."

Namun had sobered at the oblique mention of his late friend's fate, and the smile that now played about his lips was rueful. "Ah, but a saint fears earning his God's disapproval, does he not?"

In the silence that followed that observation, Jaya imagined he heard Ana's voice: "You terrify me." If Ana was not a saint, she was at least a pretender to sainthood—or perhaps a saint-in-training, he thought, more charitably. And, as the attraction between them was inarguably mutual, he represented a potential fall from the high Rohin path. If Namun was right about the fears of saints, Ana had every reason to be afraid.

An emotion not unlike pride fluttered momentarily in Jaya's breast. He smothered it in incredulity. Had he really, in that self-infatuated instant, seen Anala Nadim's ethics as a target to be hit or a barrier to be breached?

"You seem troubled, Jaya," observed his Uncle Namun, quietly. "Are you taking this thing with AGIM that much to heart?"

An upward glance showed that both Namun Vedda and Ravi were regarding him with solemn concern. "I know ... some people to whom the freedom of Avasa is somewhat more than an abstract legal issue. Recently I ... discovered that the Saroj has some offshoots on our sister world. They are not directly affected by the Guild's concerns, but..."

"Anything that affects the mining industry on Avasa cannot help but affect all Avasans," finished Namun. "Excepting, perhaps, a handful whose livelihood derives from purely Mehtaran interests."

Jaya managed a weak smile. He had not lied to his Uncle Namun since he was a small boy, and all of his childhood and adolescent lies put together paled before the one he had just uttered. "Funny," he said, "that's what Ana said just last night."

"Ana?"

"One of my Avasan cousins—Ana Sadira." He chanted a litany of falsehoods, then, about Ana's timber magnate father, and her vacation from a school where she studied forestry.

"She wouldn't happen to be a tall, rather striking young woman with deep auburn hair, would she?" asked Namun.

"Yes. Have you—?"

"We nearly met the other day, I think. She was Jivinta Mina's luncheon companion at this very table. I thought perhaps your very stubborn grandmother had taken my advice and hired a young woman to accompany her on her junkets."

Jaya pushed his jal frazie around on his plate. "Yes, well, Ana is rather fond of junkets herself. Unfortunately, she's also prone to be stubborn, independent, and risk-taking. She has a particular predilection for junketing about in the Warrows and the Nahar."

Namun Vedda's eyes crinkled with silent laughter. "Ah, the Sarojin women! She sounds quite remarkable."

"She is," said Ravi, unexpectedly entering the conversation. He glanced at Jaya. "Quite remarkable. It is a shame, Jaya Rai, that you do not get on better with each other."

Namun laughed. "Do I detect an undercurrent? What's the matter, Jaya—are you uncomfortable with a woman you can't intimidate?"

"I'm not uncomfortable with Jivinta Mina."

"Jivinta Mina is your grandmother, not a potential liaison."

Jaya suffered a moment of epiphany. He actually stopped to ponder the suggestion, which provoked his godfather into further laughter.

"You are your father's son, Jaya."

"What? How so?"

"You have his ... habit of introspection and self-analysis. I know few men who would even allow themselves to ponder a question with such humbling implications." He cocked his head. "I am seized by the conviction that you would have answered, had I not interrupted you."

"Yes. I would have. And, no, I'm not uncomfortable with Ana, merely ... at a loss to know how to deal with her. Until now, the only women of my acquaintance who haven't been intimidated by me—or by what I represent—are my grandmother, the Deva Radha and Helidasa."

There was a wonderful irony in that, which Jaya did not explore at that moment, except to note wryly that when he said Helidasa ran his household, the truth of the statement far transcended the domestic realm.

He did not wonder at Hadas's surprise at him that morning—he knew very few members of his caste who allowed their das to hold beliefs, convictions, or opinions that were uniquely their own, let alone act on them. Helidasa, he had no doubt, viewed herself as being the essence of servitude, and unimpeachably loyal to her House. He had few doubts, as well, that she thought of the Saroj in just those terms—her House—as if she, too, were a Sarojin. In a sense, he supposed, she was. There was also the very real possibility that among her predecessors there were those who had entered into sexual relationships with their Taj masters. It had intrigued him as a youth to speculate that he and Ravi might share a physical as well as emotional and intellectual kinship.

The convoluted loop of thought brought him back around again to Anala Nadim and the irony of their relationship. She was, legally, at once a member and possession of his household. She was, in a reality that transcended law, a free woman who both attracted him immensely and was attracted to him. He had no doubt a sexual liaison would be passionate and satisfying for both of them. If only she were not a dasa. If only she were not Rohin. If only she were not so stubborn. Were she what she pretended to be ...

The thought hung. Were she a Rani, he would never contemplate her, his hand on her door latch, while she slept, trusting in an abstract. Honor. He knew what that was. If he had learned nothing else from his father, he had surely learned that.

He knew and despised men who used their hold on their das to force them to the humiliating performance of acts they would never have done willingly or freely. He felt the depth of his loathing and was surprised at it. Before, he might have said, if asked, "I argue no one's right to own personal das; it is simply not for me." It seemed his feelings had not only intensified, but crystallized.

No surprise, he supposed. His grandmother had never owned any das of her own; the Saroj household das had come to her through marriage. She had raised her son to view the owning of other human beings as a questionable practice, even as her husband had taught him to assume it as his right. Jaya knew it was something Bhaktasu Sarojin had battled with internally his entire adult life. But Bhaktasu Sarojin had been a man who toiled with things that disturbed him; Jaya tended to ignore them, to abide with them held uneasily at bay, or to tell himself there would be a time to deal with such things later.

In that way, he was like his mother, he supposed. It was easy to blot out uneasy thoughts or stirring conscience in day-to-day minutiae. Now, nothing in Jaya's life was day-to-day; the minutiae was gone, leaving his conscience naked. He squirmed in the discomfort of nakedness. Perhaps he was his father's son after all.

"Do I detect," Uncle Namun was saying, "a note of pleasure in that peculiar observation?"

Jaya shook himself. "I wouldn't call it pleasure. I suppose it is gratifying to know someone—a woman, specifically—that I can trust to be honest. Brutally honest, at times. Ana does not try to score points with me. On the other hand, some situations would be easier and more pleasant if she were just a little in awe of me."

"Pleasant?" echoed Namun. "Or pleasurable?" His eyes sparkled —now green, now gray. "From the glance of her I got, I would have to call her a most attractive woman. Perhaps you can work out an arrangement whereby you can be equally in awe of each other. The carriage of passion does not draw smoothly behind a mismatched team."

"Like my mother and father?" Jaya surprised even himself.

His Uncle Namun's brows twitched upward. "What makes you say that?"

"They seem so different. Father was a man of depth. A man of ... piety and compassion. A man of ... faith, I suppose you could say."

"Yes. And your mother was a woman of faith. She had faith in him and in his causes."

Jaya made a wry face. He had not intended to, and tried to snatch it back, but Namun had caught it.

"I know. You're thinking that was only pretence, else she could not have become the woman you now know. I can tell you, having known Melantha Sarojin a bit longer than you have, that it was not pretence. She has changed. I don't suppose you noted the genesis of those changes, wrapped up as you were in your own grief. That you two drew apart instead of together after Bhaktasu's death seems a great tragedy to me—more tragic, in its way than his death, itself."

He paused and searched Jaya's face as if looking for something that would determine what he should say next. What he said was, "When you judge your mother in the light of your father's virtue, do try to remember that, in your mother's estimation, it was his virtue that killed him."

"You mean because he died a crusader?"

Namun nodded. "Is it any wonder Melantha no longer treasures his causes?"

Jaya felt another epiphany coming on. He shook his head. "No surprise. I suppose that's why she made light of them to me. Beyond that, she would never discuss my father's convictions—political or spiritual. I think Jivinta Mina has given me more of my father than mother has. Do you know much about what crusade he was pursuing when he died?"

Namun frowned. "Not as much as I would have expected. He was unusually reserved about it. I don't think he even shared much of it with Melantha, or so she has indicated to me."

"That was unusual?"

"Quite. Normally, I would have known more than I would have time to tell, or you have time to hear." Namun lay his napkin aside preparatory to leaving. "I have a most uninspiring meeting to attend. I would much rather regale you with tales of your father's various crusades, but my meeting, while dull and possibly sleep-inducing, will be lucrative." He smiled ruefully. "I am told that the presence of a real scientist in a room full of marketeers sells contracts. A bit of whimsy on the part of the Goddess, no doubt, but there it is." He rose. "I believe you provided the last meal we had together. My turn, I make it."

"Uncle-"

"I insist. It was delightful to have my opinion consulted on a matter that did not have to do with a problem of chemistry or engineering. It helped alleviate the fear that I am becoming mono-dimensional."

"An impossibility, Uncle Namun. You have more dimensions than most ten men."

Namun laughed. "Flatterer," he said and gave Jaya the respectful greeting and Ravi a cordial hand clasp, no doubt raising a few eyebrows and noses about the room.

CHAPTER TEN

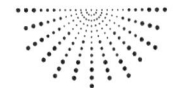

THERE WAS a promise of warmth in the air the next morning. Ana rose early, dressed, and went into the gardens for her devotions. She was watching the dance and ripple of sunlight across the surface of the pond when she realized she was being observed. Not a pompous devotee this time, she thought, and hushed herself mentally. To disdain pomposity in another was, itself, pompous.

She turned her head. Jaya, of course.

"I didn't mean to disturb you," he said, and stepped from the tiled walk into the dewy grass.

"I was finished, really. Just contemplating Ram-ji's canvas."

He quirked an eyebrow at her.

She pointed at the pond with its patterns of wind ripple and fish dart. "Water, wind, fish, and light—the palette of pakriti. He paints with life."

Jaya remembered his childhood lessons in Divine Metaphysics. "Pakriti? Maya, don't you mean—illusion? The fish aren't really made of gold, the water isn't covered in diamonds, the saroj are not emeralds—just weeds that float. You only imagine you see jewels."

"How cynical. Is that really all you see here—weeds and fish and water?"

"I see reality."

"Ah, now that is the illusion. Imagination is our spark of Tara-ji. Through that spark, we see the real. With the eyes of the body we see only the material—that is maya. The reality lies behind and within and around it."

"Can you see that?" he asked, his tone no longer sarcastic.

Ana turned her eyes back to the pond. "Yes, but not with physical eyes. One must marshall inner sight as well."

"To see the illusion."

"To see through the illusion. To see that the spirit is maya to the material and the material is maya to the spirit. If you would see both worlds, use both eyes."

"Hmm. What sage taught you that?"

"Experience."

He changed the subject. "Well, if this is Sanat-Ram's canvas, then you are certainly the center of His portrait this morning. That gown is beautiful on you. You should wear it often."

Ana responded to the compliment with a strange mixture of pleasure and unease. She smiled, smoothing the flame-hued fabric over her arms.

"Why are you wearing it this morning? Do you have some special plans for today?"

She stared at him, taken completely aback. "I ... we're ... Aren't we going to Asra today? It is Bhaktar, and tonight is the Mesha Festival..."

Jaya scratched his cheek and stared at the pond. The bright reflections hurt his eyes. He blinked at Ana as if the sight of her had the same effect.

"Ah," he said. "Well, you see, I ... It's been a while since I've been to Asra. At the New Year, I think. Jivinta goes, of course. I'm sure she's expecting to make a party of it."

"Which will not include you?" she asked bluntly.

"What would be the point? All that social jockeying and political preening is beyond me. I'd be out of my element there."

"Since when has going to Asra been about social jockeying and politics?"

"Since I can remember. Asra is like the Kiritan. People go there to be seen sitting in the best seats in their best clothes."

Ana realized she was angry. "No! Asra is a place for seeking Ram-ji, not political affiliations. If that is what Asra has become on your world, then you are wise not to go there."

His expression shifted from wry to contrite. "I exaggerate.

Don't listen to me. Of course, there are people who go to Asra to-to put in an appearance, but I'm sure there are those who really believe, even in Kasi." He smiled.

Ana stared through him, rubbing her arms, suddenly chilled. "I want to go home," she said, and fled into the House.

She was waiting for him in the broad doorway to the solarium when he reached the House, looking sheepish. "I'm sorry. I exaggerate too."

"Peace?" he asked, and gave the respectful greeting.

She returned it. "Peace."

Jaya hadn't seen the inside of an Asra for over a year (his claim to have attended a New Year devotion was an exaggeration), but it was not something one forgot. He still had a vague child's awe of the soaring lines and amplified dimensions of the overturned silver bowl; was still affected by the glory that cascaded from the central dome through a complex pattern of graceful incisions. It made one want Ram-ji to exist whether He did or not. He wondered what Ana felt as she gazed around her at the ersatz radiance of the Divine.

She was part of the radiance. The flaming silk of her garment came to life in the drifting sunlight; the gem at her forehead covered her face with a spray of crimson. Like luminous droplets of blood, he thought, then shook himself in vague horror.

They were seated just to the left of the curved fan of shimmering stone steps that descended from the altar to the Rama Fire's glorious pit. They were front row seats in a special, ornamented box reserved for the Taj Houses. A similar box sat to the right of the steps—this one, for the Holy Ones. Behind them were arrayed the Vadin and their families, and behind them sat the politicos of the Sun Crescent.

Only Sarojins and their guests sat in the Taj box now. The Royal House of Kasi had no peers in the Crescent. The Rani Melantha's noble House of birth made its home in the outlying Lake District, while the one-time warrior clan of Sivarashtra presided over Nawahr. Other minor Lords sat behind the Taj box, while further back, still, were the lesser nobles, the merchants, and the merely wealthy.

The Deva Radha, herself, led the devotions this day. She was incomparable. The sound of her voice and the grace of her movements, like the grandeur of the Asra, could almost make a believer out of a stone.

Jaya still remembered the first devotional she'd presided over at this Asra. Her hair had been jet black then and, in his adolescent mind, she was the most beautiful being ever created—and easily the most terrifying. Her eyes had been like black flames—they still were. Piercing eyes, eyes that saw through things ... and people. Was that why he found them terrifying?

While he sat struggling with that question, Ana nudged him.

"Jaya Rai," she whispered. "It's time to offer the Mesha prayers. Will you perform the Erai?"

He flushed. "I don't remember it."

She didn't embarrass him by gasping or even indulging in ocular chastisement. As the Deva Radha swung toward their box to greet the Sarojin Chieftain and escort him to the Rama Fire as clan bhakta, Ana stood smoothly and performed the ritual greeting. Her prayer beads were already draped between her fingers.

Jaya felt icy tingles like the tiny feet of chill spiders dancing up and down his spine. A brief glance around the Asra revealed just about what he expected—a sanctum full of scandalized and incredulous faces stared at the Sarojin box. Behind him, their Avasan guests seemed unconcerned and beside him, Jivinta Mina gloated.

The Deva Radha smiled and nodded her approval. She returned Ana's greeting then turned to Jaya.

"Perhaps it would be appropriate, Nathu Rai, for the Chieftain of the Saroj to join your clan bhakta at the Flame." She said it in a barely audible whisper with a smile tugging at her lips.

He nodded and followed when she led Ana to the Fire pit. She began the Erai immediately, her eyes closed, the beads still pressed between her fingers.

"There is a Spirit which is Life, Light, and Truth. He contains all works and all desires and all devotions and all perfumes. She enfolds the entire Universe and in silence loves all. This is the Spirit that is in my heart—smaller than the tiniest of particles, smaller than the atom. This is the Spirit that is in my heart—greater than Mitras' orb, vaster than Heaven itself, greater than all the worlds. This is the Spirit that is in my heart. This is Ram-ji."

False words, thought Jaya. False. There was no such Spirit. Not in his heart, at any rate. But in Ana's ... He glanced at her rapt face and had no doubt that something was there—the fire of faith ... illusion.

He recalled their conversation by the pond. Illusion and reality —which was which? Her reality was his illusion and vice versa. He didn't like that idea; it made him feel somehow insubstantial. If his reality was an illusion to Ana, then what did that make him?

He shook the gray thought out of his head and brought himself back to Ana's chanting. The verse was unfamiliar and sung in a homely Avasan dialect instead of the traditional prayer tongue. It quickly caught the attention of the other worshippers. As Ana's voice rose in the musical chant, all other voices fell away to a murmur. The Flame sizzled and hissed in its great bowl and Jaya held his breath.

"My thoughts praise You, O God, even as Mitras praises You in its rising. May I find continuing joy in being Your lover. Keep us under Your protection, forgive our sins, and never cease to love us. You made the waters to flow ceaselessly without weariness. May my stream of life flow into the river of righteousness. Sever the bonds of sin that bind me, but let not my thread of my song be cut while I sing. Let not my work cease before it is finished."

She paused, and Jaya wondered if the silence was as loud in her ears as it was in his. She smiled as if receiving some secret communion, then nodded and rose. He rose in unison with her, watching her face in the fire bath burnish. Every eye was on them. Only the most pious continued to pray. As they returned silently to the Sarojin box, the voices grew once again in strength. Minds struggled to reclaim the prayerful attitude. Eyes fluttered closed.

Jaya sat self-consciously in his grand seat, wondering what was really happening behind those fluttering lids, and suspecting he knew. Scandal—a woman serving as bhakta for a Taj House, daring to lead the Erai prayers! Heresy—the prayer beads in the hands of a female who is not even a member of Orders! He could almost hear the whispers, feel the sly looks. He would experience them again at the celebration tonight. The thought made his stomach churn.

Suddenly, the tightness turned on itself and became anger. Stupid! He was thinking like his mother—shrinking from the prejudices of his peers. He realized he had lowered his head. He raised it, eyes sweeping a nearby row of worshippers. Their gazes—curious, arch, scandalized—skittered away to the Flame.

He looked at the Deva Radha, then. Her gaze, with its buried smile, was not so timid. It held his until he was forced to look away.

There were the inevitable whispers as they left the Asra. "Did you see ... ?" "Did you hear ... ?" Some bolder friends and acquaintances smiled and said they hoped they'd see the Rani Sadira at the Mesha celebration that evening.

At length, the ordeal was past and they were on their way home. Jaya sank into the padded seat of the long-coach's ornate cabin and heaved a sigh of relief.

"Remind me," said Jivinta Mina, "to have Heli lay on more food for tonight. I have no doubt the Palace will be bursting its seams." She patted Anala's hand. "You were quite a sensation, my dear. You know, Jaya, I wish your mother would have been there today. She would have had a fit."

Jaya snorted. "At the very least."

"And your father," she continued wistfully. "He would have enjoyed every minute of it. To hear the prayers rendered so movingly..." She let her gaze wander around the interior of the cavernous coach. "It's been that long since we used this coach, you know. Spring five years ago. Just before he died."

Hadas, seated beside her, impulsively took the old woman's hand.

Jaya changed the subject. "The Deva Radha seemed to know you."

Ana blinked. "The Deva Radha?"

"Chief of the Holy Ones. Deva of the Cloud Order. Head of the Inner Circle and the Vrinda Varma..."

Ana's expression was entirely blank. "I-I told you I went to Asra. I met her then. I had no idea who she was."

Jaya was skeptical. "You expect me to believe Avasans don't know who the Deva Radha is?"

"Of course we know who she is," Hadas interjected, "but most of us have never seen her. She's very impressive."

"She is that," admitted Jaya. "Well, you'll get a chance to be impressed all over again tonight. She'll be at the Mesha Fest."

"Will I be at the Mesha Fest?" asked Hadas.

"That depends on you. Do you want to be there?"

"I'm not sure. The people from the dalali won't be there?"

Jivinta laughed. "By all the attributes of God, no! I wouldn't think of inviting them into the House Sarojin."

Hadas vacillated a moment, then said, "Well, I really would like to come to the celebration. Do you have the Time of Gifts? That's my favorite part."

Jivinta Mina chortled. "Well, we call it that, but it's more like the 'Time of Entertainment.' People here generally hire professional performers to present their gifts. It saves them the trouble of having to develop their own talents."

"But Mesha gifts are supposed to come from the spirit," objected Hadas. "How can you hire someone to give from your spirit?"

"My sentiments exactly," said Mina, and patted Hadas on the knee. "And if you want to give something to the guests tonight, then I encourage you to do so. I daresay Ana will have something to present."

Jaya was immediately interested. "Really? And what might that be?"

"Scoundrel," interjected Mina Sarojin, before Anala could answer him. "Only one of questionable upbringing asks what a gift is before he receives it. You will have to wait until tonight to hear Ana's recitation."

Wait he did. He was dressed first and, as tradition demanded, stood at the base of the Grand Stair waiting for the rest of the family to descend. Ravi was with him, acting in his usual capacity.

The Rani Melantha was the first one down. Jaya gave her a dutiful kiss on one cheek, after which she excused herself to oversee the last minute preparations. Jivinta Mina was next to appear, on the arm of Hadas. Jaya felt an absurd tickle of jealousy at the way Hadas doted on his grandmother. He fanned it away and smiled up at them.

"You're all looking quite splendid this evening," Jaya observed when the trio reached the hallway. "Where is the Rani Sadira? Taking her time, or trying to escape?"

Jivinta Mina reached up and slapped his cheek smartly with her fan. "Do not mock the effort one person takes to please others, Gauri. You have no make-up to apply but a dab or two of kohl. You have no hand-dazzles to cover your palm, no skirts to arrange, and no significant jewelry." She tapped the glittering cascade of silver lotus blossoms that fell from his left earlobe.

"Now, Jivinta, I did have to plait my hair." He turned to display how the top layer had been woven into a complex, jeweled braid that ended above the middle of his back in a clasp of Saroj crimson and gold.

"Hah! You mean Ravi had to plait your hair. You never could braid it correctly. Now! You will appreciate Ana when she descends. I am going to preside over the Entry." With that, she led her devotee out into the Entry Hall where guests would most certainly be arriving any minute.

Jaya grimaced. Appreciate Ana! He had no trouble doing that. The problem was the form his appreciation insisted on taking. He couldn't just label her a beautiful work of art and appreciate her from afar. He had yet to find a way to combat the effects of the chemistry or sakti or whatever it was that took hold of him when they shared the same room.

If the circumstances had been different, if he had not been a member of the Vrinda Varma and she had not been the daughter of Rokh Nadim, and Rohin, he wouldn't have bothered to fight that chemistry. But circumstances were what they were, and he was who he was, and she was who she was, and what either of them would have done under other circumstances was academic.

He pondered this for a moment, then, almost without thinking, embarked on a mental discipline aimed at giving him a measure of detachment. He was engrossed in that and totally oblivious to anything else when a ripple of static coursed up his spine. He nearly swore.

She was descending the staircase behind him; he knew that without looking. He applied the discipline, focusing his mind on a familiar mantra, and felt the calming influence immediately. It was true, he thought, with some satisfaction, you never forgot the lessons of the schoolroom completely.

He turned, smiling, and caught her about six feet above him on the carpeted flight. His self-mastery scattered like a flock of frightened birds—up from the ground of discipline, out the windows of his soul.

She had frozen on the seventh step (to be admired?) and was assaulting him with those eyes. He couldn't read the expression in them and didn't try. She was wearing crimson—dazzling as a sunset —with matching jewels and gold twist gleaming from here and there. Her hair was bound loosely in more twist and a large red gem dangled over her forehead from the gold and silver winged diadem atop her head.

She was all contrasts—creamy skin, crimson gown; blood and gold sparkle, fiery hair. Jaya's whole being was astonished. He heard nothing but the roaring of his blood in his veins. That, and the laughter of arriving guests in the Entry. He wallowed for a moment in confusion.

At his elbow, Ravi said, "You are the image of the Goddess, Rani Ana." Then, "Oh, but I've embarrassed you. Forgive me."

Ana, looking down, was flushing like the asok blossom. She seemed, Jaya thought, as stricken as he was.

She took Ravi's offered hand and descended the last steps to stand facing Jaya. He felt like a man coming out of a stupor.

"Shall I attend?" asked Ravi cautiously.

"Yes, yes, by all means." Jaya took Ana's hand from Ravi. "Shall we greet our guests, Lalasa?"

Ravi's eyebrows ascended in a swift echo of Ana's. He cleared his throat and moved away before them toward the Entry.

"You mock me, Nathu Rai," Ana rebuked him as they followed Ravi from the Hall. "I am not your 'beloved.'"

"I'm not mocking you, and you may stop sounding like my Jivinta, if you please. One Mina Sarojin is quite enough."

"You forget our circumstances."

"No, I only attempt to."

"Don't."

He turned to look at her as they stood, arm in arm at the head of the long Entry Gallery, under the archway. "Ana, there's something to be worked out between us. This is something we both know."

Her brows arched. "Do you speak of Karma, mahesa?"

"I speak of what I don't understand. Gloat if you like, but I freely admit my ignorance." He began to walk again, down the long, cavernous passage toward the bevy of arrivals. "I've never thought of myself ... as what I'm becoming."

Ana glanced at him, puzzled. "And what is that?"

"When I find out, you'll be the first to know."

They dined in the state banquet hall, which consumed half the premier floor's south wing. The other half was a Salon of epic proportions with six huge fireplaces and three sunken braziers—all lit. For this occasion, Jaya took his place in a throne at the head of the Taj table. Ana sat at his right hand and he wondered who had arranged for her to sit there. It spoke, at least insofar as Mehtaran etiquette had it, of betrothal or other liaisons. Jivinta Mina was the chief suspect.

Dinner was enjoyable. The company was lively, the food delicious. Time flowed in a swift stream to the end of the meal. They moved into the State Salon, then, amid laughter and chatter. Fruit wines from the Sarojin vineyard had flowed freely at the dinner table and most guests were already in high spirits. Musicians played traditional Springtime cantalons from a recess beside the raised stone semi-circle where gifts would be presented later in the evening.

Ana instantly became the object of attention as she entered the Salon at Jaya's side. She did not seem surprised, but then only a complete ingénue would have missed the flickering glances directed at her from every corner of the banquet hall. She circulated freely among the many guests, repeating the fabricated story of her meeting with Jaya to anyone who asked while Jaya watched her out of the corner of one eye, hoping she would be able to keep her glib fiction straight and wondering how a miner's daughter came to be so at ease in a crowd of the caste-conscious. It must, he figured, be a function of her own castelessness. Or perhaps it had something to do with being Rohin.

There was that paradox, too. How did a miner's daughter come to be a candidate for the Upward Path and its rigorous spiritual and mental disciplines? He'd found several books containing references to the Rohin in his library. They were conflicting in tone; one ascribed to the Rohin bhakta absurd austerities, another portrayed the women of the Discipline as little more than ritual whores with witching powers, a third extolled their honesty, devotion and pragmatism.

None of those things rang quite true. Ana had laughed at him for calling her an ascetic. Yet, she seemed to take her chastity quite seriously. She was certainly devoted to something, but Jaya Sarojin subscribed to the opinion that religion was a myth one chose to believe, which was hardly honest and arguably pragmatic.

Accessing the Kasi-Nawahr Library database in search of more information, he had gotten nothing but facts and figures and cryptic references to secret Rohin practices and powers. In the end, he was no closer to understanding what motivated Anala Nadim than he had been before. The Rohin secret was within her, and he suspected it had little to do with facts or figures or mysterious disciplines.

His eyes still half on Ana, Jaya drifted to the perimeter of a lively discussion between some elder statesmen. It centered, not surprisingly, around the situation on Avasa.

"Damn Guilders!" The deprecation, uttered in Vadin Sarad Valli's precise Durvan accent, surprised Jaya into a chuckle.

"What is for laughter, Sarojin?" Sarad asked, laying his stress on the wrong syllable.

An intentional gaffe, Jaya knew. Valli reputedly called him the "Jinn Rai" when among friends. He only wished he might have done something to warrant being labeled a demon prince.

He smiled. "Sorry, Vadin. Your vehemence was-"

"Amusing, evidently," concluded the Vadin. "That surprises me, Nathu Rai. I wud think a Lord of the Vrinda Varma wud be also vehement about the Guilders."

"You know me, Sarad. I inherited my seat on the Vrinda Varma. Vehemence about anything is beyond me."

"Now, that's not what I hear." The Vadin Bel Adivaram joined the conversation from behind.

Jaya moved slightly to take him in and lifted his beverage in salute. "Vadin."

Adivaram inclined his head respectfully. "Nathu Rai."

Sarad Valli's round face was lit by curiosity. "And what do you hear about our eccentric young mahesa? Something wort' repeating, I hope?"

"I've heard no more than what I've also observed. Which is that the Mahesa is vehement in his attachment to a certain young lady." The Vadin's eyes turned their sly gaze to where Anala held animated conversation with another group of guests.

"Do you blame him?" asked Valli. "She's an excellent hostess, Nathu Rai. Where did you find her?"

"In Kasi." Jaya was purposefully vague. He was a little weary of telling the misidentified baggage story.

"Ah, yes!" said Valli. "The Hotel Ramkasha wasn't it? An uncommon coincidence that. Serendipity, one might say, eh, Sarojin? Already in the family, too." He flashed a toothy, simian grin. "Very convenient."

Jaya caught the oblique reference with a tickle of irritation. Sarad Valli was forever reminding him of the onerous excesses of the "old families." Only in a Taj household was it not considered sinful to simply treat a female cousin or niece as if she were a wife.

"I'd call it a salvation. Ana saved my honor this morning by leading the family devotions. I had completely forgotten the Erai invocation."

Adivaram's eyebrows scooted halfway up his broad forehead. "Indeed? Isn't it unusual for a young Rani to be schooled in such things?"

"Ana is Rohin."

The Vadin's eyes protruded. "Her father honored such a ridiculous pursuit? A woman such as that should not be wasted in a monastery."

"They do things differently on Avasa. Apparently, the Rohin do not lock themselves away in retreat, and the lines of caste are allowed to blur in areas of the spirit."

"Backward little dirtball, isn't it?" said Adivaram.

"Ah, that reminds me of a joke my son tol' me this morning," began Sarad Valli.

Jaya moved away from the group before the conversation degenerated into racist humor. He had almost reached Ana's side when a hand fell warmly to his shoulder. He turned, saw who the hand belonged to and smiled.

"Uncle Namun! You came after all."

Namun Vedda returned the smile wryly. "Well, I got to thinking about a lecture your Jivinta gave me the other day about carrying sound ideas to extremes. I decided that attending the annual Sarojin Mesha Fest hardly constituted a conflict of interest. I'll be glad when this mess is all over with, Jaya," he added. "It will be good to get back to normal—not have to worry about infringing on your neutrality. I sometimes wish Vedda Technologies didn't have to do business with the Consortium at all. In fact, there are times I wish I could return to academic life and leave the business to the business-men. Had my father and his father not been businessmen, it might have been so."

"Well, I'm glad you came to your senses about Mesha Fest, at any rate. Have you spoken to Jivinta?"

"Oh, yes, and she was about to introduce me to your—cousin, is it?—when some other gentleman drew her off." Dark blue eyes crinkled at the corners. "Not that I blame him, she's extraordinary. Did I just hear you tell Adivaram that she's Rohin?"

Jaya nodded. "I thought his eyes were going to pop out into his drink. He was scandalized."

"So I noticed. Old prig. I think it's fascinating. Imagine the challenge. Imagine the will it would take to pursue something so..."

"Socially unacceptable?"

Vedda snorted indelicately. "Well, it shouldn't be. Why shouldn't the woman follow whatever path suits her? Your father was right about conformity, Jaya. It lives uncomfortably close to stupidity."

Jaya laughed. "Let me introduce you to Ana," he said. "She'll be happy to have found such a champion."

He turned to the spot where Ana had been standing only moments before, but she had been swept away into yet another group of guests. He was about to suggest they track her down, when Duran Prakash joined them.

"A joyous Mesha to you, Nathu Rai, Vedda-sama!" He greeted them both respectfully, a wide smile on his face.

Jaya fumed. Prakash was the last person he wanted to socialize with. A glance at Namun Vedda's face suggested he was having similar thoughts, but he turned the momentary grimace into a bland smile and responded graciously.

"Prakash-sama—a joyous Mesha to you, as well."

"I thank you," said Prakash and turned to Jaya, his eyes bright. "Nathu Rai, I couldn't help but notice that singular young woman you had at your right hand during dinner. A beautiful, bright thing. Is she, er, your betrothed?"

Jaya's ire began to smolder. "A cousin." Out of the corner of his eye, he saw Namun Vedda make an eyerolling, ludicrous face and nearly laughed aloud.

"Ah! A contender, then, eh? I couldn't help but notice also—well, how could anyone fail to notice against that red gown—her color ing." He lowered his voice. "Does she have Genda Sita blood, do you think?"

"Good God," muttered Vedda.

"I hadn't asked after her racial heritage," replied Jaya as neutrally as possible. He realized he had never contemplated the idea that Anala Nadim might be of the socalled "dirty white" race. She was light-skinned even for an Avasan, but hardly jarringly so.

Prakash looked sly and cast a significant glance at Vedda. "The Rani tells me she's from Avasa."

Jaya nodded. "Yes. From the Sagara."

"Ah, the Pleasure Zone. Aren't you concerned that such an, er, intimate relationship with an Avasan might compromise your neutrality?"

"Her father is in the timber business," said Jaya.

Namun Vedda exhaled explosively. "Prakash," he murmured, "this is neither the time nor the place to be discussing affairs of state. You are compromising more than neutrality to even bring the matter up. It is hardly an honorable subject for Festival."

"But, sama, the Nathu Rai's honor-"

"Should not be questioned by a guest in his home. To do so is an act of outrageous impudence. If you have some sort of accusation to make, you can damn well make it in chambers before the Vrinda Varma."

"I thought I would give him a chance to explain-"

"He is your Nathu Rai, Prakash. He owes you no explanations. You, on the other hand, owe him an apology."

Prakash appeared to be floundering in amazement. Was the bookish scientist daring to rebuke an attaché of the KasiNawhar Consortium? Jaya bit the inside of his lip and enjoyed Duran Prakash's discomfiture.

The lawyer finally recovered himself enough to offer defense. "His relations with these Avasans could very well prejudice him toward AGIM."

"Perhaps it could. I daresay you may be doing much to prejudice it, yourself."

Prakash bristled visibly. "Do you refer to my relationship with the Rani?"

"I would never make such an unseemly reference, Prakashsama.

I refer to your boorish behavior. I repeat that you owe the Nathu Rai an apology."

Prakash's face had screwed itself into an impossible tangle of outrage and embarrassment. "Need I remind you, Doctor Vedda, whose money it is that pays for your patent research?"

Namun Vedda paled visibly.

Anger prompted Jaya to speak. Prakash was the worst kind of idiot. "Prakash-sama, you forget yourself. Please try to recall where you are, and whom you address."

Prakash glanced at his host's face and backed down. "I am ... sorry, Nathu Rai. Please forgive me. It is only my zeal for justice."

Namun Vedda grimaced and looked down at his feet.

Jaya allowed none of his emotions to show. "Is that what it was? Well, Prakash-sama, I must ask you to confine it to your business dealings. If I hear that you have exercised your zeal further in this house, I will ask you to leave."

His face expressionless, Prakash bowed crisply and hurried away, leaving the other men to recover the spirit of the occasion.

Namun Vedda shook his head. "I sometimes wonder if I haven't sold my soul to demons for the sake of a few patents. By all the embodiments of God, boy, what does your mother see in that man?"

"I'm sure I don't want to know," said Jaya.

He searched the room again for Ana, and had just spotted her when the bells pealed to announce the Time of Gifts.

Jivinta Mina was Rani of the Gift Giving, deciding in what order gifts should be presented by those who had signed the silken Presentation Scroll in the Entry. She had scheduled herself last, with Jaya and Ana just before.

Most of the gifts were not actual presentations, but donations of funds or goods to Kasi charities; some gave artwork for display in gallery or Asra. There were, of course, musicians, several poets and a group of actors who had been hired to perform a traditional playlet about the creation of the Seasons. Whether performed by the gift-giver or professional surrogate, the fare was entertaining and the audience enthusiastic.

Ana was curious about what Jaya Sarojin would present. She had heard Ravi joke about his lack of singing skills; he did not strike her as a poet. When Mina Sarojin announced that her grandson would present a traditional tale "in the way of our ancestors," Ana imagined he would simply tell a story. She was completely surprised by what he did do.

From the hush of fire-lit expectancy grew a tantalizing drum beat and the drone of obas and faroons. Out of the recesses of the darkened hall came a team of six torch bearers, chanting deeply against the rhythm of the drums. They carried torches on tall poles. These they set in floor braces on the perimeters of the performers' dais. Their duty complete, they turned in a swirl of bright fabric and bowed to one knee before the audience, fisted hands crossed over their hearts.

"INDRA!"

The roar of a single voice sent the torch bearers leaping into the crowd with a shrill response. As the audience fell back in surprise, there vaulted into the torchlit platform a Being out of legend—Indra, Conqueror of Chaos. Reflected flames licked over the gleaming platelets of his armor and ran like liquid sun down the curving blade of the sword he held in gloved hands. In the radiant, gold and silver face, only the eyes were alive—dark and glittering in the recesses of the helmet's half-mask. The rest of the face was in shadow as Indra assumed the stance of a Balin warrior, ready for combat.

Drums pounded, obas keened, faroons rumbled, and bell harps sang in shrill, sharp bursts. To their music, Jaya danced the War of Sat and Asat—of Existence and NonExistence—a battle that ended when Indra, Son of the Supreme Spirit, brought light and life to the Universe.

The audience fell into the role of chorus, responding to Indra's roars with ululating cries, answering his guttural barks with the requisite chatter, joining exuberantly in the chanted passages of the Sacred Text.

Ana was swept into the fantasy. The torchlit platform vanished; Indra danced and leapt and whirled amid suns and planets and snowy galaxies of pin-prick stars. The torch bearers in their black cloaks became the forces of darkness—clouds of human corruption and doubt—seeking to extinguish the torches of divine Light. The formless horde scattered before Indra's mighty sword. With a final roar of triumph, a final stroke of his great sword, Indra brought the Sun of Divine Truth from behind the clouds of concealment and the Universe blazed with light.

The cosmos erupted in a final shout of rapture, then the fantasy fled before the rush of returning light. The universe became a vaulted room full of inebriated partiers.

Indra unmasked now, and Nathu Rai Jaya Sarojin bowed to his guests and swept sweat-damp hair from his forehead. Ari and Ravi, still in the black cloaks of the Asat forces, helped him from his armor. Many compliments and kudos later, he stood before Ana and bowed.

"What did you think of my gift?" he asked.

"I was surprised," she said in all honesty. "I would not have thought traditional dance to be ... a suitable pastime for a prince."

"I'm a Sarojin, first of all. My grandmother has always insisted that I have an appreciation of tradition."

"You danced it beautifully," Ana told him, and a small demon made her add, "If you ever tire of the indolent life of a mahesa, you might consider dancing as a profession."

To her surprise, Jaya Sarojin threw back his head and laughed. "No, no," he said, when laughter had spent itself. "Dance is, to me, a labor of love. You will think it odd, but when I dance, there were moments when I feel there is no stone beneath my feet, only the void. There are moments when ... when I felt I am no longer the dancer, but have become the dance. I have yet to feel that about government."

Ana suspected she was being teased, but said anyway, "That is the goal of all life, isn't it? Not to do, but to become." She gave him a courtly bow. "Now, if you will allow me to present my gift..." She slipped away toward the stage from which Jivinta Mina beckoned her.

Jaya heard a soft chuckle at his elbow and glanced aside. Bel Adivaram's porcine face beamed at him, tinted with the rouge of drink. His mouth wore a suggestive grin.

"You find it difficult to share your cousin's gifts, do you, Jaya?"

The tone was suggestive as well and Jaya found it irritated him. "Do not make a joke of my cousin's gifts, Vadin. She is a Sarojin."

Adivaram raised his brows. "Ah, and the Sarojin honor is unimpeachable, isn't it? 'As a lotus, though born in the muddy water, is unsoiled by it.' Eh, mahesa?"

"Even so. You will excuse me." Jaya nodded curtly and made his way to the edge of the presenter's platform.

"I was born and raised on Avasa," Ana was saying, "and as I grew up there, I came to know that despite its youth, there is a rich culture there, as on this world. There are legends, histories, tall tales, songs, and poetry. My gift to you tonight is one of the chansons of Avasa. It is called 'The Plains.'"

She began the cant:

> *"Only where some passionate, level land*
> *Stretches itself in reaches of golden sand,*
> *Only where the sea is joined to the sky, clear,*
> *Beyond the curve or ripple of white foamed crest—*
> *Shall the weary eyes*
> *Distressed by the broken skies—*
> *Broken by Asra, mountain, or towering tree—*
> *Shall the weary eyes be assuaged—and rest."*

When the final tone of the short piece faded, the applause was loud and long and accompanied by requests for an encore. Ana complied with an intimate Rohin tribute to the Kalki Avatar.

> *"The secret of love's code is never found*
> *By those who but to reasoning are prone.*
> *What rose could spring from out that brackish ground,*
> *Or what anemone from stone?*
> *O brighter than the bright sun art Thou!*
> *It is Thy light that veils Thee from men's eyes.*
> *But who has ever glimpsed Thy face, he cries:*
> *The Sun of Truth is dawning on me now!*
> *A thousand gaze upon Thy face and none*
> *Is worthy he should ever look thereon.*
> *How could I ever on Thy beauty dwell?*
> *O, this unease! Thou art not to be sung."*

It didn't sound like a hymn written to some lofty Divine Authority, Jaya thought. It sounded like a love song for someone of flesh and blood. "The secret of love's code" ... was that what he was struggling to decipher? Bhakti—devotion—would he ever be able to decipher that? Jaya shook his head. Maybe he was a stone, but would a stone feel unease "not to be sung?"

He caught Ana's eyes on his face and realized he was frowning. He relaxed deliberately, joining in the applause, but she had seen the frown, and would no doubt interpret it as atheistic disapproval or even superiority. There was a vast gulf between wanting and having.

He turned his gaze aside and found Bel Adivaram and Duran Prakash watching him rather too closely from a markedly political grouping nearby. They raised their glasses to him; he inclined his head curtly and moved away.

"You have the voice of Music, Rani Sadira," the Esteemed One said. "Very rarely have I heard chanting with such power and conviction. You are a true and sincere bhakta. I encourage you to enter the Orders. With your discipline as a Rohin, your fire of devotion, your obvious knowledge of the Sacred Texts, you would make a most worthy Deva."

Ana blushed profusely and reflexively gave the respectful greeting. "Your words are more than praise, Deva. It has always been my desire to study for Orders, but life on Avasa has not afforded the opportunity."

The Deva smiled, her eyes glinting. "I hope you will take the opportunity afforded you here. I would consider it a joy to personally oversee your instruction. You have the spirit of a Deva. All you need attain is the colors." She brushed the folds of her ceremonial stole and smiled. "And these colors would suit you. Now, Mina," she turned to the Old Rani, "you've been so patient waiting for me to finish my speech. Please continue with the gifts."

Jivinta Mina presented her gift in three parts. The first part sat in a velvet-draped display case brought to the stage by four of the Sarojin servants. The drape was removed to reveal an array of porcelain cups, bowls, goblets, trays, and vases all decorated with glowing colors and designs both intricate and simple. Guests broke into spontaneous "ohs" and "ahs," and moved forward, murmuring; jostling to get a good view of the pieces.

Standing by the display case, Mina Sarojin seemed pleased with the response her gift had brought so far. "These exquisite pieces will be here for all of you to admire ... and plot to own," she announced. "Now, the second part of the gift."

She looked off-stage, holding out a veined hand. A pretty, but frail young woman dressed in a simple gown stepped from the shadows skirting the platform and up onto its polished surface.

"This is Sushela Kapivastu. She is the creator of these extraordinary pieces." She waited out the applause that followed, then continued: "Sushela has graciously agreed to reside in Kasi and open a shop in the Sun Crescent. I am certain you will all frequent her business."

Again, there was applause.

"And now," said Jivinta Mina, smiling from her eyes, "the third and final part of the gift. Heli, if you would..."

There was a cry from the Salon's main entrance and a small girl darted toward the stage, weaving her way through the guests like a frantic shuttle.

Sushela Kapivastu covered her mouth with her hands and burst into tears. She embraced first her benefactress, then the child who vaulted onto the stage and into her arms. There was a scene of inarticulate joy and reunion through which the old Rani smiled, eyes glistening.

In a moment she turned back to her guests and proceeded to astound them further. "Dana Kapivastu was cruelly torn from her family by one of the most respected dalalis in Kasi. I had the ability and, I felt, the duty to reunite her with them. I petitioned the Deva Radha to review the child's case and restore her freedom. I am happy to announce that she did exactly that. Dana Kapivastu is no longer a dasa. She is free, by the grace of Tara-Rama and the Inner Circle."

A murmur rolled and spread through the crowd like backwash from the prow of a boat.

Ana glanced at the faces of those near her and saw everything from pleasure to uncertainty to shock, dismay, and disapproval. She began to applaud, slowly, rhythmically. Next to her Jaya picked up the rhythm. Ravi, always two steps from his side, echoed him. The Deva Radha also joined in and, with her, the other Holy Ones present. Glancing about the great Salon, the Deva moved to mount the stage next to Mina, her hands keeping up the rhythm, her face alive with something like passion. She raised her hands high over her head, calling for the other guests to applaud with her.

Many did, some nodding, smiling, joining in the spirit of Mina Sarojin's gift. Others slipped quietly away, out of the room, out of the Sarojin Palace, to places where they could talk about the old Rani's scandalous behavior.

Melantha Sarojin and Duran Prakash went only as far as the main hall.

"I'm sorry you had to witness that display." Red-faced, Melantha Sarojin did not look Duran Prakash in the eye—but then, she rarely did that, anyway.

"Nonsense, my dear," Duran murmured, laying a consoling hand on the back of her neck. "I'm more concerned that you had to witness it, since it distresses you so."

"That old woman will forever distress me with her illtimed, misbegotten social blunders. I wonder my husband was able to rise to such respect with that sort of upbringing. By all rights he should have been a royal joke instead of one of the greatest statesmen Mehtar has ever known."

Ignoring her praise of the deceased Nathu Rai Bhaktasu Sarojin, Prakash made a mew of sympathy. "You mean she has always been like this? I thought perhaps her age..."

The Rani laughed curtly. "No, Duran. The Rani Mina has always flown in the face of rita. She speaks of tradition, heritage, social responsibility—in reality they mean nothing to her. Nor does she care what anyone else must endure as a result of her maudlin effrontery. Bringing that dasa into the party as a participant! Celebrating that-that peasant artisan as if she were from the artistic Orders!"

Duran dared to remonstrate with her. "My dear, it was an act of charity. The woman does have a great natural talent."

"Don't take her side against me," warned Melantha acidly. "You have no idea what life is like with her—with my son. Neither of them will call the das by their proper names. They treat them as if they were peers. And that damned Ravidas! Jaya has insisted on making him his closest confidant since they were small boys. I thought he'd outgrow it. I was certain of it. But no! First my husband and then his mother insist on supporting Jaya in his iconoclastic tendencies."

"Iconoclasm? Oh, surely it's not as bad as that," interjected Prakash.

"Isn't it? Now he's brought that woman here. She may be a Rani, she may be a leaf of the Saroj, but—my God—raised on Avasa ... ? Well, what did I expect? I should have known when Jaya's appetites finally conquered him, there would be some 'kindred spirit' around for him to plant his staff in."

Duran mewed again. "Do you think he designs to marry her, or is it just a—well—a dalliance?"

"I'd hope for a dalliance, but the girl claims to be Rohin. Jaya does not believe in such things, but he is tolerant, to a fault, of the beliefs of others."

"Perhaps," murmured Prakash, glancing back down the hall toward the Salon, "this is merely another form of rebellion. Most men would get their pre-nuptial ... practice at the hands of a cunnidasa or someone from a lower life. In all likelihood, Jaya would consider that taking advantage of his rank. It certainly would provide little challenge. A Rohina or a Rani, on the other hand..." He shrugged. "Perhaps he merely wants a relationship with an equal."

"He's fascinated by her—that much is clear."

"Has he ... taken her to his bed, do you think?"

"Perhaps. You know what they say about the Rohin. He placed her in a room adjoining his and I've never known that door to be locked. Then again, I know also that both beds are slept in every night. But why should I care if he marries her—or merely beds her? She's a Rani, at least. I don't think she's Genda Sita—even Jaya couldn't be that foolish. Her skin only wants a little tinting. Perhaps she'll even acquire some sophistication. She's not stupid. She couldn't be and impress the Deva Radha." She glanced at Prakash and smiled. "It really doesn't matter to me, Duran. Not at all. My son may feed his appetites as he pleases and I shall feed mine."

She looked at him in a certain way, then turned her eyes to the Grand Stair just up the hall toward the Entry. "I'm going up to my suite."

"Should you be alone just now?" Duran asked significantly.

"No. I think perhaps I shouldn't."

She brushed his cheek delicately with one scented hand and left him standing in the hall.

He waited a bit—spoke to some fellow guests as they drifted by, telling them the Rani was distressed by the evening's events and had gone up to her rooms. They were sympathetic. He was on fire, but did not show it.

A quarter of an hour later, when the hall had cleared considerably, and sounds of celebration still wafted from the Salon, Duran Prakash climbed the Grand Stair with due speed and soft step. But at the landing, he turned right instead of left and scurried down the gallery to the most ornate of doors. It was unlocked.

He stepped within and stopped to take in the room. So, these were the private chambers of a mahesa. As grand as might be expected. He imagined the Rani's quarters must be even more sumptuous than her son's. Well, tonight he would know—at last.

He moved to what he suspected was the connecting door to the Rani Sadira's suite and opened it. It was a smaller bedroom than the Lord's but just as grand. He found the wardrobe and opened it.

A certain type of clothing was what he sought and—ah, there! The silken, shimmering folds of black and crimson and palest moon beams told him a wealth of tales. Women did not have such things in their wardrobes for their own enjoyment. These were for the pleasure of a man, these were proof of compromise.

Duran Prakash smiled and let his personal excitement grasp him. She was waiting for him—dare he hope—wearing something like these? He brushed a hand through the filmy folds. It collided with something a good deal heavier and coarser to the touch. He pushed aside a flimsy bit of gauze and pulled the odd piece of cloth out where he could see it.

It was an insulsuit—clean, but well worn and even mended. On Avasa one did not survive without one. He wrinkled his nose. What an offense for a woman—any woman—to have to wear such a rag next to her skin. He fingered the initials—"AN"—frowned, and shook his head. Why would she bother to keep such a rag? Her name decal had even been effaced. Ah well, perhaps it had some sentimental value—reminded her of home, or something like that.

He grunted and let go of the offensive piece of cloth, then ran his hands, again, over one of the gauzy camisoles, as if to purify them from the insulsuit's alien coarseness.

His craving soared and sent him hurrying toward the wing he knew the Rani occupied. He would be the most sympathetic of companions tonight; a listening ear, a willing provider of any pleasures she desired to experience. He prided himself that what she had experienced so far had been pleasurable enough. He was, if not a master, at least highly skilled at the Kunda arts. After all, it wasn't every man who had the opportunity (or the reason) to study the mysterious sexual disciplines of the Bogar.

Duran Prakash chuckled as he gazed appreciatively at the delicately ornamented doors to the Rani Melantha's private wing. How crazily did life behave. All the cajolery and sweetness and pleasure he had contrived to shower upon the Sarojin queen had never bought for him what her anger had now given away—passage into her intimate chambers.

Who knew? Perhaps before Mitras rose and killed the night, her anger would grant ultimate access to the most intimate chamber of all.

CHAPTER ELEVEN

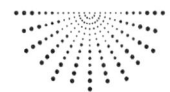

IT WAS WELL into morning when the last guests wandered from the Sarojin Palace. Jaya was halfway to his room when he realized how tired he was. Beside him, Ana let out an audible sigh.

Jaya stirred out of his own sluggish thoughts. "You too?"

She nodded. "I'm exhausted. I think I'm less tired after a day in the mines. Socializing requires much mental effort. Especially when you have to remember not only what to say and how to say it, but what not to say."

Jaya glanced at her in dull surprise. "You don't actually work in the mines, do you?"

"What else would I do?"

"I don't know, but I can't quite picture you covered in dust and man-handling drill bits. I guess I ... thought maybe you ... prepared meals..." He broke off lamely, feeling as if he'd just stepped into a sink hole.

Ana did not seem to begrudge him his ignorance. "The domestics prepare the meals. That's their job. Mine is mining. My chores run from surveying terrain and assaying ore to driving sandcats and repairing machinery. I'm a very good mechanic. The best, father says. He also says I have gaur savvy."

"Gaur savvy?"

She grinned. "I know where the ore is."

They were at the door of Ana's room. Ana glanced at it, then reached out to run her fingers over its sheeny, carved surface. "So hard to believe. I never imagined I would call anything like this 'my room.'"

Curiosity nibbled. "What's your room at home like?"

She shrugged. "It's small—compared to this, at least. Dark and warm and round, like a cup turned upside down. The walls are white clay with tiny chips and slivers of mica. At night I can open the skylight and lie in my bed and watch Upala Ratri turn the slivers into a field of stars."

"What do you watch while you lie in bed here?"

"The stars themselves." She shook her head. "Windows—you take them for granted. I've only seen them on houses in the Sagara where winds aren't so violent."

Jaya wanted to know more about Avasa and violent winds and houses without windows. He wanted her to talk about her home, but it was neither the time nor the place. He opened the door to her room.

"Go watch some stars, Ana."

She smiled, sleepily, and shook her head. "Tonight, I'll watch only my dreams."

There was an awkward moment as both of them hung between stillness and movement, then Ana disappeared into her room, the door closing with a soft click. Jaya stared at its ornate exterior for a moment, then retired to his own chambers.

The sakti wasn't so bad when he was tired. It was hot and diffuse like sunlight. Maybe if he kept himself exhausted it would go away.

Ana went immediately to her bath chamber, undressed, washed and put on a soft robe. Humming a little of a favorite chanson, she carried the opulent clothing to the bed chamber wardrobe. Her hand halfway to the intricately carved door, she paused, frowning. It might have been hours ago, but she distinctly remembered closing the wardrobe door. It was open now and the clothing disarranged. A diaphanous camisole was draped across the darker folds of the bodysuit beside it. At the end of the closet, the rough, brilliant fabric of her insulsuit protruded awkwardly from the surrounding finery. She started to tuck it back in then paused. The lapel had been pulled open, clearly revealing the initials stitched on the breast.

Ana's tired mind immediately rejected the idea that a member of the Palace staff had been through her clothes. She headed for the connecting door to Jaya's suite, flinging the crimson gown across the bed as she went. She was fully awake by the time she reached the opposite side of the room and realized the door was slightly ajar. She reached for it, then gave a shrill yelp as it opened toward her, forcing her to jump out of the way.

A bemused-looking Jaya entered her room. "Ana? What's wrong?"

"The-the door," she stammered.

He glanced at it. "Yes. I just noticed it was-"

She grabbed his hand and hauled him across the room, pointing at the wardrobe. "That was open too. Someone went through my wardrobe. They pulled this out." She tugged at the insulsuit.

Jaya stared at the bright blue cloth. "Are you sure one of Heli's girls didn't just get curious?"

"Jaya, Heli's girls have seen every stitch of clothing in this closet. They put it there. They check it and straighten it every day. And they don't leave doors open."

"Who, then?" he asked, but Ana saw a veil of suspicion fall across his face. He swore.

"It won't help to-"

He held up his hand. "Spare me, Ana. Spare me all Rohin piety. Just let me be angry ... Damn!" He paced away across the room, stopping to lean heavily against a bed post. "Someone is obviously very curious about you. And I'd say they suspect that a certain relationship exists between us."

"Who? Who would care?"

"Duran Prakash. He dropped a few unsubtle hints at the celebration."

"Duran Prakash? The Rani's..." She stalled in mid-sentence. "Friend," she finished.

"Toy," said Jaya, then made a dismissive swipe at the air. "He's the Consortium's legal representative."

"The Rani and the KNC Speaker?" Suddenly overwhelmingly weary, Ana crossed to the massive bed and let herself down onto it.

It was too late and she was too weary to have to think in political convolutions. "How strange is coincidence."

Jaya snorted. "What coincidence? Prakash is wooing the Rani because he has something to gain from it ... he thinks. She's a political link in the Kasi-Nawahr chain."

"All right. But why would Duran Prakash care if we have ... a certain relationship?"

"You're Avasan. A sexual relationship between us could be construed as a compromise of my neutrality. Which he hinted at tonight. I made a point of telling him you were from the Sagara but-"

"But now he's seen my insulsuit. Not something a woman of my means should have."

"So it would appear."

"And ... I think I may have mentioned the Kedar to the Rani."

"Delightful."

"So." She put more resignation into the word than she felt.

"So, nothing! Damn!" He struck the bed post a vicious blow with the flat of his hand. "The frustrating thing is, we can't be sure it was him. Worse, we have no way of knowing if he learned anything significant."

Ana had difficulty speaking past the lump in her throat. "He saw my initials on the insulsuit, Jaya. He learned my name isn't Ana Sadira. Even if he doesn't know Anala Nadim exists, he's going to wonder why I'm lying about my clan." She sighed. "You were right; I should have destroyed that insulsuit."

"Well, I may be in ruin, but at least I've lived to hear you admit I was right about something."

Ana glanced up at him. He was looking at her, stone-faced, only his eyes betraying irony. She laughed—and then couldn't stop. She doubled up and fell over onto the bed. She could hear him laughing, too, and that only made matters worse.

Five minutes later, they were just recovering, feeling silly and spent. Ana sat up, Jaya sat down.

Ana uttered a sigh that was heavy with laughter. "The poor mahesa. I am such an irritant, I drive him to tears."

He chuckled and wiped her cheeks with the sash of his robe. She realized the kohl around her eyes must have run; Jaya began dabbing at it.

"It's a damn good thing no one can see us," he told her. "They'd think I'd been abusing you."

"You'd never do that, mahesa."

It was something to say, but she instantly regretted saying it—most especially not in a tone of voice that sounded so coy.

He dropped the sash, gazing at her, eyes opaque. His fingers strayed into the thick fall of hair over her left ear. She shivered, relaxed, shivered again. She should stop him before he mistook the situation.

"Mahesa," she started to say, but his kiss caught the word and silenced it.

She didn't resist. She told herself she was a slave and he was her master. He had this right. Then she forgot about slaves and masters and simply began to drown.

She wanted to drown.

No, she wanted salvation.

She fought both drowning and salvation: Sense against sense. It was an age old battle: Will against attraction. She might as well fight gravity. This force, too, held the planets in their courses, ordered the universe and cemented families and nations together.

Her mind seized on an irrelevancy. How was it that the same force that ordered the universe created chaos between a man and a woman?

Chaos must be the illusion. Sakti illuminates. 'And are you illuminated, Nathu Rai?' she'd asked him.

Am I illuminated?

I am drowning, she acknowledged.

There was a pillow beneath her head now and Jaya pressed against her, over her, his hands still in her hair; her fingers were tangled in his. It was black silk; it was a spider's web.

She tried to rouse her sense of self-preservation, but felt no danger. She tried to throw her mind forward to morning—beyond, to going home—alone. She failed to push it past the moment.

Jaya's hand glided down her neck to her shoulder; caressing, gentle, pushing aside her robe. Cool air touched her breast for only a second before Jaya covered it with the warmth of his palm. The heat and pain was swift—no wonder the poets spoke of fire. She trembled convulsively and was suddenly terrified. His mouth left hers.

"No!" She forced the word between her lips.

He hesitated, then kissed her neck.

"Please," she said.

He hesitated again.

"Jaya Rai?" Ravi's voice came from the adjoining bed chamber.

Jaya groaned and rolled to his feet, pulling his robe tight around his waist. "Here." He set his back against the bed post and glanced at Ana.

She had sat up and was clutching her robe over her chest.

"Don't look so frightened, please," he murmured.

"Mahesa!" Ravi was hovering in the connecting door, disapproval in every line of face and body.

Jaya beckoned him over. "What is so urgent you couldn't ring?"

"I did ring, Nathu Rai. You did not answer." He glanced at Ana, who let go of her robe and folded her hands in her lap.

"Ana just made a rather disturbing discovery," Jaya said. "Someone went through her wardrobe this evening."

Ravi's dark eyes flickered to the open closet doors. "A thief?"

"A guest. I suspect Prakash-sama. I'd like to know for sure. Maybe someone on staff saw something."

Ravi nodded. "I'll ask them, Jaya Rai. Now, my message—which is urgent: There is someone downstairs who must speak with you. A Govinda-sama."

Jaya straightened. "Where is he?"

"In the kitchen." Ravi grinned. "Mata's feeding him leftovers."

"I'd better get down there before she fattens him up. We can't have Govi looking well-fed. It would ruin his career. Ravi, if you'd talk to anyone who's still up? And you,"—he turned to Ana —"sleep."

When they'd gone, Ana sat cross-legged on the bed, staring at nothing. She was not thinking, but there was movement. An inner sense of balance took hold and righted her capsized universe.

After a while she prayed—begging forgiveness, begging wisdom, begging further balance. Then, exhausted both physically and emotionally, she slept.

∾

"Ah! Jaya Rai!" Govi waved a fork at him and nodded, his mouth full of one of Heli's prize concoctions. "This woman—a saint! A goddess! A shame she is married and I am crazy."

Heli flushed and turned to poke at the fire in the raised hearth.

Jaya pulled up a chair and sat down opposite his indigent friend. "What's the report?"

"Mmmph," said Govi, chewing rapidly. He swallowed. "The alley behind the B&D."

"Someone has moved in?"

"No one as moved in. Moved out my cozy—boxes, everything."

"And?"

"Guards." Govi chomped into a crispy bit of finger-food. "Big, ugly guards. Armed to their eyeballs. And gates at both ends of the alley."

"Armed with what?"

"Illegals, I'd say. Oh, there's stun-fuzzies. Visible. But take my word, Jaya Rai, they've got more than stunfuzzies."

"Any traffic?"

"Yeah. Oh, yeah. Night time stuff. Little fellas pad up, slip something to the guards, pad off. Slick'n'quick."

Jaya frowned. "Slip something to the guards? What? Slip what to the guards?"

"Little somethings. Little packets. So by so." Govi indicated the size—about as big as a mailer.

"Anything else?"

"Not that I see ... yet." He grinned.

Jaya nodded and rose. "Thank you, Govi-sama." He bowed. "Enjoy your meal. You will always be welcome here. My palace is your palace."

"Nathu Rai," said Govi tentatively. "I did notice a certain loft in your coach house. An empty loft. I see it was once das quarters."

Jaya nodded. "Except for Kena, the full time staff lives in the main House."

"Might one borrow it for a night or two? I haven't found myself a new place yet."

Jaya smiled. "Yes, you have. The loft is yours—permanently. If you need anything at all to make it cozier, just ask Ari or Heli."

Govi's face became a crinkled fabric of pleasure. "Thank you,

Jaya Rai. I will repay." He shot Heli a saucy look and tucked back into his meal.

Jaya returned upstairs feeling as if something was kicking his insides to pieces. He wanted nothing in the world but to send time backwards. To relive the last half hour without Ravi's ill-timed appearance.

She'd said "no." He'd heard that, ignored it. She'd asked him to stop, but he had no doubt he could have changed her mind—overwhelmed her the way she'd overwhelmed him.

He was just reaching for his door latch when Ravi's voice called him—"Jaya Rai."

He turned, strangely disoriented. Ravi, grim-faced, strode quickly toward him, stopped, glanced over his shoulder, and gave a soft report.

"I spoke to the upstairs girls. One of them saw Prakash-sama enter the Rani's suite at about fifth hour and fifteen."

All thoughts of Ana fled. "That–" He smothered a foul imprecation. "I knew it."

Ravi frowned. "Why would he be in Sri Ana's suite?"

Jaya sucked in a sharp breath. He could hardly ignore the implications of the title Ravi had just used.

"Are you ascribing Ana sainthood now—or is that just your way of putting me in my place?"

Ravi's face suffused with color. "I would overstep my boundaries–"

"You have no boundaries. We have no boundaries. Speak plainly, Ravi."

"Anala may not be a saint, but I respect her. I wonder if you do."

Jaya felt his face tingle with ... embarrassment, he realized. "Yes. I do respect her. But ... it's more complicated than that."

"Is it? Or is it as simple as heat and hardness and a certain pain?"

My face will be singed black, thought Jaya. "No. It is not that simple."

"When one is hungry, one eats."

"It is not that simple."

Ravi waited patiently to hear how simple it was not.

Jaya sighed. "She draws me. Like ... like rain to earth. Ravi, you're making me explain things I don't have words for."

Ravi's eyes glinted. "Poor mahesa. Life is discovery."

"Now you're beginning to sound like her."

"Thank you. Jaya Rai, you owe me no explanations."

Jaya nodded. "But I do owe Ana."

"That depends on what has passed between you. I was thinking you owe them to yourself."

"Ah. 'Know what you feel before you act on it.'"

"Always good advice."

"But if I don't know what I feel-"

"Then is it wise to act?"

"I feel desire."

"She is Rohin, Jaya Rai."

Jaya exhaled explosively. "What does that mean? I've read everything I can find about the Rohin. It's all contradictory, mysterious."

"Mysterious? What's mysterious about it? It's a way of life, a path of purity, an attitude of devotion, a bhakti."

"Bhakti." Jaya shook his head. "What's that? I don't understand that either."

Ravi's eyebrows arched quizzically. "How can you not understand what you live, Jaya Rai? Bhakti is what you have for your Jivinta. That, I know you understand. Now, about Duran Prakash."

Jaya pulled his mind back from the rim of some half-glimpsed metaphysical world. "Is he still here?"

"No. He left. Father says he was one of the last to have his mitas brought around. Will you confront him?"

"No, but I want you and Ari to hire some extra security people. No one must be allowed to enter this House without being seen. And I want more surveillance points added to the system."

Ravi nodded. "Then there is nothing we can do about Prakash-sama's behavior tonight?"

"It appears not."

"That is a shame," Ravi said.

Yes, it was a shame, Jaya thought, as he wearily entered his suite. A shame on a noble House. If he was punctilious about tradition he would send the Rani packing back to her clan capitol in disgrace ... but that would mean publicly disgracing his father's memory.

He stood at the connecting door now. It was still ajar. His hand rested on the latch. He pushed gently, swinging the door wide on silent hinges. A soft pinkish light still burned near Ana's bed, shedding its glow over the occupant. She was asleep. She looked exhausted ... and troubled. Her face lacked the softness of true rest and a frown lay across her forehead like a dark compress.

Jaya let himself relive those moments before Ravi's interruption; felt Ana's lips respond to his kiss, her fingers tangling his hair, her body—warm, smooth, muscular, seductive—evoking every form of hunger he knew. He recalled the verse of Erai prayer: All desires and all perfumes and all tastes. She was that. She was beautiful. She was terrifying.

And terrified.

He remembered that, now, having somehow burned through the veil of preferred memory. He recalled her face in that second before Ravi called. That was fear. Not desire, fear.

He turned back into his own bed chamber, leaving the door open. His head hurt with fatigue. Puzzle pieces spun there, Desire, sakti, disgrace, honor, love, fear, bhakti—pieces.

Bhakti is what you have for your Jivinta.

He slept with that thought, finding it an easier bedmate than the memory of Ana's terror.

CHAPTER TWELVE

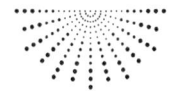

"Your report?"

"Not as good as I'd hoped."

"That's disappointing."

"No less so to me. The Rani Melantha has charms beyond her son's political position."

Duran Prakash seated himself in a pillowed cup chair and gazed out over Kasi. He barely noticed the magnificent view afforded by the height of the penthouse.

"She divested herself of any conflicting interests," he reported.

"At her son's request?"

Prakash shrugged and sipped his drink. "I have no idea. I only know that the couture called in extreme heat asking why his benefactress had withdrawn her funds."

"I see. And you've gotten her no closer to marriage?"

"I was admitted to her private chamber after the Mesha celebration."

"Ah! And?"

"And we performed ... certain Bogar rites. Rites she had not permitted me before. But that was all. She seems determined to give me only a drop more of herself at a time. I did glean some more about her son's relationship with this Avasan girl, though."

"Yes?"

"Her bed chamber connects with our Lord's, and her wardrobe

is full of the sort of whispwear a man likes to see on his bedmate. I'm certain there's a sexual liaison there and, with the position she enjoyed at table—well, I would say our Nathu Rai has a vested interest in the welfare of her family on Avasa. They are not in the mining business-"

"Irrelevant. The Avasan economy is driven by mining. Everything else is just part of the infrastructure."

"We may be able to call him on this, then, if the Vrinda Varma shares that interpretation of the situation."

There was a protesting creak of leather as Nigudha Bhrasta rose from his chair. He moved to the great window that formed one wall of the opulent office atop the North Tower of the KasiNawahr Consortium's main offices. Imbedded pieces of crystal shot a rainbow of light-darts back into the darkened room.

"It seems, then, that there may be several ways to get to the young mahesa through this woman. Which is best? Is she in a politically susceptible position?"

Prakash chuckled. "That I seriously doubt, although I suspect she is not just Avasan, but possibly Genda Sita, as well."

"Her skin is surely not that light."

"I've had the opportunity to inspect her fairly closely. Her palms are pale as cream, which leads me to think what color she has is merely sun tan. I'm having the Sadira family checked out, of course. Her grandmother was from Avasa and her grandfather from Darupur. I'm having the Avasan side of her family traced."

"I'm not sure the color of her skin is going to serve us much. Remember, a Sarojin can get away with things other men cannot. If she is Genda Sita, that means that one of them has already got away with marrying a snow-jinn. Besides which, there are elements within the Vrinda Varma that would consider raising a racial issue a petty tactic. Her origins alone may provide the tool we need. At the next session, the issue shall be raised."

"That will slow things down a bit," agreed Prakash, "but it will hardly get us the Sarojin vote. Nor will eliminating him from the vote serve our purposes."

"No, we must influence the young Taj. It appears we must resort to more obvious persuasion."

Prakash grimaced. "So it would seem. Sarojin is too arrogant to be bought and too apathetic to be pressured politically."

"No, Duran, you're wrong. Apathy is not a Sarojin trait and never has been. If it were, your Rani would not recently have sold her KNC interests. Our Nathu Rai is simply too stubborn to be pressured politically. He has that much of his father in him."

Bhrasta seated himself in the chair opposite Prakash and reached for the decanter of wine on the table between them.

"Perhaps he will respond to pressure of a more primitive sort."

～

Ana felt completely bedraggled—as if the repeating dream of tearing her way through the sweat of a Mehtaran swamp had been real. It was a child's nightmare—the endless path; green, dripping horizon at arm's length; alien sounds spurring her to a haphazard run; the continual sense of pursuit, as if some dim alien beast closed in behind.

Ana was mistress of her subconscious. She manipulated the dreams, massaged them, paused, edited and reread them. On the fourth or thousandth time through, the diadem on her head sprouted real wings and let her soar above the close, green maze.

She saw the high plains—flat, dry and familiar. She winged her way to them and perched, secure, on a low hakwood tree. Her lungs filled with sweet, arid chill. She scanned the horizon for dangers and saw only mirages—shifting, indistinct, threatening. Like dark little dust-jinn, they hung on the fringes of perception.

She closed her eyes and let the mist from the cup of hot channa between her hands caress her cheeks and eyelids. Sun wove through the trees and soothed the dim ache at her temples.

"Are you asleep?"

Ana's eyes came open and tried to focus through the steam. One of her dust-jinn had come to life.

"I'm not sure," she answered him. Then, "No. I think I must be awake. If I were asleep I wouldn't be so exhausted."

"I thought you were a career miner. Where's that famous Avasan stamina?"

"Don't scoff, Nathu Rai. You'd do no better after a day in a mine shaft."

"Undeniably true. Have you eaten breakfast?"

She shook her head. "My stomach is still asleep."

"Let's go, then."

"Go?"

"Into Kasi. I think we need to pay the Port Zone Sarngin a visit. We can get something to eat afterwards."

We are not talking about it, then, Ana thought as she followed Jaya from the House. A crimson aircar waited at the bottom of the wide steps.

Anala stopped to admire it. "Very impressive, but why are we taking it? Horses are-"

"Not nearly as impressive. I want to be especially impressive today. And I want you not to be seen."

He thumped the nearly opaque surface of the tinted window, then popped the passenger side door open. It rose with the elegance of a bird's wing.

"Your coach, Rani."

"Your manners are improving."

He bowed and helped her into the car. It was spacious and comfortable and smelled like any new machine. She was reminded of her family's sand-crawler, then laughed at the absurdity of the comparison.

"What's so funny?"

"I was just struck by the similarity between your car and our sand-crawler. It smelled new once, too."

Jaya chuckled and started the aircar's near silent engine. They were out on the road before he spoke again.

"Are we going to talk about last night or pretend it didn't happen?"

Ana's face flamed and her stomach quivered. "What needs to be said? It happened."

"And you don't feel anything?"

"I feel a great many things, mahesa."

"Name one."

"Fear."

He nodded. "I know. I saw that. What are you afraid of? Me?"

"Of drowning ... of losing myself."

He glanced at her. She made busy staring out at the passing scenery. He started to say something, then grimaced and shook his head.

"I am not an institution," he said. "I'm a human being."

Ana turned to look at him. "What does that mean?"

"It means..." He shook his head. "It means I was thinking out loud. Ignore me. Govi informs me that there's some clandestine business going on in the back alley of the Badan-Devaki."

"What?" Ana sat forward too quickly. Her safety harness snapped her back against the seat. "Ouch! And when did he inform you of this?"

"Last night. Correction: This morning."

"That was the visitor-?"

Jaya nodded. "He says the alley behind the dalali is gated and under guard now, and that couriers are making midnight deliveries to the guards."

Ana frowned. "Midnight deliveries of what?"

"I don't know. Govi just said they were small packets."

Ana put her hands on the curving, padded crash panel and stared out at the road.

"That's it, then. The thieves steal the leaf, the Sarngin pick up the victims and take them to the BadanDevaki. You told me Govi got hustled out of his alley by Parva Rishi. He must have been in the way." She frowned. "Isn't that backwards? If the dalali is paying off the Sarngin, why are deliveries being made to them? Are you sure Govi didn't see a payoff?"

"I'd trust Govi's sight—it's pretty sharp. He said the couriers were delivering, not picking up."

"But delivering what?"

"I don't know. I do know that some of our Port Zone Sarngin are on Badan-Devaki's payroll. The question is, how many and at what level of command?"

"How can we find out?"

"I don't know, Ana. I've never done anything like this before."

Ana glanced at him. He seemed suddenly uncertain. A chill skittered down her back. "You're jeopardizing yourself, aren't you—doing this?"

Jaya smiled. "Don't worry, Ana. I'm not jeopardizing anything."

The headquarters of the Port Zone Sarngin was in a neighborhood of modern, business-like splendor. Square, gleaming buildings of stone and glass lined up along the broad avenue—the lairs of officialdom.

Jaya parked the car before a particularly solid-looking block of stone with a pair of bronze eagles flanking the heavy, gilt doors. The massive birds glowered menacingly over the street as if they took their role as Sarngin symbol of Law and Order very seriously indeed. Their wings were open and arched, metal pinions nearly touching over the doorway.

"Impressive," said Ana, peering at them through Jaya's window. "Our Sarngin in Onan have a conservative little dugout with a nice flagpole. They replace the Eagle flag every month—twice in Chaitra —and the flagpole comes down at least three times a year. They'd love this. Of course, it would be entirely impractical in the Kedar outback."

"So, it would seem, is the flagpole."

She shrugged. "We have to be able to tell the Sarngin dugout from all the other dugouts in Onan. But you may be right—maybe the Onan Sarngin should get some statues. Of course, they'd have to have the wings folded or they might blow away."

Jaya shook his head. "Eagles with folded wings would hardly present the image of tireless vigilance-" He broke off and gave her a severe scowl. "You're obnoxious when you're tired. Didn't your mother and father ever warn you not to tell tales?"

Ana knew she missed looking innocent by a wide margin. "You don't believe me about the flagpole?"

Jaya unsnapped his harness. "I don't believe a one thousand pound bronze eagle can fly."

"You've never been to the Kedar. Onan is at the foot of Mount Amurpradha—merely at the rim of the High Plains. The wind gauge is a boulder on a hundred pound chain."

Jaya grimaced and popped his door open. It swung up and back with wing-like grace as if saluting the feathered guardians.

"Stay in the car," he warned. "The air system is on and the vents are open. Keep the doors and windows closed and locked. Don't get out for anything or anyone. Don't open the doors until I get back."

She watched him disappear into the headquarters. Wings. Wings seemed to have new significance all of a sudden. Wings on guardian birds, wings on crowns that became wings to escape nightmare dangers. Protection, status, freedom—an odd lot. She sighed and settled back to wait.

$\sim$

The Sarngin headquarters was very much as Jaya expected—muted and concise. Every angle was exact, every surface gleaming. The only color in the place was in the uniforms of the officers. The Patrolmen were in gray, their sergeants in black.

There were two officers approaching him already. They seemed pleased to have noticed him. He was pleased to have been noticed.

"Nathu Rai," said the senior of the two. He wore the nearly iridescent purple of a Division Chief. Both offered the military version of the respectful greeting—one quarter benediction, three quarters salute.

"We are honored," said the lesser officer—a Patrol Chief. "How may we assist the Nathu Rai Sarojin?"

"I wish to consult with your Commander about a matter of great concern to his district."

"I am Division Chief Varaza," said the D.C. "Perhaps I can be of some assistance."

Jaya weighed the advisability of revealing any more, then said, "It seems the merchants near the Spaceport are concerned about the growing number of thieves roaming the streets. I've heard reports that the crime rate is up around the Warrows—a lot of Avasan tourists are being mugged and then arrested as yevetha. An unhealthy diplomatic situation."

The two Sarngin exchanged frowning glances.

"I've noticed no increase in complaints from the area," said the Division Chief. "Have you heard anything, Kers?"

The Patrol Chief shook his head slowly. "The Warrows, you said, Nathu Rai. If I knew the neighborhood..."

"Dockrow," said Jaya.

"Ah! That's not my territory." There was relief in the man's face. "Perhaps I could-"

"Yes. Patrol Chief Kers is correct," interrupted the D.C. "That isn't his territory. I believe you want to talk to Patrol Chief Ranjit ... or to me. I'm his superior."

"I believe I already stated what I wanted, Chief Varaza. I want to speak to your superior. Is the Zone Commander in?"

A dark anger glinted in Varaza's eyes. "I'm sure I can assist you-" he started to say, but Patrol Chief Kers was already speaking.

"I saw the Commander not five minutes ago in his office, Nathu

Rai," he offered, and the D.C.'s face darkened to an unbecoming shade of purple that clashed dreadfully with his uniform.

Jaya smiled. "I'll see him now—if he can spare the time."

Division Chief Varaza smiled in return, his color returning, more or less, to normal. "I'm sure he can. If you will follow me, Nathu Rai."

A glance in the P.C.'s direction effectively dismissed him.

Jaya followed the Division Chief down a broad central corridor toward the rear of the building. The click and clatter of myriad heels on the polished gray floor sounded like a horde of summer locusts. As they crossed the large common office area given to Patrolmen and their immediate superiors, young Sarngin eyed him with unabashed envy and admiration.

How naive. They could only envy the status that went with the Sarojin tiliq between his brows or admire a reputation for ... whatever it was he had a reputation for. They had no idea what kind of man lived behind all that.

He was escorted to the glass-fronted office of Zone Commander Mall Gar and waited patiently while Division Chief Varaza went inside to announce him. In a moment he was back, holding the gleaming metal and glass door open for Jaya's entrance. The Chief glanced quickly from his Commander to Jaya, then left, closing the door behind him.

"Nathu Rai." Commander Gar bowed deeply, then gestured toward a less-than-comfortable looking couch across from his desk. "Please make yourself comfortable," he said and gave the couch a rueful look. "If you can."

A man with a sense of humor, Jaya observed. He seated himself and glanced around the office. It was neither austere nor opulent, and was tasteful, if muted, in its appointments—a thing which Gar's deep crimson uniform jacket more than made up for.

The pictographs on one wall told him of a man's career—graduation from the Academy of Military Sciences in Nawahr, awards for marksmanship, the Badge of a master level Logician. On the wall opposite, a different tale; this one told by a tripaneled antique tapestry of delicate and lush beauty. And behind the desk, a wall full of books.

Jaya took that all at a glance and turned his attention to the man. "This is quite an elegant office, Commander. You have excellent taste."

Gar's eyes widened in apparent surprise. "I am sure it can't be as elegant as what you're accustomed to, Nathu Rai." His speech was precise and carried a slight Norther accent.

"Elegance," observed Jaya, "is a function of taste and self-expression, not of wealth. Unfortunately, wealth and taste are rare partners."

Commander Gar's response was a twitch at the corner of his thin mouth and a slight jerk of his head. "What may I do for the mahesa?" he asked.

Jaya draped his cloak over the back of the couch and arranged himself to look relaxed.

"The mahesa," he said, "has been informed that muggings are becoming commonplace in the Port Zone. Especially in the Warrows."

Gar frowned and nodded, his hollow cheeks drawing in even further. A thick fringe of curly hair screened his eyes so that Jaya couldn't read them.

"The tourist areas are always the most attractive to criminals," he said.

"According to my sources, they've become suddenly more attractive."

The frown deepened. "What do your ... sources say, exactly?"

"That attacks on tourists are occurring with growing regularity."

"I've heard no such reports. I assure you, Nathu Rai, if there were more muggings being reported I would have heard of it."

"I didn't say they were being reported, Commander. But they are being observed."

"By whom?"

Jaya shook his head. "I'm not at liberty to say, but I consider my sources unimpeachable."

Gar stood and circled his desk, obviously disturbed. "If they're not being reported ... Why are they not being reported?"

Jaya met the other man's impressive gray gaze. "Because the people being attacked can't go to the Sarngin without being arrested."

Gar made an impatient gesture with one hand. "Speak plainly, Nathu Rai. I have no aptitude for mysteries."

Jaya sloughed the relaxed pose and stood face to face with the Sarngin Commander.

"Neither have I, Gar-sama. But I'm in the middle of one nonetheless. Speak plainly? I'm not sure I can. Quite frankly, I'm not sure I can trust you."

He moved away from Gar toward the interoffice window and gazed across the outer room. Division Chief Varaza and another officer were involved in conversation in a doorway across the commons. They both glanced toward Gar's office, saw they were being watched and glanced away again.

Jaya chewed his lip. Who to trust? And how far to trust them?

He turned his gaze to the Commander's reflection in the glass. The frown of deep perplexity and growing impatience hadn't altered.

"I'll try to speak plainly, Commander Gar. When I can do so without jeopardizing my informants." He turned his back on the window. "Here's the scenario: A young, attractive Avasan gets off a starcoach at the Kasi spaceport. Somewhere in the Port Zone, he or she is set upon by thieves. The thieves aren't after money or jewelry, unless it's readily gotten. They take only leaf. A matter of minutes after they're gone, a team of Sarngin come by and take the brand new yevetha to a dalali where they are processed and sold."

Gar studied him for a moment, then said, "You are suggesting this is no coincidence."

"These attacks are not taking place out in plain sight, Commander. One that I know of occurred in an alley; one happened in a side street rowhouse. In that case, the Sarngin passed the thieves on their way to make the arrest. They went right to the house, Commander Gar. Right to it."

Gar's expression was grim. "You seem very well-informed. You said 'young, attractive Avasans.' You believe they're being singled out for this treatment?"

"I do. They have no cree. Once their leaf is gone, their id is gone. Instant yevetha. Instant fodder for the dalali."

"Yes, the dalali. A particular one, you think? One you could put a name to?"

"Badan-Devaki."

Commander Gar moved to the bookshelf behind his desk and touched a small control panel. A large vicom screen came to life just above it. He fingered a menu item on the screen, then another. A map of the Port Zone filled the screen. He tapped the southern corner and the map shifted to show a portion of the Silk District. Another selection caused an irregular array of red squares to appear on the map.

"The Badan-Devaki is here, is it not?" Gar pointed to a red square situated along a broad boulevard.

Jaya nodded.

"Well, here are the Warrows." The tracing finger moved south into the Port Zone. "As you can see, the Badan-Devaki is the closest dalali. It's normal procedure to take yevetha to the brokerage closest to the point of arrest."

Jaya studied the map for a moment, then moved to plant a finger among a warren of minor streets. "One attack took place here. The victim still ended up at Badan-Devaki. The closest dalali is this one..." He pointed at a red square to the east. "The Blue Iris. I suspect the Badan-Devaki is paying to have das made for them, Commander Gar, and that some of your men are on their payroll. If that's so, wouldn't you like to know which ones?"

"Indeed I would, Nathu Rai Sarojin. And I assure you, I intend to find out who they are. I also assure you that their orders did not come from this office. If you could introduce me to your sources—let me question them-"

Jaya shook his head, turned back to the sofa and retrieved his cloak.

"Forgive me, Commander, if I hesitate to trust you. But I can't take that chance. Not yet."

Ana was nearly asleep by the time he returned to the aircar and jumped half out of her seat when he got in. She was fully awake in seconds, though, and listened intently to his report as they drove.

"Do you think he's one of them?" she asked, when he'd finished. "One of the crooked Sarngin?"

"I don't know, Ana. I honestly don't. I tried to read him. I wanted to trust him. Then he asked to question my informants." He shrugged. "I don't trust Varaza, though. He just seemed ... too perturbed by my visit with Gar."

"Maybe he was just concerned that you might get him in trouble with his Commander. After all, you did go there to complain about the rise of crime in his sector. And you went over his head to do it."

Jaya chuckled. "I guess I did. All right, so I'm not a detective."

He had just turned the car onto the drive that fronted the Sarojin property when Ana saw the graffiti. She grasped his arm.

"Jaya, look! On the wall by the gates!"

He brought the aircar to a stop. Just up the gentle slope, a red, three foot high scrawl glared down at them from the perimeter wall. "DEATH," it said. "DEATH TO AGIM. DEATH TO FRIENDS OF AGIM." The meaningless word "WoCoa" was scribbled beneath.

"Who in the name of—"

"It's fresh," said Ana. She pointed at the oozing letters.

Jaya swore violently, flipped his harness off, and popped the door.

"What are you doing?" asked Ana, grasping his arm more tightly.

"I'm going to see if they left any telltale signs."

"All right." Ana reached for her harness clip.

Jaya's hand closed over hers. "Stay in the car, Ana."

"I'm not afraid to go out there."

"Then you're an idiot. Stay in the car."

Angry, Ana tugged at the clip. The pressure of Jaya's fingers increased painfully. She glared at him.

"Do you want to take the chance that someone might be watching? Someone who might recognize you? These are your father's enemies we're dealing with."

He was right. She was being an idiot. Still glaring, she nodded.

Jaya slid out of the car and glanced around, removing his cloak and dropping it onto the driver's seat. He closed and secured the door, then rounded the sleek nose to wade through the lush greenery at the base of the wall.

Watching him, Ana failed to notice the large, silver-gray aircar that glided to a stop behind her. Failed to see the hooded men that climbed from it until they were flanking her.

A movement at the corner of her eye made her turn her head. Two figures slid by her window, close enough to brush the glass. Electrified, she let out a muffled shriek. Two more men moved by on the left. She'd flipped off her harness and was in the act of springing the door catch when she remembered that they couldn't see her.

She caught at mental cords of discipline. I can't panic. I won't be any good if I panic.

The men fanned out at the nose of the car, moving to encircle Jaya. She could just see him through the wall they created and willed him to hear them or sense them.

As if at her thought, he turned and straightened. His eyes flicked to Ana, though they couldn't see her there, behind the opaque glass. Stay, they said, then scanned the hooded ones.

"Is this your work?" asked Jaya. His hand extended toward the wall.

Ana couldn't tell if he got an answer.

What he said next was, "Who are you? What do you want?"

The answer to that was movement. They edged closer, spreading the circle to cut off his retreat.

"Damn!" murmured Ana. "Damn!"

She searched frantically for some way to hear what was happening without giving herself away. She found the controls to the roof hatch and breathed a prayer that its mechanism would be as silent as sunlight. It was.

"-jobs on the block," said a raspy, metal-edged voice. "We don't like that. We're just ... registering our disapproval."

Jaya shrugged. "What have I done that you disapprove of? I haven't voted on the AGIM petition yet."

"We want to make sure you vote correctly, that's all. We don't like the idea of your foreign friends eating into KNC payload. Which they will, if the AGIM petition passes. And the first thing to go will be the cargo handlers. The KNC won't support a team of wharfers when there's nothing for them to do. And that won't be all. AGIM threatens every honest worker in the KNC family. You vote right, mahesa, we keep our jobs. You vote wrong, we lose—and we'll see to it that you lose."

"You're not damn likely to influence my vote by painting hate slogans on the walls of my estate."

The thugs edged closer.

"We hear," said the saw-tooth voice, "you can't be bought."

"And you thought maybe I could be frightened? Think again."

"No, mahesa. You think again."

The thug took three quick strides forward and slammed Jaya against the wall with a blow to his shoulder.

Ana gasped and coiled for action, her hand hovering above the door catch.

Jaya's eyes drove her back.

They won't kill. They need to frighten, not to kill. Stay calm ...

That was far from easy. Ana knew her temper was a great personal weakness, and watching Jaya take a swift series of vicious blows taxed her self-discipline almost beyond limit. She concentrated all her will on his well-being.

His back to the wall, Jaya struggled for breath and focus. He was hemmed in—a man before him, another beside him, holding him in place. A black hood wavered before his sight, eyes like dark flares gleamed through the shadowed slits. Not quite right, those eyes. One of them was crooked. Skewed in some way—the flesh around it, puckered. Through a haze of pain and vertigo, he heard the rasping voice again.

"How do you vote now, mahesa?"

"I vote you to Niraya Hell."

"Are you sure, mahesa?" There was a surreptitious movement among the folds of the man's black cloak.

Jaya saw the thin, shining sliver of blade just before it bit into his left side. He sucked in a sharp breath and tried not to cry out.

Ana jumped as a chill dashed around her rib cage. Something was wrong. She gasped for air, fighting against a sudden stitch in her side. She tried to read Jaya's face, but his eyes were closed. They came open as her fingers curled around the door catch. She bit her lip and waited, wishing someone would come. Surely someone could sense that they were in danger. Kena? No, Ravi! Jaya's shadow. If only Ravi might have some gift of second sight.

"Am I making an impression, mahesa?" The knife nibbled its way deeper.

Caught between the knife and the wall, Jaya could not escape the pain. "Not the one you were hoping for," he said and gasped when the blade punished him for the insolence.

"I don't think this is going to convince him," said the man at Jaya's shoulder. "I think maybe another tactic might."

Sawtooth seemed to consider that, then nodded. He withdrew the knife and wiped the bloody point on Jaya's shirt.

"So you don't care about your own pain, hm? What about someone else's? What about ... oh, that Avasan cousin of yours—the Rani Sadira?"

Jaya tensed. "What do you know about her?"

He could feel the smile through the hood. "Oh, the Coalition is very interested in what you Varmana do in your private moments. Knowledge like that can be quite useful in times like these. We have quite a network set up to bring us that knowledge."

"Oh? What knowledge did you hold over poor old Adivaram's head?"

The black hood laughed. "I'm sure you'd like to know. I can tell you it was nothing like this. That old boy only cares for the dagam. But you ... I'll bet you'd go out of your way to protect your little Genda cousin, yes?"

Jaya thought frantically. Where distraction had failed, perhaps bluff would succeed.

"What makes you think I would? She's a pleasant diversion, but hardly worth jeopardizing my career on the Vrinda Varma."

"You really expect me to believe you don't care about that woman? Tsk. Nathu Rai, you're joking with us. I assure you, this isn't the time for jokes."

"I'm not joking. I don't give a damn what happens to her. I can buy five more just like her in any dalali in Kasi."

He was surrounded by unpleasant laughter.

"Buy a Rani, mahesa? I doubt even you could do that. You're lying through your eyes." He peered into them as if to flush the lie out. "It's a shame your beautiful, Rani-dasa isn't here, or we could put that lie to the test."

He didn't mean to glance at the car, but he did—and Sawtooth, with the skill of a veteran tracker, followed the trail his eyes left.

"Ah! But she is here, after all!" He jerked his head to one side. "The car."

～

Crouched on the padded seat, Ana tensed, her fingers aching in their death-grip on the backrest. She'd already thrown the door catch, already disengaged the automatic lift mechanism. Now she braced herself against the inner arm of the passenger seat, her feet resting against the door panel.

Two men approached the car. One circled to the driver's side. Ana grimaced. Thank God she'd thought of that. The man on her side drew a very illegal weapon from his cloak—a lightning gun. It occurred to her that Jaya would probably want her to start the car and shoot away in a jet of hot air. She took a deep breath. Not a chance.

The car rocked slightly. A voice overhead and behind called, "This side's locked."

Ana glanced at the driver's side monitor. This thug, too, had a weapon trained on the car. He nodded to his partner. Ana swiveled her head back around and tensed. The man above her leaned forward slightly and reached for the external hand hold.

She kicked with every ounce of strength in her body. The door flew up and back, caught the thug full in the face, and sent him crashing backward into the knee high foliage. It closed over him like a green tide. The car bucked savagely as his partner scrambled to the roof.

Ana dove through the open door into the leafy cover. She landed half atop her unconscious victim. Gun! she thought and scrambled for it among the moist shadows. It wasn't in his hand. She slithered forward, suddenly aware of sound. To her left—shouts and cries and the sound of fighting. Behind her, something scrambling, groping, seeking her out.

Last night's nightmare popped into her head. Her salvation then had been the winged crown, but the crown was gone, safely tucked away in a velvet bag. A velvet-

Heart beating loudly enough to drown out all else, Ana groped for the fallen thug's hood. She found it, grasped it, tugged. It gave slightly, then caught. Biting her lip to keep from groaning in frustration, she gave it another yank and was rewarded. The hood was in her hand. Her ankle was in someone else's.

Kicking, she struggled the hood over her head and prayed she could make her naturally husky voice sound like a man's. "Hey!" she roared and popped her head out of the greenery.

The other thug released her ankle with a disgusted growl. "Help me find her!"

She jerked her head backward. "The gun," she grunted, and submerged herself in the foliage again.

Now she crawled toward the wall, desperate. Where was the gun?

The glint of stray sunlight on its anodized casing gave it up. It had come to rest against the base of the wall, its muzzle propped in the woody crook of a fern. Two more feet and she had it in her hands. She rolled over onto her back and lay still.

It was quiet. Too quiet. Just beyond her feet she could hear the sounds of search. To her right ...

A sharp cry of pain made every nerve in her body jump.

"Tell her to come out, mahesa. Tell her to come out now. Before you lose the ability to speak."

Ana sat up and tore off the hood. "I'm here! I'm right here!"

"Come here!" ordered Jaya's captor. "Come here and save your Lord from a very sore throat."

Ana shook her head. "Come get me."

The knife tip nipped at Jaya's throat, drawing blood.

"I've hurt my ankle," she added.

The thug just below her on the florid bank started to move toward her, then stumbled. He swore, reached into the foliage and came up with his partner's hand. He started to pull, attempting to help the man to his feet.

"No!" The leader gestured violently. "His hood, stupid! She's got his hood! Leave him! I want her."

The thug nodded, straightened, took a step up the slope. Ana raised her hands out of the leafy blanket, sunlight dancing along the barrel of the lightning gun. She aimed it at his middle.

The hooded head shook. "You don't know how to use that, Rani." He made a move to draw his own weapon, tucked away during his search.

"Don't bet your life on it."

He kept moving. A sizzling bolt of light shot from the gun's muzzle and sliced past his right elbow, turning the fabric of his jacket to cinder. He grabbed his arm and dropped into the vegetation, howling in pain.

Ana was on her feet, swinging toward Jaya and his two guardians.

One of them made a dash for her just as the wounded man recovered himself and drew his gun. Faced with a two sided attack, Ana leapt backwards against the wall.

In the momentary burst of confusion, Jaya parted company with his distracted captor. A well-aimed kick threw the thug off balance, but he still had the knife. He thrust it at Jaya's face, forcing him back and away from where Ana dealt with her two attackers.

~

Distracted, Jaya tried to edge around and away from the slashing blade. The next thing he knew he was on his back in the brush, fending it from his throat. He heard the crack and sizzle of a lightning pistol and a shriek of singed agony. Above him, the knife-wielding thug swore and tore out of his grasp, leaving him to wallow in the brush. Someone ran past him, shouting.

He heaved himself up and staggered toward the car, trying to focus his eyes. Ana was there, moving toward him through the tall growth. She reached him in what seemed like hours, her hands searching for wounds. He pushed her hands aside and gathered her into a fierce embrace, kissing her hard enough to bruise his lips. She responded in kind.

"Idiot!" he called her. "Why didn't you just drive to the House for help?"

"I wasn't about to leave you out here alone."

"Stupid. You could have got Ravi-"

"I did get Ravi." She pulled away from him and looked over her shoulder. Behind her, Ravi held a stun-fuzzy on a huddled heap wearing a crumpled hood.

Jaya blinked. His arm around Ana's shoulders for support, he moved unsteadily to Ravi's side.

His friend's face was a study in anger, amazement, and anxiety. He grasped Jaya's arm with his free hand.

"Are you all right? You're bleeding."

Jaya shook his head. "I'm fine—just muddled."

"I'm deeply sorry the others got away-" Ravi jerked his head toward the empty road behind Jaya's car. "-but we've got this one at least."

"And just who is this one?" asked Jaya. He tugged the hood from the lolling head. The face was unfamiliar and would have been even if Ravi's stunner hadn't deprived it of all expression.

"You don't know him, either," said Ana, disappointed. She turned her head. "Ravi?"

"No, Rani. I've never seen him before."

Jaya sighed. "No. That would have been too easy. Well, let's see if the Sarngin can get anything out of him."

~

Jaya exhaled explosively and winced. "How long do I have to wear these bandages?"

The Asvin Suhrdam chuckled. "Until the wounds heal, Nathu Rai. A matter of, oh ... Ram-ji's good time."

He closed his kit and winked at Mina, who stood next to her grandson's couch, leaning a bit heavily on her cane.

"I'll be back in three days to check up, so make sure he doesn't slip out of them before then."

"Rest assured, Asvin Suhrdam. I shall do so," Mina assured him.

The Asvin kissed Jivinta's hand and left, humming.

She gazed after him fondly. "Such a man. I do believe I shall have him to dinner Kistn'eve. He's only fifteen years my junior. Might make a good match."

Jaya refastened his shirt, the pain-killer the doctor had given him making both his fingers and his mind slow and clumsy. "You'll have to ask him to marry you then. He'd never presume on a Rani of the House Sarojin—that would not be rita."

"I shall ask him ... if I decide it's him I want."

"Jivinta, you're incorrigible."

The old woman snorted. "And you're not? Getting yourself beaten, stabbed-"

"Just a little gouged."

"Just a little gouged," she mimicked. "Idiot."

"What was I supposed to do—agree to vote as they demanded?"

"Yes! Tell them you'll do what they want—then don't."

"That would have been a lie. Cowardly."

Jivinta's pale eyes widened. "Well, you wouldn't want to lie to thieves and assassins, would you?"

"I did lie to them." Jaya shivered. "'Ranidasa,' he called her. I pray he never knows how close he was to the truth."

"Ah! Praying now, are we? It's about time."

"She's terrified of me, you know."

Jivinta Mina took the change of subject—and bald admission—in stride. "Do you think she has no reason."

"I would never touch her against her will."

"Who said you would? She's Rohin, Jaya. She has made a covenant. She will take one husband as a lover and no others. She is not a woman to be taken lightly, nor will she take a man lightly. She is all or nothing, Gauri. Make no mistakes with her."

"If she's all or nothing, then why is she afraid of me? Afraid of losing herself, she said. What does that mean? I don't want her to lose herself."

Mina eyed him wryly. "Are you really that naive or are you merely pretending to be? No, don't answer. It must be the Asvin's potion making you so dense. She's not afraid of you; she's afraid of herself. She's a bhakta, not an Avatar—not even a saint. Her will is strong, but it's not inflexible. She's afraid of her own weakness."

Jaya let his exasperation out on a long breath. "Now I'm a weakness. By tomorrow I'll be a sin. What do I do, avoid her?"

"Do you want to?"

"No."

"Then don't. Talk to her, Jaya. Don't let the mystery of her bhakti be a wall between you when it doesn't need to be."

Jaya shook his head. "The biggest mystery right now is how Ravi knew we were in trouble."

His Jivinta smiled. "I'm not sure you'll believe the answer."

"Now you're going to tell me Ana's a mistress of the Jadu, I suppose."

The smile deepened. "She's Rohin. All true Rohin have a little of the witch about them."

"How is it you know so much about the Rohin?"

"Ah, well. There is a little of the witch about me, too."

Jivinta Mina turned and moved regally to the door, where she paused.

"There is a Rohin text: THE ONE SOUGHT. In it is a parable. The Parable of the Devi's Garden. If you were to read it, you might understand Ana a little better."

"And where can I find this obscure text?"

"In our library."

She enjoyed his surprise for a moment then left.

Ana stared at the window. Against its dark, glossy panes firelight skimmed and slipped. Tongues of flame and tiny cinders danced, jinn-like, in a ghostly replica of the room behind her.

"Sri Ana?" Ravi appeared, translucent in the rippling window world.

She turned her head. "Please, Ravi, call me 'Ana.' I'm not a Deva."

"Ah, but you should be! Sri Ana, Deva of Fearlessness."

Ana laughed and shook her head, gesturing for him to stop.

"No, it's true. I felt it. You have the Jadu—the Magic."

"Then, doesn't that make me a witch or something?"

"Jivinta Mina just told me all Rohin are witches." Jaya came into the small salon, closing the door behind him.

Ana came to her feet. "You're all right?"

"I'll wear these bandages until Jivinta is finished courting our Asvin, but other than that..." He patted his ribs gently. "It hurts."

Ana resisted the temptation to go to him—to offer comfort. Reflexively, she made a tiny stroking gesture.

A startled expression flickered through his eyes. "I'll feel better tomorrow."

"You're not going to the Vrinda Varma session, Jaya Rai," said Ravi.

Jaya's brows rose. "Of course I am. And I'm going to report our little ... scuffle. I want to see if I can bring this Worker's Coalition into open discussion—get some kind of reaction from the KNC." He touched a bruised cheek gingerly. "Now I know what Bel Adivaram meant by 'approached.'"

"Pardon, Jaya Rai, but what reaction do you expect from the KNC?"

"I'm not sure. I just have a feeling, I guess. Duran Prakash applies pressure from one direction, and these thugs apply it from another. Is it just coincidence—two parties with the same intent, using different tactics to make the same point—or is it ... ?"

"Conspiracy?" supplied Ana.

"It could be coincidence," observed Ravi. "The link between the Coalition and the Consortium is not necessarily an illegal one."

"I suppose it could be, but I'm not convinced of it."

"What do we do next?" asked Ana.

"We sleep."

Ana opened her mouth to protest.

"Tomorrow," added Jaya, "is the earliest we can expect to hear anything from the Sarngin. Unfortunately, Ravi's stun-fuzzy was a little too potent."

"I have no regrets," said Ravi.

"I have a few." Jaya glanced pointedly at Ana.

She ignored him and headed for the door. "If there's nothing more I can accomplish waking, I shall try to achieve something in dreams. Good night, mahesa, Ravi."

The door closed behind her.

"I believe I shall retire early, too," said Ravi. "I want my eyes to be sharp tomorrow, in case there are more of these WoCoa people in the bushes."

"Ravi." Jaya stopped him as he reached for the door handle. "How did you know we were in trouble? Or were you just on your way out?"

Ravi looked amused. "On my way out—carrying a weapon? No, mahesa. I came because Ana called me."

"What do you mean—called you?"

Ravi considered that in silence for a moment.

"I was in the kitchen with Mata. Suddenly, I knew you were in trouble. I even ... saw you—for a moment only—as if in a dream. I got a stunner from the lockup and I went to the lower gates." He shrugged. "All was just as I had seen it. I stunned the one man—he would have shot Ana if I hadn't. She burned the other. There is really nothing else I can tell you." He gave Jaya a thorough once over through narrowed eyes. "You won't be up too late, Jaya Rai."

Jaya shook his head, contemplating the fire.

"That was not a question."

Jaya glanced at him and smiled. "I know." He waved Ravi away. "Go on."

Ravi smiled. "Good night, then."

"Good night," Jaya said and went back to his study of the flames.

CHAPTER THIRTEEN

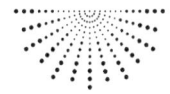

"Report on project AS17B."

The vicom terminal beeped. "Voice identification accepted," it responded. "Project AS17B code Black. Do you wish visual report, oral report, or hard copy?"

"Visual."

"Reporting."

The system displayed the report's contents on the vicom screen, oblivious to the displeasure in its master's face. Across from him, Duran Prakash looked up questioningly from his papers.

"The Sarngin have one of Subham's idiots!"

"What? What happened?"

"Evidently, Nathu Rai Sarojin and his Rani proved to be too much for them. The others escaped. Small consolation."

"But perhaps the wheel has been turned," suggested Prakash. "Perhaps our Nathu Rai has been sufficiently unsettled."

Nigudha Bhrasta looked as if he had swallowed something disagreeable. "He was slightly injured. I should thank the Avatar he wasn't killed. Fools."

"What will you do?"

"First, let me tell you what you must do. You must contrive to find out if our crude persuasion had any effect. Damn! We must have the Sarojin vote, Duran. Without it we stand no chance at all of swaying the Vrinda Varma. If those old cretins will vote with the Taj House, then we must have the Taj House in our palm." He cupped his hand before Prakash's grim face.

"And the thug? What if he speaks?"

"That's easily taken care of. See to Sarojin. I'll deal with our dim-witted associates."

"Are we now contemplating a return to subtlety?" asked Prakash. He despised the use of violence in these matters; he felt it showed weakness and naiveté. Not that he'd ever say as much to his employer. It did, however, afford him a certain spiritual and moral superiority. An offset to material power.

"It seems we must. At least, once we have seen to our current problem."

Jaya entered the Assembly chamber intentionally late. It gave him an opportunity to watch the faces in the KNC box as he picked his way to his seat. There was some reaction to his split lip, bruised cheek, and bandaged neck, but nothing he could honestly read as anything more than curiosity. He paid closest attention to the reaction to the Chairman of the Kasi-Nawahr Board. Nigudha Bhrasta was a big cadaver of a man with eyes like steel ballbearings—eyes that were perpetually narrowed. He had, Jaya realized wryly, no expression to read.

After the invocation, the Deva Radha called for a reading of the summary of the last meeting. Jaya chose that moment to press his comment button.

The Deva looked at him questioningly. "Nathu Rai, you have a comment to make?"

Jaya stood. "I have a report to give, Deva. I wish to report an attack against my person by employees of the KasiNawahr Consortium."

Now he saw a roomful of shocked faces. A murmur rippled around the chamber. Nigudha Bhrasta's eyes narrowed even further.

"An attack?" repeated the Deva. "When and where did this take place?"

"Yesterday at the front gate of the Sarojin Palace."

Again, the eddy of stunned disbelief.

"I was attacked by four hooded men carrying illegal weapons. They beat me, they held me at knife point, they threatened my life and the life of my cousin, Ana."

"Pardon, Nathu Rai," said Bel Adivaram, "but if these men were masked, how do you know they were in the employ of the KNC?"

"They told me as much. Their object was to coerce me into voting pro-Consortium."

His eyes pried at Nigudha Bhrasta's closed face. Bhrasta gazed back coldly.

Adivaram scowled. "You mean to tell me, Nathu Rai, that KNC henchmen announced themselves?"

"I didn't say they 'announced' themselves as KNC henchmen," returned Jaya. "They claimed to be members of a Worker's Coalition. An organization made up of KNC wharfers and other employees."

"Worker's Coalition," repeated the Deva. "I've never heard of such an organization."

"I think our friends in AGIM have," Jaya said. "They also call themselves WoCoa."

Taffik Pritam and his two boxmates both reacted strongly to that, sharing angry glances and pushing toward the edges of their seats.

"The Vadin Adivaram might also have had … a recent encounter with them," Jaya added.

Adivaram reddened, then nodded reluctantly. "Yes. It sounds as if they're the same people who … suggested my vote might also favor the Consortium."

"You said nothing before the Council about these socalled suggestions," observed the Deva.

Adivaram made a dismissive gesture. "Deva, the threats were so veiled, so ambiguous. I had never heard of the organization."

"They'd heard of you," said Jaya.

Adivaram paled.

The Deva turned to fix the KNC box with an intent gaze. "Have you ever heard of this Worker's Coalition, Bhrastasama?"

The Board Chairman returned the gaze with equal intensity. "I had heard that something of that sort was being organized by the Wharfers Guild, but nothing indicated its members would resort to fanatical behavior. I assure you, Deva, we are just as shocked by this as you are."

Jaya studied Bhrasta's impassive face. If he was shocked, he hid it well.

"Have you notified the Sarngin, Nathu Rai?" asked Adivaram.

"He has," offered the Vadin of the Sun Crescent, Rakesh Bithal. "We have one of the men in custody. I questioned him myself. A most stubborn individual. He would tell us nothing."

Jaya, his eyes still on the KNC box, thought Duran Prakash went a shade paler but that certainly didn't qualify as evidence of conspiracy.

"Such fortune!" exclaimed Adivaram, also watching the KNC contingent. "But, of course, the Sarngin of Kasi are unparalleled."

"My friend, Ravi, captured the man. The Sarngin merely put him under arrest."

"The Consortium officially abhors any acts of violence perpetrated by its employees," interjected Bhrasta. "We will, of course, do whatever we can to counsel our wharfers to patience."

He glanced away from the Varmana as if they had ceased to be of interest to him.

Duran Prakash stepped into the awkward silence. "May we now return to the issue of AGIM's anarchy?"

"Autonomy," corrected Sri Radha. "And I think, perhaps, this Worker's Coalition deserves a bit more consideration."

Prakash uttered a sound of sheer frustration. "Deva, this is obviously an issue that affects a broad spectrum of people. We can't expect all of those people to behave reasonably in such an emotional situation. Surely, Holy One, you would not hold the Consortium responsible for the actions of a few distraught men."

"No, we would not. However, it hasn't been established that a few distraught men are the perpetrators. I suggest this issue not be addressed until the Sarngin of the Sun Crescent have had further opportunity to interrogate their prisoner."

"I agree," said the Vadin Bithal. "Let's continue with the matter at hand. I have some questions for the Speakers."

There was general consent to that and Jaya was the first one to key in a "yea" vote. He found himself watching the doorway as the session advanced, hoping Ravi would come with a message that the thug had confessed.

They were up to their eyes in fiscal reports, examining the KNC claim that AGIM autonomy posed undue financial hardship, when Ravi at last appeared in the vast doorway of the chamber, escorted by a Chamber courier. He came quietly to Jaya's side and knelt to whisper in his ear.

"The news is not good," he said.

Sri Radha interrupted the conversation. "Nathu Rai, does your man's message bear on the attack made against you?"

Jaya looked to Ravi, who nodded.

"Then, share this information, if you would, please."

Ravi straightened, glanced at his Nathu Rai and said, "Holy Deva, my Lord will have told you that the Sarngin captured one of the men who attacked him."

"Actually, he told us you captured him, Ravidas."

Ravi merely bowed his head again. "It matters very little who captured him now, Deva. He's dead."

"What?" Jaya's exclamation was lost in the general uproar.

It took the Deva some moments to bring the meeting to order again. When she had done so, she motioned Ravi to the witness box.

"Continue with your report, please, Ravidas. How did this man die?"

"He was poisoned."

So much for coincidence, Jaya thought, and did not like the implied meaning in this sudden death.

"How did this happen?" the Vadin Bithal's whisper was heard clearly in the silent chamber.

"It isn't known yet, Vadin. The poison was contained in a capsule which was still in the man's mouth when he was found."

"Well, it sounds to me as if the fellow committed suicide!" exclaimed Kreti Twapar.

The Deva's face was expressionless. "Ravidas, have the Sarngin found any evidence to suggest that this man's death was indeed a suicide?"

"No, Deva. No conclusive evidence."

"He was searched thoroughly when he was admitted to the cell block, Deva," offered Rakesh Bithal. "There was no poison capsule found on him then."

"You mean your Sarngin didn't find one," said Adivaram. "That doesn't mean there wasn't one to be found. Perhaps he had it in his mouth all along."

"Then why," asked Jaya, "why wouldn't he have used it immediately?"

Adivaram opened his mouth to reply, but the Deva cut across him.

"Do they have any idea who he was?"

Ravi shook his head. "He carried no leaf and his cree had been ... tampered with."

"Tampered with?"

"His palm had been burned. According to the forensic Asvin, the scars were several years old."

"That seems highly suspicious," observed the Vadin Narudin.

"Such injuries among wharfers must be quite common," said Duran Prakash. "I'm sure it's just an unfortunate coincidence."

"Coincidence?" repeated Jaya.

"Nathu Rai, you're out of order," said the Deva.

"May I speak?" asked Ravi from the witness box.

The Deva nodded.

"If this man were a wharfer, then he must carry cree. With his left palm damaged, the cree would have been placed in his right. It was not. Yet, he could not have gotten employment legally without that cree."

"If the injury occurred after he began working for the Consortium-" began Kreti Twapar.

"Then the Consortium would have been bound by law to see to it that the cree was replaced," Rakesh Bithal finished. "It was not. The man's lack of identifying cree is on record. He is—was—yevetha."

The Deva nodded. "You seem to be suggesting that this man was a professional criminal."

Bithal shrugged. "That is entirely possible. One thing is clear at this point: He couldn't have been what he claimed to be ... unless, of course, the Consortium is hiring yevetha illegally."

"Or unless," said Nigudha Bhrasta, his eyes on Bithal, "he was hired by the Worker's Coalition to pursue their ... questionable goals."

The Deva sat back and clasped her hands before her in her lap. "This changes the complexion of the situation significantly. I recommend that this Council receive a full report on this matter from the Sarngin of the Sun Crescent. Immediately." She scanned the faces of the Council. "Do we have consensus?"

The Varmana reached for their consoles to indicate "yea" or "nay." Radha watched the votes register on her own console. Amid the gold lights that signaled agreement, the cluster of red ones was glaring.

"Majority carries," announced the Deva, "but I would like to know why there is disagreement. Do any of the nay-sayers wish to discuss this?"

There was a moment of silence, then Kreti Twapar cleared his throat. "It simply seemed to me that an added expenditure of time and energy when we're already involved in an undertaking of this magnitude would be overwhelming. In the scheme of things, wouldn't we do just as well to wait until the Sarngin issue a report to our noble associate?" He nodded toward Rakesh Bithal. "He could then tender it to a review council—I would gladly volunteer for such, and would recommend Bel Adivaram, since he is our senior Vadin."

"Why shouldn't I tender my report directly to the Vrinda Varma?" asked Bithal quietly.

Twapar wheezed. "Pardon, Vadin, but it appears either a suicide or a murder has occurred in the headquarters of your own District. Certainly it would not be proper for you to head any investigation into it."

Bithal's dark skin flushed, but he held his tongue.

"I think perhaps the Lord Twapar is correct," said Bel Adivaram. "That way the matter would be in the hands of objective parties and would not consume valuable Council time."

"Pardon me," said Sri Elui, "but this is a most grave matter. Does it seem suspicious to no one else that, in the midst of these negotiations with AGIM and the Consortium, the Saroj is attacked by an employee of the KNC—pardon, an alleged employee—who then either commits suicide or is murdered before he can speak? My dear friends, if this man were, indeed, a wharfer intent on survival, why would he kill himself? Why would he be killed?"

He shook his head, the bells in his long silver braids whispering across his shoulders. "It surely behooves us to search into this matter. A threat to the Saroj is a threat to our government. If it was made by desperate and ignorant men, as Speaker Prakash suggests, that is tragic. But if it was made by other than a simple group of activists..." He left the thought unfinished.

"Such an insinuation-" began Prakash, then choked off whatever he'd been going to say as Bhrasta's hand descended onto his forearm.

"I insinuate nothing," said the old Dandin mildly. "I am merely determined that we should know the truth."

In the silence that followed, Kreti Twapar signaled and was recognized. "I agree whole-heartedly with my noble colleague. We must certainly know the truth. I would like to recommend that the Vadin Bithal be required to lay a full report before our senior Vadin immediately."

The Deva looked at him steadily for a moment then said, "Let me amend the recommendation: A report is to be submitted directly to the Inner Circle by Vadin Bithal. Immediately. Discussion?"

"Deva," said Bel Adivaram, quietly, "I have also been contacted by this WoCoa. I feel that I have a ... personal interest in this development. I would welcome a chance to investigate it."

"It is precisely because of your personal interest, Bel, that you should not investigate it," Radha returned reasonably. She scanned the Council chamber. "Is there further discussion? A counter proposal?"

There was none.

"Then the recommendation stands: A report shall be tendered to the Inner Circle immediately. Consensus?" The Deva watched the lights on her console wink on. "So be it. The Inner Circle will meet as soon as the report is available."

She recorded the consensus with her light pen, then gestured for Ravi to step down from the witness box and leave them. When he had gone she favored the assemblage with an assessing gaze that fell, at last, to her folded hands.

"I have, myself, a rather disturbing announcement to make," she said. "We were expecting to be able to bring Rokh Nadim before this Council in the very near future. However, his arrival is now in question. Rokh Nadim seems to have disappeared."

In the hushed wake of that lightning strike, the Deva glanced up at Taffik Pritam who sat silently in the AGIM box flanked by two younger Guilders.

Nigudha Bhrasta chuckled.

"You have some comment, Bhrasta-sama?" asked Radha.

He shrugged. "Only that a coward is as a coward does."

Pritam started to rise, but was restrained by one of the younger men, who whispered something in his ear. He reseated himself, glaring at Bhrasta.

The Deva took a moment to arrange her robes about her.

"This situation has become quite convoluted," she said at last. "We are dealing with a matter which will affect the lives of millions. There is much at stake. There are allegations of coercion leveled at a group connected to the Consortium, and I believe there is enough evidence to warrant an investigation of those allegations. The lives of our colleagues and the members of the Guild's guiding council are too precious to endanger by prolonging consultation. I therefore recommend that this entire matter of AGIM independence be remanded to the Inner Circle for closed consultation and resolution."

There was relief in some faces, dismay in others, but it mattered little what the general members of the Vrinda Varma thought now. By laying it at the door of the Nine, Radha had effectively excluded the other Varmana from the discussion.

The members of the Circle sent their votes to the Deva's console. That it was unanimous was evident from the lack of subsequent discussion. Radha then set the next meeting of the Vrinda Varma for three days hence. The agenda for the meeting was summarily discussed and agreed upon.

Back to normal business then, Jaya thought as he rose to leave. New laws to enact, old ones to re-interpret, disputes to settle— though none so big as this one.

His console lit up, making him glance down at the screen. "Stay, please," it said.

He glanced at Radha who made a small gesture with her hand. He stayed until the hall had cleared of all but the nine members of the Inner Circle. Sri Radha approached him herself.

"You will be available to us, Nathu Rai?" she asked.

"Yes. Yes, of course."

She was studying him intently. "Your ... your cousin, Nathu Rai, is Avasan."

"Yes." He felt his stomach tighten.

"Duran Prakash suggested to me before session that he thought that prejudiced you."

Jaya relaxed. "That no longer bears on the consultation, does it?"

"No, but do you think it bears on the attack? Prejudice against Avasans is unfortunately common on Mehtar. Prejudice against the Genda Sita-"

Jaya felt exactly as if someone was squeezing his throat. "What ... makes you think Ana's Genda, Deva? Certainly, she's fair, but-"

"I noted at the Mesha Festival that her palms were unusually pale compared to the tone of her skin. It occurred to me that what little color she has may be the kiss of Mitras, rather than natural pigmentation. On Avasa, race is not the issue it has been here. There were many Genda Sita among the original colonists. Mining was one of the few types of work they were permitted to do on Mehtar once upon a time. I speak of age old prejudice, Jaya. It is alien to me and meaningless to me, except in that it may mean much to others."

"I don't think Ana is Genda, Deva. I think she's just very fair."

He caught himself, remembering, in a flash of heat, exactly how fair. He had seen the milky white of her breast—had touched it—but the sun never had. Did it matter? Did it change how he felt? Certainly, it had not curbed his desire. He made an abrupt gesture, deflecting the thought.

"I'm not blind to the possibility that my ... relationship with an Avasan could cause ill feelings. Race might bear on the attack if the attackers were what they claimed to be."

"You forget, Nathu Rai, bigotry isn't solely the province of the poor. Ignorance has a place among the well-educated and powerful, as well. It had occurred to me that Ana, being Avasan and so close to a member of the Vrinda Varma, might be the target of the attack rather than yourself. Then, maybe it was only intended to look that way. You said they threatened her life. You indicated they knew of her. Did they see her in the car?"

Jaya shook his head. "No, Deva. They couldn't have. It has opaque glass. I gave Ana away. They mentioned her and when I reacted, they realized she was with me."

"Then we must assume you were the target and it that coercion was the aim." She put a hand on his arm. "We will call you, your cousin, and Ravi to testify. Until then, may God watch over you."

The interview at an end, the Deva Radha moved away as if gliding on ice.

∾

"Tara be praised! You're here, and not out getting into trouble!"

Ana looked up from her reader and grimaced. "I was afraid to go out."

Jaya feigned astonishment. "You? Afraid? I've heard rumors of your exploits on Avasa. You can't tell me there's anything on Mehtar more fear-inspiring than a full grown—what did you call it?—a chandi cat."

"There are Mehtarans on Mehtar. The hordes of Niraya hell are on Mehtar."

Jaya didn't laugh; in his more cynical moments, he'd had similar thoughts. He crossed the study to sit opposite her at the window. "Ana, that's superstitious nonsense."

"I was being facetious." Ana looked down at the reader, marked her place with the press of a key and put the little machine down on the window seat. "What do you think the Worker's Coalition really is?" she asked.

"I'm not sure what to think."

She pinned him with her eyes. "What does your heart say? What does your spirit tell you?"

"My ... intuition tells me the Consortium is involved on some level. At the very least, Nigudha Bhrasta was silently cheering today when I told them about the attack. At the worst ... ?" He shrugged.

Ana's gaze wandered outside. "This place is so confusing. So beautiful. So ugly."

She turned her head to look at him and ambushed his eyes. He pulled them away, not wanting her to read them or know what he'd been thinking just then.

"Life on Avasa is hard," she told him. "There's always a sand blow or a cave-in or a dead-end drill. People get hurt. People die. But they die cleanly. They don't die by politics."

"They do now. Or at least they will if this situation continues."

"I wonder if my father will be the first casualty."

At the mention of her father, Jaya glanced away.

She caught the gesture and pounced on it. "What? What have you heard? What's happened?"

He raised his hands. "Ana, I can't. I can't discuss–"

She was on her feet. "Damn you, Sarojin! This is my father, not some abstract political cipher!"

"What about honor?" he asked, feeling heat. "What about fidelity? Are those just abstract spiritual ciphers? What about my responsibility to the Vrinda Varma? Am I supposed to overlook that because you demand it?"

Ana stared at him, shame clear on her face. "I'm sorry," she whispered. "I didn't realize what I was asking."

He held her gaze for a moment, then glanced away. "It's all right. I understand what this means to you, believe me."

She made an indecisive gesture. "I can always go to cousin Taffik."

"No. No, you can't. Ana, you can't be linked to AGIM. That would throw both of us into the fire."

"Then what can I do?"

The tone of her voice, the look in her eyes, brought swift empathy and opened a flood gate on memories he thought he'd safely dammed. Memories of waiting, helplessly, for hit and run death to complete its task; to leave the House Sarojin without its head, to turn his mother into a cynical stranger, to thrust him into a life of political significance.

"I'll have Ravi contact Pritam. We'll find out what's going on, Ana. I promise you."

She shook her head, subsided into her chair. "I ask too much."

"No, you don't. I sometimes imagine that you do."

His eyes were drawn to her hands, draped loosely over the arms of the chair. He noticed, probably not for the first time, how white were the moons of her fingernails in contrast to the pale gold of her skin.

She caught him staring, tucked her hands into her lap. "What?" she asked. Her pale eyes held both bemusement and suspicion.

The question pressed at his lips, willing him to ask. He found, within himself, an innocent enough way to ask it.

"The Deva Radha drew me aside after the assembly today to ask about the attack on us. She ... asked me if I thought it might be racially motivated—at least in part."

Ana shrugged. "I'm Avasan."

"That wasn't what she meant. She thought perhaps some people who care about such things had gotten the idea that you were Genda Sita. She pointed out to me that many of the original Avasan colonists were."

Ana neither replied nor reacted. Instead, she merely watched him watching her and waited. He opened his mouth to frame the words.

"Yes," she said. "Yes, I have Genda Sita blood. There are probably very few Avasans who don't. It is simply more evident in some of us than in others. Does it matter?"

Does it matter? In what context was she asking that question? In what context was he to answer it?

"It shouldn't," he said.

"Excuse me, Jaya Rai." Ari peeked cautiously around the tall, carved door of the study. "There is a Sarngin to see you. A Zone Commander Gar."

Jaya shot Ana a significant glance. "Please send him in, Ari."

Ari nodded. "I'll bring a tray."

"You," Jaya told Ana, "go into the next room."

"I want to stay."

He shook his head. "I don't trust him, Ana. If he sees you here, he just might conclude that you're my informant."

"If he sees the color of my skin, you mean."

The words froze him. "Go."

"Jaya-"

"A Kasian Sarngin is going to think it very peculiar that a young Rani is included in a discussion of dalalis, thieves, and corruption. Go." He gestured toward the door to the Court Parlor.

Ana moved quickly, scooting into the next room and concealing herself behind the slightly ajar door. When Mall Gar had entered and presented himself to Jaya, she dared peek around the slab of carved wood. The Zone Commander's back was toward her, so she allowed herself the luxury of watching as well as listening.

"You're out of uniform, Commander," observed Jaya, seating him.

"Even the Sarngin may take days off, Nathu Rai. I'm ... not here in an official capacity."

"Then what may I do for you, Gar-sama?"

Even from her oblique angle, Anala could tell the Zone Commander was ill at ease. Beneath his leather jacket, a pry-rod straight back spoke of great discomfort.

"I am not ... pleased to be here, Nathu Rai. I was disturbed by your visit. It raised my curiosity. No, it did more than that. It raised suspicion. I talked to some of the rookie patrolmen on the Warrows. I asked if they had noticed an upsurge in the number of Avasan yevetha they were finding. Some said 'yes,' some said 'no.' I asked if they had been given specific orders about where any yevetha were to be taken. Again, some said 'yes' and some 'no.'"

Jaya sat forward, not bothering to hide his interest. "And those who said 'yes?'"

"Told different stories. A few had been ordered by their immediate superior. A few had been ordered by someone further up the chain of command. Most had it suggested to them that a certain dalali was to be favored. None have admitted to being paid for their trouble ... yet. But two young patrolmen who resisted the idea of favoring a particular business with their yevetha claimed that an unfamiliar gentleman approached them while they were on patrol and put to them a deal. He would provide them with the location of yevetha and they would take them to the BadanDevaki no matter where they were found. The young men asked what should inspire them to do this and a sum of money was named. Their Patrol Chief approached them the next day and made a suggestion to them that it might be worth their while to favor the Badan-Devaki."

"They didn't report him?"

Gar shook his head, his lips pursed. "No, Nathu Rai. These were barely men—boys. Neither had gotten good marks in academy. Both were on probation for that reason. A Patrol Chief can be very intimidating when he holds your career in his hands."

Commander Gar paused and studied his own hands for a moment. "I spoke with some of the Patrol Chiefs. Their stories were also inconsistent. Some denied having said what their men claimed they had, others-" He shrugged. "But there was a common thread. The names of Division Chiefs Varaza and Nastan kept coming up—also that of a Patrol Chief named Ranjit."

"Varaza," repeated Jaya. "Yes. He seemed ... unsettled by my visit."

Gar shifted in his seat—his leathers voiced a protesting creak. "There is more. I heard about the attack on you. In view of your visit—what I had discovered—I wondered if the two things might not be connected. I went to the Sun Crescent Headquarters intending to visit the prisoner myself. He was dead when I arrived. Just. I was there, Nathu Rai, when the forensics team removed the poison ampoule from his mouth."

"Suicide?"

Gar's lips twitched. "That was suggested as a possibility by the Asvin in attendance, but he said it was by no means certain. The ampoule was of a soft, gelatinous substance. It was caught on one tooth." He paused again, then said, "You ask if it was suicide. I think not. The guards I interviewed claimed to have searched the man thoroughly and found nothing on his person. The man died while eating his dinner, Nathu Rai. I don't think he took that capsule voluntarily. I think it was in his food."

Jaya stood and paced toward the hearth. He could just see Ana behind the door, listening. Not wanting to give her away, he turned his face toward the fire.

"There is yet more," said Gar. He sounded like a man who had just bitten into a sour fruit. "Division Chief Varaza paid a visit to the Sun Crescent Headquarters less than an hour before the time of the prisoner's death."

Jaya returned to his chair. "He visited the prisoner?"

Gar shook his head. "That is not a matter of record, but he was seen entering the cell block by at least two patrolmen."

"Are visits to the cell block normally a matter of record?"

Commander Gar looked as if the fruit had become suddenly more sour. "Normally, yes."

Jaya's mind raced. Varaza. If Varaza was the one who planted poison in the thug's food ...

"It is a hard thing for me to accept, Nathu Rai, that such corruption has seeped into the ranks of the Sarngin. That a man—even such a man as that—should be murdered for the sake of petty greed."

Jaya glanced up at the Commander's face. Did he dare trust him —let him in on the larger implications of this? Or did he let him believe that it was as simple as that? He shifted his eyes from the brooding Gar to Ana, half-hidden behind the Parlor door.

She nodded. Trust him, her eyes said.

"The greed may be a good deal more than petty, Commander," Jaya said. "You're assuming I was attacked because I inquired into the corrupt dealings of some Sarngin officers and their men. I imagine you suspect Varaza of master-minding that attack."

Gar nodded.

"Are you familiar with the dispute between the Avasan Miner's Guild and the Kasi-Nawahr Consortium?"

"One hears and reads of nothing else."

"As a member of the Vrinda Varma, I was to vote on that issue. As a Sarojin, my vote carries ... an undue amount of weight. I suspect that someone would have liked to influence that vote."

"The Consortium?"

Jaya nodded. "A possibility."

"But you speak in the past tense. You were to vote-"

"The case has been remanded to the Inner Circle. I'm no longer a deciding factor."

Gar's brows disappeared under over-hanging fringe of dark hair. "Are you not? Let us assume that the attack on you was motivated by the desire to affect your vote. Did it?"

"No."

"The report states that these men claimed to be KNC wharfers in fear of being let go—members of a Worker's Coalition. Do you believe that?"

"I'm not sure. I've ... received some pressure from another quarter. From someone I know, without doubt, is connected at a high level to the KNC."

"Can we assume this person is aware of your suspicions?"

Jaya recalled the expression on Duran Prakash's face when he'd mentioned the KNC in the same breath with the word "attack." He nodded. "I think we can assume that."

"Can we not also assume that your testimony is critical to proving coercion?"

Jaya nodded again.

"And that a substantiated charge of coercion would end or severely damage the Consortium's political aspirations?"

The implications sat in Jaya's mind like huge cold blocks of stone. It had never occurred to him that the Consortium's aspirations were anything more than big business.

"You are very much a deciding factor, Nathu Rai—and very much in danger, if all this is so. But I wonder: Are these two things linked, or is Varaza simply a man of varied interests?"

∼

"Do you know what this is?" Kareen Devaki shook her fist in Ashur Badan's face, a chain dangling from her fingers.

"Off-hand, I'd say it's a necklace. Gold, by the look of it."

Kareen tossed the chain down on her partner's highly polished desk. It glinted in the light of the chandelier hanging just overhead. "Look at it. Closely."

"Ah!" he said. "Yes, it's leaf isn't it? The old etched style. We see enough of that around here, I'd say, not to get so excited about it."

"You fat toad," hissed Devaki. "Read it!"

Frowning, Badan picked up the delicately incised medallion and peered at it. "Anala Nadim—Onan. Dated: 5523-Pausha-9. ... Nadim," he repeated. His eyes met Devaki's. "You don't think-"

"I most certainly do think. Nadim is not a common name—except in Onan."

"Kareen, you're jumping to conclusions."

"Am I?" She pointed to the leaf. "Don't you think we'd better find out? We'll have to access the census records."

Ashur Badan's face was suddenly less jovial than usual. "You know what he'll say."

"Oh, he'll say we're every kind of idiot known to God. He'll say we've let an incredible opportunity slip through our fingers. And it's all thanks to that idiot Rishi. He had this for the better part of a week before he turned it over to us. This may be the end of everything, Ashur."

Badan shrugged. "You exaggerate. Our network is too valuable to him. He's not likely to toss it aside when things are going so well. He's too greedy and he enjoys our ... arrangement. Besides, how could we have known? Ah, we still don't know! She might not be any relation to Rokh Nadim at all."

"Or she might be in his immediate family. We need to let him know, Ashur. Now."

"Do we? Why can't we exploit this thing ourselves? Why not use it to retrieve our autonomy?"

"Why not? We're not big players in this game, Ashur. We're mice. Attractive, expedient, useful mice." She leaned across her partner's desk. "What if we try and fail? It's not just him we'd have to face. Remember that. This is not a game for small players anymore."

Ashur nearly pouted. "It was."

"Was, was—I'm talking about what is. We will not be let go easily. We are deeper in this every day and with this-" She snatched the id from his fingers. "With this, we are in over both our heads."

Ashur Badan shuffled the flimsies on his desk. "All right. I concede that an attempt to get out from under would probably..."

"Kill us?"

He glanced at her uneasily. "You don't think he'd-"

Devaki laughed brittley. "Him? No, not him. But his puppet-masters might. Don't judge others by yourself, Ashur. You wouldn't kill someone for the sake of maintaining our little kingdom, but they are different people playing in a different dimension and I suspect they have an Empire at stake."

"Jaya?"

Jaya barely glanced up from the buffet at which he filled his plate. "Ah, mother! It's been ages."

"It's been two days," said the Rani, moving to pour herself a cup of channa. She scooped a segmented asok from the buffet and put it on a plate. "And in two days, you have managed to turn this house completely upside down. When I got home last night I found armed guards at every entrance, men patrolling the grounds and a team of journalists preparing to storm the front gates. Can you explain any of this?"

Jaya turned to look at her and she found her hands could no longer hold her plate and cup. She put down the channa with a clatter, spilling it. Asok wedges rolled onto the sideboard.

"What happened to your face?"

"The same thing that happened to my ribs—a little bit of

campaigning on the part of ... some people in favor of crushing AGIM."

"What?" The Rani's breath stopped in her throat. "What are you saying?"

"More than I should. Excuse me." He literally fled into the gardens.

Melantha Sarojin stared after him. She was at the point of giving pursuit when Jivinta Mina entered the room.

"Well, good afternoon," said the older woman dryly. "You've been conspicuously absent. Sleeping late or were you ... out?"

"I was visiting my family in Mohan. Can you tell me what's been going on around here? What happened to Jaya?"

Mina raised her brows. "He didn't tell you?"

"He mumbled something about a campaign against AGIM and then said he was telling me more than he should. What is going on?"

"Maybe you should ask that fine man-friend of yours."

The Rani's brow furrowed. "Duran? What do Jaya's injuries have to do with Duran?"

Mina shrugged. "Maybe nothing, maybe everything. But he does have an interest in Jaya's vote."

"So does AGIM. So, probably do the Avasans living under our roof."

"Neither AGIM nor the Avasans living under our roof have dispatched a clutch of thugs to lobby the House Sarojin." Mina shrugged again and moved to sit at the dining table. "But, thankfully, lobbying—or threats—are futile now. Jaya's vote no longer figures in it."

"What does that mean?" Melantha gathered her channa and fruit and moved to the table.

"The Deva Radha has relieved the Vrinda Varma of the issue."

Melantha's felt weak with relief. "Then Jaya's involvement with this thing is at an end."

Mina made a moue with her lips. "Well, except for the small matter of the threats made to his life."

"Surely the Sarngin can handle that."

"The Sarngin!" snorted Mina disparagingly. "They've already managed to lose the one suspect they had in custody. I wouldn't expect too much of them, if I were you."

"How does one lose a suspect?"

"In this case, death by poisoning. Ah, but I've said too much." Mina smiled into the Rani's face. "The biscuits are very good, Melantha. You must try one."

~

"So. He will testify."

Duran Prakash snorted. "Of course he will testify. And we have no way to stop him—short of killing him, that is. In view of everything that's happened, that would be exceptionally stupid."

"Not if it's done correctly." Nigudha Bhrasta extracted a jellied leaf from the appetizer tray and put it into his mouth, obviously savoring the minty flavor.

Prakash bared his teeth in nothing like a smile. "Do you trust any of our 'associates' to do anything correctly? Besides which, any action against the Saroj would be immediately connected with us."

"Not necessarily." There was a flash of light from the wall monitor as it came to life. "It's the server."

They discussed inconsequential things until the domestic had served them and left. Then, Prakash's host picked up the thread of their previous conversation along with a forkful of seafood.

"Our young Lord has been pursuing certain other unhealthy avenues of curiosity. He seems to have noticed an upsurge in the number of muggings in the Port Zone that target Avasan tourists. He also noticed that those tourists are then subject to immediate arrest by our fine Sarngin."

Prakash's eyes widened. "Sarojin made that connection?"

He was favored with a grim smile. "You underestimate him, Duran. He is Bhaktasu Sarojin's son, after all."

"Hmm. But he is also Melantha Sarojin's son. With her predilection for the trivial and shallow-"

"I thought the beautiful Rani had quite captured your heart. Shallow, you call her?"

Prakash snorted indelicately. "She's captured only my lust, my friend. She has enough depth to satisfy that, if only she was willing."

"Tsk. Still not admitted to the Sacred Chamber, eh?"

"No, but at the door. You are familiar with the Bogar rites?"

"Vaguely. I have nowhere near the ... fascination with it that some do. You are considered a master, are you not?"

"I am. I find the satisfied female is willing to express gratitude if a rite is well-performed. And I do perform them well."

"Ah, and the Rani was grateful for your performance."

"Oh, yes. But not grateful enough. Still, I've gotten farther than any of her previous suitors. I interviewed them, you know. They all lied terribly."

His companion chewed thoughtfully. "Yes, you are in a most convenient position with regards to the Rani. The barometer of her fear."

"Fear?"

"For her son's wellbeing."

"She sold her KNC holdings. I'm not certain whether it was out of fear for her son or fear of him."

"Oh, I think it's fear for her son that motivates the Rani. The young mahesa is sticking his pristine horns into the corrupt business of Niraya-jinn. His mother might be convinced to warn him away from such dangerous curiosity. I doubt she would care how many Avasan yevetha are manufactured in Kasi."

"And if she fails to dissuade him?"

"Then we will at least have put in the minds of those closest to Sarojin's whelp the idea that the threat against him is from a different quarter altogether. The Worker's Coalition is perhaps a little to close to our front door for comfort."

"Ah. Sarojin dies and a handful of corrupt Sarngin are suspect. But won't that trail eventually lead to our door as well?"

"What trail? Dead men don't leave trails, and dishonored men tend to become dead men. The Sarngin are a proud lot. Even the crooked ones."

"What if the dalali is implicated?"

"There are hundreds of dalalis in the provinces, Duran. One will not be missed."

"The trail does not end with the dalali," Prakash observed.

"Our associate has been discreet. To a fault. A good thing—he is not expendable. The trail will end with the dalali.

"You wish me to warn the Rani that her son may be in danger as a result of his poking and prodding?"

"Certainly. You are her lover."

"I am her pleasure tool. I doubt love enters into it. But how am I, as Consortium Speaker, to know of this other business?"

He cringed as the shell of a resistant mollusk shattered in his companion's hands.

"You hear things, don't you? You're a legal expert. You have connections."

Prakash frowned. "I wouldn't want to raise her suspicions. She's shallow, not stupid. I-" He broke off and favored Nigudha Bhrasta with a slow, beatific smile. "I'll see her tonight," he said. "Yes ... I think I know how to handle this. I'll take care of it."

CHAPTER FOURTEEN

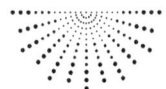

RAVI WANDERED through the Bazaar with seemingly aimless strides. He had a gaily decorated bag of roasted nuts in the crook of one arm and munched handfuls at his leisure. He examined each colorful stall, tent, and wagon with interest, stopped at one or two and asked prices, haggled at one and purchased a blue crystal on a beaded chain.

At the third booth from the end of the main thoroughfare he paused again and examined a painted bowl of great grace and beauty. He flagged down one of two girls behind the kiosk's improvised counter.

"How much is this bowl?" he asked.

"This is a very special bowl," said the girl. "It's for sale only to a very special person." She smiled up at him through eyes that glistened like pebbles at the bottom of a stream.

"I'm a very special person," said Ravi. "I have the Sight—the Jadu." He tapped his temple.

She laughed. "Do you now? Show me."

"I will tell you the story of this very special bowl. This bowl," he continued, running his hands over the satiny finish and closing his eyes, "is from another world. From a place where the wind paints the land with its own dust. A place where the sky is a frigid blue bowl and clouds are red splashes of dust. This bowl is from Avasa.

From Onan. Am I right?" He opened his eyes to see her laughing at him.

"So poetic! You're right. You are very special, indeed. The bowl is yours for twenty dagam."

"I'll take it. Have you any more?"

She gestured with her head at the wagon that formed the rear wall of the booth. "In the back."

"May I see them?"

"Surely." She picked up the bowl and signaled for Ravi to come around the end of the counter. She led him up a short flight of wooden steps and into the wagon.

Ravi surveyed the small room quickly as the door closed behind him. Three men sat at a table surmounted by an ancient wickless lamp. Two of them rose and faced him.

He bowed his head respectfully. "Pritam-sama," he said to the one man he recognized. "I am Ravidas, your servant. The Nathu Rai Sarojin sends his respectful greetings."

"You can dispense with the formality among us," said Pritam, clasping Ravi's hand. He gestured at the young man beside him. "This is Bala. And that-" He thumbed toward the table. "-is his father. Come, sit and give us your message."

Ravi took a seat across the table from Bala's father, who sat huddled in the shadows, sipping hot tea. He caught the sweet, winy fragrance of kesara. Behind him, the girl moved softly, making the wooden floor creak. She set a mug of the tea in front of him.

"Thank you," he said. He inhaled the perfume and took a sip. "I am sent to ask about Rokh Nadim. Can you tell me where he is?"

Pritam shook his head. "No, but I can tell you he is well."

"Then you know where he is. You can get a message to him quickly?"

"Yes."

Ravi sighed. "Ana-sa has been beyond anxiety. I'm happy to be able to tell her her father is safe."

"Can you give him a similar assurance? He knows of the attack on the Nathu Rai Sarojin. He is also anxious."

"I must be frank with you, Pritam-sama. We are all anxious. There are few people as bold as Sri Ana. The mahesa fears she is a danger to herself."

The man across from him was laughing—quietly, at first, then with less inhibition. He set his cup down on the table with a thump and guffawed. Pritam and Bala also seemed amused.

"What have I said?" asked Ravi.

"Sri Ana!" rumbled the old man's hoary voice. "That a Nadim should be ascribed sainthood by a Mehtaran! How rich an irony! You're a good man, Ravi." He brought his mirth under control. "Tell us more about your bold saint. Is she well?"

"She is very well, sama, and in the bosom of our family. She wishes to know that the family of Hadas Gupta has been notified of his safety."

Pritam nodded. "Tell Ana they were informed. They are grateful and send their thanks. But, Ravi, they are a mere handful. Reports are now coming in from all the settlements. Twenty-six families have reported members missing on Mehtar—wives, husbands, children. Forty-one people in all."

Ravi nodded, empathetic pain twisting his gut. He had never been separated from his own family. "I don't need to guess what happened to them. The same thing that happened to Hadas Gupta."

"Except that we know where Hadas is and that he is safe. We know nothing of the others. Not even how to find them."

"I promise you," said Ravi, "my mahesa will try. He's already gone to the Sarngin about it and may have an ally in that quarter. Could you get him a list of names?"

Pritam nodded. "If you think it would help, you shall have a list. We should be able to receive it during our next trans-chat home. That will be tonight."

The young man, Bala, made an impatient gesture. "You spoke of danger to Anala. Can your mahesa guarantee her safety?"

Ravi frowned into his tea and shook his head. "The people who were sent to frighten the Nathu Rai Sarojin quickly discovered that the way to the Sarojin is through his Avasan 'cousin.' I'm afraid that his attachment to Ana will be used as a weapon against him. I'm afraid that, through him, she has also become a target."

Bala's father stirred. "His attachment? You imply that your mahesa is fond of Anala?"

"Yes, sama."

"Do you believe she returns his affection?"

"I used a poor word, sama. One doesn't risk one's life for mere attachment. Have you a message for her from her father?"

The older man leaned into the light from the table lamp, the hair Ravi had thought gray and white becoming a curling carpet of garnet streaked with gold. His eyes shone like the noonday sky from a face the color of sun-washed sand.

"Tell Ana," he said, "that her father is alive and well and in Kasi, and that he will not leave without her."

Ravi rose and gave the respectful greeting. "May I tell her that I saw you, Nadim-sama?"

The older man chuckled, the sound rolling and rumbling deep in the broad chest. "You may. And take her my love."

"And mine," said Bala.

Ravi bowed and left, the potter-girl going before him. At the bottom of the steps, she handed him the bowl, her eyes sparkling with humor.

"Don't forget your special bowl," she said.

He grinned. "Ah, that would look suspicious, wouldn't it?"

She nodded, smiling. "We must not have suspicion." She leaned forward and kissed him on the lips.

He blushed.

She laughed at him, not unkindly. "You are special."

"What ... what is your name? In case I should need to find you again."

"My name is Lila ... and I'm easy to find. Look for the laughing Sun." She tipped her head toward the wagon, smiled at him, and went back to peddle her wares.

Ravi stared at the place she'd been, his eyes finally finding focus on the jovial, painted face of Mitras that decorated the wagon's curved door.

Lila, he thought. The laughter of the Divine. He glanced up at the real sun, playing hiding games with the clouds, then gazed past it to Something beyond.

"Smile on us, Tara-ji," he murmured. "Smile on us all."

"Father is in Kasi?" Ana started from her chair by the fire.

"Yes, Ana-sa. He and Bala send their love."

"Bala, too? Where are they, Ravi? Take me to them!"

Jaya put a hand on her shoulder and pushed her back into her chair. "Right now we're the only four people outside of his retinue who know your father is here. Do you want to take a chance on someone else finding out?"

"But there must be some way-"

Jivinta Mina leaned across from her own chair and laid a hand on Anala's arm. "Jaya is right, Ana. Your father's life is already in danger, and that danger increases every time one of us visits his hiding place."

His eyes on Ana's face, Ravi said: "I'm supposed to return to get a list of the missing Avasans. I could at least ask if it might be arranged for her to see him."

Jivinta raised her eyebrows. "In Lila's wagon? And what would someone like Anala want with an amorous young vendress?"

Ravi blushed slightly. "Lila also reads the stars and stones. I saw that painted on the side of her wagon."

"Ah!" Jivinta nodded approval. "Now that's something. Who'd notice an eccentric old woman going to have her fortune read? When will you return to Bazaar, Ravi?"

Ravi smiled. "Tomorrow morning. They were to trans-chat the list of names tonight."

The old Rani peered at him through bright and narrowed eyes, a smile curling the corners of her mouth. "So eager, Ravi? Am I to think you have developed a belief in the telling of fortunes? Or is it the pottery that makes you smile?"

Ravi blushed again and excused himself, claiming unspecified household duties to attend to.

Jivinta Mina announced that it was time to dress for dinner and moved with a sprightly gait to the door. She paused there and turned back.

"Hadas is in the Game Room," she said. "You might want to hurry him or he'll miss an enjoyable meal. The Rani will be dining with Prakash tonight, so we can have as much fun as we please."

She grinned saucily and exited, cane tapping lightly on the tiles of the hall.

Jaya grinned wryly and studied the pattern of the carpet. "I have to admit, I'm a little jealous of Hadas."

"Jealous?"

He shrugged. "He seems to have replaced me as her favorite grandson."

"That's ridiculous. No one could replace you in Jivinta Mina's heart, Jaya. Besides, Hadas is temporary. When all this is over, he'll go home to his family on Avasa. You'll always be here."

He glanced at her. "And you? Where will you be when this is over?"

She stared at him, eyes prying at his. After a moment at that futile task, she looked away.

"With my family, I hope."

"You could stay here, with us. It feels as if you've always been here."

"But I haven't always been here. I've always been on Avasa." She folded her hands together and pushed them between her knees. "I feel ... comfortable here, in this house with Jivinta and Ravi and his family ... and you—but your people, your city, your world—they're all so strange to me. I have no purpose here. It's not home."

"Is home a place, then? I always thought it was ... something else."

"It is something else. I just–" She shrugged, her eyes darting away from his. "I don't have words for it."

"I'm not sure I do either." He smoothed the front of his tunic, which didn't need smoothing. "Ana, do you really want to study for Orders?"

She glanced up at him. "Yes. Yes, I do."

"With the Deva Radha?"

She smiled and he could see her eagerness. "That would be the opportunity of a lifetime."

"Which would give your life here a purpose."

"Yes."

"You take your commitment to the Path seriously."

"Of course, I do." She made an impatient gesture. "Speak plainly, mahesa. I'm sick of skirting the issue. You ask how serious I am. What you want to know is if I would be willing to spend some moments in your bed. Long enough, say, for you to satisfy yourself before I embark on my devotions."

She shocked him into a half-considered reply. "No! Not moments. I don't want mere moments. I want you to stay."

"Then command me to stay and have done with it." There was challenge in her voice, in her eyes.

"I don't want that."

"Of course not. You want me to enslave myself willingly."

"I don't want you to enslave yourself at all."

"Nathu Rai, I know you don't understand this, but my freedom is in my bhakti. Ram-ji is my Lord, not you, not your passions, not mine. I would be a fool to burn up my freedom and the passion of my soul in a physical fire." Her eyes strayed to the door. "I believe in another Fire. A Fire that warms instead of burning; a passion that purifies, like the Fire and passion of bhakti. No, not like bhakti—it is bhakti, but devotion to a human beloved. I would gladly give my soul into that Fire, not for annihilation, but for union. I want to know a union with my human beloved that is a reflection of my union with the Divine. You don't believe in a Divine."

He didn't argue his belief or lack of it. He was suddenly sick of arguing. "Do you believe this is only a physical fire?"

"I don't know. But if it is, it will die out and leave ashes."

He took a step closer to her chair, raised a hand to her hair, and stroked it. "I don't think it will die out."

Her eyes glinted. "So you want me to stay until you're sure? You want me to give my body to you until you're certain you love the soul that goes with it?" She shook her head, her mouth twisted wryly. "You asked me once if your honor was just a spiritual abstract. What about mine? Should I just put it aside while you come to some decision? Should I become something other than what I am?"

Guilt gnawed sharply at his stomach. "No. No, you're right. I can't ask that of you ... or demand it. But I have to be honest and admit that I want to demand it ... Laldasa."

"That's what I'd always be, isn't it—your beloved slave."

She held her left hand before his face, then took his and lifted it to the same level. Raicree and dascree faced each other between them.

"We are unequal, Nathu Rai. And inequity cannot be brought to union."

Jaya grasped her hand with his own, bringing their marked palms together. The touch sent a thousand tongues of flame through him.

"These marks mean nothing. They're just so much pigmentation. You are more than my equal, Ana."

Her eyes met his again over their entwined fingers. "I hear the words, Nathu Rai. I have to ask myself if you truly believe them."

She pulled her fingers from his and slipped away.

Jaya Sarojin had to ask himself the same thing.

~

Duran Prakash arrived at the Sarojin Palace precisely on time and was therefore nearly ten minutes late by the time the security team had gotten through checking his id and searching his car and person. He was convinced Jaya Sarojin had given them special instructions to make the experience as embarrassing as possible for him.

He dined with the Rani Melantha in one of the smaller private parlors on the premiere floor—the Room of Moons she called it, since the dominant color was a soft, silvery whisper reminiscent of moonlight. She was not her usual talkative self and Prakash hoped that signified some anxiety over Jaya's run-in with the WoCoa thugs.

Over dessert she confirmed his hope, but not quite as he expected.

"Duran," she said, "what do you know about the attack on my son? Were you responsible?"

He nearly dropped a cup of scalding channa in his lap. "Melantha, what can you be thinking? Who would have put such a vicious idea into your head?"

Her eyes were on the fire in the half-moon hearth. Her fingers toyed with the folds of her gown.

"You wanted to influence his vote."

"I wanted him to vote sensibly and justly. I believed, and still do believe, that once all the facts were revealed he would have found the Consortium's case to be the stronger. I assure you, I sent no thugs to intimidate him."

That was probably the last truth he would tell this evening.

"Can you assure me that your masters didn't?"

"The Consortium doesn't conduct its business that way, Melantha, surely you know that. I shouldn't be discussing this with you."

"No one will discuss it with me, Duran. No one. Jivinta Mina said this afternoon that you knew why Jaya was attacked, then closed up as tight as Greed's jewel box."

"That I-?" Prakash was quite realistically shocked. Who'd have thought the old woman was half aware of what was going on?

"I supposed she must have meant the KNC was responsible."

"Ridiculous!"

"Is it? Who else would want to pressure him into throwing the Sarojin vote behind Kasi-Nawahr?"

"The Worker's Coalition."

"And who are they?"

"Only a simple group of fanatical and misguided souls acting out their fear. They're desperate men doing desperate things and we regret that heartily. You must not believe the Consortium condones their actions."

The Rani stood. "How desperate are you, Duran? How desperate are Nigudha Bhrasta and his Board of Directors?"

"Melantha, I assure you, the Directors of Kasi-Nawahr Associates have not been plotting to influence the Sarojin. By God, how could you think it? Nigudha Bhrasta is above reproach in his business dealings. Ask Namun Vedda, if you won't believe me. He's dealt with Bhrasta for years. Can you honestly picture him consorting with someone who'd send a troupe of henchmen after his godson?"

"No. Honestly, I can't. But Namun's dealings with the KNC do not make him privy to the secrets of its directors."

"The Board of Directors is innocent of this, Melantha. Nigudha Bhrasta is innocent of it. I give you my word."

"Ah. Your word." She nodded and moved away from the table toward the pale, arched mantelpiece. "How much is that worth, do you think?"

"Melantha, your distrust wounds me. I-" He cut off as the chamber door swung open and Ari appeared.

"Pardon, Rani, but the Vadin Bel Adivaram desires an audience with you. He says it's urgent."

The Rani's brow furrowed and she made a sweeping gesture with one hand as if to bat the intrusion away. "Adivaram? What could he want? Show him in, Aridas."

Ari bowed and moved silently back through the door. He returned seconds later with a distressed looking Bel Adivaram. The Vadin went directly to the Rani.

"My dear," he said, clasping her hand, "I must speak to you about your son."

The Rani's gaze flickered to Duran Prakash, drawing Adivaram's after it.

"Prakash-sama," the Vadin greeted him curtly. "My apologies for interrupting your obviously pleasant evening, but I must ask to have private words with the Rani Sarojin. I assure you it is important."

Prakash rose and bowed. "Vadin, your apologies are not necessary. Excuse me, Rani, I'll be in the Court Parlor."

The Rani nodded to him, then moved to sit on a couch flanking the hearth. She motioned Adivaram to a chair opposite.

He did not go to the Court Parlor. He went only as far as the corridor just beyond the chamber doors, which he left very slightly ajar. From his vantage point, he could see the back of the old Vadin's head and Melantha's face.

"You say you have some urgent business that concerns Jaya?" the Rani asked.

Adivaram spread his hands in a broad gesture. "To be completely frank, my dear, this could be a matter of life and death. Ah, I know," he said, apparently reacting to her expression of disbelief. "The old man loves to exaggerate. I assure you, dear Melantha, this time I do not. Jaya is embarking on a very dangerous exploration into things I fear he is ill-equipped to handle."

"What do you mean? What things? He's no longer involved with the case against AGIM."

"Oh, only incidentally. Besides, that is a matter of record with the Vrinda Varma and the Inner Circle. I would take any fears associated with that case to them. No, no. This has nothing to do with that."

The Rani's brows winged gracefully upward. "No? I thought everything had to do with that."

"Unfortunately, this is an entirely separate matter, one it would do me little good to take to the Vrinda Varma. It came to my attention as a matter of, em, internal Zone security."

"What did?"

"Your son has taken it upon himself to champion the cause of Avasan yevetha."

"He what?" The Rani's relaxed pose became suddenly rigid. She flushed, shook her head and made a languid move to rearrange her silken skirts. "How is this a matter of life and death?"

"There are people who have, shall we say, an interest in the, ah, disposal of these yevetha I mention. People who would rather that their disposal not be investigated."

"Don't be mysterious, Bel. It irritates me. What people?"

Adivaram cocked his head to one side as if about to impart a great confidence. "It has come to my attention, Rani, that a ring of thieves are plying a very lucrative and very specialized trade in my Zone. They are waylaying travelers as they wander the Warrows and stealing their id. The beneficiaries of this activity would seem to be one of our more prosperous brokerages. Your son is attempting to apply the leverage of his station against the masters of this illegal enterprise."

The Rani shrugged. "So tell him to leave off. Tell him it's for the Sarngin to sort out."

"Ah, I wish it were that simple. Your son, Rani, noble as he certainly is, is also stubborn. It would seem his, er, liaison with your stunning Avasan clanswoman has made him particularly tenacious about exposing these conspirators. The warnings given him by my officers were useless." He leaned forward, elbows resting on pudgy knees. "We suspect, Rani, that there are people of high position in the business community who derive much material wealth from these activities, and Jaya is placing himself in direct conflict with their interests. I do not exaggerate when I say that these people may be very dangerous. They have much to protect."

He leaned back in his chair and gazed at her in silence for a moment. Duran Prakash could well imagine the expression of deep concern on the old man's face.

"Believe me, if my authority extended over the members of the Taj House, I would order him to leave this matter to the Sarngin, but..." He shrugged. "Unless he does something illegal—which we both know is entirely unlikely—my hands are tied. You, my dear, were the only person I could think of in a position to influence the Nathu Rai. Please, I urge you, for your sake as well as his, make him see reason. I can do no more than pray he comes to no further harm."

The Rani glanced at him sharply, her eyes glittering strangely in her porcelain face. "Further harm? Are you linking the beating with this other business?"

"Those thugs were not what they seemed to be, Rani. I know that as well as Jaya does. They weren't KNC wharfers, you know. They were yevetha."

The Rani rose and moved to the mantelpiece, putting her back to her guest. "Why would they claim to be KNC wharfers if they were involved in this other business?"

"Can you think of a more perfect or ready-made cloak? You remarked on it yourself—it seems that everything is about the KNC and AGIM."

The Rani was silent for a moment, toying with a mantelpiece decoration. "What you say makes some sense. And I must admit, Bel, I am afraid for Jaya right now. I ... I have already lost my husband. I don't want to lose my son, as well."

"No, no. Of course not."

"I'll speak to him," she said. "He'll accuse me of meddling, of course, but I will try."

"Good." The Vadin nodded, rising. "I have no desire to see Jaya follow his father's path to the tomb. Well, my dear, I thank you for hearing me out. I must be going."

The Rani, still finding her mantelpiece of more interest than her guest, waved her hand dismissively. "Yes. Yes, of course," she murmured.

Bel Adivaram rounded the sofa and moved toward the door; Duran Prakash slid silently away from the door.

The Rani asked: "You mentioned Avasans in particular—Avasan yevetha. Why?"

Prakash paused to hear the answer.

"Because, of course, they become yevetha most easily, do they not? No cree."

Prakash hurried away down the hall to the Court Parlor before the old Vadin might see him. He was waiting there for Melantha, sipping wine when she arrived several minutes later. He set down his drink and came to take her hands as she stepped into the room, leading her solicitously to her throne. He liked to see her there. It reminded him how important their liaison was.

When she was seated, he knelt at her knee and gazed into her face. "My dear, you look troubled. Has the Vadin Adivaram brought you bad news?"

"He has brought distressing news. It seems my 'noble' son has gotten himself embroiled in the affairs of some Avasan yevetha at the behest of his so-called 'cousin.'"

"So-called?"

She shook her head and waved him aside. "Ah, the girl is a gaur-mouse, I'm sure of it. Snuggling up to a powerful relation."

Prakash raised his eyebrows. "The Vadin came to warn you about that?"

"No, the Vadin came to warn me that he suspects Jaya has angered or frightened some very unscrupulous people by threatening their livelihood, which has something to do with manufacturing yevetha from Avasan visitors so they can be sold to local dalalis. That's what I inferred, at any rate. He ... he said he was afraid for Jaya's life. He thought I might be able to influence Jaya—convince him to leave the matter to the Sarngin." She laughed. "Can you imagine that? He wants me to influence my son!"

"I take it he has tried to make the Nathu Rai see reason and failed?"

The Rani nodded. "There's nothing he could do, of course, except suggest politely and with all due respect that Jaya not endanger himself ... or interfere in the Vadin's jurisdiction."

Prakash gazed at her for a moment, losing his train of thought in the way the soft lighting in the room reflected in the silky, woody sheen of her hair. He shook away a wave of hunger and reached up to touch her temple.

"Melantha, your voice is as cool as moonlight, but I would be a fool to believe this façade of serenity. Can't you tell me, just once, what you're really feeling?"

She met his eyes for perhaps the first time since he'd known her. He could see the anxiety in them as clearly as if it had been written there. Her guard was slipping, finally.

"I'm frightened, Duran," she said. "Jaya is beyond my reach. In the last five years, he's slipped further and further away from me. Day by day. Inch by inch. I've built my wall; he's built his. I can't talk to him without it turning into an argument. We're adversaries locked in an uneasy truce, and even that collapses from time to time. And now ... God, if I come to him pleading concern, he'll laugh in my face—and with every right. What do I do, Duran? What can I say to him?"

A tear raced down her cheek, leaving a dark trail.

Prakash was astounded. Reflexively, he moved to catch the tear before it fell from her chin.

"Hold me," she said, and it was not a command, it was a plea.

~

Bel Adivaram arrived home and checked the messages on his private vicom. There was one—an audio message. The woman's voice said, "Bel, we must meet immediately. Tonight, if possible. It's urgent."

He checked the time. It wasn't late. He supposed a trip across town wouldn't be too much of an imposition, especially if there was some sort of compensation at the end of it.

He took his aircar and drove himself to a car park in the Silk District. He took a lift basket down to the sub-level and strolled the private, well-lit promenade that ran beneath the street. Once across, he selected another lift basket and emerged into a small parlor at the rear of the Badan-Devaki foyer. He'd barely seated himself in the sumptuous little room when Kareen Devaki appeared in response to the sensor that had chimed his presence.

"Well, Kareen, what brings me out this evening?"

"Something we should discuss privately. My parlor?" She gestured toward the lift.

He rose and followed her, frankly admiring the way her body caused the fabric of her gown to ripple and flow. He began to have delightful thoughts about her and was disappointed when it turned out that Ashur Badan was waiting for them in her private quarters.

"So," he said, ensconcing himself in a large cup chair, "it's business after all, is it?"

"I said it was urgent," Kareen told him.

"Yes, you did. And what is it, my dear, that seems so urgent to you?"

"This." She handed him the id necklace; watched carefully as he turned it over in his hands and read the inscription.

His face went through a rapid series of expressions. Finally, he looked up at her.

"You think this woman is a member of Rokh Nadim's family?"

"A distinct possibility, wouldn't you say?" asked Kareen. "Does he have a daughter?"

Adivaram nodded. "Yes. Yes, he does. I don't know her name, but I can certainly find out." His eyes glinted. "This is incredible! Where is she?"

Kareen made an uncharacteristically uncertain gesture. "We're not sure. The thieves didn't get this to us immediately. All of the females we processed that week have been placed."

Adivaram paled. "You mean, you've lost her?"

"No, no, Vadin!" Ashur leapt to reassure him. "It's simply a matter of tracking our sales for that week and contacting the owner. I'm sure we can find her."

Adivaram nodded. "Hmm. An inconvenience then, not a disaster. Well, let's find out if we even need to bother finding this girl. I'll need to use a vicom terminal."

"This way." Kareen led him to the terminal in her private office.

Personal information on the AGIM Chairman was harder to come by than he expected, but in about twenty minutes time, Bel Adivaram was looking at a list of names culled from the Avasan Census Base—they belonged to the members of Rokh Nadim's personal compound. He requested the names of only immediate family members and was rewarded with a list of six.

"There!" exclaimed Kareen, pointing over his shoulder at the display. "Anala Nadim. His daughter!"

Bel looked up at her and smiled. "Now, you must find her."

CHAPTER FIFTEEN

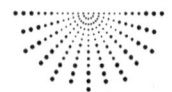

LILA SEEMED VERY pleased to see Ravi again and made much of him when he came by her kiosk. She took his arm and pulled it intimately around her waist, then walked him to her wagon, calling to one of her co-workers to carry on without her.

"I believe this young man wants me to read his stars and stones," she laughed and led him inside.

Taffik Pritam was alone in the wagon, seated at the small table. As they greeted each other, Lila moved to pour out some tea. Pritam removed a data wafer from his wrist bag and placed it on the table before Ravi.

"The list of missing Avasans is on this wafer. It has now grown to over fifty names. I wish you Tara's fortune in finding them."

Ravi took the wafer and slipped it into an inner pocket. "I have a message from Ana," he said. "She wants desperately to see her father."

Pritam frowned. "It could be dangerous for her to come here. Dangerous for both of them."

"We have an idea, sama, of how she might come here if not inconspicuously, at least safely."

They discussed the plan over their tea, coming to agree on a simple sequence of events. At last, Ravi rose to leave, but found Lila blocking his path, a blue bowl full of small stones in her hands.

"You must let me cast your fortune, Ravi-sama."

Ravi's face suffused with color. "I am Ravidas, memsa," he said. "I don't wish to cause offense, but I don't believe the future lies in either stones or stars."

Lila's dark eyes glinted. "Neither do I," she told him. "But I do believe it lies in each being's kriya-sakti. Your soul has intimations of your future, Ravi. I can read only what your soul allows me to read."

She held the bowl out to him. "Choose five stones. One each for body, spirit and soul; two for Ram-ji."

He hesitated a moment, then reached into the bowl and selected a handful of small, smooth stones.

"Now, hold them in your hand—tightly."

He did as she directed, glancing obliquely at Taffik Pritam, who sat at the table nursing his third cup of tea. The Avasan was smiling at him.

"Humor her," he mouthed.

Ravi turned his eyes back to Lila. "What now?"

Her smile was sweetly sly. "You have never done this before?"

"No. I told you, I don't believe in it."

She nodded, then moved to the table. She set the bowl down on a chair and spread the top apron of her many-layered skirts on the table.

"Cast the stones there," she said.

He did, and watched Lila bend her smiling face toward the stones to read them. Taffik Pritam now seemed openly amused and Ravi was certain he did not like being a source of humor. Still, he bore with it; he had no choice.

Lila held a hand over the random arrangement of stones, fingers spread. "You are a man of patience and honesty. You like order in your universe and you abide by order's rule. You are greatly trusted by others."

Taffik Pritam chuckled. "Please, Lila, tell the man something that is not patently obvious. Of course, he is patient; he is putting up with this distraction. We know he's honest, since he told you what he thinks of all this. As for order and trustworthiness,"—he shrugged—"he would need both to be in charge of the Nathu Rai's household."

Lila colored. "The stones should never be read before an audience. The next time you come, Ravi, I'll read them for you, alone."

She gathered up the stones and put them into a small bag that dangled at the waist of her skirt, then slipped the bag beneath her waist band.

"Now, I must go back to my pottery and give Irini a break. I will see you again, Ravi."

She stretched up to kiss him, then left the wagon.

Pritam chuckled. "Ravi, my friend, you are a marked man. By tossing the fortune stones on her skirts, Lila has just claimed your future. You are betrothed."

~

Sitting at Jaya's personal vicom terminal, Ana pored over the list of names, then pointed at the screen. "Feirkald. I know that family; they're from Tadushk. And this one—Saed Kala—he lives on the southern side of Onan with his wife and children. He's foreman at Fardana Mines."

"You mean, he was foreman," said Hadas, from behind her. "Now he's probably-" He broke off with a strangled cry and thrust his finger onto one of the names, his face ashen. "Purus Betiq! Ana, she's my ... she's one of my sister's best friends! She left the settlement about a week before I did. She was supposed to come over with Belia, but her family didn't have the price of passage then."

He straightened, eyes grim and glittering with tears. "If only she had been with Belia. Neither of them might be lost."

Ana rested a hand on his arm. "We'll get her back, Hadas. We'll get them all back."

"How? How can we even find them? They're spread all over this city by now. Maybe even all over the continent. God knows what might have happened to them. They may not even be alive."

"Stop!" Ana rose from her chair, grasped his shoulders, and shook him. "Listen, Hadas. For every person on this list there is a record in the Badan-Devaki. I'm sure of it. Maybe not names—I'm not sure they care about names—but descriptions, identifying marks, probably even images."

Hadas took a deep breath, nodded. "Yes. Yes, of course. You're right. Badan-Devaki is a business—a big business. They must process a lot of people; maybe hundreds every month. That's inventory. Businesses track inventory. My father and mother keep inventory for the inn on the vicom. Every stick of furniture, every towel, every plate in the channara. The dalali will do no less. They did take my image while I was there, and asked me my name."

Ana tugged at her lower lip, glancing down at the vicom screen. "I wonder how I can get into that place without being noticed?"

"Simple. Put on your insulsuit and go for a stroll in the Port Zone."

Ana grimaced. "No, thank you. I've done that once already."

She sank back into the chair, while Hadas perched on the edge of Jaya's desk.

"You could go in as a customer," he suggested. "Try to get lost in the right place-"

Ana shook her head. "Where's the right place? I don't know my way around that building—I've only seen a small portion of it. And if I got caught..."

"What about the Nathu Rai?" asked Hadas. "Surely he's been to their private offices. He's a mahesa, after all."

"Jaya is rather unorthodox, as you've no doubt noticed. I think, when he took me there, it was the first time he'd ever been inside the place."

Hadas made a frustrated noise. "Well, you came there to get me —that makes you a customer. Wouldn't customers be invited to auctions? If you could get inside..."

The names blurred before Ana's eyes. Get inside, yes, but how?

～

She was distracted all afternoon, barely touching lunch. Immediately after that tense meal, she confronted Jaya.

"Take me to the Badan-Devaki," she demanded.

"What?" He paused in the act of skipping a stone across the pond.

"I have to get in there, Jaya. I have to get into their files."

He looked back to the pond and flipped another stone at its rippling surface. "It's that list, isn't it? You want to see if they've got one that matches it."

"That's reasonable, isn't it?"

"Certainly. And dangerous. And futile."

Her ire flared. "Why, futile?"

"Let's say you find the names of even some of the people on that list in the B&D's files. What then?"

"Then, you tell Commander Gar and he gets the people back to their families and puts Badan and Devaki where they belong—in prison."

"How, Ana? How does he do that? With what proof?" He turned to look at her. "So, they processed Avasans, and we suspect those Avasans were targeted and we suspect some Sarngin are being paid to collect them. How do we prove it? We'd have to connect Badan-Devaki to the thieves—solidly and irrefutably—and if we wanted to get any of the bent Sarngin, then we'd have to connect them, as well. Getting into their files won't do that."

"But it will locate those people. My people. Children, some of them. Younger than Hadas. Hadas has lost his sister and one of their closest friends to that lot. Don't you care?"

He gazed at her balefully. "What do you think? Of course, I care. But finding those people—and they're as much mine as they are yours—won't make everything right. This thing is like a growth, Ana. Like sour-wort root. The more of it we dig up, the more we find branching out in all directions. This goes further than Badan-Devaki and some greedy Sarngin. Somehow the Worker's Coalition is involved, and possibly the Consortium."

"So, what then? We just do nothing?"

"No. We proceed, but cautiously. We figure out what kind of evidence we need and we try to obtain it."

She studied him suspiciously. "You and Gar have a plan?"

He made a non-committal gesture with his head, "Nothing so definite as a plan."

"Tell me!" she insisted, planting herself right in front of him.

He opened his mouth as if to demur, then said: "Gar still doesn't know you're involved in this. It's not that I don't trust him, exactly. I'm just not sure on what level he's committed to uncovering this ... conspiracy. Right now, I'm inclined to think it's just a matter of personal and professional pride."

Ana shrugged. "So, he doesn't need to know I'm involved. Just tell me what you're thinking."

Jaya sat cross-legged on the grass and signaled Ana to join him. When she'd dropped down across from him, he said, "Ask yourself something: If the thieves aren't taking money—or at least not much —how is Parva Rishi financing his high life?"

"He's being paid by someone. I'd guess Badan-Devaki."

"Ah, but how do they know what to pay him? I doubt he's on salary."

"Don't patronize me, mahesa. They pay by the head—that's the only way that makes sense. And the next question you will ask is: How do they know what to pay, since not every yevetha that's brought in is Rishi's work? And the answer is: The leaf that's being taken must serve as redemption tokens. The thieves get paid for the number of id leaves they present to the Badan-Devaki."

Jaya nodded. "That's what we thought, too."

Ana's brows arched. "Then you've introduced Gar to Govi?"

"It seemed important that I produce at least one informant, so I chose Govi. Govi described what he'd seen behind the dalali and that was when I had the thought that the packets being delivered might be the stolen leaf. Gar was especially interested in the weapons Govi saw. He thought that might give just cause to investigate the doings in the back alley."

Ana's heart blazed with raptor fury. "That's it, then. That's the evidence we need to tie Badan-Devaki to the thieves!"

"We?" asked Jaya wryly.

"You're not going to leave me out of this!"

"For your own safety, yes. No, listen, Ana!" He laid a finger across her open mouth. "This is Gar's investigation."

"Then introduce me to Gar and let me in on it!"

"I can't. I can't forget that there are some dangerous people involved in this. Someone was willing to commit murder to silence that thug. I don't know what they'd do if they knew Rokh Nadim's daughter was within reach."

Ana shivered as a sudden realization struck. "Forgive me, mahesa, but if we're right about the leaf being exchanged for money, then someone knows I'm in reach already."

Jaya had gone into seclusion with Mall Gar and Govi, leaving Ana to her own devices.

Unwise of him, Ana thought.

She played some card games with Hadas and Dana, then went into a secret meeting of her own with Mina, Ravi, and Heli to plot a clandestine visit to the Bazaar. She longed to see her father, yearned for home and family as she had once yearned for water while stranded in a sandcat during a red blow.

Yet, prayer and meditation had led her to know that her future was on Mehtar—not with Jaya, but at the Asra, with the Deva Radha. She was Avasan, casteless and, worst of all, Genda Sita.

She hadn't trumpeted her racial heritage, but she'd made no secret of it either. The Deva Radha and Jaya Sarojin both knew what she was. She was aware that if origin nor caste nor race mattered to a religious Order, it most certainly mattered to the Nathu Rai of Kasi, despite his talk of equality. He could not marry himself to the casteless daughter of a gaur miner—a Snowflake— even were he to desire such a union. She knew with certainty that if she stayed with him in any other capacity, she would immediately cease to be the person for whom he claimed both desire and respect.

Desire and respect. Ana found wry humor in that peculiar juxtaposition of emotion. A paradox, surely. "Laldasa," he'd called her—his beloved slave. That patronizing endearment had wounded, but Ana was willing to forgive. She loved Jaya Sarojin and would freely admit it to him. She would gladly die for him—but she would not, could not, betray her bhakti for him.

When thought proved unproductive, Ana wandered into the library in search of something to read. She'd just seated herself in the window seat with a reader when she spotted a familiar bound volume sitting on the adjacent serving table. THE ONE SOUGHT was embossed in silver across the midnight blue cover.

She picked it up and opened it, finding a marker at the Parable of the Devi's Garden. She frowned. Who, in this household, would be reading a Rohin text? Had Jaya's curiosity about the Rohin Path prompted him to this?

She grimaced. No doubt he was looking for a hole in the fabric of her faith. She chastised herself immediately for the petty thought, knowing it was motivated by her own sense of outrage that the color of her skin or the place of her birth mandated that he see her as an inferior.

"Ah! Here you are!" The cool female voice came from the open doorway.

Ana glanced up to see the Rani gazing at her, her smooth face adorned in its customary impenetrable expression. The older woman closed the door behind her and glided into the room on a breeze laden with exotic perfume. She came to the center of the soft mulberry and cream carpet that lay before the window seat and faced Ana with icy hauteur.

"Who are you?" she asked bluntly.

Ana froze, barely even blinking. "I don't know what you mean."

"You are obviously not a Rani of the House Sadira—if such a House even exists ... are you?"

And closed the little book and clutched it tightly in her hands. "No, Rani. I am not."

Melantha Sarojin's perfect brows rose in mute surprise. She recovered her aplomb swiftly and pressed on. "You're not a Rani at all, are you?"

"No. How did you know?"

"A friend of mine told me that my son was championing the cause of Avasan yevetha. He happened to mention that Avasans, when deprived of their leaf become instantly yevetha because they have no cree. Though you are Avasan, you have a cree. A dascree, unless I'm very much mistaken."

Ana shook her head. "You're not mistaken, Rani."

"I thought as much."

The Rani seated herself in a chair across from Ana, smoothing her pantalons.

Ana had the strong impression she'd sat down because her legs were shaking. She watched as the Rani took a moment to adjust the impressive collection of rings on her delicate fingers. Their eyes collided as the older woman raised hers to Ana's face.

"Why didn't you lie? You could have told me that since your family was originally from Mehtar you had a raicree."

"I may not be a Rani, but I am Rohin. That much is true. I won't lie to you. I hate lies. I've disliked this subterfuge. I was resigned to being a dasa in this household. Your son wouldn't accept that. He felt it was unjust. This is the way he ... dealt with the injustice."

"How, then, did you get your dascree?"

Ana sighed. "I came to Mehtar to buy mining equipment

unavailable on Avasa. On my first day in Kasi, I was attacked by a band of thieves. They took my money and my leaf and left me lying in a woodland near the Bazaar. Jaya happened to see me stumbling across the grounds and came to my aid. If he'd been two seconds later the Sarngin would have had me. As it was, they knew I was yevetha. They followed us. Jaya had to take me to a dalali for processing while they watched to make sure it was done."

"So, you became his cunnidasa."

Ana's abdomen twisted into a knot. Her cheeks flamed. "No, Rani. Your son has never demanded it. He's made me the keeper of my own honor."

"Hmm. And your Avasan friend—he's also das?"

"Yes."

The Rani nodded. "So now you've gotten my son embroiled in trying to keep any more Avasans from falling into the evil clutches of some dalali."

Ana struggled to control her temper in the face of Melantha Sarojin's facetious tone.

"It's not the dalali I'm worried about, Rani. It's what becomes of them when they leave it. Jaya allied himself with us willingly. We didn't 'embroil' him in anything."

"Us?" repeated the Rani. "I think Jaya allied himself to you. I must give you credit. I've never seen him so completely beguiled by anyone. Or should I say 'enchanted?' I've heard things about you Rohin..." The Rani was studying her again.

Is that it then? Ana thought, when the other woman fell silent. Is she content to believe I'm just an unfortunate witch?

She was not. "So then, if you are not the Rani Ana Sadira, who are you?" Her eyes were sharp, demanding.

Ana didn't answer.

"Well?"

"No one of any importance."

"If you are important to my son, for whatever reason, you are important to me. Who are you? What is your name?"

Ana licked her lips. How parched they were.

"Anala Nadim," she said.

The Rani shook her head, an odd expression twisting her mouth, then, incredibly, she began to laugh. It was one of those laughs Ana had read about in legend—pure and high and flute-like

—and she wondered if one could be born with such a laugh or had to cultivate it. When Melantha Sarojin had gotten her mirth under control, she sat back in her chair and gazed at Ana through dark, glistening eyes.

"You are Rokh Nadim's daughter?"

"Yes."

"What an incredible vise that must have put Jaya in politically!"

"And morally," observed Ana. "That's why I couldn't be Anala Nadim. If anyone knew I was in his household, they'd think he was biased toward AGIM."

The Rani chuckled. "But, of course, he wasn't, was he?"

"No. But he was trying to help me out of my personal predicament—along with the fifty some odd other Avasans who have disappeared in Kasi in the last several months."

The Rani was visibly stunned. "As many as that?"

"More, by now."

"That's why he was beaten—because someone doesn't want their dirty little business disrupted?"

"No. That was a result of the clash between the Miner's Guild and the KNC."

"Was it? My friend says not and, frankly, I have more reason to trust his word than I do yours." She studied Ana speculatively. "This has suddenly gotten very interesting. Do you know who Duran Prakash is?"

Ana's eyes shifted involuntarily aside. "He's the KNC legal representative."

"He's also my ... lover. Do you have any idea what he might do with this information?"

Ana knew her face must be as pale as Mehtar's three moons. "Yes."

"Can you think of any reason I shouldn't go to him and tell him everything I know?"

Ana brought her eyes back to Melantha Sarojin's face. "I know you don't care what happens to me or my father or my world, but I think you love your son. And I think you know what it would do to him if this came out."

The Rani rose and moved to the door, stretching the moment unbearably.

"It's something for me to think about, I suppose. Perhaps I'll let you know what I decide." She paused with her hand on the latch, her back still to Ana. "My son won't marry you, you know."

"That has never been a possibility."

The Rani's shoulders shifted. "You underestimate yourself—but you must realize that the children of such a union would be ... unacceptable. Pale half-castes. Accursed."

"Not on Avasa."

Now the Rani turned, her eyes black and glittering as the jet beads at her tawny throat. "Jaya will never go to Avasa. His place is here—as the head of the Saroj, Nathu Rai of Kasi and One of the Nine, in his time."

"I know that."

"As long as we understand each other," said the Rani. Her departure was silent and sweet-smelling.

Ana closed her eyes and slumped in sudden exhaustion. "I will never understand you," she whispered.

∾

THE PARABLE OF THE DEVI'S GARDEN

A bhakta was set by Ji upon the Upward Path to tread it in search of his Beloved. He carried a gift for her near his heart which he would give her when she said to him the hidden Word which only the Lover, the Beloved, and the God of All know.

One day he passed by a garden of great beauty and heard a sweet voice singing strange songs. He entered the garden and found in it a fountain of the most delicious beverage. The color was golden, the scent was of the jambu, the sound it made as it fell into its bowl was the song he had heard.

How the bhakta thirsted for the taste of the drink! How he longed to bathe in the golden liquid! But he had taken a vow not to rest but in the Garden of his Beloved, not to drink until he reached the Fountain of his ultimate desire.

He turned to go, closing his ears to the song of the golden water, and saw the most beautiful of fruits hanging from the most wonderful of asok trees. He realized suddenly how hungry he was.

A voice like a soft rain spoke, saying, "You may have the fruit, O bhakta, and the water also, if you give to me the gift you carry near your heart."

The bhakta turned and saw a Devi—the Essence of Beauty—standing before him. His heart told him to leave the place, but he sat down in the shade of the asok tree where the golden fruit of non-sorrow hung just before his face and where he could see the fountain and the Devi who sat on its rim. The longer he sat, the more beautiful the garden seemed and the more at home he felt there.

"Perhaps," he told himself, "this is my Beloved. Perhaps I am supposed to be here. But she has not said she is my Beloved. She has not revealed the hidden Word. How can I know for certain?"

He pondered his dilemma a bit more, then thought, "If I taste the fruit and the water, surely then I will know if this is the right Garden. Surely then she will tell me the Word."

So the bhakta took the fruit from the asok tree and bit into it. The taste was as wonderful as he had imagined. He went to the fountain and drank—just a sip at first, then he drank his fill. He ate more of the fruit and drank more of the water. Then, sleepy and content, he lay down and slept while the Devi stroked his hair and sang.

When he awoke, the garden was gone, the Devi was gone, and his gift was gone with her. He no longer had it to give to his Beloved. More horrible still, was that the Path was no longer clear, for the sand of the desert had covered it.

He found its traces and stumbled along it, alone and afraid, hoping for a glimpse of the Devi. He journeyed long and, with every step, the taste of the fruit and the memory of the song twisted themselves more deeply into his heart until he found that whatever garden he passed by, he compared it to that first one, and found it lacking. And because he was afraid of finding his Beloved in each one, but had no gift to give her, he never dared to step within.

So he wandered, carrying the memory of the Devi's Garden always in his heart. The taste of that fruit and that water had ruined for him all other refreshment. So, he said, "The fruit I ate was not asok (non-sorrow) but asat (nothing)."

CHAPTER SIXTEEN

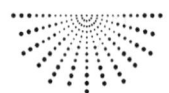

"I REGRET, Nathu Rai, that I am unable to trust more of my men."

Mall Gar gazed out the mullioned doors of Jaya Sarojin's private study, his eyes only vaguely registering the vernal glow of growth beyond.

"You can trust mine," Jaya assured him. "How many will we need?"

"A small group for the inside work. If you can give me seven, maybe eight men, that should suffice. If we need reinforcements they can be called out at the last minute—so that they can give nothing away."

"I think I can manage that many, including myself."

Gar turned, appalled at the suggestion. "You, Nathu Rai? You can't take part in this raid. It's unthinkable."

"It's unthinkable that I not be part of it. I have ... a somewhat personal stake in this. It's a matter of honor and of something more than honor."

"That being?"

"Friendship."

"Your other informant?" guessed Gar.

"My other informant. Everything dear to that person is threatened by this in ways I'm only dimly beginning to understand."

Gar nodded, then glanced at Govi, who sat by the fire, looking more like a well-fed mahesa than a beggar. Or at least, Gar thought, like a mahesa's well-fed pet.

He gestured at the table where he had placed a folio of maps. "Summon your men and we shall begin," he said, only belatedly realizing he had issued an order to his Nathu Rai.

He glanced at Jaya's face, his mouth open in apology, but saw only amusement there.

"You remind me of my father, Commander," said Jaya. "He was also a decisive man."

He rang for the others, who appeared within minutes, and they began, Commander Gar leading the discussion of timing and tactics.

"We have done some reconnoitering," he said with a nod at Govi, "and have located a vantage point here." His finger pressed a spot on the detailed map of the Silk District's main avenue. "From a point on the roof of the building facing the Badan-Devaki across the alley, the rear entrance is in plain sight. The guards' activities are clearly visible, as are any visitors to their post."

"Traffic?" asked Jaya.

"Only service wagons," said Govi quickly. "Refuse wagon, twice weekly at dawn—Kistna and Mu'ad; linens weekly on Sakya; food-stuffs pretty regular—first, fourth and eighth day of each week, plus special deliveries." He shrugged and tilted his head. "A busy alley—but on a schedule."

"Ah," said Jaya, "but has the schedule changed since you got hustled out of the alley?"

Gar raised an eyebrow. "It should be easy enough to find out about the refuse wagon, but we have no way of knowing who delivers their foodstuffs and linens, short of asking them."

"Tripura," said Govi. "Tripura brings the food; Lipyate, the linens. Oh, and there is a couture—Akala House—that delivers clothing and toiletees."

"That's 'toiletries,' and you were a very nosy neighbor," observed Jaya.

"The air wagons were not as I'd call slinkers-in. They made a big old blow where I'd tucked up. So, I had frequent occasion to read them."

"You read?" asked Gar, surprised.

Govi made a rude gesture at his own head. "Crazy, not ignorant," he said.

Mall Gar smiled. "Then, thanks to you, we shall know these schedules and determine how best to use them."

～

"This description matches none of the young women the Sarngin brought in last week."

Ashur Badan made a frustrated noise between his compressed lips and scrolled the data past his eyes again.

"Ah, well, here—this one has dark reddish hair, but dark skin, as well. Not even Avasan ... from some loggertown. These are Avasan, but all the wrong coloring, wrong names..."

"She might well have lied about her name," said Kareen Devaki.

"But not about the color of her skin, eyes, and hair."

Kareen jingled her bracelets impatiently. "Then perhaps someone else brought her in. Maybe-"

Ashur's eyes met hers on a shared recollection.

"My God, how could I have forgotten?"

"Or I," said Kareen acidly. "I recall thinking I would sell my pride to spend one night in her Genda skin ... in that House."

Ashur snorted. "In his bed, you mean. Ah, yes! That must be her, the Sarojin's find. Then we're looking in the wrong place." He patted at the keyboard. "There she is! Nameless girl, private processing, Jaya Sarojin's personal cree."

Kareen leaned over his shoulder to peer at the full-face and profile images taken during the quick-processing.

"That's the woman. Damn."

"Ji, she's exquisite!"

"Don't drool—think! How are we going to get her out of that House?"

"We could buy her back."

"What reason could we give? She was never ours to begin with. And why should he sell her? He certainly doesn't need whatever money we might offer. Besides which, there's every possibility that he knows who she is. Send for Adivaram."

"He's already here. He came in about half an hour ago for the private auction. Dare we interrupt his enjoyment?"

"Dare we not?"

The Vadin, when he arrived in Kareen Devaki's office, was already rubbing his hands together, gleefully.

"Well? Where is she?"

"In the Sarojin Palace," said Kareen.

"In the-" The Vadin's glee was blown to the four winds. His face suffused with violent color. "By the mount of Indra—it-it must be the same woman!"

"The same woman, Vadin?"

Adivaram made a cyclic gesture with one hand. "The one he's been parading around as his 'Avasan cousin.' A Rani of the House Sadira; some obscure branch of the Saroj. A rare beauty; cherry-colored hair, eyes like the snow clouds. Yes! Damn! I sat at table with her just days ago and had no idea-" He cut off in mid-sentence, his hands fidgeting with the silk shawl that covered his shoulders. "Ji! If this is the woman ... ! She will testify!" His eyes snapped to the dalal. "Your vicom."

Kareen Devaki gestured at the device then herded her partner toward the doorway. There, they stopped, hovering. Adivaram was already on the link, using the earpieces for privacy, his face intent on the screen as he spoke.

"Believe me, I do not interrupt you frivolously, so cease glaring at me like a fractious child. Your 'friend' will want to hear this, too, so have him gather 'round. The so-called 'Rani' our Nathu Rai has been embellishing his presence with is a dasa processed by Badan-Devaki."

The Vadin waited silently while this news elicited a response at the other end of the comlink. Watching, Kareen Devaki smiled, grudgingly admiring how Adivaram played his fish. She did not move to see the face he studied so archly. She suspected whose it might be, but was not permitted to be certain.

"I'm gratified you find the news so titillating," said Adivaram dryly. "Now let me tell you who this dasa is. Her name is Anala Nadim. You are familiar with that name?"

He sat back in his chair and nodded, fingers laced over his expansive girth. "Yes, I thought so. I would wager she is at the heart of our young Lord's sudden interest in the affairs of those unfortunate enough to wander Kasi without the proper identification. She was, you realize, the 'clanswoman' who was with him during the attack of the Coalitionists."

Kareen could hear the vicom audio spike from across the room.

Adivaram winced, then said, "Yes, and she will probably be called to testify in the next day or so before the Inner Circle."

He pulled the earpieces away suddenly and gave them a baleful glance. "Damn it! You're deafening me! ... Yes! Yes, I know, but she is also Rokh Nadim's daughter and, I assure you, that will count for something with the Circle. ... No, I would not recommend that. You were lucky once, but I think a repeat would raise suspicions. You don't need Sarojin dead, you need him in your pocket. ... It can be done—he's not his father—and I think the woman is the key to all of it. If you have her, you have not only the Nathu Rai Sarojin, but Rokh Nadim, as well. And if you have Nadim, you have the Guild. So now, the question is: How can you have the woman?"

There was a moment of silence, during which the Vadin nodded and made rumbles of agreement. At last he made a dismissive gesture and said, "I'll wait here for your call."

He removed the earpieces and tugged at his ears.

"Your puppet-masters play the big game, don't they?" asked Kareen.

Adivaram's glare quashed her curiosity. "That is absolutely none of your business, and if you know what's good for you, you'll keep it that way."

"I don't care who they are," said Ashur Badan from the doorway behind his partner. "What are they going to do?"

"They are thinking," said Adivaram. "We should all pray their thought bears fruit."

Duran Prakash stared at the kinetically moving palette of one of his spectacular collection of light paintings, but failed to enjoy the display.

"A.N.," he said. "Damn! It was right there for me to see, but I was so drunk with that Sarojin witch, I missed it."

"What are you babbling about?" asked his companion.

"At the Mesha Fest when I went through that girl's wardrobe, there was an insulsuit hidden among the whispwear. It was well-worn and had the initials 'A.N.' on the breast. The girl's name being 'Ana,' I simply assumed the last letter had been torn away."

Nigudha Bhrasta gazed at him steadily, eyes dark with acid. "You never mentioned this insulsuit before. Didn't you think it significant?"

"I ... I..."

Bhrasta shook his head and laughed. "Damn you to Niraya Hell, Prakash! Are you so besotted with Melantha Sarojin that you didn't even think to question the presence of such a garment in the wardrobe of a Sarojin clanswoman?"

"She's Avasan. Avasans wear insulsuits."

"The working classes wear insulsuits. Miners wear insulsuits. Did it never occur to you that a Rani would not?" Bhrasta couched the question in a light purring tone that made Duran Prakash sweat.

"But she-she has a raicree! I saw it when she greeted the Deva Radha."

"Avasans don't have cree. Unless they've been made das. I should think you would know that. You purport to be our legal expert."

Prakash flushed. "My area of expertise is corporate law. I never had occasion to study caste law."

"No doubt you were too busy studying the Bogar to have the time ... or the energy. Sometimes you disgust me, Duran. Indulging in such unsavory and pagan practices."

"It didn't disgust you when you thought my mastery of the Bogar was an asset. It's an asset that's availed you and the Consortium very well, my friend. Or have you forgotten how useful it's been in my dealings with the Rani Sarojin?"

Bhrasta seated himself. "Is the Rani now of the opinion that her precious son's injuries were the result of his prying into the other matter?"

Prakash nodded, forcing himself to relax back into his chair. His temper had come close to being uncorked and that, with this man, would have been disastrous. Friends they might be, but he was still an employee. He had not to forget that ... though it rankled.

"I arranged for Adivaram to interrupt our dinner the other night with his concern for the young mahesa," he said.

"Then she's of no further concern to us."

Prakash smiled. "She is of concern to me. I am now her lover."

His companion seemed less than impressed. "How important

you make it sound. Lovers! Next I suppose you'll tell me you've attained surata with her, as well."

"Isn't that the point of it all?"

Bhrasta regarded him with renewed interest. "Have you attained it, then—the Bliss?"

"Yes. Why should you care?"

"I don't, but we have a mutual friend who is also most interested in these ... mystical quests and chimeras. He'll be delighted to hear you were finally able to achieve your ... heart's desire. Unfortunate that you will no longer be able to grant the Rani that level of attention."

"What?" Prakash nearly held his breath.

"You will no longer pursue intimacy with Melantha Sarojin. At least not until things are under control."

"You can't ... order me-"

"I certainly can. I just did. You are lust-drunk around that woman. Stay out of her bed and keep her out of yours until we are in control of this situation. Now, let's get down to business—how are we going to lure the Rohina out of the Sarojin Palace?"

"Hasn't it occurred to you," said Prakash, forcing his voice to remain even, "that the Rani may be useful to us in that endeavor? If she thought the woman was dangerous to her son, she might drive her out of the Palace for us. My relationship with her gives me a distinct advantage when it comes to credibility."

He leaned forward across the desk, his fist clenched as if around a jewel. "She cried in my arms that night. She bared her soul to me."

"And then her body, eh?"

Prakash sat back abruptly. "You have the soul of a purchasing clerk. The point is she trusts me. No man has made love to her since Bhaktasu Sarojin. No man but me!"

There was a long moment of silence during which Duran Prakash watched the darkly thoughtful face, waiting to know the effectiveness of his ploy.

At last Bhrasta spoke. "Tell her you have proof the woman is an impostor. Tell her the woman is an AGIM agent sent to gather information and sway the Sarojin vote. Tell her the woman is being investigated by the Inner Circle. That ought to put a different complexion on their 'invitation' to testify."

Prakash nodded. "I guarantee you, she will be only too eager to get the 'Rani Sadira' out of her house. She has no love for the woman, believe me."

"I believe you. But, in the event that the Rani's disaffection for her isn't effective, we need to have a contingency plan. Perhaps Anala Nadim's fascination with rescuing her fellow Avasans can be made to serve."

"Shall I contact Adivaram at the dalali?" asked Prakash, nodding toward the vicom.

"By all means. His devious mind should be able to concoct a suitable plan."

Prakash smiled, relaxing again. "I'm sure. Though I doubt it will be necessary."

"As long as it results in me getting my hands on that Nadim woman, I don't care whose idea it is."

It was an odd-looking entourage that parted the morning crowds at Bazaar. The old-fashioned covered palanquin was richly ornamented and draped with the Sarojin blood and flame. Borne by four men, it rocked down the main sward, preceded by Nathu Rai Jaya Sarojin and his steward, Ravidas, and surrounded on all sides by the shimmering music of the hundreds of tiny bells woven into its glittering valance.

Passers-by assumed that the old Rani, Mina, rode within, but it was Anala Nadim who sat in the canopied box.

The palanquin came to rest at a wagon decorated with the smiling Sun. Outside, Ravi announced that the Rani Sarojin would have her stars and stones read. A girl's voice answered lightly and with laughter that she'd rather read his stones instead.

Jaya took Ana's arm and helped her from the box, murmuring to her as he would to his Jivinta. She saw the bright-tented kiosk and the wagon behind, with its smiling portrait of Mitras, and her heart leapt in her chest. It was all she could do not to not to straighten her body and run to the wagon, but the bent and frail do not run. So she gritted her teeth and dug her fingers into Jaya's forearm and prayed for patience.

At last she was up the stairs and within the confines of Lila's wagon, which were dominated by the two tall men who stood in the center of the long, narrow room.

Ana straightened, at last, and threw back her hood. "Father!"

Her father and brother both embraced her at once, enveloping her completely in the warmth of their greeting. After moments of tears and endearments, they pulled apart.

"You are wonderful to look at, Ana," said Rokh Nadim, then offered his hand to Jaya. "Thank you, Nathu Rai, for taking such good care of my daughter, and for returning her to me safely."

Ana glanced up at her father. His eyes were on Jaya's face, reading it. For his part, Jaya clasped the offered hand in a firm grip.

"You wish Ana to go into hiding with you then, Nadimsama?"

Ana held her breath.

"That would only increase her danger. No, I have at my disposal a small vessel lent to me by friends. In it, Ana may return to Avasa and the safety of our family compound."

Ana stared at him; her heart seemingly still in her breast. "I can go home? Now?"

He nodded. "You may go home. If you wish. Mata says I must tell you she misses you terribly," he added, "and that she's afraid for you."

"And I for her. It's been so hard not knowing what's happening at home. Not seeing you and Mata; not even knowing where you are."

Rokh Nadim nodded. "All that can be over now. You can go home."

She listened carefully to the words—weighed the tone and the force of them. She felt as if there was a shaft plummet where her heart should be.

"If I go home, who will look for the others? The Lost Ones?"

"I will," said Jaya. "I promise you, I'll do everything in my power to find them."

Ana protested. "You endanger your life—"

"Some things are worth endangering one's life."

She tried to read his face, to penetrate his eyes. Yes, she thought, some things are.

She turned her eyes back to her father. "I can't go home, Father. I have testimony to give before the Inner Circle about the attack on the Nathu Rai."

"Is that necessary?" asked her brother.

"Bala, it is necessary that I be willing to do what I can in these circumstances. Jaya has made great sacrifices for me—for us. I, too, must be willing to sacrifice. This isn't something I can run away from."

"I can give my own testimony before the Nine," Jaya said. "My word is worth a good deal in Kasi."

Ana fidgeted. The rich layers of clothing she wore suddenly felt claustrophobic and binding.

"The Rani knows who I am, Jaya. She threatened to tell Prakash. If she does, your word is worth nothing."

Jaya stared at her, his face frozen and expressionless. "How?" he asked. "How does she know?"

Ana made an impatient gesture. "Someone warned her about your involvement with the missing Avasans. He happened to mention we have no cree." She raised her hand. "I do."

Bala made a hissing sound and turned his face away. Their father closed his eyes and whispered something too softly to be heard.

"But, that wouldn't tell her-" Jaya began.

"She asked me who I was," said Ana. "I couldn't lie to her. And I can't lie now." She turned to her father. "Father, I'm not going home. I have to stay in Kasi and testify. I have to tell the Inner Circle who I am."

After a moment of inscrutable study of his daughter's face, Rokh Nadim smiled and laid a large hand on her shoulder. "Yes," he said, "I think that would be best."

She looked up at him, still troubled. "I won't compromise you?"

"No, Ana. You won't compromise me. You've made a good decision. The Circle must hear what you have to say."

"I think, sama," said Jaya, "that they also must hear what you have to say."

Nadim tilted his head to one side and looked nowhere in particular. "Oh, they will. I promise you, they will."

She found him waiting in the Court Parlor, pacing the room and looking distraught. She paused in the doorway to watch him. He pretended not to see her, but continued his fretful pacing until she spoke.

"Duran! This is a surprise! I didn't expect to see you."

Nor, he wagered, did she expect the fervid embrace she found herself enveloped in.

"Melantha," he whispered against her cheek, "I had to see you."

She pulled away from him and studied his anxious face. "Why? Whatever is wrong? You look like your world is about to collapse."

"It's not my world I'm worried about, Lalasa. It's yours."

Melantha laughed. "Mine? What are you talking about?"

He led her to her throne and seated her in it, still holding her hand. "I'm talking about that girl your son has brought into your house. She's not what she seems to be, Melantha. She's an impostor."

"An impostor!" Melantha stood and moved away, putting her back to him. "What do you mean?"

"She's not the Rani Sadira. She's an agent of AGIM, sent here to gather information and sway your son's vote. Or, barring that, to compromise his position."

Melantha paused by the central hearth to run a manicured fingernail along its polished surface. "What an incredible story! How did you get this information?"

"My intelligence network uncovered it. I know it's stunning, but it's true. Their meeting at that Hotel was no coincidence. It was a set up—conceived by AGIM to throw them together."

Melantha turned her head, watching him from the corner of her eye. "Are you sure of that?"

He nodded, hoping he looked suitably weary and rueful. "I have witnesses who will swear the girl paid a baggage handler to bring her luggage to the attention of the concierge just as the Nathu Rai was leaving the Hotel dining room. Naturally the concierge thought the bag belonged to the Nathu Rai, it appeared to have his crest on it. It was a set up."

"Was it, indeed? Tell me something, Duran..." The Rani turned to face him, leaning her elegant body against the huge, white expanse of the hearth face. "Do you love me?"

"What?" Prakash blinked at the non-sequitur. "Of-of course I love you. Why else would I be here?"

"Why indeed? Why are you here, Duran? Why are you telling me this?"

He moved toward her, willing his face to be solemn, earnest. "Because I love you, Melantha, as I know you love your son. I want to protect you, as I know you want to protect him."

"And what shall I do now, Duran, to protect my son from this woman?"

Ah, good. She did not prolong the game, he could move more quickly.

"Get her out of the Palace and away from him. Before she can influence him further. Before she can hurt him."

"How can I do that?"

"Confront her. Expose her. Put her in a coach and send her away."

"How earnest you sound."

"I am earnest, Melantha. This is a more dangerous situation than you realize."

Melantha was looking down at her hands, rearranging her rings. "Well, I've already confronted her, Duran. And putting her in a coach and sending her away is out of the question ... since she's my son's dasa."

"She–" He was thunderstruck. "How–?"

"How did I know? I asked her. She has a cree. Avasans don't have cree as a rule. So, I confronted her with that fact and she admitted she was Jaya's property and not a long lost cousin."

Prakash licked his lips. "You must have been furious."

She shrugged. "At first—but of course, I have to be fair and lay the lie at my son's door. I can hardly believe she coerced him."

"Really? A woman can exert a great deal of power over a man. Especially one such as that."

"You mean a Rohin woman?"

"They are said to have the Jadu—or at least to think they do— and I've heard they are schooled in Kunda disciplines that make the Bogar rites seem like the play of innocent children."

Melantha's mouth twitched. "Truly? Should I fear for my son's sanity, then? I would hate to have him go mad from too much pleasure."

Prakash scowled. The reins of this interview were no longer in his hands. "It has been known to happen."

She stared at him, bright-eyed, then threw her head back and laughed.

He colored, embarrassment rising from his gorge. "You take this much too lightly, Melantha. The girl is not only Avasan, she's Genda Sita. She's involved him in dangerous undertakings. Surely, you must want her out of your household."

"No, I don't. And do you know why I don't? Because you seem so very much in favor of it."

Prakash could only stare at her as if she'd started speaking an incomprehensible dialect. "I-I don't understand..."

The Rani shook her head. "I'm not surprised. You stupid man. Do you think I can't tell when I'm being used? Do you think I'm so dim-witted I don't realize I'm being lied to?"

"Lied to!" Prakash felt the blood drain from his face. "The girl may be a dasa, but I assure you, she is also an AGIM agent—owned by AGIM, it appears."

Melantha Sarojin moved back to her throne and seated herself regally, her gaze eloquent with scorn. "Avasans don't own people, Duran. I've spoken to my houseguests enough to know that. Oh, and one other thing: You say your witnesses will swear she arranged their meeting at a Hotel near the Spaceport? They didn't meet in a Hotel. There was never any confusion over baggage because she didn't have any. They met at the Bazaar where Jaya apparently just kept her from being arrested as yevetha. But the Sarngin refused to let the girl out of their sight—he was forced to have her processed. Poor Jaya, he's always hated the whole concept of das. Another way in which he is like his father."

Prakash stared at her for several seconds, his body stiffly upright. "You knew all this and yet you let me go on with my ... accusations. Why?"

"I was curious. I wondered how many lies you could tell in the space of five minutes. I counted three."

"I lied about the girl's identity. I admit that."

"That was the first lie."

"I only repeated their lie about the way they met."

"And added the lie that there was a witness. That was the second."

"What was the third?"

"That you love me."

He put his hands out to her, ready to beg, to grovel.

"Melantha, please, I"

"No, don't. It's not important. Just a matter of pride. Bhaktasu always said pride was a fool's surrogate for selfrespect. He was right."

Prakash dropped his hands to his sides. "What else do you know about the girl?"

"I assume I know at least as much as you do. I know who she really is ... above and beyond being Jaya's dasa."

His eyes raised, hopeful. "Then you know I'm right about the danger to your son. I assure you, I am neither lying nor exaggerating when I tell you his life is in jeopardy."

"I believe you. Now, get out of my house, Prakashsama, before I'm forced to have Aridas and his inestimable sons throw you out."

He left without protest, in a haze of stunned disbelief.

Melantha Sarojin sat for a while in her throne, her hand on the arm of the one next to it, her eyes trained sightlessly ahead. She recalled a time when that second throne had been occupied. When she and her husband had greeted guests from the Taj Houses of all Mehtar, from the most illustrious and Holy Orders, from the most prestigious schools of Law and Science.

She'd felt respect then—and if it was not directed at her, at least it came to her by way of the man who occupied the other throne.

By God, he'd respected her ... and loved her, too.

Perhaps Jaya was right. Perhaps she'd been a different woman then. A woman worthy of this seat. Worthy of respect ... and selfrespect. Now, she didn't have even a fool's pride to solace her.

"Stupid," she whispered, and allowed her self to weep.

CHAPTER SEVENTEEN

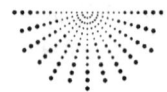

BACK FROM BAZAAR, Jaya secluded himself in the study, buried himself in the depths of a cup chair and tried to think. Ana would stay, at least for the time being, at least until this tangled web was sorted out. His own feelings and thoughts were so bound by that web that he felt sticky, muddled.

Closing his eyes, he tilted his head back against the padded comfort of the chair and took a deep, centering breath. There was yet another confrontation on his schedule for the day and he was not looking forward to it.

His eyes opened on the ceiling with its tastefully muted woodland mural. They fastened on the night sky of one panel.

What did Ana see when she looked at the night sky? Or Ravi, or Jivinta or any of the other believers in some unific Deity. If they saw in the world around them jewels and lights and a fabric of dreams, what did they imagine they saw beyond that world, in those 'other worlds' they spoke of? Where was the Abode of Ramji? Where was —what had that little book called it —the "Garden of the Beloved?"

"I wish I could believe in You," he murmured. "I could use the consolation ... and some advice." Feeling slightly foolish, he dropped his gaze to the carpet.

How I wish Father were here.

He rose and went to find the Rani.

~

In the library's adjoining game room, Hadas had pressed Ana into a match of Pariyanti. The board game was unfamiliar and served to distract her from the warring senses of anticipation and boredom. Hadas was beating her soundly when Aridas entered, carrying an envelope on a carved wooden tray.

"A message for you, Rani Ana," he said and offered it to her with a deferential bow before leaving the room.

She took it almost gingerly and stared at it, then broke the seal with a fingernail, slitting the dark packet. Inside was a single page. The note was written in tiny, hurried strokes on the back of some sort of form. Ana turned it over. It was an inventory sheet from the Badan-Devaki.

She gasped, then reddened when she saw the nature of some of the form's fields: "Hair Color," "Eye Color," "Teeth - good/bad," "Height," "Figure/ Build," "Attractive Features." The last was followed by a series of numbers so the person making out the form could grade the inventory item to a numeric category. There were some other fields as well, of an even more intimate nature, but she ignored them, turning the flimsy over quickly to read the note.

My name is Vanam Sanoh. I am Avasan. I have been taken by force to the Badan-Devaki and made dasa. I was training as an upstairs serving girl, but a patron inquired about me and I am to be sold at private auction tomorrow morning. I am terrified. My training isn't complete, so I know it's not a serving girl he wants. I heard talk among the workers about the Rani Sadira who has made it her cause to help Avasan prisoners—how she freed Hadas Gupta. I thought Tara-ji had at last heard my prayers. So, I bartered with a Salon guard to send this letter to beg you to help me—to free me as you did Hadas. I can't let myself be sold into dishonor. I have bartered my body once in the hope of being saved; I will not have it abused daily. Help me. My life is in your hands. Your Servant, Vanam Sanoh.

"Vanam Sanoh," repeated Ana. She was already heading for the Library vicom terminal.

Hadas followed her. "Is she-?"

Ana, viewing the list of missing Avasans, nodded. "She's here. Vanam Sanoh, eighteen years, from the Tash settlement."

"Should we tell Jivinta Mina or Jaya Rai? Will you go bid on her?"

Ana took the note and studied it again. "I don't know ... Somehow..." She shook her head.

Hadas's eyes narrowed. "Don't you believe her?"

Ana glanced at him sharply, then turned back to the vicom. She keyed it into communications mode and requested an audio-only link to the Badan-Devaki dalali. Hadas, his face like stone, sank into a nearby chair, watching her.

"Good-day, sama," she said when she was connected with the dalali's receptionist. "This is the Rani Ana Sadira. I've heard there is a private auction tomorrow morning. Is that so?"

"Yes, Rani," returned the pleasant male voice. "Our schedule does show a private auction at fourteenth hour in the Blue Salon."

"Wonderful! I'd like to attend, if that could be arranged."

"Ah," said the voice. "Well, unfortunately, the schedule shows that auction as being closed—by invitation only."

Ana made her voice sound slightly peeved. "I see. What must one do to receive an invitation?"

"Well, I..." There was a momentary hesitation, then the man cleared his throat. "Perhaps, if you spoke directly to one of the dalal. Devaki-sa is in the Parlor this morning."

Now it was Ana's turn to hesitate. The thought of holding conversation with Kareen Devaki was daunting. She still dreamed of her—tall, elegant, her coldly assessing black eyes glittering from a statue's pale, perfect face. But she'd gotten this far ...

"Yes," she said, willing her voice to sound confident. "Yes, please let me speak to Devaki-sa."

"As you wish, Rani. One moment, please."

It was less than a moment. Kareen Devaki was on the line immediately, crystalline voice pleasant. "Rani Sadira! How delightful to hear from you. How are you enjoying the gift the Rani Mina purchased for you?"

It took Ana an embarrassing moment to realize she meant Hadas. She laughed, her voice husky. "Oh, he's-he's just wonderful!" she enthused. Hadas glanced away.

"I'm so pleased. How may I serve?"

Words! thought Ana. What words?

"You can invite me to a private auction," she said lightly. "Your receptionist tells me there's one tomorrow morning at fourteenth hour. I've never been to a private auction. It sounds ... exciting."

"Ah! Well, my dear Rani, the auction was at the special request of a certain patron—a very valued patron, you understand..." Her voice dripped her regrets. "However,"—the crystal brightness was back—"as co-owner of Badan-Devaki, I can invite whomever I please to our auctions. Yes, it would please me very much to invite you to this one."

"Why, thank you, Devaki-sa. I'm looking forward to it."

"Rani, may I..." Devaki paused, her voice tinged with reluctance.

"Yes?"

"Pardon me, I beg you, if I seem presumptuous, but it has long been common knowledge that the Nathu Rai Sarojin despises the buying and selling of das. Does he approve of your patronizing our dalali?"

"Oh, he doesn't know!" exclaimed Ana in a breathless voice. "That's what makes it fun! Why, he thinks the young man we bought last week is my cousin, can you believe it?" She laughed again.

"I see. Well, then I will look forward to greeting you personally tomorrow morning. Will there be others in your party?"

"Oh, no. Just me, I think."

"Very well, then. Until tomorrow, Rani."

"Thank you, Devaki-sa," said Ana and cut the connection.

Hadas gripped her arm. "Take me with you, Ana. Please."

"You could, if I was going, but I'm not."

"I don't understand. You said-"

Ana shook her head. "It didn't feel right, Hadas. That's why I called. I wanted to talk to one of them—to hear a voice. She didn't even ask how I knew about this private auction, but she did make sure I wouldn't be bringing anyone with me—especially Jaya."

Now Hadas's eyes were mere slits. "You think it's a trap?"

"Well, think of it, Hadas—how did I get a reputation at the Badan-Devaki as a redeemer of lost Avasans? As far as anyone knew, Jivinta Mina bought you for me as a toy. The same kind of toy Vanam Sanoh would be for this 'client.'"

"Perhaps some rumor of what happened at the Mesha Fest ... ?"

Ana shook her head. "It feels like a trap."

"What if you're wrong? What if Vanam Sanoh really is in the dalali? If we don't do something-"

"I didn't say I wasn't going to do something. I said I wasn't going to the auction. That place is a business, not a fortress. I'm sure there are ways to get in. Especially since they're expecting me to walk in through the front door, not sneak in the back unannounced."

Hadas came to his feet, his face flushed with excitement. "You know Jaya Rai would never permit you to do this."

"Jaya Rai can't prevent what he doesn't know about. And you are not going to tell him, are you?"

"I wouldn't think of it ... because I'm going with you."

"No. It will only take one person to slip in and check their files."

"Check their files?"

"Even if Vamam Sanoh is no longer there, I can still get into their database and see if their 'inventory' matches our list. I want to know where the Lost Ones have gone."

He perched close to her, on the arm of her chair. "How? How can you access their files? They could have a whole different system."

"I've seen the terminals. They're just like these." She patted the top of the vicom. "Paran 50's. We use the same model at home. Chances are they use a commercial database for their inventory. I know a fair amount about databases, having been responsible for tracking the equipment for a mining compound for the last five years. Even if the software is unfamiliar, I can set the terminal for audio input. Then I won't even have to use entrance codes, I can make plain verbal requests."

"But what if someone hears you?"

"I'll whisper."

She got up and tucked the note into the waistband of her pantalons. "Now, I just need to talk to Govi."

Hadas was nothing if not persistent. "What if the terminal is voice imprinted and doesn't acknowledge you? It could set off an alarm."

"Hadas! In the name of Tara-ji, don't be so paranoid. Voice imprinting would be highly unlikely in files that have to be open to the Census. Alarms! That's something out of fiction."

"You're being naïve. They're running an illegal business-"

"I'm sure the files that track their payments to the thieves are coded up as tight as a sunburn. But it's legal for them to buy and sell yevetha—Avasan or otherwise. They'd have no reason to put a lock-out on their inventory files. As a matter of fact, if they did, it would probably arouse suspicions somewhere in the Census Ministry. Now, calm down and go talk Ari or Dana into getting beaten senseless at Pariyati."

She started to leave, but found his hand on her arm.

"Take me with you, Ana. You need someone to back you up. Please. I can't let you do this alone."

She shook her head. "I can't ask anyone else to jeopardize them-selves, Hadas. This is my crusade."

"No, it's our crusade. I'm Avasan too. And you're not asking—I am. I may have led a softer life than you have, but I'm a good athlete. I can climb, run, swim."

"Thank you, Hadas. But I don't think I'll be doing any swim-ming. Now, come on. Let me go see Govi."

"Then at least let me in on the plan," Hadas begged. "Just in case something goes wrong. I could tell the Nathu Rai."

She hesitated, then gave a reluctant nod, acknowledging the wisdom of that. "All right. But you tell no one what I'm doing."

He nodded in solemn agreement, then followed her in search of Govi.

～

The Rani met Jaya in the salon of her suite, dressed impeccably in pale amber silks that set her tawny complexion off to great advantage.

"Going out?" he asked coolly.

"I have a dinner engagement in Kasi." She checked the time-piece on her wrist. "How long will this take?"

"That depends on you."

"Oh dear. I recognize that voice. Well..."

She moved to a low couch and made herself comfortable on it. "There, I'm ready. What are we going to snarl at each other about today?"

"Ana."

The Rani nodded exaggeratedly. "Oh, yes. Ana."

"I'll get right to the point. You know Ana is Rokh Nadim's daughter. You know she's been made dasa. Now, what do you intend to do with that information?"

The Rani studied her presently golden fingernails. "You mean, will I tell Duran Prakash?"

"Will you?"

She looked up at him. He was standing in an almost defensive position; rod-straight and tense, as if facing a physical threat.

He must have stood like that outside the gates the day they attacked him—whoever "they" really were. Faceless, cowardly—how dare they touch him, the Sarojin Prince—her son? She nearly cried out aloud at a sudden intense desire to hold him; to gather him into her arms as if he were still her little boy—as if he were not a tall, threatening stranger.

She tried to make her voice sound cold and distant, but didn't manage it well. It came out hushed and strained. "I'm afraid that's rather academic at this juncture, Jaya. He already knows."

Jaya's face drained of color. "How?"

She shrugged, still struggling for composure. "I have no idea. He wanted me to get her out of the Palace. He said she was an agent of AGIM or some such nonsense. I told him I didn't appreciate being lied to and threw him out."

"Lied to? I don't understand. You know she's Anala Nadim, why not believe she's an AGIM agent?"

"She told me everything; how you met, how she got the dascree."

"You believed her?"

"She's Rohin. Her story made sense. His didn't." She shrugged again. "He admitted he was lying."

Jaya shook his head bemusedly. "So you threw him out. For good?"

"Permanent exile. That will no doubt bring tears of joy to your eyes."

"I'm celebrating already."

"Hmmm. Well, the fact remains—he knows who your 'cousin' really is. He stated, quite bluntly, that her presence here is endangering your life."

Jaya lowered himself to the arm of a chair opposite his mother's couch. "He knows who she is, yet he hasn't told the Inner Circle. He suggested to the Deva Radha that I might be prejudiced by my relationship with her, but that was all. Why, I wonder?" He glanced at the Rani. "And you—you didn't help him remove her. Why?"

"I can't really say. Pride, I suppose—the wounded variety. Or maybe ... the vestiges of self-respect. Or maybe because I knew if I did help him, my son would never forgive me. You couldn't forgive me for that, could you?"

"No. No, I don't think I could."

"She's important to you, this Avasan?"

He nodded.

"Well, then, it seems I've done something right, after all."

Jaya exhaled sharply and stared at the carpet between his feet. "Thank you, mother."

"You're welcome. Is there anything else?"

He glanced up at her. "Yes. You told Ana someone warned you I was getting involved in an investigation of some Avasan kidnappings. Who was it—Prakash?"

"No, not Prakash. It was Bel Adivaram. ... What? What's wrong?"

Jaya had risen slowly to his feet, his face eloquent with astonishment.

"Is that so surprising? He's been close to the family since your Father-"

"What did he say to you? Tell me everything, Mata. Everything you can remember."

"He said you were—how did he put it—'championing the cause of Avasan yevetha,' and that you were putting your life in danger by doing so. I swear, Jaya, if one more person tells me your life is in danger, I'll scream."

"Mother, please-"

She waved him down. "All right, I'll attempt to stay to the point. Bel said he was investigating these kidnappings, as you call them, as a matter of Zone security. He said a ring of thieves were stealing Avasan id to benefit one of the local dalalis. He said he suspected some of the involved parties were highly placed politically and that you were putting yourself at odds with them. He said his officers had tried to warn you off, but that you wouldn't listen. He asked me to try to influence you to..." She stopped, staring at her son's nearly gray face. "I thought ... I thought he was just being ... a friend."

"All lies," said Jaya, his voice barely above a whisper. "Or at least, most of it. Yes, there are kidnappings; yes, there are probably highly-placed people involved—but I know of no investigation except ... mine, and no one warned me about anything. If Bel Adivaram knew about my concern over the Avasans, he kept it to himself when I was around."

"You never discussed it with him?"

"Never."

The Rani nodded. "He said something else, too. He said—or rather, he implied—that those so-called Worker's Coalitionists who attacked you were nothing of the kind. That they were sent to dissuade you from prying into this kidnapping business because you were a threat to the people behind it."

Jaya shook his head. "The first time I even mentioned the kidnappings to Adivaram's Sarngin was the morning of the attack. In fact, we were on our way back from the Port Zone Headquarters when it happened. There was barely enough time for anyone to decide I was a threat and send out those thugs. No, Mata. That attack was staged on behalf of the Consortium—either directly or indirectly—I'm not sure which. Someone thought they could frighten me into voting pro-KNC. All they did was induce the Deva Radha to throw the case out of the Vrinda Varma and place it before the Circle."

"Bel knew that?"

"Of course, he knew that. He was in Chambers."

"But he wanted me to think otherwise ... for some reason."

"Yes. For some reason."

The Rani knew a desperation born of fear. "Jaya, what is happening here? What is Bel doing? What is he part of? Is he—is he a friend or an enemy?"

"I don't know."

"My God, Jaya, who can we trust?"

His eyes met hers—huge and brilliant in his ashen face.

"Apparently, no one," he said.

They sat in silence for a moment, each trying to absorb meanings and ramifications. Trying to remember who had said this or that. Trying to sort friend from foe.

At length, the Rani had had enough of the silence. "What will you do?"

"I'll make sure our security is tight. I'll have everyone who tries to enter searched twice and I'll take an armed guard to the Asra Complex tomorrow. When we testify, we'll tell the Circle everything we know."

"That ... could ruin a few people."

"I'm beginning to hope so."

"One of them could be your Uncle Namun. If the Consortium is ruined, it will be very hard on Vedda Technologies."

"Uncle Namun once observed to me that he feared that to deal with the KNC was to deal with demons. If the KNC is a Consortium of demons, then they deserve ruin."

The Rani grimaced, shaking her head. "Ji, it must run in the family."

"What?"

She shrugged away a wave of fondness. "You're just like your father. You remember how it was with him—he was always in the forefront of some crusade. Sometimes I teased him about believing he was the God-defender of the Down-trodden—the Guardian of Every Right." She smiled wryly. "The Consortium was no great friend of his, either."

Jaya nodded. "I seem to recall that. I didn't really understand that—how he could be so close to Namun and yet throw himself into a pitched battle with the institution that was the source of so much of Uncle Namun's working capital. I don't recall that there was ever a bit of strain between them over it."

The Rani shrugged. "Both of them had a rare ability to see the difference between people and institutions; between people and their actions, even. A rare form of detachment. It kept your father's crusades from becoming vendettas. It also kept him from destroying treasured relationships."

"I didn't understand that, either, then—the crusading."

The Rani shrugged. "You were a boy. You had other things on your mind than fair wages for hard labor or the disposition of sonless widows and orphans."

Jaya grimaced. "I wish I'd paid more attention. I might have learned something about how to conduct a crusade."

"You could always consult his journals. He took notes on everything. There should be a plethora of material there on the how's and why's of being a successful crusader."

"I think I understand the why's now," Jaya said. He took a deep breath. "I'd better go set up our security arrangements for tomorrow."

"You'll need my testimony, too, won't you?" It was more statement than question.

"Yes. Yes, I think we will."

She nodded, resigned. "I believe I'll cancel my dinner plans and stay in this evening. I'm not sure it's safe to be a Sarojin in Kasi just now." She shivered, touched by the chill of that thought. "I'll be glad when this is over."

"So will I," murmured Jaya. He turned and started for the door.

"Jaya."

He paused in the doorway to her entry.

"When this is over, you're going to free her, aren't you?"

"Ana? Of course. Her family can easily produce id for her, once the danger to them is past. Removing that obscenity from her palm should just be a formality."

"Remove it? Or do you have plans to replace it with another obscenity? Don't you mean to exchange that dascree for the Sarojin raicree?"

The aloof stranger had returned. "I don't think this is the time to discuss that. When this is over, I'll stop and I'll think."

"I hope you'll make a point of thinking clearly."

Now the dark eyes glittered with heat. "Meaning?"

"Meaning: You should think long and hard about marrying across caste boundaries."

"I don't believe in caste boundaries."

"No, but the world around you does. Think, for a moment, of what life would be like for her once everyone knows she's not a displaced Rani of the Saroj, but an just Avasan miner's daughter—a common, colorless, ore-digger."

"She's not 'just' anything, Mother. Least of all, common. And if I did marry her, she'd be a Rani of the Saroj, after all."

"Not to them." She jerked her head toward Kasi. "Not to me."

"I care, very little-"

"Ah, now!" She rose and moved toward him, praying he would see reason. "Now, you care very little! But how much will you care when it begins to affect the way people look at you, speak to you, or speak about you behind your back? How much will you care when time passes and the pallor of her skin doesn't fade? When you realize it wasn't the climate that blanched it, but her ancestors. When she gives you children marked by the same heritage. She's Genda, Jaya—born from of the bowels of the world, a child of the creatures that live in darkness."

" That is the most ignorant, superstitious pack of nonsense I've ever heard you preach. Those are fairytales—legends. We're all products of earth. Every last one of us."

She felt swift, certain denial. "There was a time," she said, "when the Sarojin men were little less than gods. To the people around them, they were gods."

"They were never gods. They were men. My father was a man. I'm a man. Ana is a woman. We're equals."

"Equals! She's a Genda slave!"

Jaya held up his hand. "Stop. Ana is not my slave. Not in any real sense. And don't suggest that I make her a cunnidasa. I have no interest in it. None."

She knew better than to believe that. "None? You've never thought about it? Never thought about walking through that unlocked door into her bed?"

Her son's face gave up secrets that were no secret to her.

She laughed. "The Crusader-Hypocrite? Come, Jaya, admit it. You have thought pleasantly about that pretty piece of property. And she is your property. Believe me, she could hope for no greater honor than to be a cunnidasa to the Sarojin. If I were in her position-"

"You're not in her position, Mother, and never could be. Oh, you might have been born to a poor house, even to the family of an Avasan miner. You might have found yourself enslaved and alone on a strange world full of strange people. But you could never, never be in her position, because to be in her position, you'd have to be honest and honorable and selfsacrificing, and I doubt you are any of those things." His eyes spat rage at her from their depths.

She had to allow it was her own fault. A heavy weight pressed upon her heart and she pressed her hands over it as if they could lift the weight away.

She smiled wryly. "Well, I seem to have done it again. Forgive me. I realize it all sounds like bigoted nonsense to you, but the sanctity of a Taj line is something I was raised with—something I was taught to respect and believe in. Other men might corrupt themselves or pollute the stream of their heritage with lowlife marriages, but not men of the Taj. There are always human needs, physical desires. That's what makes men—even Sarojin men—less than gods. Those needs can be fed. But I was raised to believe that people of caste must marry to their station. How else is the quality of the line to be preserved?"

"Quality of the line? What quality? What quality of character does Ana lack that should keep her from being accepted as a Rani of the House Sarojin? She's passed well as one so far."

"She has passed. That doesn't make it so." The Rani shook her head. "This isn't her world, Jaya. It is foreign to her. You are foreign to her."

His face flushed. "No. No, I'm not. This world may be foreign to her—is foreign to her. She's told me as much. But not me. That's part of my dilemma, Mother. I feel as if I've known her for centuries, and I know the feeling is shared."

"You are part of this world. She is part of another. In a very literal sense, an alien."

"I don't want to be part of this world, damn it! I never have! I exist in it, I glide through it. It never touches me. Nothing has touched me. Until now. Now, I've been touched. By her; by those people whose lives my world is shattering. All I want right now is to get to the end of this tangled yarn and find out whose hand holds the skein. I want to find Ana's 'Lost Ones' and reunite them with their families and I want to dig the corruption out of Kasi. You talk to me about caste boundaries? Well, I want to shatter them. Every last one of them. They're stupid, artificial walls and I want them broken!"

Dear God, he was shaking! The Rani applauded, laughing. "Oh, wonderful speech, Nathu Rai Sarojin! Well spoken! And with such admirable passion. If that's all you want—Ji!—the purging of Kasi; the destruction of age old custom? A mere wave of your hand should suffice."

She advanced on him suddenly, anger leaping like black flame in her heart. "Do you have any idea how long your father struggled to accomplish just that? Do you have any conception of how many nights I slept alone because he was at the vicom, or skulking in some alley, or interviewing some lowlife in an attempt to dig the corruption out of Kasi? Can you imagine your father, the Nathu Rai Bhaktasu Sarojin, on his knees, weeping into my skirts because one of his yevetha informants had been killed or because he could not produce the proof of labor abuses he knew were occurring?

"You-you pup! You upstart! You have no idea what it is to be a mahesa. You speak of crusades and justice and honor and you've only just discovered they exist! You are a poor mirror of your father's light. A poor copy of the original!"

Jaya stood motionless, staring at her. In a moment, he managed to find his voice. "I'm not trying to imitate Father, Mata. I'm not a copy of him—poor or otherwise. I am myself. I am Jaya Sarojin and that makes me the mirror of both my father's light and yours."

Melantha shrunk away from him, folded in on herself. "Ah, now that's a poor heritage. Half god and half Niraya-jinn. It's no wonder you're confused about your role in life."

Jaya's expression softened. "I'm beginning to sort through the confusion, Mother. You could help by not throwing such conflicting signals at me. I swear, for the past five years I've been the most confused over who you are."

"Well, so have I. If I throw conflicting signals at you, it's only because I am in conflict. I loved your father, Jaya. I loved him with a passion I swear few people are privileged to know. And he returned that love, every last grain of it. I worshipped him and he ennobled me. I admired the crusader in him as much as I begrudged it the time it took from me. Whenever he was able to bring justice out of chaos, I was the first one to adore him for it. But when he died ... out on one of his crusades..."

She dug her fingernails into her palms, seeking composure through physical pain, but it was an ineffective discipline against inner agony and she cried, sounding pathetic even to her own ears. "By God, Jaya, you're all I have of him! If I lose you-"

He reached for her, folded her into his arms. She recalled both Paradise and Hell in that embrace. Her son was hers again, for a moment, but Bhaktasu was lost to her for the rest of her life. And at the end of that fleeting dance, could she honestly hope for reunion? She realized that in the past five years she had forgotten how to pray.

"Don't leave me, Jaya," she begged him. "Don't leave me alone."

"I won't, Mata," he promised.

~

Ana yawned and stretched, trying to bring her eyes back into focus on the detailed floor plan of the Badan-Devaki. She closed them and discovered that the picture was imprinted on her retinas. She chuckled. That would be great if it would last until she was finished with this bit of espionage, but already the image was fading.

One thing remained fixed in her memory—the small, black square drawn into the alley wall that represented admittance to the sub-levels of the building. It was listed in the architect's index as an "inspection access" and was intended to afford the City Development Corps a commanding view of pipes and conduits and any structural weakness of the sub-flooring. To Ana it was just another dark shaft, and since she had virtually grown up in dark shafts, she greeted it with almost a sense of welcome. That, at least, was her element.

From that entry way, there were several trap-door routes up into the dalali. One opened into a kitchen storage area, another into a long rectangular room with no particular designation. From its lay, Anala figured it ran behind the staging areas of the two premier floor public Salons. She pondered it for a moment, then decided it correlated to the wardrobe/dressing area she had seen during her processing.

She checked the time. It was getting close to dinner. She printed a copy of the floor plan, then bundled it up with the list of names, the schedule of deliveries, and some notes she had taken from Govi's sagacious input. Considering herself prepared, she folded the flimsies away into a pocket and hurried upstairs to store them in a safe place.

Later, she would plan her entry route and look over her notes. Then, she would just have to pray she was ready.

~

The journal hadn't been easy to find. In the end he'd asked the Rani for clues as to where his father had kept it.

Old Recipes from Vatapur, the faded, hide-bound cover said, but when Jaya opened it, the book was hollow, and in the carefully cut hole was a hand-sized com-journal. He powered it up, then sat down with it and scanned the entries. There were some files with cryptic names, others merely carried dates.

One of the named files had the initials "KNC" in the title; he tried to open it. The file was locked.

"Enter id," the machine told him, and a small red light came on above an oval depression in its black face. He didn't know where his father's leaf was, so he used his own, pressing the crystal face down into the depression.

"Access granted," said the journal, and proceeded to open the file. He began to read.

CHAPTER EIGHTEEN

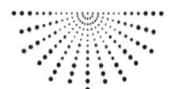

ANA SLIPPED, silent, into the dim hallway—cautious, but not surreptitious. Her dark robes murmured silkily; barely loud enough to be heard above the rapid beating of her heart. She was sure that would bring the walls down. At the bottom of the staircase, she glanced away up the broad hallway. The flat panel of light squeezing beneath the door of Jaya's study confirmed that his meeting with Mall Gar was still in progress. She continued on her way, exiting the back of the house and heading for the long, two-story stable.

In that darkened building, she stopped to let her eyes grow accustomed to the gloom and listened to the soft midnight whispers of the horses in their boxes. She moved down the rows of stalls to the area where the carriages were kept.

She had just laid her hands on the tongue of the bike she'd targeted as an appropriate vehicle when a sharp sound from behind froze her. Common sense told her it was one of the horses rattling the door of its luxurious cell. Common sense told her she was being paranoid. Still, she listened to the dark stable the way a gaur-witch listens to a new mine shaft—all senses pointing outward.

When nothing else stirred, when she had convinced herself that fear was out of place here, she dared move. Behind the padded bench seat of the two-wheeler, her hands found the closure of the stowage cowling and opened it, groping within. The little pile of equipment she had secreted earlier in the evening was still there: the coil of rope, the palm-lamp, the small leather satchel.

She slipped the palm-lamp under her robe and clipped it to the belt at the waist of her black body suit, then moved back to the front of the bike. Grasping the tongue in both hands, she rolled the little carriage out into the middle of the harnessing arena, then selected and harnessed a dark horse. She checked each buckle, quietly tugged at the traces, then paused to murmur a quick prayer.

A moment later she was driving across the yard, a blaze of pinkgold light washing over her, heading for the main gate. The guards had been instructed to keep people out. No one had said anything to them about keeping anyone in. They were not party to the whys and wherefores of their job, so when Ana called out something about visiting a friend in town they merely exchanged uneasy glances and let her go on her way unchecked. She sang on the drive into the Silk District. She'd done all her thinking; had tried on every "what if" she could think of. There was no sense in worrying it to death.

A block from the Badan-Devaki, she pulled the bike up to a public tie-down and secured the horse to one of the many empty rings. Light from a corner street lamp flooded the area with unwelcome light; she had to slip into the bike's shadow to pull off the robe. She flipped it onto the seat, then went to the rear of the vehicle to retrieve the rope and the satchel. She was dismayed to find she hadn't secured the hood to the stowage, relieved to find that it hadn't resulted in the loss of her equipment. The rope went over one shoulder; she clipped the satchel to the front of her belt and slid her fingers into the soft web of the palm-lamp.

As she melted into a pool of shadow along the tie-down wall, her memory called the maps to mind; the sketches and print-outs folded in the satchel at her waist. She found the mouth of the alley that ran behind the Badan-Devaki. There was a gate across it.

She hunkered down in the shadow of a trash bin and checked the time, cupping the palm-lamp above her timepiece. Ten minutes to wait. She chafed at the seeming endlessness of it, wishing she had cut it closer. She was building up a charge of fear. That was dangerous.

She took a deep breath and began a shallow discipline; not involving all her senses—she needed to hear the street—but just deep enough to calm her mounting pulse and massage some patience into her apprehension. It was an effort well spent; when her ears caught the sound of something shuffling along the wall to her left, she did not jump out of hiding, but only stiffened with a sudden chill, senses flung outward, straining.

Another sound intruded from the right, growing louder—the rush of an air wagon. She strained her hearing back to the left, but the shuffling was swallowed in the wash of the wagon's jets. She could feel its warm breath on her face and hands. She gave her entire attention to the wagon. It had a two seat cabin, rounded and skull-like, that gave the vehicle the look of a mythical beast. It was a tractor rig with a pleated tongue between cab and trailer.

Ana's eyes seized on the narrow hitch. There was enough room there for a slender passenger, she decided, and coiled herself, waiting for the wagon to pull abreast of her cover. The aperture appeared almost too quickly and Ana bolted into a low leap, landing, cat-like, on the synthetic fabric of the telescoping joint. She would be lucky, she realized, if she wasn't crushed by the two halves of the rig and prayed the wagon wouldn't meet with any obstacles in the alley.

It didn't. It glided on its cushion of air up the throat of the alley, the photonic gate opening and closing silently before and after. Ana watched brick and masonry flicker in its forward light bar.

The wagon soon slowed. Ana made herself as small as possible in her dark nest, her eyes on the bath of light around the Badan-Devaki service entrance.

She realized, with a freezing jolt, that the wagon would glide right by that well-lit portal and present its rear doors. When it did, her precarious perch would be flooded with light. She rolled from the hitch and was swallowed by the trailer's shadow. She walked beside it, stopping when it stopped; it blocked her from the view of the B&D security guards.

Her back against the trailer, she glanced back, down its long, smooth flank. The service entrance lights flooded the alley behind, opening a broad fan of illumination across the worn paving—a fan that lay between Ana and her access to the dalali's sub-regions.

The snick of a door catch brought her attention back toward the cabin. Less than three steps away the cabin door swung open and a shadowy pair of legs thrust out. She moved swiftly, silently, toward them—one long step and a pivot and she'd swung back into the breach between cab and trailer. Curled into a ball on the nearly collapsed tongue, Ana squeezed her eyes closed and hugged her knees fiercely, barely hearing the driver and his companion pass by the dark slot. Several deep breaths and a numb prayer of thanks later, she opened her eyes and glanced up toward the cab.

In the mirror surface of the window of the driver's open door, she could see the transparent, distorted images of the two draymen and a handful of B&D guards. They were armed.

One of the guards pulled open the building's service door. It swung outward and stopped, turning the delta of brilliance Ana must ford into a mere canal. She peered at it hopefully. That was little more than a meter in width. Dangerous, yes. But not deadly.

The draymen opened the rear doors of the trailer. It bobbed as they boarded and began unloading. Ana slipped off the hitch and moved silently down the dark side of the wagon. From beneath the ramp, she could see the guards. There were three. They were not watching the alley. They were talking and chewing pramada sticks, which meant their faculties would be cloudy at best.

Encouraged, Ana waited until both draymen had disappeared into the broad entrance, then took two long strides across the glowing river of roadway. The flash of light hit her full in the face before she plunged into darkness and stopped, stone still, listening.

The mumble of voices and the shuffle of feet continued behind her. Someone chuckled. She relaxed and moved the last few steps to the wall of the building, resisting the temptation to collapse against it in relief.

Summoning her concentration, Ana turned away from the light and put a hand against the cold brick. She'd taken three steps when something scraped the hard stone of the alley floor barely two meters in front of her. She hung between advance and retreat, imagining horrors; imagining Parva Rishi leering at her from the sooty beyond.

No, it could just as easily be a rodent of some sort—a citizen of the alley, itself terrified of alien intrusion. Something small. Something harmless. It was, even now, backing away in fear. Turning to give her one last, wild-eyed glance. Skittering away to safety.

The scraping repeated itself, was followed by shuffling and the clatter of pebbles against stone. Wings fluttered.

Ana expelled a silent breath of relief. A night bird, that was all. Hunting, as she was hunting. She calmed herself and moved cautiously to the access shaft.

She crouched by the small rectangle of absolute darkness and reached a hand tentatively into it. There was no covering to be pried away; it was open to the alley. Open too, said a small, annoying voice, to whatever lived in the alley.

Ana swallowed a tingle of apprehension. She'd faced worse on her own world. She thrust her legs into the opening and rolled onto her stomach, letting herself backwards into the aperture. Her toes touched gritty bottom. She lowered herself to the floor, then turned slowly, putting her back to the access. She took a deep, centering breath and a long moment to orient herself to the void. The place smelled of wet and rusty metal.

She recalled the computer rendering of the sub-structure. This should be a rough square, about four meters to a side. The opposing side funneled into a narrow passage hemmed by pipes and conduits. She tried to imagine that; tried to overlay an illuminated map on the lightless place. It was difficult and she wished for a miner's helm with the computer image in memory. But she didn't have one and so began a measured pace toward the opposite side of the imagined square, counting each footstep under her breath, her hands outstretched. Even in the soft shoes she'd chosen for the adventure, each step seemed to emit a crunchy shriek as it crushed unseen debris.

In fourteen deafening steps, her fingertips touched cold, curving metal. A large pipe. She felt to the left. The pipe took a sharp upward angle. She felt to the right. The pipe turned away and ran before her into the dark. She followed it, finding herself in the pipe-hemmed pathway that led into the bowels of the dalali. The floor plan had given the width as half a meter. She stretched out her arms. Good. The floor plan was accurate.

It was too soon for the palm-lamp, she decided, and continued her blind, fingertip progress to her immediate goal—a second pipe-bound chamber with a trap door to the regions above.

Above the rush of her own breath, above the crackle of her footfall, she heard, or rather felt, something behind her. She froze, found herself listening to nothing but the rhythm of her heart, thudding in her chest. She isolated it, closed her mind to it.

Other sounds scurried forward to take its place—the gurgle of water in the pipes, a slow drip from somewhere ahead and to the right, a sporadic creaking from over head, a pervasive hum and, on the periphery, minute noises like the whisper of tiny feet on the gritty floor. She refused to put form to it.

Ears ringing from the intensity of her listening, she took a step forward. Paused. Nothing. She took another step, her hands nearly gripping the cold, filthy pipes that ran level with her head.

A long scrape of sound shrieked at her from the blackness. She shot forward, her hands braced before her at eye level, struck a large pipe, rebounded, spun, stumbled to the right and half-fell into a corner. She hung there, barely daring to breathe, her arms lying atop the cross-piece of some bit of framework.

The blackness was absolute. Nothing existed in this place with her. Nothing but dripping, scurrying, screaming blackness.

She took hold of her panic with the firm, callused hands of a veteran miner. Whatever was sharing this alien cave with her was at least five meters away and around a corner. That is, she thought wryly, unless it was small enough to glide under the pipes.

She pushed herself upright, listening. The nerve-flaying sounds were gone. For now.

Ana struggled to reconnoiter. She had known where she was when she'd started her sprint—just below the first corner. The forced right turn was all right, but the next turn should have been a left only a meter and a half along this corridor. She must have stumbled twice that distance to the corner, which meant she'd have to work her way back down the passage.

Grit crunched softly somewhere in the darkness. Somewhere back the way she'd just come.

Her jaw clenched painfully. She willed it to relax. It was only three steps—four, at most. A quick right turn, then another quick jog to the left.

Just put one foot in front of the other, Anala, she told herself, and did that, feeling for the junction and curve that would signal the turn.

One step. Two steps. Three. Her hand met the raised collar of the junction fitting and ahead of her in the dark, something brushed the dust.

She slipped around the corner as silently as possible, sidling, listening. Her hands sought signs of progress—another curving juncture slid beneath them. Her right hand, extended at arm's length met a wall—the "T" intersection that butted against the lift shaft. She padded left; three meters later, she turned right.

She stopped. Now she had to measure carefully or turn on the lamp. She turned her head toward her back trail, listening. Nothing.

Biting her lip, she took what she hoped was a half-meter step, then another and another. She stopped, turned and fanned her fingers against the wall. The metal framework she expected to find was not there. She felt left and right. Nothing. Had she gone too far or not far enough?

Above the sudden clamor of adrenaline, her senses told her something was moving in the peaty gloom, advancing on her up the pipe work maze. Denying her fear the power of form, she thumbed on the palm-lamp and scraped its golden beam across the wall.

Not far enough! She dove at the spider-work of metal braces the light revealed—a manual cantilever stairwell. Ana gave the mechanism a swift glance, saw the oil-packed chains that supported the closest end. She shut off the palm-lamp and, before the image of the stair frame could fade from her eyes, lunged for the bottom end of the narrow steps. Under the sudden weight, the mechanism groaned, resisted, then gave, lowering in a ponderous glide. She willed it down. When it was still a meter from the floor, she flung her body onto it and crawled upward toward the seemingly unreachable trapdoor.

It was not unreachable, but it was set at an a awkward angle to the steps. She ended up lying on her back along the metal frame, pushing upward with increasing force. Thought of the unseen Something Behind nearly made her frantic, but she fought the urge to pound on the trapdoor and kept her pressure on it firm and consistent.

It gave, at last, and swung away with what seemed like a deafening protest.

She sat up, poking her head into a darkness as complete as the vat of black below, yet radically different. Close, cottony warmth pressed against her face and neck. She scanned for a light source, but hadn't found it when the metal beneath her vibrated.

The gentle touch of the unknown electrified her, sent her flying up through the trap and onto the floor above. She scrambled, rolled and felt something feathery brush by her in a direction she took to be up. She struck something solid—a frame of some sort—and used it to stop her wild roll.

She lay silent now, tangled up in herself, cursing the folds of fabric that had fallen on her from overhead. She felt movement from that direction—rhythmic and diminishing. She reached up a hand. It met cloth—soft, silken cloth. She was lying beneath a clothing rack.

She dragged the swinging clothes into noiseless submission, begging total silence—and it was silent here. No scurrying, no scream and crash of dripping water; just solid, dust-covered silence.

Still waiting for Something to drag itself out of the sublevel abyss, she moved carefully into a more or less upright position, then slid whatever had fallen on her to the floor. Using the clothes rack as a landmark, she tried to pinpoint the trap door. With help from some God-sent trickle of light, she made out its squared edge toward the center of the room. It was still angled upward just as she'd left it.

Orienting herself, she guessed her back was to a wall that abutted the backstage area of the main Salon. That put one exit on her left, and two somewhere along the wall at her back. It was that left-hand one she wanted. It fed into a connecting corridor to the rear foyer, from which she had her choice of lift basket or back stair. She got her feet beneath her and started to rise.

A door opened somewhere on the periphery of her senses. The lights came on. She froze, not so much as breathing on the fabric hanging about her face. She couldn't see who was shuffling toward her hiding place from the unseen doorway in the wall to her left; she could only hear their tuneless humming and the swish-scuffle of their feet across the floor. What she could see, between barely parted veils of color, was the trap door. It was shut.

She tried to make herself believe in some well-lubricated, fully automatic mechanism; some system of counter-weights that had just now came into play. Something she'd failed to see when she forced the door. She didn't believe in it.

The shuffle-hum was closer now, making her shiver with tension. It stopped not two paces off.

"MM-hm," murmured a female voice. "Blue. Bl-ue." The rack

trembled and creaked, hooks scraped wood—closer, then closer. "Blue, blue, blue," the voice chanted.

Ana could see the woman's feet—silver-shod—through the diaphony to her left. Dear Tara-Ji ...

"Ah! Blue!" The rack jolted. There was a moment of silence, then, "Ah! Tsk!"

A hand appeared between Ana's knees. It reached for and grasped the fabric that lay over her toes, whisked it away. The voice muttered about dirt. Then, the shuffle-hum commenced again and moved away. The lights went out, the final stream cutting off as the door closed.

Ana slid to the floor. Three seconds later she made a mad, but silent dash for her far away target—the door to the outside corridor. It took all the courage she possessed to open it into the empty rear foyer; more than that to navigate the length of that to the back stair.

Reaching that goal with ragged nerves, she slipped upward toward her goal.

∾

It's a strange and startling coincidence that the very evening of the day I poke my photonic nose into the accounts of the Kasi-Nawahr Consortium, Scar-Eye and his companions cross my path. Cross it! By God, they very nearly cut it in two. Scar-Eye is short on both patience and gentility, but fortunately the bruises do not show when I'm fully dressed, and if I constrain myself around Mel (a damned hard thing to do), I might be able to hide them from her as well. That much is imperative.

I am now fully apprised of my mortality and weakness of character. The confrontation gave me pause to wonder why I must go on with this, suspecting, as I do now, that it could cost me more than a few bruised ribs. Yet, if what I suspect is true, if the Consortium is trying to grapple the reins of government, must I not go on? Must I not obtain some proof the Inner Circle can use to prosecute the grapplers?

I have spoken only to Sri Radha about this latest development. She, alone, has a transcript of the conversation I intercepted two evenings ago, and I am not certain, but only hope she is to be trusted. That the KNC has gotten to the Vrinda Varma is clear. What is not clear is which members they own.

I'm certain Duran Prakash is serving as the agent of the person or persons at the head of this dragon. I am not certain whose face the head wears. I had even begun to suspect Nigudha Bhrasta before Ram-eve, but Namun tells me he was in Vatapur recovering from a surgery. Bhrasta's heart is not good, Namun confided, and I can tell from the irony in my friend's eye, I am invited to take him metaphorically. Of those present at the banquet that evening, I remember only that three people were absent from the room when I entered the study and caught the outgoing message: Sarad Valli, Duran Prakash, and Ranjan Vrksa, Bhrasta's able lieutenant. There may have been others and I curse my memory for its inattentiveness. I suspect that Prakashsama or even Vrksa may have been the sender of the message. Perhaps both of them are implicated.

There may yet be a way to attempt a retrieval of the log file they so carefully erased. If I can retrieve that, I can track the call.

Gar looked up at Jaya from the amber glow of the com-journal's little screen, his eyes strained. "Are you supposing, Nathu Rai, that the Vadin Adivaram is one of those owned by the KNC—and that Prakash-sama may be the purchaser?"

"I'm inclined to fear that, yes."

The Sarngin shook his head. "What prompted your father to embark on this investigation?"

"He thought he was seeing an unhealthy trend in Vrinda Varma consultation. Some of the junior members would back a particular opinion so stubbornly, it would block resolution. Things would get tabled or just drag out interminably. It wasn't anything he could pinpoint precisely enough to warrant an investigation, so he didn't say anything, just took notes on the various issues that seemed to cause the most trouble.

"Then, Duran Prakash suggested to him that his friendship with Namun Vedda should also extend to the Consortium. There was a particular issue on the Council docket that indirectly affected Vedda Technologies and Prakash indicated that if Father was really a loyal friend he'd throw his vote toward the KNC. Father rejected the idea so thoroughly, he didn't expect to hear any more about it. Then he started thinking about that trend in consultation and looked at his notes. The issues that caused the most contention, the ones the junior members were so stubborn about, were all issues that affected the KNC either directly or indirectly, through their various suppliers and contractors.

"After that, Father wondered if he should have cultivated the situation with Prakash—led him a little to see how far he was willing to go to own the Sarojin vote. He had some thought of getting Prakash into a compromising position, then reporting him to Uncle Namun."

"Uncle Namun, you call him. He is not really your Uncle."

Jaya shook his head. "My godfather and an old family friend—fanatical in his insistence that government, business, and friendship be kept in their separate spheres. He would have decapitated Prakash if he thought he was trying to coerce Father into throwing his vote, perhaps even default on his contracts with the Consortium."

"Which would have devastated his own company," observed Gar.

"Namun Vedda is a man of principle. He has always put family, friendship, and honor before business interests. Something that has never endeared him to the members of the KNC board."

"This conversation your father intercepted—he never discovered who the participants were?"

Jaya shook his head. "Evidently he had a house full of guests. Father was in the study when he caught the outgoing message on the vicom. It was startling enough that he monitored it and traced it to the terminal in the library, but by the time he got to the terminal, whoever placed the call was gone. There were about four members of the Kasi-Nawahr Board here that night, plus quite a few members of the Vrinda Varma, some of whom were, according to the message, Consortium targets."

Gar nodded, tapping the com-journal with one finger. "He says he was peeking into their accounts. He was then looking for—what—pay-offs?"

"He wondered if money was moving out of KNC coffers into the accounts of individual Varmana. He used his Council access rights to try to track that."

"And he found ... ?"

Jaya shrugged and lifted the com-journal from Gar's hands.

"This entry was made less than a week before his death. I don't know what he found ... if he found anything at all."

"Who is this Scar-Eye he speaks of? It occurs to me that this is not unlike your description of one of the alleged Workers' Coalitionists who attacked you."

Jaya glanced at the journal. "'A man with a scar running across his right eye,'" he read. "Yes, it occurs to me too. Only, five years ago, there was no Workers' Coalition."

"How did your father die, mahesa?"

Jaya felt the muscles of his chest constrict. "He was run down by an aircar left sitting with its engines idling. The Sarngin called it an accident. I'm beginning to have my doubts."

Hunger was what finally drew Govi to the kitchen of the House Sarojin. He satisfied that, but found a full stomach did not completely still the dim anxiety that wriggled somewhere in his shaggy head.

Aridas was there, sharing a cup of channa with his wife. They had spoken and fallen silent to watch steam wraiths escape their mugs. Govi twitched his shoulders and threw a chuckled comment onto the table.

"That Ana creature," he said.

Heli looked up from her channa. "That Ana creature?" she repeated. "What of her?"

Govi shied away from the defensive gleam in the woman's eye and shrugged his shoulders. "She's a curious curiosity."

"That's about as clear as a closed door," said Heli dryly. "Before you explain it, know I won't hear insults to the Rani Ana."

"Insults? No. No insults," Govi promised. "Compliments, only. She's just not molded to rita. Not ordinary, I mean. Full of questions ... like a man, see."

Ari produced an odd grunt and Heli's brows ascended.

"Like a man?"

Govi raised a calloused hand. "Now, don't run off at the brain. I just mean she—well, she comes to me asking all this and that about my alley. How this lays and that. What time this happens and that. Same things the Nathu Rai and his Sarngin friend are asking. Now, what the Niraya Hell's a woman be doing with that? Putting it in her chatbook?"

Ari and Heli were now looking at Govi in such a way as to make him wish he'd kept his mouth shut.

"She asked you these things?" Heli asked.

"I said so, didn't I? She asked and I told." He shrugged.

Heli leaned toward him across the table. "Did you tell Jaya Rai?"

"No. Why should I? What's she going to do, after all? She's a woman."

Heli sat up. "She's not a Mehtaran woman, Madman. She's Ana."

"And that means what?"

Ari pushed back his chair with a loud scrape and stood. "It means you'd better tell Jaya Rai, Govi-sama. Because this woman is like to do anything at all."

The corridor was empty. At least, there were no people moving through it—but it was full of sounds and aromas and auras that extruded into the red velvet hall from beneath the closed doors. Chatter, laughter, sobbing. Foods and perfumes. Desire and satiation. Fear.

Ana shivered and retracted herself from the swirl of sensation. There was no business done on this level.

After a moment of thought, she decided the top floor was the most logical place to lodge the private zones of such a business. Taking the stairs, she by-passed the next two floors and made her way directly to the penthouse, where she was met by a sturdy wooden door whose polished plaque told her she was about to violate a private area. An equally polished handle told her the door opened on a manual slider.

She scanned the edges of the door for any sign of an alarm system or surveillance network. There didn't seem to be any, but the situation dictated caution. She got to her knees and slid the door carefully aside, hunkering into the lowest crouch possible as she slipped through. She glanced down the corridor; it was opulent and empty. Everywhere was the product of Avasan gaur mines. Door handles gleamed with it; it adorned cornices and moldings; it dripped from light fixtures.

The fruits of our labor.

She shook the anger out after a moment and checked the doors here for surveillance gear. She saw none. What she did see were more golden plaques. They labeled the private quarters of Ashur Badan and Kareen Devaki, their respective offices and a shared Salon. An ornate lift cage reposed midway down Ashur Badan's side of the hall.

Ana moved to the door with Kareen Devaki's name on it. She laid her hand on the door handle, then closed her eyes, whispered a prayer and turned the handle, gently. There was no click, no creak, no groan, just silent mechanical obedience. The door opened.

Ana took the luxurious but business-like place at a glance, saw the vicom terminal and the connecting door to what must be Kareen Devaki's private suite. She moved into the room, closing the door behind her. The terminal was active, displaying what appeared to be a tally of the day's receipts. She slid into the chair, a smile beginning to curve her mouth. She recognized the program. Her father and mother used the same software to track their accounts.

It was almost too easy. She hadn't dreamed she'd actually find the system opened to a module of the very program she needed to access. The thought that struck next wiped the vestigial smile from her lips. All this might mean that Devakisa had just left the terminal for only a moment—that she was even now in the next room and had every intention of returning to complete her late-night work.

Ana put her fingers to the keyboard. She exited the accounting module and called up the inventory. It was a continual shock seeing the familiar layout of fields detailing the acquisition and disposal of goods filled with the names and descriptions of human beings. She found Vanam Sanoh easily enough in the database—simply running a search for the girl's name—but, reading the entry, she knew she would not find her in the dalali. Vanam Sanoh had been sold at public auction the day before she had supposedly sent her plea for help.

It was chilling knowledge—that a trap had been deliberately set for her. The mixture of fear and fury made her brain and fingers fly. When a search for "none" in the cree field yielded too many records, Ana added "fair" skin tone to the logic and netted a more manageable group. She eliminated several more on the basis of their descriptions then made a quick cross-check against the list she pulled out of her satchel.

There were still more fair-skinned id-less people in the dalali's database than were accounted for by the list, but Ana couldn't afford the time for a detailed comparison. She looked around, a little frantic, and saw the imager on a nearby table. She keyed the program to scan her list and enter them into a table she could check against the database records ... and all but jumped out of her skin when the machine responded with a low hum.

Her eyes fastened on the door she assumed led to Devaki's private salon. She fully expected it to swing open at any second. She was so intent on it, she almost failed to hear the sly sound that penetrated the door from the outside corridor.

At the exact moment she realized there was someone just outside the office, the imager disgorged its list. She froze for an instant, her hand already reaching for the printout flimsy, her eyes now on the external door. In that instant, the door handle turned.

She grabbed the flimsy from the imager's output tray and flung herself out of the chair. She went toward the door, not away from it, and was barely behind it when it swung open.

Whoever was there didn't move for a moment, but hovered with an uncertainty that Anala felt as a prickling sensation on the side of her face and neck. She tried to swallow the knot in her throat, but the muscles seemed paralyzed. She gave up and settled for taking a deep, silent, shaking breath.

There was a warm crackle of movement from the unseen one; a sliding of fabric on fabric, an intake of breath, a shift forward into the room.

Come in! thought Ana. Just come in and let me slip past you!

He/she did come in—swiftly, suddenly—and closed the door behind. Exposed, Ana recoiled, cold adrenaline pouring through her core. Then she lunged forward, whipped out a hand and grasped a black-clad arm.

"Hadas! What in the name of Ram-ji are you doing?"

He whirled around and half raised an arm in defense. His face showed immediate relief.

"Ana! Thank God!" he whispered. "I thought I'd lost you!"

"No, only your senses. What are you doing?" He opened his

mouth to answer, but she shook her head. "Never mind. I know what you're doing."

"I couldn't let you do this alone."

"So now no one knows where either of us are."

"I left a note on my bed. If they think to look for me, they'll find it. Do you have the list?"

Exasperated, Ana took a deep breath and nodded. She patted the satchel. "Right here. Let's get out of here."

"Why don't we make another copy of it?" Hadas suggested. "I'll take one—you take the other. That way if anything happens to one of us..."

She grimaced. "You really take to this skulk and scurry business, don't you?"

He shrugged. "It makes sense, doesn't it?"

Ana nodded. "Keep an ear to the door." She crossed to the desk and started the imaging process again. The machine responded with its sonorous hum and slid out a second copy of the records. Ana took it, then returned the vicom program to the accounting module, leaving it (she hoped) the way she'd found it.

She moved back to the door and handed Hadas the flimsy.

"Now, we've got to get out of here. Quietly and quickly. We'll go back the way we came. There's another airvan due in about-"—she glanced at her timepiece—"-twenty minutes. That's our ride out."

"Vanam Sanoh?"

"Already sold at auction. She couldn't have sent that note."

Hadas nodded, then tilted his head toward the door. "All quiet."

"Let's go."

The hall was empty. Ana slid through the door with Hadas right behind. They hurried to the exit, slipped through and started their downward journey. It was still except for the muffled hammering of rhythmic music from the levels below.

They were perhaps halfway between the first and second floor when the door just above them opened and closed. They now shared the stairwell with an unknown someone.

Ana pushed Hadas downward, her eyes raised to the second level landing. He glided gracefully the remaining steps to the first floor. She followed and just saw someone round the corner of the second landing as she slipped around the corner of the first. The footsteps above them moved deliberately and swiftly downward.

Ana shoved open the door to the foyer and pushed Hadas through, following him into the dimly lit interior. It stretched before them in a seemingly endless tunnel of wood paneling and carpet. The backstage storage area was half the length of the building to the right along that tunnel, but at least the tunnel was empty.

"Run," Ana whispered and gave Hadas a gentle shove. Together they sprinted toward the opposite end of the hall.

Ana heard a shout go up behind them, but ignored it, her eyes on Hadas's back as his greater speed pulled him ahead of her. She was hungering for the black warmth of the storage area when someone stepped out of a doorway into Hadas's path and collided with him.

The man grabbed the Avasan's arms and held him, a scowl building on his broad face. Ana slowed, readying a sassy remark, and glanced back over her shoulder. Three men pursued them up the long foyer. One of them was Ashur Badan.

Barely thinking, Ana launched herself at their roadblock, hitting his elbow and jarring his grip. Hadas moved at the same time, kicking the fellow square in his sturdy shins. He wrenched free and pelted off down the foyer. Ana tried to follow, but found a hand wrapped solidly around one wrist. Terrified and furious, she put her head down and bit the man's forearm as hard as she could. He shrieked and let go, grasping at her shoulder. He caught the rope that hung there instead. Ana let the rope go, slipping out of its coils and twisting away.

Hadas had disappeared and she made a flash decision not to draw their pursuers after him. With Badan's men nearly on her heels, she threw herself through the next open doorway. Three doors confronted her in the semi-darkness. She chose one and catapulted into an unlit room that echoed every breath, every footfall. She was lost in a barrage of harsh, ambient sound.

She ran and collided with hard, cold surfaces, fell and scrambled up and went on. She met maze-like walls that herded her in square coils so that she lost all sense of direction. She could hear her own breathing—loud, rasping. She could hear the sound of feet on the unyielding floor and voices flinging themselves against the chill walls.

Someone was very near. She recoiled and staggered along yet

another smooth, patterned wall this one studded with painful obstructions. She bumped her shoulder, her breast; bruised her ribs and hands.

Without warning, a spray of freezing water hit her full in the face. She screamed and recoiled and was met by a stinging spray from another direction. She screamed again and ducked out from under it, stumbled and slipped and came down against a wall. The water was beneath her, too, cold as Niraya Hell.

On her knees and soaking wet, she felt along the wall for a way out. Trembling, she didn't dare rise; didn't dare poke her head up out of the black pocket of spray. She put her hands against the tile surface and began to creep along to the left.

Oh, God, should it be to the left?

A prickling ran up her back, colder than the water that lapped around her knees. He was right behind her, standing in the stinging spray and maybe he could even see her there, groveling at the wall like a pilgrim before a shrine. She started to turn and rise and was knocked down again by a blaze of light.

White. White room. White light gleaming and glittering and shining viciously off of every surface—tile and polished chrome. Her eyes watered from the glare. She knew this place, this deadend corner. She'd been here before, stripped naked and cleansed of Avasan soil.

He blocked out the light when he stood over her, and she dared, stupidly, to look up into his face. Anala Nadim experienced, then, for perhaps only the second or third time in her short life, a moment of real fear.

CHAPTER NINETEEN

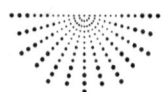

STANDING in the hall with Hadas's note clutched in his hand, Jaya felt as if his internal organs had been sucked out and put back rearranged. There was a sudden rushing of blood in his ears and through a peculiar tunnel of black mist, he could see everyone frowning at him, waiting for him to say something.

When he didn't say something, Govi shrugged uneasily and said, "I guess I should have given tale before. Didn't know the memsa was liable to craziness."

"Kena says there's a two-wheeler gone," said Heli quietly.

Jaya nodded, struggling for decisiveness. "Ravi, call down to the gate station and find out what time she left."

Jaya carried the note back to his study where Mall Gar pored over his surveillance team's reports of back-alley activity.

Gar got to his feet, eyes intently on Jaya's face. "What has happened?"

Jaya swallowed; it was difficult. "You know I have a second informant. One I was reluctant to reveal to you."

"Yes, Nathu Rai?"

"Her name is Ana. She's Avasan—dedicated to locating and freeing the Avasan das. She's been secretly keeping track of our research, monitoring our activity."

He hesitated, then held out the note.

Gar took it, read it, then glanced back at him, his eyes now showing honest concern. "She has gone to the dalali herself? With this young man, Hadas?"

Jaya's reorganized insides twisted. "Apparently so. I suspect she thought we weren't as avid in pursuing the missing Avasans as we were seeking a connection between the dalali trafficking and the Consortium. Or maybe we just weren't moving fast enough for her."

Gar frowned. "We must move very fast, now," he murmured. He pulled a palm-sized comlink from his belt and keyed a coded sequence into it. The response from the recipient of the message was immediate. "Voice link," Gar said to the small unit. "Report, Srestha."

A male voice answered. "Sir. Everything seems normal at this end. The linen wagon arrived on schedule, unloaded and went on its way. There should be a catering vehicle along in about ... ten minutes."

"Nothing unusual?"

"No, Commander. Haven't seen any of the couriers tonight, but they're pretty irregular."

Gar nodded, watching Jaya fidget by the door. "We have reason to believe a couple of young Avasans may try to penetrate the dalali's security in an attempt to rescue some of their compatriots. Don't take your eyes from the back of that building, Srestha. If you see anything that seems at all suspicious, contact me immediately."

"Yes, Commander."

Gar broke off the link and stared at the carpet.

"What do we do?" asked Jaya.

"We could raid the dalali now—tonight. But then, if this young woman is successful-"

"If she's successful it won't matter one way or the other. If she gets caught-"

Gar nodded. "Yes. Then, it makes a great deal of difference. You are supposing these people would kill her? Would they not take note of her id and send her home to repent of her mischief?"

Jaya stirred uneasily. "Her id is fictitious. She's wearing a doctored dascree. She has no leaf."

The Commander's eyebrows shot upward and lodged in his curly hair. "A dascree of the House Sarojin?"

"A dascree with my personal seal. Ana was yevetha. I managed to get to her before the Sarngin did, but only by a matter of seconds."

"Then they must surely return her to you, since you're her legal owner. To do otherwise would only give you more reason to pry at their affairs. Unless, Nathu Rai, there is another revelation you have yet to make about the young memsa?"

Jaya came all the way into the room and sat heavily on the corner of his desk.

"Yes. Yes, there is. And I'm afraid it's a revelation I should have made earlier. Ana is Rokh Nadim's daughter." He watched Gar react to that, then continued. "Judging from what Hadas said about Ana suspecting a trap, I would assume that there is someone connected with the dalali who knows who she is. Someone who would very much like to get their hands on her."

"Then her death is not the object."

"I would say that the death of AGIM is the object, Commander."

"Rokh Nadim will be asked to choose, then, between his daughter's life and the life of his organization?"

"Between his daughter's life and the life's blood of his people and his world," Jaya amended. "The Consortium is interested only in a return on their investment."

"I must disagree with you, Nathu Rai," Gar observed. "Judging from your father's discoveries, I would say they are interested in a good deal more than that. Has it not occurred to you that the person or persons who pursue Anala Nadim might be the same persons who arranged your father's untimely accident?"

Jaya felt as if he stood on a high, Avasan snow-plain surveying an uncompromisingly bleak landscape.

"It had occurred to me," he said and shivered.

~

Hadas shook with a cold that had nothing to do with the temperature of the black box he stood in. He peered out of the square access and wished he was any place but here—prayed unsuccessfully for the courage to go back up into the dalali and free Ana.

His eyes snapped into sudden focus. A diffuse beam of light

skidded down the alley from the direction of the gate. He strained his ears and caught the whine of airjets braking to a stop. The illumined face of his timepiece told him this was not the airwagon he was expecting, unless it was seven minutes early.

He stood on tiptoe and tried to see around the sill of the access. The vehicle was a long, low, dark luxury car not unlike the one he'd seen the Rani Sarojin drive out in. Its lightbar scraped the alley slab, leaving darkness in its wake; its rear running-lights glowed dull amber.

Hadas watched it glide past, hesitated, then levered himself up and out of the sub-level into the aircar's warm rear exhaust. It was easy to keep up with it at this speed and he padded along, bent over, one hand riding lightly on the aircar's rear deck. He slowed as the car slowed, doubling over further as it reached the dalali's service entrance. He stopped and settled with it into a full crouch, his eyes straining for a chance to see and recognize the passengers.

The guards had disappeared within the building. It seemed peculiar that the entrance should be completely unguarded in the presence of an obviously important guest. The driver of the car got out first and opened one of the rear doors. The man who exited was tall, imposing and thick-looking in a full, heavy coat. His face was first in profile, then averted, and Hadas was disappointed that he couldn't see more of it.

He watched a second man get out, then a third. Like the first, they wore furs and tall hats that covered all but just a fringe of hair. Both were smaller than the first man—one short and slight, the other tall but slender. They were also vaguely familiar, but Hadas couldn't remember where he had seen them.

The men turned their backs to the rear of the car as a short, fat fellow Hadas recognized from the Mesha celebration came out to meet them. A Vadin, Hadas remembered.

"You've got her?" asked the tall one. His voice was deep, rough, and dry, like rocks rolling down a slope.

"We have."

"You're sure she's Nadim's daughter?"

"Positive. Please, come in and meet the young lady. I would recommend that you wear these." The Vadin held out something to the three, which they accepted. They removed their hats, then pulled on velvet hoods, making any further scrutiny on Hadas's part futile. They disappeared into the dalali after the Vadin. The door closed.

Before Hadas could decide what to do next, he heard the approach of another aircar from behind and knew he would be exposed if he didn't move quickly.

The guards had returned to their posts, the driver to his seat in the front of his grand vehicle. There was only one direction Hadas could flee—down the right flank of the luxury aircar to its nose. Barely shielded by the car's bulk, he watched a catering van advance until it lay practically nose to tail with the big aircar. The driver shut down his lights and disembarked from his cabin, entering into an earnest discussion with the guards and the other driver. The thrust of the conversation was clear: The catering draymen wanted the car moved so they could unload their perishables.

Hadas glanced up at the cabin of the airvan. It was empty. Hadas took a deep breath and began a swift creep down the flank of the car toward the catering van. He reached the haunch of the car and rolled across the irregular gap between the two vehicles. Pausing only a moment, Hadas reached up and pushed gently on the airvan's passenger door latch. It clicked, hummed, and the door slid open, disappearing into the rear wall of the van. The smell of food wafted out of the gap.

Hadas stuck his head inside and peered back between the seats. He praised Ram-ji silently. There was a walk-through to the storage area. Quickly, he climbed into the cabin and closed the door behind, then slid through into the van's fragrant interior to seek a place of concealment.

"My men will approach the front of the building and cover all exits." Mall Gar pointed to three separate spots on the vicom's holographic extrusion of the Badan-Devaki dalali. "There will be two men on each exit, plus the team of four who will enter the main foyer and initiate the search."

He gave a terse verbal command and the vicom rotated the image until the small audience was looking down into the building as children through the open roof of a doll house.

"You and I, Nathu Rai, will bring the second team in through the back. An armored unit will cover each end of the alley. We will make the surprise complete by coming in through these previously blocked doorways." He indicated two points on the abandoned facing building where his teams had been obliged to pull apart the debris and hasty hammer-work put in by the building's latest owners —Badan and Devaki. "We will not move until the street side units are in place."

"How long will it take us to get there?" asked Jaya.

"Not long. Ten minutes." Gar glanced at the assembled forces. "Are we ready, then?"

There were nods, grunts of assent. The vicom had sucked up its holograph and Gar had opened his mouth to give moving orders when his comlink demanded immediate attention. He thumbed it on.

"Voice link," he said.

"Reporting as ordered, Commander." It was Srestha. "The dalali has some special visitors. Three men in a luxury car."

"Who?"

"Can't tell, sir. They put on hoods right away. But I think ... Well, sir, the man that met them looked like the Vadin Adivaram. I don't suppose it could have been."

"Anything else?" asked Gar, only half seeing the intent faces that peered at him across Jaya's study.

"Yes, sama. At the same time this car showed up, we thought we saw someone sneaking around in the alley beside the vehicles."

"Vehicles, Srestha?"

"The, uh, the catering van showed up right on schedule, Commander. It's parked behind the aircar at the moment. I think our skulker climbed aboard."

"Aboard the airvan?"

"Yes, sir."

Gar glanced at Jaya. "You only saw one person concealed in the alley, then? Male or female?"

"Just one, sir. We couldn't tell what sex from here. Too dark."

"Hold your position. We're on our way." Gar signed off and passed Jaya a significant look. "Perhaps our raid will net some very big fish, Nathu Rai. Shall we go?"

~

Ana winced and tried to pull away from the pressure of the fingers gripping her jaw. It was futile. The couch she lay upon offered no escape. The thick ring on the man's hand only bit further into her skin, forcing her to gasp.

"Ah, sorry, dear." He spoke in a voice that might have been soothing under any other circumstances. "But you would resist my admiration."

One of his companions moved to stand at his shoulder. He seemed towering, alien—the only thing human about him the eyes that pierced his hood's black velvet fabric. They pierced Ana's courage, as well.

"She's very beautiful for a Snowflake," he said and his voice was like cold stone. "I wonder, is that the pallor of the cave, or is she Genda Sita?"

The first man made a clucking sound through his teeth, turning Ana's face into the light. "She has eyes the color of a three moon sky. The eyes of the Jadu." His finger traced the line of Ana's jaw, making her shiver.

The remaining two men hovered in the background. Now one of them stepped forward and asked, "Sama, what do we do with her?"

"You don't do anything with her, Vadin," said the tall one. "She is now ours. You may go back to your business concerns ... but do try to be more discreet."

A Vadin! Ana nearly gasped at the enormity of it.

"Will being more discreet save me from exposure, do you think?" the hooded Vadin asked.

"Ah, you mean, of course, your insidious dabbling in illegal enslavement. Well, I seem to recall that if you'd had any discretion to begin with, you wouldn't be in this position. But I don't think you need to worry about exposure just now, old man. With this young woman in our hands, we can stop the overeager Sarojin dead in his tracks and Rokh Nadim and his rabble of yevetha with him."

"And if Sarojin won't stop? Then what? Am I to be sacrificed to the ... to your interests?"

"What—after we've worked so hard at winning your loyalty? You have too much work to do, Vadin—you and that little toad who calls himself a Lord. You are our strong and steady voices on the Inner Circle. We need you. If anyone is to be sacrificed to our best interests, I think it will have to be Jaya Sarojin."

Ana gasped and nearly stopped breathing. The hand on her jaw tightened.

The Vadin made a strange sound in his throat. "He is much like his father."

"I had noticed. You seem reluctant to see him disposed of. In fact, you've resisted the idea of killing him since the subject first came up. Do you have some political reason for that, or just a soft spot in your heart?"

"Bhaktasu Sarojin was my friend," said the Vadin almost petulantly. "And yes, I have what amounts to a 'soft spot' for the young Nathu Rai."

"Ah, so of course you would rather sacrifice yourself than the son of your friend."

There was a pause of some weight. The silent man near the door fidgeted, his attention shifting between the other players in the scene.

"I didn't say that," murmured the Vadin at last.

Ana's anger overcame her sense of judgment. "Worm," she said before she could stop herself.

The tall one chuckled. "A woman of strong opinions. I think I'll enjoy her company."

The man beside her turned his hooded head and his fingers left her chin. "When she has served your purpose..."

The tall one shrugged. "Then she may serve yours."

Jaya picked his way through the dusty, dank interior of the shuttered building behind Mall Gar, wishing teleportation was a technological fact instead of a theoretical abstraction, or that they could simply make time stand still. There was too much of that precious commodity being spent just getting into position. Any moment Gar's watchers could hail him and say the big, midnight blue aircar was gone.

They reached the barricaded doors in a matter of seconds and

Gar stopped to check in with his street-side forces. That done, he turned to the men behind him in the abandoned building.

"The others are in place. Are we ready?"

"Dammit, yes," said Jaya and tightened his grip on the stunfuzzy in his hand. He heard Ravi and Kena give their assent.

"Then, we go."

The remaining barricade, held lightly in place by several propped beams, folded to Gar's wiry strength and the Commander led his force of four into the alley. They emerged several meters behind the catering van. Up-alley, another quartet of men appeared from a second doorway. This group was led by a trusted Lieutenant and included Aridas and two of Jaya's private security men. At Gar's signal both groups converged on the service entrance.

The Badan-Devaki door guards dropped their weapons and surrendered, several more were captured in the corridor along with the driver of the car and the draymen emerging from the airvan.

There was much shouting and protest and confusion as the raiders overran the dalali. The Sarngin and their civilian assistants fanned out and conducted an exhaustive search, gathering everyone they found into the largest of the dalali's showrooms on the premiere floor.

Jaya, Gar, and Ravi went directly to the penthouse and cornered Badan and Devaki in their sumptuous private Salon. The pair seemed merely surprised and annoyed, and gave no indication they wished to escape. Ashur Badan blustered about Sarngin arrogance and Kareen Devaki spoke dispassionately about legal action.

Jaya Sarojin lost his temper and shouted them both to silence.

"Where is she?" he demanded and felt like committing mayhem when both of them stared at him blankly and said, "Who do you mean, Nathu Rai?" almost in unison.

Gar intervened. "The mahesa is asking after the whereabouts of his young cousin, Ana. We believe she is here."

Kareen Devaki looked at her partner with well-feigned innocence. "I certainly haven't seen her. I can't imagine what she'd be doing here at this time of night. You must have misunderstood her, Nathu Rai. She's been invited to a private auction tomorrow, but-"

"That's enough," snapped Jaya. "We know she was coming here tonight."

Devaki shrugged. "Apparently she never got here."

"We'll see what our search reveals," said Gar mildly. "Yes, Lieutenant?" He turned to the young officer who hovered in the doorway.

"The search is complete, Commander. We've found a lot of young women, but none of them seems to be Anala Nadim."

Gar caught the glance the two dalal exchanged. "I see the name lights."

"Nadim? Of course it does," said Devaki. "But what in the name of the Goddess would Anala Nadim be doing in our dalali?"

"Checking your files, memsa," said Gar quietly, "to see how many Avasans have passed through your doors on their way to becoming das."

"Our trade is quite legal, Commander," returned Devaki.

"So. But it is not legal to manufacture das by intentionally stealing the leaf of people who bear no cree. Haroon, you have finished with the offices? What have you found?"

"This was in the lock-up, sir."

Officer Haroon, graying, craggy and dour-looking, held a box in gnarled hands. The sight of it excited the most incredible expressions on the faces of the two brokers.

Jaya reached for it reflexively.

Haroon hesitated, but gave up the box at a slight nod from his Commander.

Jaya tried the lid. It was set with a micro-encoder and refused to admit him. He handed the box to Devaki. "Open it, memsa."

She hesitated, then grimly did as he'd commanded, entering her private code to loose the lid. She hesitated, again, to hand it back and he took it roughly from her hands, spilling a portion of its shining contents onto the polished wooden floor of the salon.

Haroon bent to pick up the fallen items and held them up to the light; a necklace and two bracelets glittered in his stubby hand, the leaf they carried tinkling musically as they jostled together. He squinted, then separated the necklace from the tangle and handed it to his Commander.

Gar turned the leaf over in his hands. "Anala Nadim," he read. "Lying right on top where you must have just put it, eh, memsa? Now, you could tell me you don't know how these got into your possession or into your lock-up but, of course, I wouldn't believe you. I wouldn't believe you, because I know how they got into your possession. I even know the name—or should I say names—of the man who put them there. Pidar Rel, I think, or Parva Rishi or— But I'm sure you've heard them all."

Kareen Devaki's face was a horrid shade of gray and a white aureole encircled her pursed lips.

"Where is she?" asked Jaya again.

"I will admit," said Devaki archly. "That we have used rather questionable methods to ensure our business has the finest and most exotic stock. However, I will not admit to kidnapping this Nadim girl, or whatever it is you're accusing us of having done. You may be able to prove that she was processed by this dalali some time ago and on your behalf, but you cannot prove that she was here tonight."

"Whose car is that parked behind your building?" asked Gar abruptly. "What special visitors do you entertain?"

"All of our clients are special," countered Devaki. "Many of them come to us in chauffeured aircars."

"Who has the woman?"

"I don't know." Devaki shot Jaya a sideways glance. "He had her. If he lost her, that's his fault, not ours."

Gar made a grinding sound with his teeth. "Downstairs," he said. "Let's go and see what the rest of our team has turned up."

They had just stepped out of the lift basket on the premiere level when one of Gar's officers approached escorting a crumpled young man in a black body-suit.

"Hadas!" Jaya shouldered his way past Gar and Haroon.

"Nathu Rai!" Catching sight of Badan and Devaki being led from the basket, he pointed a finger at Ashur Badan, his cheeks flushed with anger. "He's the one! He's the one who chased us! He and his-his-" He stammered, searching for a word, then gave it up. "Where's Ana, Nathu Rai? Tell me she has come to no harm."

Jaya stared at Hadas, feeling the gnawing of defeat at the inside of his stomach. "We haven't found her yet, Hadas. Do you have any idea where she might be?"

The Avasan shook his head. " they know," he said, moving his eyes to the dalal. "And those other men."

Jaya grasped his shoulder, ungently. "What other men, Hadas?"

"In the alley. They came in a big, dark blue aircar. Three of them. I didn't know them," he offered before either Jaya or Gar could ask. "Although ... one of them, I think I've seen somewhere—it must have been at the Mesha Fest. They were both wearing hats, then the Vadin came out gave them hoods to put on."

Jaya jerked his head around to catch Kareen Devaki's reaction. She'd gone completely white. Ashur Badan just stared at the floor.

"What Vadin?"

"I saw him at the Mesha Fest, too," Hadas said. "Jivinta introduced me to him, but I don't remember his name."

"The boy is lying," said Devaki. "He didn't see anything."

"I saw the men get out of the car."

The dalal sneered. "Lots of men get out of lots of cars at our back door if they wish to be discreet. This is that kind of business."

"They came to see Ana. One of them asked the Vadin if they had the woman."

"We have a house full of women-"

Hadas rode over her sarcastic retort. "Then he asked if the Vadin was sure she was Nadim's daughter. Then they put on hoods and went inside."

"Who were the men, memsa?" Gar leaned close to Devaki's face. "Who was the Vadin?"

"I don't know."

Ashur Badan glanced at her, then shoved his gaze back to the floor.

Gar studied the two of them momentarily, then turned to Haroon, who hovered at his shoulder. "Find the driver of the aircar and bring him to me."

Haroon bowed smartly and disappeared in the direction of the dalali's public showroom. Gar turned back swiftly and caught Kareen Devaki staring after the man as if her gaze could topple him to the ground.

"Who were the men, Devaki-sa?" he asked again. "And who was the Vadin? Was it, by any chance, Bel Adivaram?" Gar's eyes were tight against Kareen Devaki's face, clamping it in a brilliant vise.

She held his gaze coolly, trying to look down her nose at him. "I don't know. Several auspicious Vadin frequent our business. It could have been any of them."

"Do they all behave as if they own the place? Greet your discreet visitors at the back door and introduce them to young women?"

"They rent facilities for their own private parties quite often. We don't pry into their affairs."

Gar nodded. "Ah, well, I think you must have known what this Vadin was about. After all, the young lady he was introducing his guests to was very recently in the possession of Badansama—isn't that right, Badan-sama?"

The dalal jumped and glanced swiftly to Devaki. He tried to meet the Zone Commander's eyes but his gaze slid from that intense scrutiny and escaped back to the carpeting.

"This young man saw you, sama."

Badan sweated.

"We know she was here in Hadas Gupta's company. We know the two were pursued by you and your men. We know that Hadas escaped, but Anala Nadim did not. We know that three men arrived by car and were greeted by a Vadin. We strongly suspect that Vadin was Bel Adivaram. Those men were here with the express purpose of seeing Anala Nadim—who was last known to be in your possession."

Jaya's entire anatomy recoiled from that last word. It was wrong. It shouldn't be spoken in the same breath with the name Anala Nadim ... or any other name.

"Ah! Haroon returns with the driver."

"It was Bel Adivaram!" Ashur Badan spat the words from his mouth, his fear making them sound vicious.

Devaki was on him in an instant. "Ashur, you idiot! What are you doing?"

"I am not going to freeze in Niraya Hell for the sake of that old lecher, Kareen." He turned to face Gar. "The Vadin who met the our ... guests was Bel Adivaram. He instructed us to lure Anala Nadim here so she could be captured."

"To what end?"

Badan made a gesture of frustration. "Some ... political scheme. Some grand design—I don't know. We did as the Vadin asked."

"And the other men?" asked Jaya over Gar's shoulder.

"I don't know." Badan raised his hands before either Jaya or Gar could protest. "That is the truth. We have only seen them hooded.

We have never been permitted to know who they are. We have never even heard their voices. Adivaram knows."

"They have the girl?"

"Yes."

"You idiot," repeated Devaki.

"Where are they now?"

"Gone. I don't know where because I don't know who they are."

Gar's eyes narrowed. "Are you lying again, Badan-sama? Is there not some hiding place where they might be secreted?"

"There is a private lift shaft. It goes directly from this level to a small foyer at the back of the building. From there, one can cross beneath the street to the carpark-"

Gar made a sudden shift in attention. "Haroon! Leave the driver with Lieutenant Bharta for questioning. Take two men and search this passage and carpark."

"Sir!" Haroon snapped like a wire puppet and obeyed instantly.

Gar turned back to Badan and Devaki. "I think we will be more comfortable in one of your lovely parlors. We have much to discuss."

Jaya opened his eyes and stared, unfocused, at the patch of sunlight that crept slowly across the table top. He watched a thin veil of golden motes ripple through the radiance—tiny, dancing jinn that hypnotized with their chaotic frolic. When a curl of steam invaded the bright aura, he realized someone had put a cup of channa in front of him. He mumbled his thanks and automatically lifted the cup to his lips, trying to reorder his thoughts. That was futile just now, because there was nothing around which to organize them.

He got up stiffly, stretched, and went to the couch that occupied the bay window in Kareen Devaki's private parlor. Below, the street was coming to life; merchants rolled up their gates and rolled out their awnings; street-keepers swept and curried the glistening composite walkways; aircars began to tour the avenue. People were chatting amicably, enjoying their morning channa, deciding what to eat for breakfast.

The pleasant scene would make it difficult for the average person to imagine that somewhere out there, there was fear and uncertainty—terror, even. That there was a darkness in Kasi this morning that had not lifted with the rising of the sun.

No, he corrected himself, remembering where he was, not just this morning. Every morning. But this particular morning, the darkness had reached out for and found Jaya Sarojin. This particular morning, he was experiencing it firsthand.

Jaya shook himself. He had to concentrate on the positive. Whoever had Ana wanted her alive—had to keep her alive, in fact—at least, until some demands had been made and responded to. He couldn't see what that person or persons had to gain by taking her captive. How could they possibly hope to issue their demands without revealing who they were—without making the whole exercise futile?

He turned from the window as Mall Gar re-entered the room, his face still clothed in its irritatingly dispassionate mask. He'd admired that dispassion when he first met Gar, now it aroused in him the conflicting urges to emulate the Sarngin's detachment and to fly into an hysterical rage. Jaya Sarojin was not given to either hysteria or rages, so he simply watched Gar cross the room.

"The driver's story checks." The Sarngin allowed himself a minute gesture of frustration, raking the fringe of ringlets back away from his forehead. "He has been employed by the Air-Spirit Agency for four years. They consider him one of their most reliable and discreet drivers. He doesn't know the identity of last night's fare because, by company policy, the identity is only given at the client's discretion."

"Then the company records-"

"Show only that a call was placed to rent a luxury car under the name Singh. Since there is no more common name in Kasi..."

Jaya nodded. "But the car was paid for-"

"In cash, by a man who fits a description so general as to be no description at all. He wore a pair of tinted eyeshades—Mitrex brand, according to the Air-Spirit cashier. She volunteered that she's always wanted a pair. I gather they are considered fashionable," he added wryly.

"I'd buy her a hundred pair if she could give us a worthwhile description."

"Would it help? I think we can assume the courier was Parva

Rishi or one of his cohorts. I've got Govi-sama and some of my men out digging around his known haunts already."

"So, what do we have?"

Gar expelled a sharp breath and sat on the arm of a chair near the window. "We have Badan and Devaki, who are still being inter-rogated. And we have the Vadin Adivaram ... if we can find him; he has yet to return to his home. And we have Varaza and his Lieu-tenant, if we can connect them solidly enough to this business."

"No one here saw the men Adivaram brought in?"

"No one. Adivaram removed all the guards from the entry and made sure the catering draymen stayed in the kitchen during their passage. Hadas Gupta and the driver are the only two people to even glimpse these men and the driver has made discretion such a habit, he didn't even look at their faces when he picked them up."

Jaya straightened. "Picked them up? Where?"

"In a public tiedown in the Jewel District—and before you ask, yes, I had the tiedown searched and all vehicles accounted for. On the surface there is nothing suspicious there. There were a number of aircars, two carriages and a single horse. They all belonged to merchants on the row. So, Nathu-Rai, tell me—precisely who is it we are attempting to corner?"

"What makes you think I know?"

"Ah, not know, perhaps, but suspect—" He tilted his head and waited for Jaya's reply.

"Obviously, I suspect Duran Prakash, if not of conspiracy, at least of complicity. And ... I have to admit I'm suspicious of both Nigudha Bhrasta and Ranjan Vrksa. I have to wonder if it was coin-cidental that Bhrasta just happened to show up in the KNC box the morning after I'd gotten my ribs kicked in."

Gar nodded. "A sensible suspicion. Do you think you have enough evidence to accuse them of this complicity before the Inner Circle?"

"With my mother's testimony and my father's journal, I can at least raise the suspicion that Prakash is part of a Consortium attempt to manipulate the outcome of Vrinda Varma deliberations. If Hadas can identify him as one of the men that was here last night, we've got him on suspicion of kidnapping, as well."

"Theft, you mean. The memsa did have a dascree in her palm, Nathu Rai. Yours."

Jaya winced at the jibe and knew that, coming from Gar, it was not accidental.

"I would suggest," continued the Commander after a moment, "that the best use of your time would be to lay out your case and that the best use of mine would be to find the missing Vadin."

Jaya nodded and pulled himself to his feet. "I've got just enough time before the Circle Call to bathe and change clothes. I suppose I should go home."

"May I recommend that you also take breakfast? You will be of little use to the cause of Nadim-sa in a sugar coma."

~

The Cause of Nadim-sa. Jaya made a wry face at the roof of the Sarngin aircar that ferried him home. He had little interest in Causes just now and every interest in Nadim-sa. Her disappearance had turned his insides into a deep pit full of cold ash, and an emotion that had nothing to do with Causes and crusades dug its raptor claws into his soul and shook it.

He relegated all causes to Niraya Hell. He only wanted Ana back.

The thing with its claws in him shook a little harder and demanded recognition. Bhakti is what you feel, said Ravi's voice. Bhakti is what you feel.

Ana could speak of bhakti and passion in one breath and feel both for a Being she could neither see nor touch. Could she feel them for a man—for him? Ana believed in Causes. Ana fought crusades. It was as much a part of her as her Rohin devotion or her inherent courage or that hint of the Jadu that lurked in her eyes. He could not have Ana and eschew Causes.

Liar.

The Voice was sharp and clear and came straight at him from deep in the ashy pit: You could separate the woman from her Causes if you wanted to but you don't want to. You don't want to, because they were your father's Causes and they came to you in your blood. They've been part of you since you formed in your mother's womb.

He knew it was true and, for the first time, did not embark upon denial. The thought that followed that revelation was even more sobering: It was his responsibility to tell Rokh Nadim that his daughter had been kidnapped.

By the time he left for the Asra Complex Jaya knew that Bel Adivaram was the key to Ana's whereabouts. Varaza and three of his minions had folded under interrogation moments before, but Adivaram's was the only name any of them seemed to know. From Adivaram, Varaza claimed, came the order to poison the jailed thug. He had even provided the poison. Ashur Badan was also induced to reveal his suspicions that the Vadin's puppet-masters were Consortium officers. Hadas, shown a selection of pictures, quickly recognized Duran Prakash as one of the men he had seen the night before.

"I am not certain," Mall Gar had told him, "whether it is ignorance or fear that has so effectively tied Devaki-sa's tongue, but I suspect she knows more than she's saying."

"Or maybe she only pretends to know," said Jaya. "Still, if you can keep her alive, you might learn something from her."

"Yes, if. Perhaps," Gar mused, "the thought of being accessible to her master's masters will jog her memory."

Jaya prayed that it would. He was not looking forward to trying to untangle this skein of intrigue before the Circle in his present state of exhaustion. A breakthrough from Gar would be welcome.

He found the Deva Radha in her private chamber.

"Nathu Rai Sarojin," she greeted him. "You're here quite early. Is your cousin with you?"

"My 'cousin' has been abducted, Deva."

Radha rose from her chair, her shock visible on her fine-boned face. "What? By whom?"

"Last night. By Bel Adivaram and two men, one of whom was identified as Duran Prakash."

She sank back into the chair. "Adivaram? Are you certain?"

"Yes. He was identified by two witnesses last night and implicated by the owners of the Badan-Devaki dalali who seem to have been involved in some illicit dealings with him."

Radha shook her head as if trying to shake astonishment from it. "Illicit dealings? What sort of illicit dealings?"

"The Badan-Devaki has been ... enhancing their chances of snaring prime das by bribing Sarngin patrolmen to bring any attractive yevetha they've arrested to their dalali—regardless of what district they're found in. We suspect that about two dozen patrolmen have been involved. Apparently, when a few of these men were found out by their superiors, the officers did not report them, but instead demanded to be in on the take. Somehow, this came to the attention of Bel Adivaram who, for his own reasons, became their ... overlord and protector."

The Deva raised a hand to her heart. "This is ... this is incredible. Horrific."

Jaya grimaced. "It gets worse, Deva. To make the system even more lucrative, the group hired an ambitious thief named Parva Rishi to put together a team of thugs for the sole purpose of creating yevetha for the Sarngin to arrest. At some point, some KNC officials became involved and the thieves were told to concentrate on Avasans. Ashur Badan suspects these anonymous officials discovered Adivaram's dealings and used the knowledge to control him."

"Badan-sama has confessed to his part in this?"

Jaya nodded. "Mall Gar, Commander of the Port Zone Sarngin, is heading the investigation. I've found him to be trustworthy."

The Deva closed her eyes. "I must admit to having had my suspicions that Adivaram was currying favor to the Consortium. I did wonder at his reaction to the attack on you—his insistence that he filter Rakesh Bithal's report." She shook her head. "Corruption ... everywhere you turn. But not here, I thought—hoped. Certainly not here. And the cruelty! Corruption is bad enough, but to benefit from the enslavement and pain of other souls—that is times worse than corruption."

"Ashur Badan is fond of reminding me that buying, selling, and owning das is legal on Mehtar."

She looked at him. "Our ancestors made it legal. The business sector works hard to keep it legal. So much of our economy rests on the shoulders of das laborers."

"Forgive my impertinence, but are you making excuses, Deva?"

Her lip curled. "I do believe I am. Making excuses for the inaction of the Inner Circle and the silence of the Orders. We are more timid than we once were. More timid than Tara-Rama meant us to be. Timid and corrupt." Radha uttered a deep sigh. "Have you told Nadim-sama?"

Startled, Jaya glanced at her. Her sharp eyes were on his face. "Told him-?"

"That his daughter is missing."

"Not yet. Ravi is attempting to contact him now. How-?"

She shook her head and raised a hand to silence him. "That won't be necessary, Nathu Rai. Rokh Nadim is here, in the Complex."

Jaya flailed about for something to say, then sat down in the nearest chair.

"I'm lost," he said.

She cocked her head a little to one side. "Rokh Nadim has been under the protection of the Orders since Taffik Pritam informed me that his daughter was missing. At first, he was insistent that we do something to find her, then, suddenly, it seemed no longer to matter. He knew where she was, he said, but our sources on Avasa confirmed that she wasn't there. And that confirmed what I already suspected. I knew Ana was no cousin of yours, Jaya. I saw the cree in her palm. It looked wrong to be a dascree, yet if she was born and raised on Avasa as she said, it couldn't be raicree. There was this sense of ... freedom about her. A sense even you or I don't have. I think it has to do with these." She raised her left hand, revealing the small, Cloud and Star cree of the her Dandin Order.

"When we brought Rokh Nadim to Mehtar," she continued. "I asked about his daughter. He described her as a resourceful young woman who was following the Upward Path and showed me a holo-pic of a beautiful little girl with hair the color of black cherries and skin like golden cream. There was little doubt that your Ana Sadira and his Anala Nadim were one and the same."

Jaya felt as if he was floundering in a fast current. "You brought Nadim to Mehtar. He was never really missing, then."

She looked vaguely apologetic. "No. We felt it was necessary to protect him by making it seem as if we'd lost him."

"We?"

"The other Dandin of the Circle. We felt the need for complete secrecy. None of the secular members of the Circle know."

"Then you believed Nadim's life was threatened."

"Oh, yes. We just weren't certain who was issuing the threats.

The Consortium has made a good case that the Worker's Coalition is the real source of danger to the AGIM associates and to you. Now, it looks as if the seeds of deceit have been sown on a higher plateau. With Adivaram involved..."

The Deva was silent for a moment, thinking. "How high up does this go?" she wondered, finally. "Who else among the Nine besides Adivaram might be doing the Consortium's bidding?"

He studied her pensive face for a moment then brought the com-journal out of an inner pocket. "I've been reading my father's journal. It contains notes on his suspicions that the KNC was trying to pressure Varmana into ... showing favoritism."

The Deva's eyes were riveted on the machine. "He kept notes? Nathu Rai, you have no idea how grateful I am that he did. How did you find them after all this time?"

"Mother knew where they were. She thought I might find them interesting. I did. Did he share any of this information with you?"

"Yes. That is, he shared his suspicions but gave me little recorded material. He thought Duran Prakash might be involved. Prakash had suggested to him that his friendship with Namun Vedda somehow ought to imbue him with loyalty to the Consortium."

"So I read."

She looked clearly disgusted. "Partisan politics have no place in government. Nathu Rai, we must go to Rokh Nadim. Shall I tell him?"

Jaya shook his head. "No, I will. Ana was—is my responsibility."

The Deva searched him with her lustrous black eyes. "She is not dead." It was a statement of fact.

"No," he said and new that to be true. "But she's terrified." That was also true.

Ana's fear threatened to suffocate her. Bound, gagged and blinded by a velvet hood, she lay sprawled across a bed in a room scented with spices. Of her location, her senses had told her only that it was high up in a building with an underground carpark.

She tugged at the manacles on her wrists, but found them tight and secure. She tried to listen to the conversation muffled by the closed door, but it came to her in swaddled mumbles. She wanted to scream and cry with the frustration of being blind, nearly deaf, and senseless. Instead, she fell back on her discipline and worked at restoring calm. Finally, overcome by exhaustion, she slept.

She sensed someone in the room before she was fully awake, adrenaline kicking in like an alarm system. She turned her head, struggling to hear through the hood.

"Ah, you're awake."

The voice was smooth, warm. Ana knew it was the one who had hovered over her so at the dalali and was glad it was not the other— the big man whose voice was like metal grating on stone, the one who had spoken so bloodlessly about "sacrificing" Jaya. She shivered, thankful for the present darkness.

"Are you cold?" he asked. "Or do I frighten you?"

"I'm cold," she answered, her voice muffled.

"I'm glad I don't frighten you. I would not like you to be frightened of me." He was silent for a moment then said, "You're extraordinarily beautiful."

"Thank you, sama." She sounded like a dutiful child accepting a treat.

"I wish I could see your face."

"I wish I could see yours."

He laughed. He sat down next to her, the bed sagging slightly under his weight. Ana tried not to roll toward him, but failed. She could feel the warmth of his body through the fabric of her unisuit and knew her fear would be transmitted along the connection.

"Did you know that I also find you extraordinarily desirable?" he asked.

She said nothing.

"What? No 'thank you, sama'? Yet, you react so strongly." His hand touched her thigh, rested on it, caressing. "Either I've offended you or I've frightened you. Which is it?"

She didn't answer and he went on, his hand massaging the sleek fabric covering her leg. "Or could it be that I excite you as much as you excite me?"

She let out a crack of sound intended to be a laugh. "I don't even know what you look like."

"What? Are you that shallow? Is appearance so very important? Surely, what's in a man's heart counts for something."

"You have a heart?" she asked before she could stop herself.

"Now you're teasing me. Are those the words of a Rohina?" He breathed the word, making it sound like a seduction. "Now it is true that my friend—whom you will also come to know quite well—has no heart. No soul. No conscience. To him, you are a hostage, a bargaining chip, a moment of pleasure and, of course, a means of wounding Rokh Nadim. I have no interest in any of these things. My interest in you is rather more ... spiritual. You see, I've studied the Rohin ways—especially the ways of Rohin women. I know of the mysterious disciplines you practice, the potent magics you possess. They say you can make love to a man's very soul. They say you have the Jadu. Do you have the Jadu, Anala Nadim?"

Was he superstitious or merely curious? A little of both, perhaps.

She said, "Yes. I'm very strong with the Jadu. It's in my eyes—the second sight and the power of Seeing Beyond and Within."

"Ah, I can believe that. You see, I have seen you weave your magic, if only from a distance. I'll wager you can strike terror into a man's soul—bend him to your will."

"They say so."

"Does he say so—Jaya Sarojin? Do you stare into his soul when he makes love to you? Do you have him bewitched?"

She shivered again. "Of course."

"Oh, I hope so. In fact, I'm counting on it."

"Meaning, I'm bait."

"To my rather insensitive friend, yes. To me, you are ... a Goal." He drew in a deep breath, his hand gliding to her hip. "I have envied Jaya Sarojin. Now, he can envy me. I have the woman with the Jadu in her eyes. What a pity I can't see them just now. I shall console myself with other delights."

Before she could raise her knees to fend him off, he had grasped the lapels of her unisuit. The closes parted in his hands; tearing open to her waist.

"My! What delicate under-garments miners wear these days."

Ana wished heartily that her "delicate undergarments" were made of steel mesh. Especially when he twined a finger through one of the thin straps of her silken camisole. She could not pull away; he was leaning across her body. All she could do was lie, blind, beneath him, and wait. She felt sweat trickle from her temples.

"No," he said and sat up. "I only torment myself. I have a promise to keep. So, until later, my dear Rohina."

He leaned over, kissed the hollow at the base of her throat, then rose.

"My dear friend's dasa will see that you bathe and dress in something more suitable. Then, you must eat. And then, I would like to finish our conversation. I want to know all about the Rohin ways, Anala, and you shall teach me."

CHAPTER TWENTY

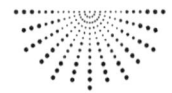

"DURAN PRAKASH HAS LEFT KASI."

Mall Gar made his report before the three other members of the Inner Circle in whom the Deva Radha had placed her trust. They were two Dandin and the Vadin of the Port Zone, Rakesh Bithal, who was, himself, head of the Balin Order. Also in attendance were Hadas Gupta—in his capacity as a witness—and Rockh Nadim.

"At least, so his aide informs me," the Zone Commander continued. "He was allegedly called away yesterday morning on some urgent business in Kalimpur. I asked to speak to Vrksa-sama, who gave me the same story—that he dispatched Prakash to Kalimpur. So, I called the KNC offices there. They confirmed his arrival and claim that he is presently in conference with the branch managers."

He glanced at the Deva sitting regally in her carved and ornamented chair and found he was still awed.

"Yesterday morning?" Sri Radha frowned. "Apparently Prakash-sama is establishing an alibi."

Sri Elui squinted at Hadas, who sat uneasily in one of the box seats reserved for visitors to the Inner Chamber. "Are you sure Prakash-sama was the man you saw?"

"The holo the Commander showed me was the man I saw at the dalali," he replied. "I'm certain of it."

"That man has my daughter," said Rokh Nadim. His back to the assemblage, he gazed from the chamber window to the courtyard below. "We must find him and get her back."

"I'm not certain he has your daughter," said the Deva, "but if he is in Kalimpur, we must certainly bring him back. Vadin Bithal, I would like to send a small detachment of Balin to Kalimpur to see to this detail."

The door chime sounded before he could respond and the Deva touched her console, causing a holographic image of the visitor to appear before her seat. It was an Asra courier, seeming to look wide-eyed into Radha's face. She clutched a piece of drawing mat.

"Yes, Rua?"

"Pardon, Holy One, but this message was found sitting on the Holy Book in the Hall of Honor. It is addressed to the Inner Circle."

"Bring it to us."

Radha banished the image and caused the door to open. The courier scurried in, bowing, and handed the crude, folded bit of mat to the Deva. She thanked and dismissed the girl, waiting until she was gone to read the message.

She frowned, her face creasing delicately. "It appears that Prakash-sama has more than an alibi. The Workers' Coalition claims that they have Anala Nadim and that they will kill her if Rokh Nadim does not withdraw the Guild's petition."

"How can they know we're involved?" Nigudha Bhrasta adjusted his hood so he could see his eyes, then studied his reflection in the glass above the sumptuously laid sideboard in his officesuite.

Behind him, Duran Prakash made a chopping gesture with his hand, anxiety oozing from his every pore. "The Sarngin contacted my office-"

"Yes, I know. And you have an alibi. Kalimpur confirmed you were there. You can't be in two places at once."

"Damn you! How can you be so calm? Bel Adivaram knows we're involved and they're searching Kasi for him right now. If they find him-"

"If. ... I am terrifying in this hood, aren't I? Do you think our little Avasan friend is impressed?"

"I think you have more important things to contemplate than how much fear you inspire in the women you control. There have been Sarngin at Adivaram's house. Rishi reports that the dalali is crawling with them. All asking questions about the Vadin's habits. There are even Balin patrolling near his residence. Balin, do you hear? Do you know what that means? That means the Circle is alerted. We have awakened Indra, my friend, and He hunts us."

His companion poured himself a cup of tea. "No, He hunts Bel Adivaram. We are protected."

"Protected by what?"

"By a Rohin witch, perhaps."

"Now you're mocking me. You don't believe-"

"No, but you do." Bhrasta's nod took in Duran Prakash and the third man who sat silently in the window casement, staring absently through the tinted glass and stroking the black velvet hood in his hands.

"The woman is a hostage, not an amulet," Duran protested.

The man in the window spoke. "The woman is more than a hostage, Duran. She's a fountain of sacred power."

"There, you see? The Mystic has spoken."

Prakash stared at his superior, increasingly uncertain of the direction his mind was taking.

"Listen to me," he said. "Adivaram isn't one of us and he's soft. He's a slave to his greed. If that can make him compromise his loyalties, imagine what abject fear and humiliation will do."

Bhrasta nodded. With a parting glance at his reflection, he turned to face Prakash. "If the Circle suspects our good Vadin of heinous sins, then he has outlived his usefulness to us. We have no choice but to cut the connection."

"Cut-?" Prakash shook his head, pretending for a moment not to understand. "And just how do you propose to do that? Adivaram is a member of the Vrinda Varma and One of the Nine, not some barely literate yevetha."

"Yet, he is just as prone to frailty as that accursed yevetha, is he not? You concentrate on handling our business with the Circle. That's paramount, Duran. AGIM must not break our hold on Avasa. Nor can we afford to relax our efforts to control the Circle's legislation in that area. If those miners gain any real independence, our empire will collapse."

"I'm well aware of the ramifications."

"Now that you've established your alibi and the Workers' Coalition has assumed responsibility for the Nadim woman's abduction, we're covered. Anything they can squeeze out of that Sarojin Rani is just supposition and hearsay. Unless, of course, you admitted more to her than you've told me."

"Absolutely not."

"No, I think I would know if you had."

Prakash fixed his companion with a direct gaze. "Tell me something, old friend. If worse came to worst, would you cut my connection, too?"

He was vaguely aware of a stirring from the direction of the window; perhaps the answer to this question was also significant to the so-called Mystic.

"I'm not a fool, Duran. And I know your worth. You're simply not expendable to me. Besides, as you said, we're friends."

"I had thought so."

"Good. Please continue to think so." Nigudha Bhrasta deftly loosened the hood and pulled it off, smoothed his graying hair, and sipped his tea. "You look worn out. Go to your office and rest. Handling the Circle will take all your wits."

"He's a very anxious man, Nigu," observed Bhrasta's companion when Duran Prakash had made a hurried exit.

"He is also possessed of a supreme sense of selfpreservation. He will do nothing to compromise me."

The Mystic nodded, then glanced down at the hood in his hands. "The woman ... you will not harm her."

It might have been question or command. Nigudha Bhrasta glanced at the speaker with a mixture of amusement and irritation. "Don't worry, I won't wring the Jadu out of her."

The other man rose from his window seat and smiled. "Nigu, you are an irreligious blasphemer. The fact is that you couldn't 'wring the Jadu out of her' if you tried. You don't believe, you aren't disciplined, and you have no capacity. I simply don't want her harmed."

"You care about her, do you?"

"Deeply. She is not only beautiful, but brave. And she is a kindred spirit—called to a spiritual path, as am I."

Bhrasta uttered a sharp laugh. "You have a damn strange definition of spirituality, my friend. You entangle yourself in subterfuge, treachery, the blackest of politics, gross violence-"

The Mystic shrugged. "All illusion, Nigu. All steps in an insignificant dance. The wealth and power you think is an end in itself is merely a means to an end. It is not a destination, but a path."

"So? What is at the end of your path, my oh-so-spiritual friend?"

"Surata, for one thing—that consuming Bliss that is at once physical and spiritual—and power of a different sort than your rather limited appreciation can afford you."

Bhrasta shook his head and sighed in feigned aggrievement. "Why do I tolerate your sanctimonious abuse? In all the years of our acquaintance, I have never really understood you. What power can possibly be more worth having than what I command as the head of this very material empire?"

"Consider, Nigu: you have a certain power, and the members of the Inner Circle have a certain power—most especially someone of the spiritual stature of the Deva Radha. Whose power do you think is greater?"

"Mine, of course, but you will tell me I'm wrong."

"Indeed. You command the material assets of men, and thereby, influence their physical existence. Our Deva commands the spirits of earth and heaven—the devas, the jinn, the atman itself—which, in turn, have a great influence on our baser material existence. Therefore, her power more is complete. I, too, have a certain power over—or at least an intimate and refined knowledge of—the elements and workings of the physical world. The greatest power would be a combination of these things, would it not?"

"You think coupling with our captive Rohina will grant you that mighty combination? Why will it not grant me the same? Yes, yes, I know—I lack the faith, the discipline, and the capacity."

Nigudha Bhrasta shook his head yet again and favored his friend with an indulgent smile. "I sometimes think your mysticism has completely overwhelmed the very shrewd and logical mind I so admired. No matter. I admit, between the two of you, you and Duran keep me quite entertained with your visionary and occult prattle. I wish you all the surata you can tolerate."

The other laughed softly. "I thank you. You know, Nigu, every soul is drawn to the unearthly. Even yours. You cannot deny that our occult prattle, as you call it, compels a certain fascination. Otherwise, you would not this moment be so nervously anticipating a union with your hostage."

Bhrasta set down his tea cup with a clatter, knowing his hands had been visibly unquiet. A bit of the liquid sloshed onto the top of the sideboard. He wiped it up with his hood, irritated.

"Nonsense. She's beautiful, as you yourself pointed out. And, yes, brave. And exotic. A heady combination. I find her sexually compelling."

"You are surrounded by sexually compelling women, Nigu. Admit it—is there not, in your heart of hearts, the tiniest expectation that this woman will be different? That you will find in her deeps your prior conquests did not have?"

"If I do, it is only because you and Duran have so filled my head with your arcane ... "

"Prattle?"

"Ah, but look ... " He glanced down at himself and laughed. "See what you've done with all your talk of surata and 'deeps?' I am not nervous, but I am aroused. You will excuse me..?"

The other pressed his palms together and bowed slightly, mockingly. "You will do her no harm," he repeated.

Ana lay on her back on the bed, staring at the embroidered awning above it. A tether now ran beneath her from her manacles to the head board. The manacles kept her arms at her sides with a connecting "leash" that also ran beneath her body.

She was clad in a gown of nearly liquid red with golden clasps at the shoulders and bodice. It was a wedding gown, and at any other time she would have thought it beautiful, but not here, not now.

She had considered trying to escape when the dasa had come in to bathe and dress her, but the woman had been accompanied by a huge, stone-faced guard who made it very clear that resistance would be instantly punished.

In the bath, she had tried to sway the dasa, but the woman was intractable. Taciturn and nearly silent, she went about the business of giving Ana a thorough scrubbing. She pulled her hair while washing and combing it out, nearly burned her while drying it, and must surely have left welts with her long nails while fastening the gown and reattaching the manacles.

"Please," Ana begged her. "Just help me get out of here. You must realize what they're going to do to me. Can you just let that happen?"

The woman fixed her with a dark, almost passionate gaze and said, "Sure, I know what they're going to do. I have no choice but let it happen." She paused, then added, "My only solace is that you won't enjoy it."

Ana received a bizarre epiphany. "You're jealous, aren't you? Then, you have every reason to want me gone. If you help-"

"They'll only find you and bring you back. I know. Then, when he's finished with you, he'll punish me for helping you. He is not a pleasant man when he's angry."

Ana thought of the large, terrifying man with eyes like glaciers and shivered. She felt sudden and overwhelming sympathy for the dasa, a sympathy that closed her mind to the idea of escape. If there was any way out of this situation, it was beyond human agency to engineer it.

She had been laid out on the bed then, like an over-sized doll—perfumed and curried, her gown arrayed appealingly, her hair carefully arranged on the saffron-colored pillows, a necklace with a gleaming gold amulet around her neck.

Now she waited.

He came in so quietly she didn't hear him. Her eyes were closed in prayer and when she opened them, he was simply there, watching her—a man-mountain in a black velvet hood and a silken dressing wrap of the same hue. She could feel his smile through the fabric of the hood, could see it in the chill eyes that gazed at her from the slits. He was something from a childhood jinn-tale—huge, dark and hellish.

"I must commend my friend's sense of ritual," he said. "He did not lie when he said that red and gold become you—with that milky skin-" He took a step toward her, his eyes taking her in. "I have never had someone of your race, my Snowflake. This will be a novelty."

Her mind raced. Red and gold ... she had worn those colors at the Mesha Fest. Had his 'friend' been among the guests? Surely not. Surely she would have remembered his stance, his voice, his sense of command.

Ignoring her silence, he moved to the bedside table and filled the golden censer with herbs from a small crystal box. He glanced aside and caught her watching him. He held up the box.

"A family heirloom," he told her. "Cut in a single piece from the largest bhasvata crystal ever brought out of my family's first mine. In the Lake District, it was—closed down now—worthless to everyone but a sect of mystics. A beautiful place. And this..." He crumbled another pinch of the herbs into the censer's bowl. " ... is a special potion my friend concocted for me. He is, shall we say, an expert at such things. It, em, frees the Kunda powers, enhances the quest for the Bliss of surata ... or so he says."

He studied her face. "Since you are, by his account, a witch and should be able to tell, I am going to admit to you that I have never tasted the Bliss. I'm not sure I believe in it. I'm a skeptic. But I am sure if surata is real and can be had, you shall make me a believer."

Somehow, Ana found her voice. "You cannot attain surata with me, sama. There is no love. Where there is no love, surata is impossible."

He lit the incense, fanned it and closed the lid of the small brazier.

"Ah, but I will try."

He turned, his eyes marking every atom of her, making her squirm inside. "I think I would like to believe. I must admit, I hope my friend is less a superstitious fool than I think."

He lowered himself to the bed, his chill eyes on her face. "It's true—I don't love you. But perhaps such a great lust is elevated almost to love." He chuckled. "Well, let's call it passion, shall we? A nobler word."

He inhaled deeply of the wisp of smoke that rose from the censer to waft across the bed.

"Lights down, two," he said, and the lights in the room dimmed. "Flicker," he added.

That, too, was done, making the place appear to be bathed in the light of a dozen torches. He appreciated Ana's startled reaction.

"I spare no expense in surrounding myself with the most current technologies. Still, all in all, I am an old-fashioned man. A traditional man."

He slipped a hand under the pendant that lay, heavily between Ana's breasts; held it, cupped, in the snowy valley. She shivered, revulsion roiling beneath his touch.

"This, for example, is very traditional. It's a wedding charm lent to me by my friend—the Mystic, I like to call him. An interesting fellow —fancies himself an historian, or perhaps a mythologist. I expect you'll find him fascinating, if he doesn't talk your ear off. This is a family heirloom apparently. I'm surprised he would lend me a thing of such obvious sentimental value, but I suspect he intends I be converted to his ... beliefs. Of course, he, himself, will use it in the appropriate spirit. For me, it is merely another prop in his imaginary bridal bower."

He held it up by its chain, dangling it before Ana's eyes as if inviting her to study it. The smoke from the censer made study difficult. She blinked and tried to focus her eyes on the thing. It was a traditional kunda-oil flask, fashioned in the combined shapes of lingam and serpent. Seeing it, Ana realized for the first time what was to become of her in this 'bridal bower.' She had never even thought the word rape; never let it enter her conscious mind; never associated it with herself. Now it flooded her with simple terror.

Rohin discipline failed her, or perhaps she failed it; her mind raced uncontrollably in all directions. She wished she'd killed herself or goaded the guard into doing it for her. There must have been a chance of that. She wished she'd been weaker of will that night with Jaya; wished Ravi had never interrupted them. Then, at least, if her chastity had been violated, her soul would not have been.

No, that wasn't right. Her eyes began to fill with tears of fear and despair and rage. She was losing her ability to think, to focus; she was losing her will to fight. Perhaps that was just as well.

"Tears, Rohina? Now, now. Let me set your mind at rest. I have promised not to harm you." The admission seemed to cause him some annoyance. "I intend this to be the most pleasurable of nights for both of us. Unless, of course, you should do something to anger me, such as acting like an insulted virgin. Come now, surely you've shared your delights with your mahesa already."

She shook her head, unable to muster words.

"You expect me to believe that Sarojin isn't your lover? The reports..." There was honest surprise in his voice, a sudden increased tension in his touch. "Tell me the truth—are you a virgin, Anala Nadim?"

He might have been asking if she were made of chocolate, she thought, and wished it were in her power to laugh.

"Yes," she said.

There was a sharp sound from the door. It swung open and a second hooded man entered the room. Her captor was on his feet with more grace than she would have expected of a man his size.

"What in the name of Indra are you doing in here? You were to wait-"

"I must speak with you. Now." The other's voice was tight and urgent.

"Can it not wait?"

"No. It cannot."

"You presume upon our friendship. Get out."

"You also presume. May I remind you that I possess certain things you very much want and need ... dear friend?"

With a sound that was half-grunt, half snarl, the big man followed his 'friend' from the room.

Ana lay in silence and thanked Sanat-ji for the reprieve. Perhaps now, perhaps any moment, she would be rescued. The surly dasa would return to help her, Jaya would find her. But time fled and the incense burned down and sounds of argument came and went in the outer room and no rescue arrived.

Ana thought her body and spirit were separating like egg white and yolk; for brief moments she floated above herself and looked down, wondering how she, who had always been so strong and resilient, could seem so pathetic and small.

∿

The remaining members of the Circle filed into the chamber and took their seats. Each noted the presence of the Nathu Rai Sarojin and the Rani Melantha. Each raised their eyebrows at the dour Sarngin Commander. Each glanced curiously at the Avasan gentleman who sat beside Taffik Pritam; several recognized him. None knew the young man with the Sarojin, though a few recalled having seen him at the Mesha Fest. All checked their agendas to see if they could determine why those persons were here.

The Deva Radha spoke. She announced the abduction of Anala Nadim without passion, her eyes on the faces of her peers. She went on to reveal the ransom demands of the Workers' Coalition. When she related how the abduction had taken place at the Badan-Devaki, there was a rustle of surprise. The Deva's eyes were on Kreti Twapar and didn't miss the sudden contortion of his features.

She back-tracked then, explaining their Nathu Rai's part in Ana's subterfuge, outlining what was happening to her fellow Avasans. Describing the tactics of the dalali, the involvement of a member of the Vrinda Varma, of Duran Prakash. The last incriminating the Consortium at its highest levels. She glanced at Twapar. He was white as a summer cloud and beginning to glisten with perspiration.

"Who is it?" Lord Mandal demanded to know. "Who, on the Vrinda Varma, is involved in this?"

Her eyes still on Twapar, the Deva answered. "He is also a member of this Inner Circle. A member conspicuous in his absence."

All eyes moved to the empty seat usually occupied by Bel Adivaram.

"No!" Kreti Twapar half rose, his voice a barely audible wheeze. "You can't be so certain! Surely the testimony of an unscrupulous dalal-"

The Deva silenced him with a gesture. "As you will see, we have testimony from several quarters. Hadas Gupta, would you speak, please?"

The Avasan nodded and rose from his chair on the floor of the Chamber. "I was with Ana when they discovered us. We were separated trying to escape. I waited in the sub-level of the dalali until a dark blue air-car came into the alley. Three men got out. They put on hoods. One of them was Prakash-sama. I don't know who the other men were—I couldn't see them very well—but the man who came out to meet them and brought them the hoods was the Vadin Adivaram."

Twapar made a whining sound in his throat. "Deva, please, are you so ready to condemn a beloved, respected peer on the strength of the testimony of this Avasan?"

"There is also," said Jaya, "the testimony of my mother, the Rani

Melantha, who can link both Duran Prakash and Bel Adivaram to an attempt to get Anala Nadim out of the House Sarojin. The testimony of the dalal implicates your respected peer in all sorts of ... intrigue."

Twapar subsided, twitching, his eyes darting from face to face.

Next to him, Lord Mandal asked, "Will we receive a full report, then? Will we hear from the Rani Sarojin?" He nodded toward where Melantha Sarojin sat, silent and pale, beside her son.

"Shortly," the Deva assured him, "but now I must ask the Lord Twapar some questions."

"Me?" Twapar gasped. "What could I tell you?"

"You could tell us if you know anything about Bel Adivaram's involvement with the dalali."

The old Lord's eyes shrunk to tiny jet beads among the sallow folds of his face. "How could I know such a thing? He ... he spent some time at the dalali. He has a large estate, needs many das to care for it."

"You're his closest friend, Lord Twapar," observed the Deva. "I thought perhaps you might have been taken into his confidence. Do you know anything about his involvement with the Consortium?"

"The Consortium? No! He had no dealings with the Consortium."

"The Consortium had not approached you—either of you—with suggestions that you should show them favoritism in this or any other case?"

Twapar cringed. "No, no. It was the Workers' Coalition that threatened Bel—they threatened me. It wasn't the Consortium." His eyes jerked frantically about the room. "Although ... although I believe—I believe the Consortium may be-" He broke off and closed his eyes.

"May be what, Lord?"

"I have no proof," he whined, sweating.

"Proof of what?" demanded the Deva, gently.

"The Workers' Coalition is a well-organized group of zealots. Perhaps they are hiding behind the Consortium's skirts—taking advantage of an implicit connection. You must admit, the Consortium's refusal to condemn their actions has lent them tacit support. Perhaps, we, em, need to actively enlist the aide of the Consortium in retrieving this situation. Perhaps, now that it's come to this—

kidnapping—they'll be willing to condemn the Coalition's tactics and help get the Nadim woman back. If we entreat Nigudha Bhrasta-"

"What?" Jaya nearly snarled the word. "Have the KNC act as intermediary for a kidnapping they masterminded? That's obscene!"

"Nathu Rai." The Deva's tone was warning.

Jaya ignored her. "Adivaram is the only one who knows where Ana is! He gave her to them!"

"No!" Twapar's gnarled hand knotted into a fist. "I will not believe it! I will not!" He broke off, wheezing horribly.

"Nathu Rai, you will stand down," the Deva commanded. She turned her gaze to the old Lord. "You are not well, Lord Twapar. Perhaps you would like to be dismissed. I can see this has all been too much for your frail health."

The old man nodded. "I am feeling rather weak, Deva. Bel is my dearest friend. I ... find it difficult to believe about him what you are asking me to believe. I think I would like to go home."

"You may go then, if the Circle agrees." She looked to the remaining members who, to a man and woman, nodded their accord.

Twapar rose shakily, looking as if the breeze created by the opening of the doors might fell him. He gazed around the room, his eyes glistening with emotion, then hobbled to the doors.

Jaya watched him leave, torn between suspicion and pity. So pathetic, the old man; dry as parchment mat, frail as cobweb. Could he be such an actor? Could he be party to what had happened to Bhaktasu Sarojin, to Ana?

Thinking of Ana, Jaya found himself caught, suddenly and inexplicably, in the coils of a vision so vivid, the council chamber seemed to disappear from around him.

Crystal. A box cut of bhasvata crystal. A wedding dress of red. The scent of incense. A flicker of light. The feeling of being utterly trapped. The taste of fear. His heart hammered against his ribs.

"Commander Gar," the Deva was saying, "if you would be so good as to make certain the Lord reaches his home? Without letting him see you, of course. The Balin are at your disposal. Please use them."

Gar rose, bowed to the Deva and swiftly exited the room.

Jaya watched him as if through a fog, his breath coming too quickly, and tried to bring his mind back to reality.

"Do you suspect Kreti of some part in this conspiracy?" asked the Deva Paramaya.

Sri Radha shifted in her seat. "Perhaps I simply want to make certain he arrives home safely. Nathu Rai Sarojin, if you would be so kind as to give the Circle your testimony." When he did not respond immediately, she gave him a searching glance. "Nathu Rai, is something wrong?"

Jaya brought his eyes into focus on her face. Everything was wrong.

"I'm sorry, I ... just had a strong ... impression of Ana."

How was one to describe such a thing? He felt ridiculous.

Radha was not laughing. She leaned forward in her chair, hands clasped before her. "What sort of impression, Jaya?"

"A room with flickering light, the smell of incense. A man's hands holding a box made of bhasvata."

"That is all?"

"Fear."

"You do not recognize the room?"

"No, Deva. How could I? Surely the place exists only in my imagination."

The Deva sat back, nodding. "I believe you have some additional evidence to offer, as well as your first hand experiences?"

Jaya's breathing steadied. "I do, Deva. I have the Journal my father kept before his death. I have found it most enlightening."

"Then enlighten us also, Nathu Rai."

When, at length, the door opened, Anala only vaguely cared. Perhaps it would be Jaya or Father or the Sarngin. It was none of those. It was a hooded man. She wondered which one. When he spoke, she recognized him as the one her previous visitor had mockingly called the Mystic.

"So," he said, "you haven't passed on the power..."

Unexpected words. "What do you mean?"

The man held out his hands as if in supplication. "For the love of Rama—a Rohin virgin! Do you realize what you are?" He cocked his head, as if reading her. "I assure you, I do, if my poor friend does not. As he told you, he doesn't believe. He thinks it's all Bogar nonsense. He is an ignorant man in some ways, interested in pleasure, power and now in humiliating your father. So, I have assured him, it matters not which of us first pierces you—it will pierce Rokh Nadim and Jaya Sarojin to the heart, as well. This is important to him—this act of humiliation. More important, I sometimes think, than his political aims. Little did he know that he had the instrument for the fulfillment of his every desire right here in his bed."

What was he saying? Ana licked parched lips. "You were listening?"

He came to the bed now and lowered himself onto it. "I had the opportunity to have certain electronic devices installed in this chamber. I took it. He doesn't know, of course. He merely thinks I ... experienced sudden and ill-timed change of heart and an uncharacteristic inability to curb my desires. He does not appreciate..." His voice roughened with emotion. " ... he does not realize, sweet Rohina, what you are. He looks at you and sees only a desirable body, a hostage, a political pawn. I look beyond the material and so see what neither my friend nor your mahesa can see—an indomitable spirit, a disciplined soul, a fountain of power. I will draw the power that Jaya Sarojin has so foolishly squandered and I will use it to free myself."

His voice was warm, smooth, almost sweet, and strangely hypnotic. Ana's mind swum in the flickering light and the mingled scents of the incense and her own perfume. Her body trembled as if every atom in was being shaken by minute hands. This man was mad.

"Free yourself?" she repeated.

He made a strange gesture with his head, as if shrugging off a noose.

"I call him 'friend'—in some ways he is my captor; in some ways, I am his. I have the advantage in that I recognize that all this—the politics, the entanglements, the relationships—are illusory. The game is bigger than my friend supposes it to be."

Ana marshaled her thoughts, struggling to follow, perhaps to lead. "And what can I give you?" she asked.

He tilted his head and gazed at her almost fondly, the eyes behind their hooded slits, soft and yearning. They were the same color as Jaya's eyes, but there the resemblance ended. Madness had never peeked at her from Jaya's eyes.

"You can give me yourself, dear Rohina," he said. He moved his hands to her neck, caressing. "And, in so doing, grant me power over the world of creation. Now, I manipulate ghosts, illusions. With your gift, with the Jadu, I shall manipulate realities. Let us begin."

A chill sliced through Ana's heart. She opened her mouth to dissuade or distract, but he silenced her with a finger to her lips.

"No more questions. Let us begin." He fingered the topmost close of the gown. "The old myths say the Genda Sita are children of the God of Darkness. This is one reason I have dressed you in red, you know—the color of the Sacred Flame, Indra's color. I thought it ironic."

"What other reasons?"

He seemed amused at her question. "What? Have I discovered a secret vanity?"

"I only seek to understand the man I join with."

The answer apparently pleased him. He nodded. "Red is traditional for a wedding gown, of course. And though we will not be man and wife in the more traditional sense, this will be a marriage of sorts—a marriage of souls." He paused, then added, "Then too, I have simply observed that red becomes you. Now, no further questions, Anala. We must begin."

He loosed the first clasp, speaking to her as if he were a teacher giving a lesson. "Being the children of Darkness, say those old tales, the Genda Sita are born in the bowels of the world where their flesh never knows the saving and enlightening rays of Mitras."

He parted the second clasp. "The myths also say that the bowels of the world are heated by the fires of Niraya Hell and that when a man makes love to a Genda Sita woman, he can feel the fire. She offers to warm him against the chill of her flesh, then sears his soul and paralyzes all sense of good and evil—all will. Fire and snow. A most paradoxical combination."

His eyes met hers, fondly. "Of course, in this day and age, we have knowledge those ancient myth-makers did not. We know that even the children of Darkness have red blood flowing in their veins, and so, are no more or less human than we."

He loosed the third clasp and parted the translucent folds of cloth.

"Ah!..." He laid his hand, palm down, on her breast, fingers splayed. "How dark my flesh seems against yours. And I am fair for one of my race. Fairer, even, than your beloved Jaya."

At the sound of Jaya's name, Ana closed her eyes, letting the tears squeeze out beneath her lids, remembering that he, too, had touched her there. Had he also noticed how pale she was? Had he thought to himself of fire and ice and the bowels of the world? Or had he thought only of flesh and blood?

She cried silently, her body quaking. She had once dreamed for herself the gift of flight. She wished she only might have for a moment the power this madman accorded her. She would stop the beating of her heart and fly from him on the wings of Yama.

"Open your eyes," he said softly.

She couldn't. Couldn't look again at that hooded head, looming above her—couldn't meet its feverish eyes.

"I said, open your eyes!" This time it was a demand.

"I can't," she whispered.

"I will not have you rob me of that, Rohina. At the moment of surata our eyes must meet. Otherwise there can be no union—no passing of the Jadu between us. It is written: 'The Jadu passes through the eyes in the moment of Bliss as through an open doorway between rooms.'"

He wasn't sane. He couldn't be sane.

"There can be no union!" Ana sobbed. "I'm a stranger to you. You don't know me. You don't love me. This isn't union, it's rape!"

He seemed appalled. "No. Not rape. A marriage of souls. A sharing of power."

"I can't pass the Jadu. It can't be done."

"Oh, but it can. I've made a study of the Bogar ways, lived among them in the secret caverns, steeped myself in their knowledge. I've learned these things from the highest priests of the Bogar. I know that while their priestesses can confer only the pleasures of the body, the Rohin can reach into the very soul, can confer not only pleasure, not only Bliss, but spiritual power. I have learned this, waiting for the day when I would find a Rohin woman who had yet to share herself with a man. Who had yet to relinquish her power."

"Myth and lies! The Rohin have nothing to do with the Bogar!"

"You must not deny me this! Open your eyes, I beg you! Look at me! Look at me!"

He grasped her shoulders and shook her, desperation pouring from him in a torrent that overwhelmed her senses. He was weeping, and his tears fell upon her like salt rain.

She squeezed her eyes more tightly shut, twisting her head away from him. In swift response, his hands went to her neck, fingers biting her flesh.

Yes, she thought, abstracting the pain. This is better. Let him kill me.

She was losing consciousness when she heard a chime. The pressure suddenly eased and his weight lifted. She heard his voice, disembodied, muffled, still sobbing: "What is it? What?"

"We have a visitor," answered a man's voice. It seemed smug, triumphant. "The Lord Twapar is here to see us."

∼

The Circle Chamber was silent, its occupants absorbing the evidence they had just been presented. Jaya fidgeted in his seat, the Rani stared at her hands.

"We have evidently," said Rakesh Bithal at length, taking his eyes from the visual display before him, "been the target of this subtle— and not so subtle—coercion for sometime. Can Bhaktasu Sarojin have been the first to suspect it?"

"Perhaps only the first to suspect who was not inclined to either ignore it or fold to its pressure," said Sri Elui. "I would like to put it to the Circle. Has anyone here been approached by anyone seeking their support for legislation or adjudication?"

There was a long silence in which many pairs of eyes traded glances full of question.

Rakesh Bithal's expression as he surveyed his peers was particularly dark.

"Come, now," he said at last. "It doesn't take the Jadu to divine that there must be members of this Council who have been tested by the Consortium. Even I can feel it. I will testify that I have not, to my knowledge, been approached by any 'lobbyists,' but there is no shame in having been."

"Isn't there?" asked Narudin. "Doesn't it imply that you are perceived as being weak, malleable, corruptible?"

"Were you approached by the KNC, Vadin?" asked Sri Radha.

Narudin scowled and fidgeted, glancing at Bithal. "Yes. I was—to my shame. I felt ... filthy. To have them think I might be swayed by their enticements!"

"You were not," said Bithal. "Glory in that."

"I, too." It was Lord Mandal who spoke, looking as shamefaced as Narudin. "And I must admit it has prejudiced me against the Consortium. The 'enticements' that came my way were delivered anonymously, but I couldn't help but attach them to Kasi-Nawahr. Until this Workers' Coalition stepped forward to claim them, I assumed some faction within the Consortium must be responsible. I was ashamed to have been approached in such a manner. I was more ashamed that it impaired my objectivity."

"And so," Radha finished for him, "you didn't report it."

The Vadin flushed deeply red. "How do you report a speculation? A man said to me, 'If you proceed in this way, Ramji will certainly shine on you.' How am I to bring that to the Inner Circle? When I said the words aloud it sounded inane. It was only in the manner of the words that I heard the bribe, felt the threat. How am I to report that?"

Radha nodded. "Is there anyone else?"

Save for the shaking of a few heads, there was no response.

"So," mused Sri Elui, "the Consortium gets to Bel Adivaram through his dealings with the dalali. And through Adivaram, the Sarngin that have already been corrupted by Badan-Devaki are used to further terrorize our Avasan brethren. Heinous. We must determine who is ultimately responsible for them. The evidence points to at least one member of the Kasi-Nawahr Board of Directors. The questions now is, which one—or ones?"

Bithal nodded. "We will call them all in for questioning, but that doesn't answer our most pressing problem—finding Anala Nadim. We must find Bel Adivaram and/or Duran Prakash immediately."

"Where shall we look?" asked the Deva. "We must suspect that Prakash-sama is not in Kalimpur, or that, if he is, he arrived there somewhat later than we were told. Discovering that takes time."

Jaya shook his head, a sudden irrational fear pushing up beneath his resolve to remain calm. "We don't have time. The evidence points to someone within the KNC Towers. The Towers are where we should begin the search, not in Kalimpur. Kalimpur is a smokescreen, just as WoCoa was a smokescreen."

"I agree with the Nathu Rai," said Bithal.

A light flashed by the chamber's large main view screen and Mall Gar's face appeared on it, drawing everyone's complete attention.

"You have a report, Commander?" the Deva asked.

"Indeed, Holy One. We followed Lord Twapar as you suggested. His gait was much more elastic once he left the Council Chamber. He did not go home. He went by car into the heart of the Industrial Zone. The vehicle disappeared in the block between Blossom and Nawahr Cross."

The Deva nodded. It was no surprise. "The KNC Towers. Commander, how many men are with you?"

"Five, Holy One."

"Leave three of them to collect Lord Twapar and apply yourself to finding Bel Adivaram. I would like both of them brought to the Circle."

"As you wish, Deva."

He signed off, leaving the Deva to gaze pensively at the screen. "So, it appears our colleague has gone straight to the jinn's lair."

"To warn the jinn?" suggested Jaya. "Now, will you send the Balin to search the place? Adivaram may be hiding there, as well."

"Think, Nathu Rai," said the Vadin Bithal. "The KNC complex is vast. It would take an army of Balin to search it with any hope of finding Nadim-sa. Who can say but that the attempt to find her might not mean her death? We could, however, send a smaller force to conduct a search of Prakash-sama's office." He turned his eyes to the Deva.

"If we wait but minutes, we may have Lord Twapar to guide our search," she said.

The words were so rational, yet Jaya had suddenly no room in him for rationality. He was terrified and the terror enraged him.

He slammed his fist against the arm of this chair. "She's there, dammit! She's in that complex! I know it!"

"How do you know?" asked Radha sharply.

"The same way I know she's not dead. The same way I know she's terrified and hurt–"

He teetered at the edge of that precipice. Yes, she was hurt. He knew it as surely as he knew that everyone in the chamber was staring at him. Breathing became suddenly difficult. An image formed behind his eyes that he could not shake away.

The Deva's eyes narrowed and she leaned forward in her seat. Light from the colored panes high up in the chamber's curved walls rippled in rainbows across her silver hair.

"Are you ill, Nathu Rai?"

Jaya barely heard her. The image in his mind was expanding in terrible detail.

The red wedding gown; the flicker of lights. Terror. Revulsion. A touch. Pain.

Jaya grasped the arm of his chair tightly enough to bruise his hands. Air refused to come to his lungs. He gasped and fought to draw himself out of the vision. It was gone suddenly, like the popping of a soap bubble, leaving him winded and shaking and aware that the fragile contact had been lost.

The Deva started out of her seat. "Jaya!"

He met the Deva's eyes. "I can't stay here and wait for them to catch Twapar. I swear to you that Ana is in immediate danger. I felt it. I saw it. Will you invoke the Power of Indra and order those offices to be searched or must I search them myself?"

The Deva hesitated. In that moment of hesitation, Jaya began to move toward the doors. Mall Gar's face appeared again on the view screen, stopping him in his tracks. Gar was visibly disturbed.

"Deva," the Commander said, "my report is ... not a happy one."

The hesitation was jarring and, for a chilling moment, Jaya thought Gar would tell them Ana was dead. The air in the room seemed suddenly thick and suffocating.

"We have heard very few happy reports today, Commander," the Deva said. "Please continue."

Gar glanced down, then back at his com-unit. "We have found the Vadin Adivaram, Holy One. He is dead."

In the silence that followed, Jaya dared to breathe again. Ana was not dead. Ana was alive. But the vital link to her was still broken.

"How did he die?" the Deva asked, her voice barely above a whisper.

"He was apparently run down near the Spaceport by an aircar. There was no sign of the vehicle, but I suspect it must have sustained considerable damage."

Run down. Jaya closed his eyes. Those were chillingly familiar words.

He sensed a stir in the room and heard the Deva speak. "I, Radha, Deva of the Cloud Order of the Holy Dandin, take into the hands of this Circle the reins of the Power of Indra."

"Indra!" repeated Sri Elui, standing.

"Indra!" Each Circle member in turn pronounced the holy name and stood, giving consensus to the Deva's declaration of autonomous power.

When all had spoken, Radha turned back to her com-unit. "Commander Gar, please take as many men as you can spare to the KNC complex. I want you to search every building. You will need no formal writ. I will meet you there and officially pass to you the Seal of Indra."

Movement in the room brought Ana fully to herself on a surge of panic, but the person in the room was not one of her male tormentors; it was the house dasa now in a flurry of preparation. She was no longer sullen. A smile played around her lips. Ana lay still and watched her, trying to divine what was going on. At length the woman glanced over and saw she was awake. She paused in her activity.

"You angered the Mystic One. I did not think it possible. I have never seen him like that. What did you do?" Her mobile face displayed real interest.

Ana tried her throat. It hurt, but she managed to say, "I wouldn't ... open my eyes."

The dasa seemed puzzled. "Not open your eyes? Why should he care if your eyes are closed?"

"I have the Jadu," Ana whispered. "He thinks if he ... He wanted me to give him the Gift—to pass it from my eyes to his. I wouldn't."

The other woman's tawny face paled. "The Jadu?" She made a superstitious gesture. "Then you'd own his soul."

There was real fear there. It was a fear that Ana leapt to exploit.

"Yes," she said, trying to make her failing voice sound forceful and arch, "but, I didn't want him. So, instead, I drove him to fury—to madness. It is your master's soul I want, for he is a powerful man. Once I have his soul, he will never seek you out again. No other woman will even attract him. He will find you repulsive. He will send you away."

The dasa smiled. "I think not. You see, he is sending you away."

Ana was immediately wary. "What do you mean?"

"They are afraid. I don't know why. Perhaps they have seen what you can do to a man's mind. But they are taking you away. You will not be able to reach him. He will be here, with me, and you shall have only the Mystic One to play with your Jadu." She all but spat the word. She rose, then, and resumed her duties.

"Where?" Ana asked. "Where are they taking me?"

But the other woman only continued to pack clothing and to smile. Ana was about to plead, when the door opened and the Mystic stepped through it. He was still wearing the hood, still terrifying. He waved the dasa out of the room. Ana began to shake all over. She couldn't see his eyes—couldn't see how much of his former madness lay there.

"So. You were not alone at the dalali, Rohina. One of your friends was with you. The old Vadin failed to mention that."

His voice held no anger; indeed, he seemed amused.

"He saw us, you know. Just for an instant, but that was enough. Now he sends us away, you and I. You cannot be found here. It would ruin my friends."

Reaching behind Ana's back, he loosed her tether from the bed frame and looped it around her neck, fashioning a crude collar. He pulled it tight with supreme gentleness, holding the free end in his other hand.

"You, Rohina," he said, his voice equally gentle, "will give me what I desire. Because it will become your desire as well. You will share with me the power of the Jadu. Do this, and I will see that my so powerful friend harms no one."

Ji, forgive me my lies, Ana prayed. "Yes," she whispered aloud. "Yes, I'll give you the Jadu."

"You are a brave woman, Anala Nadim. A selfless woman, to sacrifice all for those you love." He gazed at her for a moment more, then said, "Do this for me, and I promise I shall use my new power on behalf of your father and his associates. You see, not only do I have certain things my friend needs, but I also possess knowledge of his dealings that would be damaging were it to be known to the Circle or the Vrinda Varma."

"But your friend ... is part of the Consortium. If you helped my father..."

"It would mean ruin for my friend, yes. All part of the dance. Empires rise and fall and rise again." He released his hold on her tether. "Jitah, please attend us."

At the sound of his voice, the dasa appeared so quickly, Ana was certain she'd been listening.

"Jitah, please get her ready to move."

He left them.

Please, he had said. To a dasa. What sort of man was this who could be so cruel and yet so gentle?

When Jitah had made certain he had gone, she spoke in hushed, hurried tones. "He will take you to his safe place. To a place no one can find you. A place you will not be able to escape."

She moved quickly, pulling the loosened loop from Ana's neck and closing the clasps of the wedding gown. Then, she freed Ana's hands and pulled them to the front where she manacled them tightly together.

"Now," she said. "These only seem tight. If you twist your wrists so-" She demonstrated with an inward, then outward roll. "-they will part. Try it—quickly."

Stunned, heart thumping with sudden hope, Ana repeated the movements. A carefully arranged loop of the composite cord slipped free, allowing her wrists about a half-meter of play.

Jitah quickly rewound the loop, then withdrew a small, ivory lozenge from her sash. It looked like a woman's lip brush. She held it before Ana's face and pressed a tiny red-jeweled button in the left eye of the creature likeness—the paruta again. From its mouth sprung, not a brush, but a thin finger-length blade. Jitah pressed the dragon's opposite eye—a golden one—and the blade retracted.

"Red for blood. Remember," she said, and tucked the knife carefully behind the broad clasp at the waist of Ana's gown.

"Why are you doing this? He's sending me away. It's what you wanted."

"You heard him—he would cause my master's ruin, and that would cause mine. Now," she said, "one more thing. Master told me to drug you, but I won't."

She took a small vial from the ornate rack on the bedside table and opened it. Then she poured its contents into the little censer where it was quickly absorbed by the ash. She set the vial down again in a conspicuous place.

"You must make to sleep," she told Ana.

"How soon?"

"Soon. A minute only."

Ana took a deep breath and exhaled it slowly, calming her pulse, soothing her heart. "Thank you, Jitah."

"I do this for me and mine. You have no need to thank me. I'd as soon see you dead." She started to return to her packing, then paused. "If they kill you trying to escape, will you haunt me?"

Ana could not quite smile at that. "No, Jitah. I won't haunt you."

The dasa nodded her satisfaction and went about her duties. Ana closed her eyes and prayed. It was a simple prayer: Give me the strength to take what I am given, and if I fail to escape, let me die in the attempt.

CHAPTER TWENTY-ONE

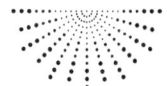

ANA KEPT HER EYES CLOSED. She had no choice, really. Her head rested upon her guard's muscular shoulder, her face was turned up into his. If she dared so much as flicker her lashes, he'd see it. So she hung limp in his arms and prayed for a chance to glimpse even a tiny tell-tale view of her prison. They went down long corridors, they descended in lift baskets, they emerged into the echoing vastness of a carpark.

The guard carefully lowered Ana into a vehicle. She smelled Jitah's perfume.

"No, no. Put her here, next to me," said the voice of the Mystic.

The guard grunted and moved her to the rear-facing seat. She dared crack an eyelid.

Jitah, her face inscrutable, slipped sideways so she was facing Ana across the carpeted interior. The large man sat next to her. Were they coming along, after all? The guard glanced at her, then got in and sat next to his master.

"Close the door, Jitah."

Jitah obeyed, activating the door control near her elbow with a bland gaze at Ana. The door was an inset slider that closed swiftly, creating an airtight seal.

Ana's heart turned a somersault in her chest. She thanked Ramji for the fortune and begged for the presence of mind to be able to signal Jitah when to open the door.

She dared open her right eye a bit wider. She couldn't see well outside the car, lying as the guard had put her. Her head was tilted forward, chin to chest, and canted very slightly toward the door. Instead of straining to see and taking a chance on giving herself away, she waited, impatiently, for an opportunity to change her position.

It came as the aircar navigated the passageway leading up from the carpark. There was a fairly sharp turn at the top and the car rocked slightly in taking it. Ana moaned a little and rolled toward the door, letting her forehead strike it solidly. She moaned again.

"Jitah, please see to her."

At the sound of the Mystic's low but urgent voice, Jitah moved to steady Ana, lifting her head and bracing it against the window so that she could see her surroundings. And she could see quite well, despite the dark tinting of the car's windows.

They were pulling away from the artfully sculpted rear face of a grand building. It was shimmering, glass-like, and familiar. Ana had seen it in travel brochures; the "Asra of Industry," they called it— Headquarters of the Kasi-Nawahr Consortium. It was what she'd expected, but somehow the certain knowledge that there was corruption and inhumanity high up in such a socially powerful and respected organization as the Consortium shocked her as if she'd only just discovered it.

They were gliding down a broad avenue bordered by trees and tall shrubs when the master of the situation chuckled. "Look, Jitah. Look at all the Sarngin and Balin scurrying about their business. I wonder if they're searching for our beautiful guest."

Jitah twisted in her seat, straining to look, then turned back to Ana, her eyes wide. She moved her hand to cover the door control switch plate beneath her right elbow. Ana tensed, making a tiny gesture with one thumb.

"Oh! So many of them!" exclaimed the dasa, twisting around again. Her hand punched the control.

The door slid back into the wall of the car and Ana threw herself out into the street, twisting her wrists free as she fell. She landed painfully across the curbing of a grassy island and scrambled to her feet. She screamed and, screaming, raced out into the middle of the avenue.

All was chaos. The aircar in which she'd been imprisoned came to a gliding halt and pivoted. Other vehicles swerved to avoid it. The guard shot out of the back seat and pursued her, cutting between her and the approaching group of Sarngin and Balin aircars. He was armed.

Ana had no time to think. She pulled out the little knife, then threw herself into the shrubbery. The guard fired the stunfuzzy as she dove into the bushes. The near hit tingled across her back. Struggling upward, she ducked behind a tree, clawed her way past a tall bush. Behind that, she swung about, straining to peer down the street behind her. The tether between her wrists pulled suddenly tight, bringing her to the chilling realization that the cord of her manacles was tangled in the stemmy growth.

She fumbled the knife, pressed the paruta's eye button—red for blood—and was rewarded by the appearance of the short blade. She turned it on the manacle cord, hacking at it fiercely, frantically, the bush shaking with every move. It was futile; the cord would not be cut. Like an animal caught in a hunter's snare, she could only cower when her pursuer towered before her.

Seeing her caught there in the torn wedding dress, he grinned. Then he holstered his stun-fuzzy, reached for her with his big, sinewy hands, grasped her shoulders and pulled her toward him.

Ana drove the little knife into his stomach. Warm blood covered her hands and made darker blotches on the crimson fabric of the ruined gown.

With a bellow of pain and rage, the guard released her and wrenched away, his eyes wide with disbelief. He looked from Ana to his bloodied stomach and back, his eyes finally fixing on the tiny dagger she still held in trembling fingers. He drew another weapon from inside his jacket. No stun-fuzzy, this, but a lightning gun.

Terrified, Ana wrenched at her bonds. "He'll kill you!" she whispered hoarsely. "If I die, you die!"

He hesitated, then raised the gun, aiming it at her left hip.

"Then I won't kill you," he said reasonably.

He put his thumb over the firing button, then made a funny shrugging gesture, his eyes going from wide to completely blank. He buckled at the knees, falling forward in slow motion. The lightning gun scraped down Ana's side as he fell against her and dropped to the ground. His head came to rest between her feet.

She stared at him, feeling a faint static tingle down her torso and legs. A sound made her cringe and glance up. Where the guard had stood was Mall Gar, a stun-fuzzy in his hand. He graced Ana with a startled appraisal, then turned his head and shouted toward the street. "Here, Nathu Rai! She is here!"

Ana closed her eyes and gave up control of her body to whatever spirit was willing to grasp it. Upright, but quaking, she listened for his footsteps. She would not open her eyes. She would not see his face when he came through the hedge and found her torn and bound and bloody, with Jitah's little dagger in her hands. She would not.

She did. And because she did, she saw the mingling of relief and horror, of joy and rage, of love and hatred. She felt it, too, in the quick current that flowed through the narrowing gap between them. Then, she saw another thing; she saw him weep.

Somewhere between the time he took her in a painful embrace and the time they emerged onto the street, someone had removed the manacles from Ana's wrists, checked her carefully for wounds, and put a cloak around her. Stepping down into the street, she took the clutter of Sarngin and Balin vehicles in a feverish glance. There were at least seven of them—the blue of the Sarngin, the white of the Balin—pulled into a haphazard pattern that blocked the avenue. But among them, one vehicle was conspicuously absent.

Ana stopped at the curbing. "Where is it?"

"Memsa?" Gar was at her side instantly.

"The big car. The blue one. The one I escaped from."

"I regret, memsa, that it eluded us."

Jaya swore.

"Two units gave chase," Gar continued, "but without success. Do you have any idea where they were taking you?"

Ana stared up and down the road with something like despair knotting her stomach. Jaya took her shoulders and turned her to face him.

"Who was it, Ana? Do you know who it was?"

He spoke as if to a child, so gently, but with rage boiling just beneath concern. Ana felt it there, and thought of the hotsprings at home ... and then just of home. She swallowed, dropping her eyes away from his.

"There were two of them. They wore hoods. I never saw their faces. I only know that one of them was connected to the Consortium. He could have been anyone high up in the company. He had a serving girl named Jitah. The other, they called the Mystic. I didn't know him at all."

Caught by the fluttering of her gauzy skirts, her eyes lowered further, taking in the dirt and blood and nakedness beneath the sheer wisps of torn cloth. A group of Sarngin stood nearby, staring at her. She started to shake again.

"Please, Nathu Rai," she said. "Please, take me home."

Jaya's touch seemed suddenly distant. He nodded silently and glanced at Gar.

"We can use my vehicle." The Commander gestured at a plain blue aircar in the center of the broad way.

"No, Commander. I think you have a search to conduct. Anala and the Nathu Rai will come with me." The voice was Sri Radha's.

Ana grasped it as a lame man grasps a walking stick. Lifting her head a little, she started to step off the curbing, but her shoeless feet and suddenly weak legs refused to obey her. She fell into the Deva's arms.

Radha supported her in a motherly embrace to a Balin aircar while Jaya and Mall Gar followed in their wake. An officer moved smartly to open the door for them. The Deva helped Ana in, her embrace never faltering.

"We will catch these men, Nathu Rai," said Gar. "We have that bodyguard—or so I assume him to be—we will track down his master."

Jaya glanced down at Ana, curled like a child in the Deva's lap. "Better you find him than I do, Commander. Because I would kill him."

"They were always hooded," Ana said, looking at her knees.

She would not meet his eyes now, Jaya noticed, as if she had committed some transgression that would be discovered if she did. The examination by the Asvin Suhrdam, as kindly as he was, seemed to have caused her further strain. So, too, had been the tearful reunion with Jivinta, Hadas and her father.

"Neither wore any sign of rank." She spoke in what Jaya could only describe as a careful monotone. "The Mystic wore a plain, gold ring. I didn't see any holo-pics or any other images in the room. The Mystic's eyes were dark hazel; the other's were like steel or the under-belly of a cloud."

"There is this," said Mall Gar, dangling the paruta flask by its chain.

Jaya shivered and thought Ana did the same.

"The paruta is a common clan totem," said Jaya. He glanced at Ana, trying to pull her eyes to him. At last, he succeeded and watched memory flair in her eyes.

"Red and gold ... the wedding dress! The big man said his friend had noticed red and gold became me. So I ... I asked him—the Mystic—why he had dressed me in red and gold. He said it was the color of Indra, first of all—and therefore an irony."

"An irony?" Jaya repeated.

She turned her eyes away from him. "An irony for a Genda Sita to wear the color of the Sacred. The red was also for our wedding, of course, and because he recalled that it became me. As if he'd seen me in red before."

Jaya nodded. "The Mesha Fest. That doesn't narrow it down much. We had a house full of guests." He hesitated, then decided to take a step toward the mystical. "What about the box? A box made of bhasvata crystal?"

Ana's eyes widened. "One of them showed me a box cut from a single huge crystal. He said it came from his family mine. How did you-?"

"His family mine?" The Deva stirred from her window seat.

"Yes." Ana nodded. "He said the family mine was in the Lake District."

"Ah!" Mall Gar was already on his way to the study's vicom. "That narrows things down a great deal."

His fingers flew over the keypad, bringing up screen after screen. At length, he shook his head.

"Ansar. That is the family name of the mine upon which the Kasi-Nawahr Consortium's fortunes were built. But that is not the name of any family or business currently attached to the director-ship. The mine is now closed and has been let to some minor reli-gious sect as a shrine."

Radha moved to stand at his shoulder. "Perhaps he was lying, then. Or perhaps it was the mother's family who owned the mine, or even the grandmother's. If that's the case..."

Gar made an explosive sound of frustration. "This must not be a dead end," he said, as if he could threaten reality into obedience.

"Excuse me."

The Rani Melantha stood in the doorway. When all eyes turned to her, she seemed to flicker like a candle flame at the point of guttering.

She cleared her throat delicately and said, "I'm afraid I must admit to eavesdropping. You're trying to locate a place in the Lake District. I was born and raised there. Perhaps I can help."

"Do you know of the Ansar mine, Rani?" asked the Deva.

"Of course. Through that mine, Ansar became the first family of Vatapur."

"Then how is it they are not the first family of the Consortium?" asked Mall Gar.

The Rani's perfect brows ascended. "They are, in a manner of speaking. Ansar was the family name until about sixty years ago. There was no male heir in that generation, so the property passed to the eldest daughter—oh, I can't remember her name."

"And to a husband?" asked Jaya.

"Yes, to her husband. But he'd married into her family property so the Ansar name stayed with the mine. How does any of this bear on-"

"One of the men who kidnapped Ana claimed to be the Ansar heir."

The Rani's eyes widened slightly. "Nigudha Bhrasta," she said.

"Ah," said Mall Gar. "Not merely one of the members of the Consortium, but its head."

The others digested the news silently. Jaya could not claim surprise. He moved to pick up the paruta flask.

"But the serpent isn't the totem of either Ansar or Bhrasta families."

Ana shook her head. "No, that belonged to the other. The Mystic. It was a family heirloom."

The Rani's head jerked as if someone had slapped her. Her eyes, huge, dark and glittering, fastened on the flask.

"Namun." She whispered the name, and for five seconds all sound was sucked from the room.

Jaya, too, stared at the flask and felt the world rock. "Namun Vedda? Uncle Namun? That's impossible. As I said, the serpent is such a common..."

The Rani lowered herself into the nearest chair. "Has it wings?"

Jaya looked at it again. "Yes, it has wings."

"The wings of a butterfly?"

He did not answer. The world, which had made little sense just recently, now failed to make any sense at all.

"Excuse me, Nathu Rai," said the Deva softly, "but I believe Commander Gar and I need to inform our forces that they have a new target."

She nodded at the Sarngin and they removed themselves to the privacy of the small parlor next door.

Jaya could no longer stand. He lowered himself into a chair across from his mother, holding her gaze, linking them in a mutual agony of disbelief.

"That man," murmured the Rani at length, "has been in this house countless times as your father's friend. Pretending. Pretending to be his friend. Eating at his table. I had thought of him as..."

"Family," Jaya finished. "My 'Uncle' Namun. God, I should have known. Somehow, I should have known."

The Rani covered her face with her hands.

"Where might he go?"

Rokh Nadim's voice jarred Jaya and brought him back to the reality that Nigudha Bhrasta and Namun Vedda were still free. He opened his mouth to say nothing.

It was Ana who spoke: "A safe place. Jitah—Bhrasta's dasa—said the Mystic would go to his safe place."

"Which could be anywhere on Mehtar," observed her father.

"Or anywhere on Avasa," noted Mall Gar as he re-entered the room. "He has a private starcoach and there is also a corporate one at his disposal." He raised his hand as Jaya would have spoken. "The Vadin Bithal has already sent men to the Spaceport. He has also requested that no private KNC vessels be allowed to depart."

The Rani lifted her head. "Just outside of Vatapur on the Lake of Jewels, very near the mine, Namun had a residence. He spent holidays there. Sometimes we would go with him. Jaya, you remember. I was there over the Mesha festival the year your father..." She uttered a sharp laugh at the self-inflicted pain. "He said it would restore me."

"You know where this residence is?" asked Gar. "You could show me on a holo map?"

She nodded, rising. "I would be happy to, Commander."

"The Bogar!" murmured Ana.

Nadim-sama turned to look at his daughter with incredulity etching his weathered face. "What possesses my daughter to utter such an obscenity?"

Ana shook her head. "He—Vedda—said he'd studied with the Bogar, lived with them in the secret caverns. Bhrasta talked about letting some minor religious sect let the mine."

The Rani was nodding vigorously. "Yes! He joked about it. Don't you remember, Jaya? He used to tease you about them sacrificing children to their dragon god. You were terrified, but it kept you away from the mine. He told me he was afraid you might fall"

"That's our best possibility then," said Gar, bending back to his business. "I will inform the Vadin Bithal."

Jaya rose and offered Ana his hand. "Come outside with me?"

She glanced at him, warily he thought, and then at her father, whose expression was neutral, if interested.

"There's nothing we can do here, right now," Jaya told her. "This is in Gar's hands, and the Deva's."

She nodded, rose, took the offered hand, and let him lead her out through the ornately leaded glass panels, onto the long ledge of tiled patio that ran behind the wing. Outside, the afternoon sun played warmly on the pale tiles, picking out sparkling bits of mica and crystal.

They stopped in unison at the balustrade and gazed over the formal garden and the fountain with its jeweled fish. He thought he might have found his voice, and turned to her to speak, but the look on her face stopped him. There was anguish there, the lost look of someone who had—he dragged in a deep breath—someone who had just been through a de-humanizing and terrifying ordeal.

He raised a hand and stroked her bruised neck. It looked horrible—a dark ring of purple and black with a contrasting scarlet collar from the tether's chafe. He knew from the husky whisper of her voice that her throat must still ache when she spoke. His own throat ached as if in empathy. Tears welled and refused to be dammed.

Ana's face showed her amazement. "For me, Nathu Rai?"

Before he could formulate words, she lifted his hand from her neck and kissed the raicree in the palm. A flash fire of pure desire struck him. He showered it with shame. Desire was inappropriate just now. It would be the last thing she wanted from him. The last thing.

"Do you know what I thought," she said, holding his hand against her swollen throat, "when I believed I wouldn't escape that place?" She laughed. It was a tight, painful sound. "Well, I thought a great many things—that I might grow wings and fly away; that I might stop my heart from beating-"

"No," he murmured.

"That I might be able to call out to you."

"You did."

"So it seems. What I thought, Jaya Rai, while I lay in that room, was that I wished Govi had not timed his visit to you so poorly, a certain evening. That Ravi had not come looking for you because of it." Her eyes met his, direct and fearless. "I wanted you to know that. I thought: better to lose one's self to kindness than to cruelty."

Jaya was surprised to hear himself say (and mean), "I will be forever grateful for both Govi's poor timing and Ravi's interruption. I wasn't ready for that. You weren't ready for it. I didn't understand you then."

She studied his face, a glint of something impish deep in the pale eyes. "And you do now, you think?"

"I don't know. But I do know that I didn't then—that's something, isn't it?"

He smiled—or, rather, tried to. He realized vaguely that she was waiting for something from him. Perhaps it was the same thing he was waiting for.

"The Deva Radha has told me that she would like you to study for the Cloud Order," he said.

She nodded. "She said the same to me."

"You'd like that?"

Again, she nodded. "It's one of my deepest longings."

"Could a Deva also be a Rani of the House Sarojin? Could she be a wife, a member of a family as well as a bhakta?"

Her eyes narrowed. "Are you serious?" she asked, peering up at him. "How can I be a Rani and still have my mice and my mountaintop? You have some very peculiar ideas about religion, Nathu Rai."

She was teasing him. He was unsure whether it was meant to acknowledge their bond or put distance between them. Afraid of distance, he tried to bridge it physically. She still held his hand; now he took hers and performed the same simple ritual she had performed, turning the palm to his lips and kissing the doctored dascree.

"Pardon, Nathu Rai."

Once again, Jaya found himself holding a broken moment. He turned and met Ravi's inquiring gaze. At least this time there was not so much obvious disapproval in it.

"Pardon, but the Commander has sent me to tell you that an accident has occurred at the Spaceport. It appears that Bhrastasama has been killed attempting to leave Mehtar."

CHAPTER TWENTY-TWO

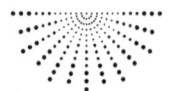

AN ACCIDENT HAD INDEED HAPPENED at the Spaceport. As the order to stop all KNC related flights came into the Flight Console Administrator, two vessels—one, a KNC starcoach, the other a private skycoach owned by Namun Vedda—were preparing to lift from the field. The skycoach had already demagnetized its docking cradle and was waiting on anchors for the go-ahead. ConAdministrator Pangel ordered it to hold. It did, but the pilot of the starcoach continued with lift-prep, ignoring him completely.

When it was apparent the ship meant to take off, Con-Administrator Pangel called for a desperate and dangerous maneuver. With his own hands, he over-rode the de-magnetization process and froze the cradle of the starcoach Gauri Star.

The vessel attempted to lift anyway with unexpected consequences; instead of merely having her mag-keel holed, she exploded in a wash of blue-green flame. In the panic that followed, the skycoach Black Paruta lifted above the blast and sped away on a course that did not match the one registered with flight control.

Twenty minutes later, on the flight field next to the still smoking wreckage of the Gauri Star, the Vadin Rakesh Bithal summarized the situation for Nathu Rai Sarojin and his companions.

"There were three people aboard the vessel, it seems—a pilot, Bhrasta-sama and a woman. The pilot abandoned ship before the explosion and has vanished. I have enlisted the aid of the Port

Sarngin to find him. This was no accident, I think, Nathu Rai. Vedda-sama is not here."

Jaya ground the sole of his boot into the resilient surface of the flight pad. "Then we have to assume he's on the Black Paruta."

"If he is," said Rakesh Bithal, "we will track him down."

~

The Balin cruiser carried eight of the elite militia men including their Supreme Commander, Rakesh Bithal. It also carried Mall Gar, Jaya Sarojin, Anala Nadim and Ravi. They had been in the air only minutes when a report from the Spaceport informed them that it appeared the Gauri Star had been intended to carry an additional passenger.

Among the remnants of baggage and various belongings in the smoldering wreck, searchers found clothing for two distinctly different men—different in stature; different in taste. There were also, reported the officer in charge, some odd icons, deformed somewhat by the blast. They appeared to the officer in charge to be the sort of icons one might find in an Asra's prayer niches, but with subtle differences. He described them as erotic, for want of a better word. They had been saved complete destruction by virtue of being in a steel case etched with the initials D.P..

"So," Bithal concluded, "it would appear Prakash-sama was supposed to have been on the Gauri Star and, presumably to have died with it."

"Perhaps that is Uncle Namun's solution to every problem," said Jaya.

His voice was bitter and Ana felt a chill pit open up beneath her heart. She wanted to weep for him, for his father, for this betrayal, but realized it was neither the time nor the place for grieving.

They found the Black Paruta approximately where they expected they would, on a small private landing field carved out of the mountainous terrain not far from Namun Vedda's summer house on the Lake of Jewels. The Balin pilot set his cruiser down next to her and they debarked.

Ana, one of the first off, paused to listen to the mountainside. It was barely spring at this higher elevation and little pockets of snow still peeked from beneath evergreens and pooled around the bases of rocks. A vague whisper at the periphery of her hearing, a vague tugging at her consciousness made her orient herself toward the bow of the ship. She took several steps in that direction without realizing she had done so.

"South." Bithal checked the map on his hand-held unit. "The computer agrees with you, Nadim-sa. Good. I would not like to have to choose which to trust." He gave Ana a wry glance and nodded in the direction she faced. "The mine is that way. Does that surprise you?"

Ana blushed. "No, Vadin Bithal. I hear wind-singers."

"Ah."

He turned to his Balin and issued orders for their armament. They carried clubs and stunfuzzies set to maximum range and power. Bithal, himself, carried an ice pellet gun as well—a weapon legal only to the Balin. Jaya and Ravi were issued stunfuzzies; Ana went unarmed by choice.

Bithal led his party through the dense brush with Jaya and Gar flanking him. They found themselves almost immediately in a draw between two steep hills, tracing an old stream bed.

The random melodies of the wind-singers grew louder as they moved toward the mine. At length, a slight bend in the trail allowed them to see the entrance, cut into the hillside by the hands of men, barred from access by the same. A lurid depiction on the arching gate announced the nature of the sect. The windsingers hung on a pole thrust into the ground next to the entrance.

"I take it we must ring to be admitted," guessed Bithal. "If you would rather not enter, Nadim-sa..."

She laughed. "I've been in worse places, Vadin Bithal. Besides, I think I can help find him."

The Vadin nodded and moved to give the chimes a hard shake. There was no response. He shook them again. Nothing. With a chuff of impatience, he pulled his pellet gun and took aim at the spot where the latch met one thick supporting beam. The latch made a sudden clunking noise and the heavy wooden gate swung wide open.

Bithal holstered his weapon and entered. All eyes strained to pierce the gloom. The darkness was not absolute, but eddied and coiled in a dance with firelight that seemed to come from every-where and nowhere. It bled up the walls, lapped at the vaulted ceiling of the manmade entry and rushed in waves across the stone floors.

It took Ana a moment to realize that someone stood before them several steps up a broad, shallow rise of stairs. It was a man in a blood colored robe and he was watching them through narrowed eyes. A Bogar priest. Ana could feel suspicion radiating from him; could almost see it run in rivulets through the creases in his face.

The Vadin Bithal saw him too, and made a small gesture at Jaya. Together, they moved up the steps to stand directly before him. That gave the Bogar priest the opportunity to read the emblem of status on Jaya's cloak and the Seal of Indra hanging across the breast of Bithal's flight suit. The Bogar did not look pleased to observe that his visitors were led by One of the Nine and a Taj Prince, but he bowed deeply to both and gave the respectful greeting.

There was no respect in him, Ana knew. None. Only suspicion and arrogance. She extended herself outward, imagining tendrils of thought reaching into the sooty recesses of the cave. She was aware of some other people here, close by, but not Vedda. She would know if he was near. She found her eyes drawn to the darkness beyond the three men now holding conversation on the top step.

There. He had passed this way and left a trail of anger and frustration. Red. She could nearly see it—a bloody, roiling smudge in the dark.

"Namun Vedda has studied and worshipped among us in the past, Nathu Rai," the priest was saying, "but we haven't seen him for some time."

"Still," said Jaya, "we would like to search the caverns. He may have entered without being seen."

The priest smiled. "Namun-sama is a Master of the Bogar. A man of great power, strong forces. The Virgin would know if he entered her sanctum, and what She knows, I know. Namun-sama is not here. Besides, the gate is always securely latched and only priests of the Order possess keys to it."

Ana moved lightly up the steps. "He was here, Jaya. He went back through there." She pointed into the ruddy blackness of the main passage.

"That's absurd-" the priest began, then broke off to fix Ana with a penetrating gaze. "Who is this?"

Jaya cut him off with a wave of his hand, not taking his eyes from Ana's face. "Are you sure, Ana?"

"Yes. He—he left a sort of trail."

Jaya peered into the gloom. "You can see it?"

She nodded, then shivered as the eyes of the Bogar priest seized her.

"You have the Jadu," he said. "Why do you seek Master Namun?"

Ana turned her own eyes on the man, willing herself to hold his gaze brazenly, arrogantly. Her stomach twisted, but she forced the words out. "He seeks me. I am the end of his quest. You know this."

The priest's face lit, the creases smoothing, sucking up their runnels of disdain. "Then you will pass the Power to him here?" He bowed deeply. "We are honored, Rohina. It isn't often that your Path crosses ours. I must assume that the Master has gone to the womb of the Virgin to prepare for you. I am sorry, but I don't know which of the passages he might have taken, which of the shrines he might visit on his way. The middle path is the shortest."

Jaya glanced, again, into the flame-fanned darkness. "How many passages are there?"

The priest did not take his eyes from Ana's face. "Three. All lead to the same place, eventually. Why do you bring these men with you, Rohina?" His eyes were sharp, suspicious.

Before Ana could answer, Jaya did. "I don't think, priest, that it's any of your concern. We are here to see Master Namun, and to see that he obtains what is his." He put a hand on Ana's shoulder.

The priest took in the ambiguous gesture, venom dripping from his eyes. "As you bring the fulfillment of my brother's quest, I can hardly stand in your way. Or more to the point, in the way of the Seal of Indra. That is license to do whatever you wish. I ask only that you refrain from disturbing the bhakta during their devotions and studies."

"We wouldn't think of it," Bithal told him, and signaled the group below him to come up.

He waited until the priest had adjourned to one of the side chambers, then posted two of his men at the entrance to the cave. Then he led the way through the long, broad main corridor into the cavern.

The first junction came about fifty meters along the

downsloping main shaft. From a sand-carpeted juncture with the smooth, polished surfaces of a cauldron, a second passage sprouted suddenly to the right. Narrow and curving, it was lit with glowing disks attached to the water-carved walls instead of the torches used in the main tunnel.

Rakesh Bithal studied the passages with some skepticism. "How far should we trust the directions of our esteemed priest?"

Ravi snorted. "I should say, very little. Why do you ask?"

"It occurs to me that Vedda-sama might be somewhere other than we have been informed, and that the brother's directions were intended to stall, to confuse, or to divide."

Jaya made an impatient gesture. "Do we have any choice? We must divide, if we're to search effectively."

"Perhaps, but we need not divide blindly." The Balin commander looked to Ana. "You saw his trail before. What does your Sight tell you now?"

She searched the walls, the sand, the ceiling. Odd. The tell-tale bloody smudges were absent here. "I don't see anything," she said.

"Perhaps he did not come this way," suggested Mall Gar. "Perhaps there is another way into the mountain."

Bithal sent two Balin to the right and instructed Mall Gar to lead two Balin down the straight path. Then he looked once more to Ana. "Now, Nadim-sa. Perhaps if we back-track, we can determine where our man has really gone."

They headed back toward the entry hall in silence and Ana listened intently to the sounds of the cave. She could hear them even above the whisper of their collective breathing and the slip and crunch of feet over sandy rock and the guttering of the torches, ensconced at intervals along the curving walls. There was water dripping constantly, insistently. Somewhere the water did more than drip; it splashed and hissed and thudded over rock molded by its persistent travels. Beneath that was a deep, musical sighing, as if the cave itself breathed along with its human denizens.

She felt suddenly like some alien bacteria, invading the body of a titanic, living beast. She recalled telling her parents quite firmly at the age of seven that the mountains men carved their mines out of were alive and really ought not to be disturbed by explosives, drills, and picks. She put out her hand to caress the cool, slick wall and imagined that they made their way through a major artery toward the heart of the mountain—a heart pulsing with the life of the planet itself.

She was still absorbing her surroundings, or being absorbed by them, when the corridor broadened and ascended into what was ostensibly a hall of sanctums in which the devotees studied the arcane and erotic arts.

Ana paused and scanned the doorways. There were four cut into the rough walls—two to the left, two to the right. One of them showed, if faintly, what she had taken as signs of Vedda's passing. She gritted her teeth, almost cursing the priest for his obvious misdirection. His warning against disturbing the students had caused all of them to completely overlook these portals.

Without speaking, Ana led the way to the suspect doorway. Within she saw red light flickering against mottled walls. She hesitated there, waiting until men had drawn up around her. Rakesh Bithal moved around her, his eyes grazing her face as he passed. One by one, the others past, except for Jaya. He drew level and took her hand.

"You don't have to do this. You can go back to the ship and wait. I'll send Ravi with you. We'll find him."

She shook her head, lips curling wryly. "I was not made to sit and wait, Nathu Rai. I'll come along."

She started to move forward, but he did not relinquish her hand. "If we were to marry," he said, "could you be persuaded to forget that I am the Nathu Rai?"

"If we were to marry, could you be persuaded to forget that I am Genda Sita?" she asked, challenging him.

His eyes were grave and very direct. "I had already forgotten," he said, and led her into the room.

It was not empty. In the smoky, red-gold light, several devotees sat in a group, poring over a scroll. They all started at the disturbance, looking like a startled flock of birds—beaks open, eyes wide. There was a flurry of whispers, then one of them hiked his robes and fled for the outer corridor.

Rakesh Bithal watched him leave with sanguine eye. "We'd best be quick about our next move. Nadim-sa?"

Ana was already studying the room, searching for a point of egress. There were two and both felt of Vedda's presence. She moved to one, then the other. Through the first was a well-lit corridor that seemed to be flanked by a series of small cells. The warm scent of incense wafted here—familiar incense. Sounds also carried from the cells—whispers, guttural chanting, the rhythmic play of music, trills of pleasure. Through the second doorway, a dark, narrow corridor made a sharp descent. From this dim hole came only the whisper of water.

"Both of these are marked," Ana said, hovering near the darker passage, glancing down it.

"But you believe he has gone this way," Bithal observed.

"He used both doorways. I have no way of knowing in what order."

The Balin grunted and made a quick decision. He sent two of his remaining Balin into the cells and led the remainder of the group down toward the sound of rushing water.

They drew their weapons now: Bithal, Jaya, and Ravi. Ana, unarmed, brought up the rear. When it seemed that the rocky corridor had gone on forever, the path was suddenly blocked. They stopped in consternation for a moment before the obstruction, watching the fire eddies perform an oily dance across its immense, polished flank. Jaya stepped forward for a closer look. He turned back, the obvious relief on his face beckoning the others forward.

"It's wide enough to pass on both sides. There's a chamber beyond. A large one, I think. There's mist or steam coming up from it."

Bithal nodded, then signaled them to divide, two to a side, and continue on around the obstruction.

Treading softly behind Jaya, Ana moved cautiously along the wall and into the cavern beyond. The temperature rose and mist kissed her face. She spread her senses outward, feeling of the slick, carved surfaces that flung away above, below, on all sides.

The chamber was a natural one, but bore the traces of men's prying. And it was large—large and sloping and filled with the mysterious hulks of a myriad stalagmites. If she blinked, they would become creatures of myth—squat, cowering, menacing. Some had formed columns with stalactites from above; in the flicker of torch-light, they suggested to Ana trapped souls, frozen in the act of fleeing the bowels of the Mountain. The pale stone was so close to the color of her own flesh, she could understand the legends that had arisen around the genesis of her race.

She followed the line of one such column to the vaulted ceiling. It was laced with the wriggling lines of torchlight reflected in water, for this was a chamber of pools. Hot pools, judging from the billows of warm mist that hung in the air. Some of the pools were in use.

Rakesh Bithal and his Balin weapon quickly and effectively convinced the bathers to forego their ablutions and depart. The baths were empty in a matter of moments.

Meters away, at the bottom of the chamber, was the largest pool of all. At its center sat a huge altar carved from the native stone. Its pale flanks were streaked with a darker color that hinted at green and glistened with water. Behind the altar was the most monstrous formation of all. It had once been a natural shape, like the others, but the workings of men had transformed it into the twin, hermaphrodite deity of the Bogar Orders. Feral and triumphant, it was joined to itself forever in the embrace of primal passion. It had no name that could be spoken, for it was said to exist only in the inarticulate sounds of passion's highest fever. The sound, the Bogar would say, of surata. Water poured over it from someplace above the deity's head, adorning it in a perpetual glistening sweat.

Ana freed her eyes from the carving and swept them to either side of it. To the right of the idol, she could just make out the entrance of another passage. There was as yet no sign of any of their other parties. Ana suspected those paths did not come this way and wondered how long it would take them to find their missing companions when this was over.

She glanced to her left and saw Ravi and Bithal making their way down the opposite wall of the chamber. At Jaya's urging, she moved toward the altar. The play of water drowned out all other sound; their torches were mute and their footfalls, silent. The play of light and darkness brought demons to life; the surreptitious movement of their small figures were lost in the phantasm. So, Ana discovered, was her awareness of anything beyond the sensual roil.

The two groups met before the altar.

"He's not here," Jaya said. Even in the crawling light, Ana could see the tension on his face, the blackness in his eyes.

"Then he must be in there," said Bithal, nodding toward the lower passage.

"Unless he is hiding in the cells," suggested Ravi. "Perhaps one of us should return to the room above and see what has become of the searchers there."

"Ah, no need," said Bithal. He looked up toward the top of the chamber and beckoned.

Ana turned to see the two Balin he had dispatched to the other corridor making their way swiftly downwards, their heads swiveling this way and that, taking in the awesome chamber.

"Well, what did you find?" he asked when the men reached them.

"It was," reported one of the Balin, looking distinctly uncomfortable, "a place where the devotees ... practice their lessons. The cells were small, separate. There were no other passages leading out."

"Ah," said Bithal. "I hope you did not disturb these devotees. We were warned."

"I don't think," said the second Balin, "they even noticed us."

Rakesh Bithal proceeded to take command of the situation. "Nadim-sa, have you any intimation of where our man has gone?"

She shook her head. "This is ... too chaotic. I can't sense anything here."

"Well, then—we have one corridor to search," he noted. "There is no telling how many divisions it suffers before it reaches its end. Therefore, we shall proceed thusly: I will take two men with me into the corridor. You will allow me the use of your man, Nathu Rai?" He nodded at Ravi. "I should like to leave one of my men here with you in the event that we flush Vedda-sama out and he is forced to flee through here."

"I do not consider Ravi to be my property, Bithal-sama. You may direct either of us as you need."

"Could he be hiding in here somewhere?" Jaya murmured when the Balin commander had led his group into the gloomy passage. He glanced from the altar to the amphitheater with its misshapen stone audience.

"No," said Ana. "I think I'd feel him—even through the noise."

Jaya shook his head—a sharp, spasmodic gesture, as if someone had just poured cold water down his back. His eyes asked her if she would always feel him, a leering haunt. She had no answer.

"I suggest," said the Balin, whose name was Datta, "that we hide ourselves within sight of this passage."

He suited action to word and found for himself a lump of molten-looking stone to hide behind. It gave him a clear view of both the upper and lower passages.

Their back-trail thus covered, Jaya positioned himself to the right of the corridor's mouth. Ana tucked out of sight above it, and to the left—just beneath the Bogar deity at the rim of its reflecting pool. From the upper entrance, she was screened by the altar itself, from the lower passage the bulk of the idol's natural pedestal obscured her.

She squatted there disciplining herself to calm. She contemplated the water that poured from above, eternally filling the pool below. Eternally filling and emptying again.

Emptying to where?

Ana turned her head to stare into the gloom between the idol's feet. The water of the pool flowed into darkness there. She put a hand into the pool. The current pulled strongly enough for her to feel it.

Silently, she turned on her haunches and began a slow, cautious descent into the shadow of the Bogar god. Between the legs, she saw it—a triangular slot barely a man's height. Water cascading down the wall behind the idol created a translucent curtain there, as if the god wore a watery cloak. A glimmer of light wavered behind the curtain.

Ana glanced down. The rock she squatted on was worn; many feet had taken this path. She edged forward. Reaching the mouth of the passage, she paused, hunkered down beside it, heart beating a prayer tattoo in her chest, mouth dry. She took a deep breath, steadied her thoughts and slipped beneath the filmy water fall.

She was soaked with warm water when she came out on the other side; it cooled quickly, the breeze flowing back from the orifice chilling her where she crouched, up to her ankles in a stream. She rose slowly, cautiously.

The passage before her was half-lit by amber and red glowdiscs making it seem as if she stood at the gate of Niraya hell. There was a narrow path along the right hand wall, slick with water. She moved up onto it and edged forward, still in a half-crouch. She had gone perhaps three meters when she saw the great yawning darkness at the end, unlit by torch or glow-disc. She hesitated, then moved forward again to the edge of darkness.

It was a chamber, smaller than the one behind her, closer and shallower. As she rose to her full height, Ana sensed the presence in the chamber and felt the hot wave of exultation sweep over her from much too close at hand.

"Be assured, Sri Ana," said the Mystic's sweet, soft voice almost in her ear, "that the joy of my soul knows no bounds to know you have sought me."

He moved to stand at her shoulder, coming into the watery light that floated from the passageway, and she saw his face. Not for the first time, she realized, for she had seen him at the Mesha Fest among the celebrants. Somehow, they had not been introduced, a thing that had worked distinctly to his advantage. His eyes were dark with passion and triumph, his teeth showed in an incongruously sweet smile. There was a dagger in his hand. He laid the long, cold blade against her neck.

"I only seek you to see that you are punished for what you've done," she told him, "to Jaya's family, to me."

"Revenge? A delusion, Anala. You will learn, very soon, that you have really sought me for an entirely different reason."

He was insane—she knew that. Perhaps her best defense lay in playing to his madness. She lowered her eyes, watched the stream disappear into the darkness before them. She took a deep breath, shuddered.

"Perhaps ... perhaps you're right. After all, I did come in here alone, knowing you were here. I could have—should have brought someone with me."

The knife blade lowered. "Jaya—you could have brought Jaya with you. But you did not. You left him behind."

She chewed her lip. That much was true. "If, as you believe, you and I have a destiny, what will you do when you have the Jadu? How will you use it?"

"Perhaps I will use it on behalf of what you hold dear."

"How? You don't control the Consortium."

"I could. I could first control Ranjan Vrksa, and he would recommend me for a position on the Kasi-Nawhar Board. That is how it might begin, at any rate. But all this can be of no interest to you. I give you a promise, Lalasa, that I shall find a middle way to protect the interests of both the KNC and AGIM. You see, Bhrasta failed because he lacked, among other things, balance. He wanted

368 | MAYA KAATHRYN BOHNHOFF

but one thing, single-mindedly. Power was not to him, a means to an end, but an end to itself. And so..."

"And so he died."

"Yes. He lacked vision, a sense of the common good. That is not true of me."

She turned to face him. "You must assure me of this, Vedda-sama. For I am called upon to judge you."

She had surprised him. "Judge me?"

"Your motives must be pure, sama, or the Jadu cannot be yours." She glanced up and about the dark chamber. "We are in the place of my Father-Mother. The god of Darkness. I was born here. This is my sacred chamber. It's fitting that we meet our destiny here, isn't it?"

He licked his lips, his eyes fevered. "My name is Namun. Speak it."

She looked him squarely in those eyes, shuddering inwardly. "Namun."

He smiled, shivered as if in anticipation. "I must finish my preparations. Come, sit."

He urged her ahead of him into the chamber, laying out glow-discs as he went. The room's features began to emerge from the darkness. In the moment that she took her attention from Vedda to plumb the red-gold gloom, he slipped manacles around her wrists and clasped them.

Fear, complete and sudden, ripped through her. She shot him a glance she hoped was imperious, not terrified. "Why do you restrain me? I won't resist you."

He sighed. "It seems we still do not trust each other, beloved. After, there will be trust. For now, the other end of this—" he lifted the manacle's chain, "fastens there."

'There' was a ring in what appeared to be an altar roughly three feet high and four feet long. Vedda left Ana's side momentarily to light a series of braziers set around the altar. The chamber blazed with light and the walls came to lurid life. They were covered with murals depicting various Bogar rites and the play of the twin god. The dominant color was red. Ana looked away into the fire.

Vedda was before her again, then, his hands going to the closes of her coverall.

"Are you prepared to judge me, Rohina?"

Ana swore she could hear the beating of her heart above the gurgle of water and the roar of flame. She had been willing Jaya to her—why was he not here?

"This must be done according to ritual, Namun Vedda. According to the ways of the god of Darkness."

His face was radiant, seeming lit from within by secret rapture. He raised her chained hands, kissed them.

"Instruct me, my goddess."

She needed him at a disadvantage. She also needed to be rid of these damned manacles.

"Your clothes. Remove them. You must be innocent of clothing."

He bowed and obeyed. He removed his garments slowly, making a ritual performance of the act. Ana did not watch, but focused on her next move. Once naked, he bowed before her again. He was fully aroused. Ana bit down on her fear and strove not to notice or react.

She raised her manacled hands. "I must also disrobe. You'll have to remove these."

He seemed amused. "You will not attempt to escape?"

"I give you my word—the word of a Rohina."

He shook his head, smiling.

"If this is not done according to Rohin ritual, you will neither attain surata nor receive my Gift, surely you understand this, Master Namun. You have studied the Bogar disciplines. Is the status of Master reached without attention to ritual?"

"No. You're quite right. But, you see. I can cut the fabric away." He retrieved the dagger.

Ana transmuted her fear into anger and gave him the full brunt of that. "Do you not want this Gift? According to ritual, you must undress me with care and gentleness. You are to become my lover, Namun, before the eyes of my god."

She jerked her head in the direction of the vivid effigy on the wall that curved over the altar. "How will my god—my father—sanctify our union, if he sees you rip the clothes from my body as if I were a common slave?"

He seemed to consider that. He set the dagger aside again and put his hands to the manacles.

Ana breathed again in relief. The moment her hands were free,

she thought, that dagger would be in them. She would not escape—
she had promised that—but she had not promised she wouldn't take
him prisoner.

He removed the manacle from her right wrist, but instead of
turning to the left one, he slipped the top close of her coverall.

"Tell me how it will be," he breathed, continuing his task.
"Where will I receive my Gift?"

Damn him! Ana began to doubt he was as mad as he seemed.

"On the altar." *Where I might be able to spill that brazier full of
hot coals on you.*

He assumed she meant to be taken to the altar, and so led her to
it. She turned and sat, her eyes on the passage to freedom, the
brazier at her back. Vedda continued to unfasten her coverall.

She turned her attention to the manacles. They were not locked,
but the catches were intricate and would require both time and
attention—or inattention, she thought, with a glance at Namun
Vedda's intense expression.

"In the joining," she said, struggling to keep her voice soft and
low, straining to keep it from shattering. "I will taste of your very
soul and know if it is sweet or bitter. In this way, your motives will
be judged, your actions, your life. Not just by me, but by the god of
this dark world. I must warn you, Namun, I have already tasted
bitterness in your touch."

As she had hoped, the remark stopped him in the act of tugging
the sleeve from her arm.

"What do you mean?"

"My neck still aches from the bite of your fingers."

His eyes moved to the bruises there and widened in stunned
anger. "Who did this to you? Did Jaya Sarojin do this?"

He didn't remember. Did she dare remind him? Most likely not,
but she could attempt to make the lie instructional.

"Your friend Bhrasta," she said. "He tried to take the Jadu from
me by force, without the ritual. That is the reality behind his
death."

He studied her momentarily, his eyes locked with hers, then he
said, "Instruct me, Deva."

A final tug at the sleeve bared her shoulder. Clever. Or hungry.
Or both. She shivered. It wasn't cold here, but the air was heavy

with mist and her camisole already soaked through, its azure muted to a dark and indeterminate shade.

"Continue." She held up the other wrist. "Slowly. Gently."

As she expected, he took the precaution of returning the first manacle to its place before loosing the second. Where were Jaya and Bithal?

"I am a balance," Ana told him as he worked. She found it difficult to keep her eyes from his rapt face with its expression of mixed adoration and lust. "I weigh a man's soul. I weigh his life. Each touch reveals more and more of him to my inner Sight."

The top of her coverall now lay about her hips and Vedda was preparing to refasten the second manacle.

"I must be able to embrace you, Namun, to touch you according to the ritual."

He hesitated, then let the manacle dangle. He reached for the folds of the coverall to complete his task.

Ana leaned forward and put her lips to his ear. "In the moment of surata," she breathed," when our eyes meet, the weighing will be complete. The god and I will know you through and through and will place on each side—the good and the evil—all the thoughts, the acts, the motives, the intentions. If the balance tilts to the good, the Jadu will flow from my body to yours—but if the balance tilts to the evil, your soul will be sucked away into the eyes of Darkness."

She looked straight up to the curve of wall above the altar, directly into the fierce painted eyes of the deity. He followed her gaze and froze.

"We must hurry," she whispered. Her lips grazed his ear, making him gasp as if shocked. "Jaya and the Balin must not stumble upon us here before the weighing is complete."

His eyes caught hers, indecision worrying their depths. She rose and let the coveralls slip down around her ankles. They revealed the azure sheen of silken leggings that clung to her damply. She stepped out of them and raised her hands to the contorted effigy above, her eyes studying the catch of her remaining manacle.

"Oh, Nameless One, your daughter prepares herself for your pleasure."

Now, she looked at Vedda, still on his knees beside her, his eyes on her face.

"Supplicate the god, as I have done. Do not rise," she added sharply, when he would have done so. "It would not be seemly. You beg a Gift, Namun ... to be my lover."

She didn't gag—a triumph. She forced her voice to be sweet, soft, caressing, her lips to curve in a smile.

He raised his hands. "Oh, Nameless One, your son prepares himself for your pleasure."

Ana smiled at him. "Now rise," she instructed him, "and lie upon the altar."

He rose. "Shall I not continue ... ?" He motioned toward her partially clad body.

"According to ritual," she said, "you must complete your task upon the altar. Lie down, my lover, and I will mount you."

He was quivering with desire now; his eyes were bright with it; his skin was flushed with it. He lay down upon the damp, glistening altar to await his Gift.

Ana, calculating how far she would have to leap to get the dagger, raised her eyes to the god-effigy again.

"Oh, Nameless One, the Moment of Weighing is near. Prepare to give of your soul ... or to receive this man's soul into yourself."

She shifted her weight as if preparing to mount the altar, then leapt for the dagger. The manacle chain snapped taut before she reached the weapon, sending a shockwave of pain through her wrist and arm. She ignored it, lunged again, and had the thing in her hand.

There was no time for triumph. Another hand wrenched the dagger away and flung it into the steaming gloom.

Ana's eyes flung upward into the pale, sweating face of Duran Prakash.

"My dear Duran..."

Ana and Prakash turned in unison to the altar.

Naked as he was, quivering and still visibly aroused, Namun Vedda was yet in possession of his dignity. He rolled over onto his side and continued pleasantly: "What in the name of God are you doing here? You're supposed to be speeding toward Avasa."

"You mean I'm supposed to be speeding toward Niraya Hell. I am here, dear Namun, to repay your kindness to me—and to Nigu."

Prakash lifted his left hand into the current of light that lapped over the altar stone. There was a lightning pistol in it. He stopped the movement when the delicate, pencil thin muzzle pointed at Vedda's groin.

Fear poured over Ana from the sudden fountain of it in Vedda's soul. It surpassed her own, numbing her.

"What are you talking about?" the fear puzzled. "Do you insinuate that I betrayed you?"

"You did betray us—with your very careful arrangements for our escape from Kasi. You betrayed Bhaktasu Sarojin and his son and Bel Adivaram. How was I to believe you wouldn't betray us? I followed my instincts, Namun. I knew you had your own plans for escape. I figured my best recourse was to stay as close to you as possible." He smiled. "I was in the guest cabin of the Black Paruta. I tried to convince Nigu to join me, but he, alas, died believing you his loyal friend."

Vedda shook his head. "I was his friend. I saved him from ignominy—from the punishments the Circle of Nine would doubtless heap upon him when they caught up with him."

"So, instead, you sped him into the punishments of Niraya."

Prakash glanced about the cavern a strange smile twisting his lips. "This place is close to Hell—or so say the priggish Rohin."

He eyed Ana, who could only stare back, praying he hadn't noticed her toying with the latch of her manacle, which she now held together with her free hand.

"What do you say, Rohina? How close to Hell do you reckon we are?"

"Very close, Prakash-sama."

Vedda stirred. "Duran, I assure you-"

Prakash jiggled the pistol. "Save your lies. I know what you are. A betrayer. You'd betray your own god—you have betrayed it. Such hypocrisy: reviling me for my study of the Bogar, while you, yourself, were a secret devotee."

"I tread a higher Path than a mere-"

"Oh, of course, you are Master Namun. The priests here worship you. Would that have anything to do with the drugs that pour out of your laboratories—drugs these poor fools inhale to increase their ecstasy? Look at you: cowering beneath your god's loins, waiting for some kind of power to drip from them; trying to squeeze it out of this woman. You defiler. You deserve to die."

Vedda trembled like water in wind, but his voice remained deceptively calm. "Duran, must I beg you not to do this?"

"Oh, don't pray to me! Pray to your god! Pray to this sleeping womb!" He cocked his head to one side. "But pray now."

The gun barrel rose.

Ana chose that moment to gouge Duran Prakash's ribs with a well-aimed elbow. The pistol flared, melting through the base of a nearby brazier and sending a shower of coals and flame to the floor.

Prakash dodged the searing stuff, slipped on the slick stone of the floor and fell headlong into the stream.

Ana shed the manacles, kicked her feet free of her coveralls, and bolted for freedom. The corridor was dark after the brightness of the red shrine. She couldn't keep her feet on the narrow path, but slipped and fell again and again, clawing her way upright, growling in frustration, gasping for breath. The corridor seemed endless.

When she had begun to think herself lost, she saw the triangular portal with its veil of water. Beyond was the chamber of pools—and Jaya. Her cry of relief twisted into a roar of fear and rage as someone tackled her from behind.

Violent hands dragged her upright and the sharp point of a dagger pricked her belly.

"Ah, my beloved," murmured Namun Vedda in her ear, "it appears we must complete our destiny elsewhere. It is time to leave. Move forward please."

"Jaya is out there," she warned him. "And the Balin."

"Yes, I know. But unless I am very much mistaken, they will not train their weapons on me while you are in my arms."

~

Jaya's heart felt as if it had been scoured out by fire. He was beyond panic. Ana had been up at the feet of the statue waiting, and then she was gone—and wherever she was, she was terrified. He'd alerted the Balin, who had at first been bemused by his certainty that something was wrong. But Ana was not where they had left her at the edge of the reflecting pool.

They searched the chamber, but came up with nothing more than hostile stares from a group of Bogar priests who had come to stand protest in the upper access to the chamber. When Rakesh

Bithal returned with his party, they still had not found her, and Jaya was in agony. Trills of sheer terror alternated with equally terrifying silences during which Jaya's imagination all but gutted him.

They were holding council in the center of the chamber, when Jaya's attention was drawn forcibly to the altar with its hideous god. Without knowing why, he moved toward it, his steps swift.

"Nathu Rai?"

Bithal's voice barely registered. She was there, she was near. He was at the rim of the pool when she appeared from behind the glistening altar, soaking wet, her hair clinging in wet tendrils to her undergarments, her coverall gone.

He had started to mount the verge of the pool when he realized she was not alone. His godfather peered at him over her shoulder.

It was only when they had cleared the altar, wading out into the knee-deep pool, that he realized two things in stunning succession —one was that Namun Vedda was naked, the other was that he held the tip of a long dagger to Ana's ribs.

"Ah, nephew!" said Vedda conversationally. "If you would be so kind as to tell your militaristic friends to stand aside, I should like to go up to my cell and put on something more suitable for travel."

The sudden flurry behind him told Jaya that the Balin were already reacting to the situation.

"No, no!" called Vedda. "That is not at all what I meant."

The dagger jerked and Ana uttered a choking cry. A dark stain spread downward through the blue fabric beneath her left breast.

An echoing stab of pain shot down Jaya's side. "Damn you, Namun, let her go!"

Vedda shook his head. "She's my insurance, nephew ... and my beloved traveling companion."

"If you need a hostage, take me. Leave Ana here."

Vedda laughed pleasantly. "A kind offer, Jaya. I'm sure your lovely dasa appreciates the sentiment. Alas, while you are a delightful companion, she has many qualities you lack. Besides, she has pledged herself to me. Does that surprise you? It shouldn't. After all, while she is your slave; she is the lover of my soul. Aren't you, Deva?"

"Yes, Namun," said Ana on cue. In her eyes, a flame had gone out. Drained of color, they reflected only the fire of torches.

Jaya's throat constricted. "Why are you doing this? Why did you do any of this?"

Vedda's expression softened. "Ah. What you really want to know is why I killed your father. Well, I'll tell you, because I want you to know. Bhaktasu Sarojin was everything and had everything I dreamed of being and having. He was all that and had all that without ever having to work for it. No discipline did he follow; no Path did he tread. It was simply given to him by blind gods of Providence. He befriended me in school the way a man might befriend a lost dog. And I was lost. My family had nothing. I had nothing. Nothing but my native intelligence and a natural talent for the sciences, which served to get me into the finest technical school in the seven provinces. Bhaktasu, who had so little natural ability it was painful, simply bought himself a place in class. I tutored him; I was his crutch and he took the poor, low-caste misfit under his royal wing.

"Don't think I was not grateful. To his credit, he was a generous soul; he helped me out a great deal. Helped me find lucrative work, later helped me start my own laboratory. But, odd as it may seem, the more he did for me, the more resentment warred with my gratitude. Of course, I felt great shame at my resentment. The shame, turning to guilt, gave birth to further resentment.

"Then, there was Melantha. We both loved her. Bhaktasu won her. I pretended it was because of his social station, but I knew it was not that, but his qualities as a man. Your father was a good man, Jaya. I wish he had not been."

He paused, shaking his head, as if another path had opened up in this mind and he hesitated to take it. He recovered himself, though, and continued. "You may think me a man without ambition, but that is not the case. I decided that I was going to someday enjoy the kind of power you and your father owned by birth. That I was going to do it in my own way, on my own terms, using my native talents. I was well on my way to that goal when Bhaktasu stumbled across the means I had chosen to attain it."

"So you had him killed."

Vedda shook his head. "That would have been unworthy and cowardly. I killed him myself. I owed him that. It seemed dishonorable to send a mercenary stranger to kill a friend."

Jaya's soul gave up an inarticulate cry of anguish. "Friend? You dare call yourself-"

"Enough," said Vedda, "kindly move out of our way."

Jaya didn't move. "Leave Ana and you can go. We won't follow."

"You're not a good liar, Jaya. You never have been. Besides, I think you understand that she is more than just a hostage. I need her—want her. I wanted her when she was merely a theory. And, when, at Mesha Fest, you showed me the reality, I knew you had unwittingly given me the greatest gift I have ever received—the other half of my soul. I thank you."

The gratitude was sincere—Jaya could see it in the glistening eyes. Mad eyes. They were at an impasse. Jaya had no threats to make, no weapons to use, nothing. He moved his eyes to Ana's face.

"Ana."

She trembled.

"Ana, what do I do?"

"Let us go," she told him. Her gaze held his in a painful grasp. "He won't kill me. He needs me. He loves me. Don't you love me, Namun?"

"With my entire being, Deva."

"You see? I'm safe with him. You can let us go."

Light-headed, Jaya turned to the watching Balin. "Move back. Let them go."

The Balin fell aside, leaving a straight path up past the pools, through the grove of stalactites and the columns of lost souls, to where the Bogar priests hovered.

Jaya, too, stepped back, never once letting go of Ana's gaze.

Vedda prodded her to the edge of the pool. She was stepping out of the water when an explosion of sound erupted beneath the Bogar idol. With a cry of pain and rage, Duran Prakash appeared behind the altar. His right arm hung, limp, at his side; blood from a ragged wound spread across his shoulder. In his good hand was a lightning pistol.

He did not waste time.

As Jaya leapt forward, shouting, as Namun Vedda turned in disbelief, as Ana tumbled into the pool, a sizzling bolt of lightning cut Namun Vedda nearly in two and cauterized the wound as it went.

Jaya felt searing heat break over him and winced at the wash of brilliance that flashed from the weapon's muzzle.

Vedda screamed—the horrible, strangled sound of a soul being ripped, unprepared, from its body—then crumpled into the pool, nearly on top of Ana. The smell of charred flesh washed up in a curl of steam.

Sobbing, Ana pulled herself to the side of the pool and retched. Before Jaya could reach her, she slid beneath the water.

∿

There was cold water in her face, cold water in her mouth. She swallowed. Her throat shrieked in bruised, abraded agony, but she swallowed again and again, worshipping the icy liquid. She was cradled in arms that shook with the palsy of recent terror.

She took a deep breath. The cut below her breast stung. She put a hand there and found the wound had been bound. Another hand covered hers.

"Jaya." The name came from her throat dry and lacerated. She put up her hand and touched his face. It was wet. "Poor Nathu Rai," she murmured. "I am such an irritant I drive him to tears."

He kissed the hand, held it against his lips and whispered something into it that sounded like, "Laldasa."

"What?" she asked.

He rubbed the dascree in her palm with his thumb. "My mother accused me of wanting to replace this with the Sarojin raicree. She was right."

She opened her eyes then, and looked at him. Tears still chased down his face. "Crazy," she called him.

"Nearly."

"Are those my tears?"

"Yes. Lalasa," he called her. "Beloved."

"Then, thank you. You asked if a Deva can be a Rani. She can, but the cree of the Order goes here." She pressed his thumb into her palm with her fingers. "Not the raicree."

He nodded. "Understood."

"I'm Genda Sita," she said. "You said you had forgotten."

"Yes."

"The Rani has not."

"It enrages the Rani. Let it. It's good for her soul."

"Crusader."

"Rohin witch."

She stared up, then, at the glitter of the ceiling—of all the tiny presumably worthless crystals that grew there. "How did you know about the bhasvata crystal?" she asked.

He blinked at the non sequitur, but answered. "I saw it ... through your eyes, I think. A crystal box with herbs in it. The red wedding gown, the paruta flask, the room ... the hooded men."

She was incredulous. "You saw all that? How?"

"I don't know. I just did. I knew you were in the KNC Towers. I knew you were hurt, frightened. Just now, I felt your fear. I even ... felt Namun's fear through you. It seems you really do have the Jadu."

"Perhaps we both do. Perhaps we are of a kind."

She studied his face, caught him looking back at her and, for just a moment, saw herself through his eyes, felt herself through his touch. It was a revelation that took her breath away. What intimacy, she wondered, might be discovered by two who could sense as one?

"Of a kind," he repeated, as if reading her thoughts. "I hope so, but..." His eyes swept the steaming chamber. " ... this is hardly the place to discuss such things."

"A shrine to the senses, not the place to discuss the sensual?"

"I had thought," he said, rising and helping her to rise, "that I spoke of the spiritual."

"The spiritual? Are you now a bhakta?"

"Let us say, I am now aware of certain possibilities."

He steadied her as they made their way up toward the chamber entrance. His eyes took in her state of undress. "Will you tell me what happened in the shrine ... with Vedda?"

She tried to grab back the dart of residual terror and disgust before he felt it, but saw in his eyes that she had failed. She offered him a rueful smile.

"Nathu Rai," she told him, "this is hardly the place to discuss such things."

END

GLOSSARY

asat
nothing -- as opposed to sat
channa
a coffee-like drink
cree
a mark carried in the palm of all members of Mehtaran
    society
dalal
one who runs a dalali
dalali
a showroom, auction house for the sale of slaves
das/dasa
slave
dascree
the cree carried in the palm of all slaves
kaladan
a brothel
mahesa
lord
Nathu Rai
Lord Prince
raicree
the cree carried in the palm of the Taj class

rita

the order of things

Rohin/Rohina

an aspirant on the Upward Path; a spiritual devotee

sat

something -- as opposed to asat

varna

the caste system of Mehtaran society

yevetha

Unmarked by a caste mark or cree. Legally this makes one a non-person

ABOUT THE AUTHOR

Maya became addicted to science fiction when her dad let her stay up late to watch *The Day the Earth Stood Still*. Mom was horrified. Dad was unrepentant. Maya slept with a night-light in her room until she was 15.

She started her writing career sketching science fiction comic books in the last row of her grade school classroom. She was never apprehended. Since then her short fiction has been published in *Analog, Amazing Stories, Century, Realms of Fantasy, Interzone, Paradox* and *Jim Baen's Universe*. Her novelette, *The White Dog*, was a finalist for the British Science Fiction Award.

Her debut novel, *The Meri* (Baen), was a *Locus Magazine* 1992 Best First Novel nominee an a finalist for the Crawford Award. She has been a sometime collaborator with Michael Reaves, with whom she's penned three Star Wars novels, and a Del Rey original, *Mr. Twilight*. Their collaboration, *Star Wars: The Last Jedi* was a *New York Times* Bestseller. She has also authored detective fiction, including her debut detective novel *The Antiquities Hunter*.

Maya lives in San Jose where she writes, performs, and records original and parody (filk) music with her husband and awesome musician and music producer, Chef Jeff Vader, All-Powerful God of Biscuits. The couple frequently serves as Guest of Honor at science fiction/fantasy conventions and at filk music gatherings, and has been honored with Pegasus Awards for Best Parody and Best Performer. They've produced five music albums: *RetroRocket Science, Aliens Ate My Homework, Jeff and Maya's Grated Hits* and *Schrödinger's Hairball* (parody), and the original music CDs *Manhattan Sleeps, Möbius Street* and *I Remember the Rain*. To top it off, they've also produced three musical children: Alex, Kristine, and Amanda.

Maya's website can be found at: *mayabohnhoff.com*.

Jeff & Maya's music website can be found at: *jeffandmayabohnhoff.bandcamp.com*.

ABOUT BOOK VIEW CAFÉ

Book View Café Publishing Cooperative (BVC) is an author-owned cooperative of professional writers, publishing in a variety of genres such as fantasy, romance, mystery, and science fiction.

BVC authors include New York Times and USA Today bestsellers. Our authors have won and been nominated for numerous awards, including: the Agatha, Campbell, Hugo, Lambda Literary, Locus, Nebula, PEN/Malamud Award, Philip K. Dick, RITA, World Fantasy, and Writers of the Future awards, and the Academy Nicholl Fellowship.

Since its debut in 2008, BVC has gained a reputation for producing high-quality ebooks, and now brings that same quality to its print editions. Find out more and sign up for our newsletter at:

www.bookviewcafe.com